3 5⁰

PENGUIN BOOKS
OUT OF INDIA

Ruth Prawer Jhabvala was born in Germany of Polish parents
and came to England at the age of twelve. She graduated from
Queen Mary College, London University, and married an
Indian architect. They lived in Delhi from 1951 to 1975. Since
then they have divided their time between Delhi, New York
and London. *Out of India* is a selection of her favourite stories
taken from four previous volumes: *Like Birds, Like Fishes, A
Stronger Climate, How I Became a Holy Mother* and *An Experience of
India*. Her novels include *To Whom She Will, The Nature of Passion, Esmond in India, The Householder, Get Ready for Battle, A Back-
ward Place, A New Dominion, Heat and Dust* – winner of the 1985
Booker Prize – *In Search of Love and Beauty* and *Three Continents*.
In collaboration with James Ivory and Ismail Merchant she
has written scripts for film and television, including *Shakespeare
Wallah, Autobiography of a Princess, The Europeans, Quartet, Heat
and Dust, The Bostonians* and *A Room with a View*, which won an
Academy Award in 1987. Ruth Prawer Jhabvala won the Neil
Gunn International Fellowship in 1978 and the MacArthur
Foundation Award in 1986.

Her writing has won widespread acclaim: C. P. Snow wrote,
'Someone once said that the definition of the highest art is that
one should feel that life is this and not otherwise. I do not know
of a writer living who gives that feeling with more unqualified
certainty than Mrs Jhabvala,' and the *Sunday Times* called her,
'a writer of genius . . . of world class – a master storyteller'.

OUT OF INDIA

SELECTED STORIES

RUTH PRAWER JHABVALA

PENGUIN BOOKS

PENGUIN BOOKS

Published by the Penguin Group
27 Wrights Lane, London W8 5TZ, England
Viking Penguin Inc., 40 West 23rd Street, New York, New York 10010, USA
Penguin Books Australia Ltd, Ringwood, Victoria, Australia
Penguin Books Canada Ltd, 2801 John Street, Markham, Ontario, Canada L3R 1B4
Penguin Books (NZ) Ltd, 182–190 Wairau Road, Auckland 10, New Zealand

Penguin Books Ltd, Registered Offices: Harmondsworth, Middlesex, England

First published in Great Britain by John Murray (Publishers) 1987
Published in Penguin Books 1989
1 3 5 7 9 10 8 6 4 2

These stories were selected from the following collections and
are arranged chronologically:

Like Birds, Like Fishes (1963)
A Stronger Climate (1968)
An Experience of India (1971)
How I Became a Holy Mother (1976)

"The Widow," "The Interview," "Passion," "The Man with the Dog," "Rose Petals,"
"Two More Under the Indian Sun," "Bombay," "On Bail," "In the Mountains," and
"Desecration" appeared originally in *The New Yorker*.

The Introduction, "Myself in India," first appeared in *London Magazine*.

"A Spiritual Call" first appeared in *The Cornhill*.

"The Housewife" first appeared in *Cosmopolitan*.

"My First Marriage," "An Experience of India," and "How I Became a Holy Mother" first
appeared in *Encounter*.

Printed and bound in Great Britain by
Richard Clay Ltd, Bungay, Suffolk
Filmset in Baskerville

For C.S.H.J.
as always

CONTENTS

OUT OF
INDIA

INTRODUCTION:
MYSELF IN INDIA

I have lived in India for most of my adult life. My husband is Indian and so are my children. I am not, and less so every year.

India reacts very strongly on people. Some loathe it, some love it, most do both. There is a special problem of adjustment for the sort of people who come today, who tend to be liberal in outlook and have been educated to be sensitive and receptive to other cultures. But it is not always easy to be sensitive and receptive to India: there comes a point where you have to close up in order to protect yourself. The place is very strong and often proves too strong for European nerves. There is a cycle that Europeans—by Europeans I mean all Westerners, including Americans—tend to pass through. It goes like this: first stage, tremendous enthusiasm—everything Indian is marvelous; second stage, everything Indian not so marvelous; third stage, everything Indian abominable. For some people it ends there, for others the cycle renews itself and goes on. I have been through it so many times that now I think of myself as strapped to a wheel that goes round and round and sometimes I'm up and sometimes I'm down. When I meet other Europeans, I can usually tell after a few moments' conversation at what stage of the cycle they happen to be. Everyone likes to talk about India, whether they happen to be loving or loathing it. It is a topic on which a lot of things can be said, and on a variety of aspects—social, economic, political, philosophical: it makes fascinating viewing from every side.

However, I must admit that I am no longer interested in India. What I am interested in now is myself in India—which sometimes, in moments of despondency, I tend to think of as my survival in India. I had better say straightaway that the reason I live in India is

13

that my strongest human ties are here. If I hadn't married an Indian, I don't think I would ever have come here for I am not attracted—or used not to be attracted—to the things that usually bring people to India. I know I am the wrong type of person to live here. To stay and endure, one should have a mission and a cause, to be patient, cheerful, unselfish, strong. I am a central European with an English education and a deplorable tendency to constant self-analysis. I am irritable and have weak nerves.

The most salient fact about India is that it is very poor and very backward. There are so many other things to be said about it but this must remain the basis of all of them. We may praise Indian democracy, go into raptures over Indian music, admire Indian intellectuals—but whatever we say, not for one moment should we lose sight of the fact that a very great number of Indians never get enough to eat. Literally that: from birth to death they never for one day cease to suffer from hunger. *Can* one lose sight of that fact? God knows, I've tried. But after seeing what one has to see here every day, it is not really possible to go on living one's life the way one is used to. People dying of starvation in the streets, children kidnapped and maimed to be sent out as beggars—but there is no point in making a catalog of the horrors with which one lives, *on* which one lives, as on the back of an animal. Obviously, there has to be some adjustment.

There are several ways. The first and best is to be a strong person who plunges in and does what he can as a doctor or social worker. I often think that perhaps this is the only condition under which Europeans have any right to be here. I know several people like that. They are usually attached to some mission. They work very hard and stay very cheerful. Every few years they are sent on home leave. Once I met such a person—a woman doctor—who had just returned from her first home leave after being out here for twelve years. I asked her: but what does it feel like to go back after such a long time? How do you manage to adapt yourself? She didn't understand. This question, which was of such tremendous import to me—how to adapt oneself to the differences between Europe and India—didn't mean a thing to her. It simply didn't matter. And she was right, for in view of the things she sees and does every day, the delicate nuances of one's own sensibilities are best forgotten.

Another approach to India's basic conditions is to accept them. This seems to be the approach favored by most Indians. Perhaps it has something to do with their belief in reincarnation. If things are not to your liking in this life, there is always the chance that in your next life everything will be different. It appears to be a consoling thought for both rich and poor. The rich man stuffing himself on pilau can do so with an easy conscience because he knows he has earned this privilege by his good conduct in previous lives; and the poor man can watch him with some degree of equanimity, for he knows that next time around it may well be *he* who will be digging into that pilau while the other will be crouching outside the door with an empty stomach. However, this path of acceptance is not open to you if you don't have a belief in reincarnation ingrained within you. And if you don't accept, then what can you do? Sometimes one wants just to run away and go to a place where everyone has enough to eat and clothes to wear and a home fit to live in. But even when you get there, can you ever forget? Having once seen the sights in India, and the way it has been ordained that people must live out their lives, nowhere in the world can ever be all that good to be in again.

None of this is what I wanted to say. I wanted to concentrate only on myself in India. But I could not do so before indicating the basis on which everyone who comes here has to live. I have a nice house, I do my best to live in an agreeable way. I shut all my windows, I let down the blinds, I turn on the air-conditioner; I read a lot of books, with a special preference for the great masters of the novel. All the time I know myself to be on the back of this great animal of poverty and backwardness. It is not possible to pretend otherwise. Or rather, one does pretend, but retribution follows. Even if one never rolls up the blinds and never turns off the air-conditioner, something is bound to go wrong. People are not meant to shut themselves up in rooms and pretend there is nothing outside.

Now I think I am drawing nearer to what I want to be my subject. Yes, something is wrong: I am not happy this way. I feel lonely, shut in, shut off. It is my own fault. I should go out more and meet people and learn what is going on. All right, so I am not a doctor nor a social worker nor a saint nor at all a good person; then the only thing to do is to try to push that aspect of India out of sight and turn to others. There are many others. I live in the capital, where so much is going on. The winter is one round of parties, art exhibitions, plays, music and dance recitals, visiting European artistes: there need never be a dull moment. Yet all my moments are dull. Why? It is my own fault, I know. I can't quite explain it to myself but somehow I have no heart for these things here. Is it because all the time underneath I feel the animal moving? But I have decided to ignore the animal. I wish to concentrate only on modern, Westernized India, and on modern, well-off, cultured Westernized Indians.

Let me try and describe a Westernized Indian woman with whom I ought to have a lot in common and whose company I ought to enjoy. She has been to Oxford or Cambridge or some smart American college. She speaks flawless, easy, colloquial English with a charming lilt of an accent. She has a degree in economics or political science or English literature. She comes from a good family. Her father may have been an I.C.S. officer or some other high-ranking government official; he too was at Oxford or Cambridge, and he and her mother traveled in Europe in prewar days. They have always lived a Western-style life, with Western food and an admiration for Western culture. The daughter now tends rather to frown on this. She feels one should be more deeply Indian, and with this end in view, she wears handloom saris and traditional jewelry and has painted an abnormally large vermilion mark on her forehead. She is interested in Indian classical music and dance. If she is rich enough—she may have married into one of the big Indian business houses—she will become a patroness of the arts and hold delicious parties on her lawn on summer nights. All her friends are there— and she has so many, both Indian and European, all interesting people—and trays of iced drinks are carried around by servants in uniform and there is intelligent conversation and then there is a superbly arranged buffet supper and more intelligent conversation, and then the crown of the evening: a famous Indian maestro performing on the sitar. The guests recline on carpets and cushions on the lawn. The sky sparkles with stars and the languid summer air is fragrant with jasmine. There are many pretty girls reclining against bolsters; their faces are melancholy, for the music is stirring their hearts, and sometimes they sigh with yearning and happiness and look down at their pretty toes (adorned with a tiny silver toe ring) peeping out from under the sari. Here is Indian life and culture at its highest and best. Yet, with all that, it need not be thought that our hostess has forgotten her Western education. Not at all. In her one may see the best of East and West combined. She is interested in a great variety of topics and can hold her own in any discussion. She loves to exercise her emancipated mind, and whatever the subject of conversation—economics, or politics, or literature, or film—she has a well-formulated opinion on it and knows how to express herself. How lucky for me if I could have such a person for a friend! What enjoyable, lively times we two could have together!

In fact, my teeth are set on edge if I have to listen to her for more than five minutes—yes, even though everything she says is so true and in line with the most advanced opinions of today. But when she says it, somehow, even though I know the words to be true, they ring completely false. It is merely lips moving and sounds coming out: it doesn't mean anything, nothing of what she says (though she says it with such conviction, skill, and charm) is of the least importance to her. She is only making conversation in the way she knows educated women have to make conversation. And so it is with all of them. Everything they say, all that lively conversation around the buffet table, is not prompted by anything they really feel strongly about but by what they think they ought to feel strongly about. This applies not only to subjects that are naturally alien to them—for instance, when they talk oh so solemnly! and with such profound intelligence! of Godard and Becket and ecology—but when they talk about themselves too. They know modern India to be an important subject and they have a lot to say about it: but though they themselves *are* modern India, they don't look at themselves, they are not conditioned to look at themselves except with the eyes of foreign experts whom they have been taught to respect. And while they are fully aware of India's problems and are up on all the statistics and all the arguments for and against nationalization and a socialistic pattern of society, all the time it is as if they were talking about some *other* place—as if it were a subject for debate—an abstract subject—and not a live animal actually moving under their feet.

But if I have no taste for the company of these Westernized Indians, then what else is there? Other Indians don't really have a social life, not in our terms; the whole conception of such a life is imported. It is true that Indians are gregarious insofar as they hate to be alone and always like to sit together in groups; but these groups are clan-units—it is the family, or clan members, who gather together and enjoy each other's company. And again, their conception of enjoying each other's company is different from ours. For them it is enough just to *be* together; there are long stretches of silence in which everyone stares into space. From time to time there is a little spurt of conversation, usually on some commonplace everyday subject such as rising prices, a forthcoming marriage, or a troublesome neighbor. There is no attempt at exercising the mind or testing one's wits against those of others: the pleasure lies only in having other familiar people around and enjoying the air together and looking forward to the next meal. There is actually something very restful about this mode of social intercourse, and certainly holds more pleasure than the synthetic social life led by Westernized Indians. It is also more adapted to the Indian climate, which invites one to be absolutely relaxed in mind and body, to do nothing, to think nothing, just to feel, to *be*. I have in fact enjoyed sitting around like that for hours on end. But there is something in me that after some time revolts against such lassitude. I can't just *be*! Suddenly I jump up and rush away out of that contented circle. I want to do something terribly difficult like climbing a mountain or reading the *Critique of Pure Reason*. I feel tempted to bang my head against the wall as if to wake myself up. Anything to prevent myself from being sucked down into that bog of passive, intuitive being. I feel I cannot, I must not allow myself to live this way.

Of course there are other Europeans more or less in the same situation as myself. For instance, other women married to Indians. But I hesitate to seek them out. People suffering from the same disease do not usually make good company for one another. Who is to listen to whose complaints? On the other hand, with what enthusiasm I welcome visitors from abroad. Their physical presence alone is a pleasure to me. I love to see their fresh complexions, their red cheeks that speak of wind and rain; and I like to see their clothes and their shoes, to admire the texture of these solid European materials and the industrial skills that have gone into making them. I also like to hear the way in which these people speak. In some strange way their accents, their intonations are redolent to me of the places from which they have come, so that as voices rise and fall I hear in them the wind stirring in English trees or a mild brook murmuring through a summer wood. And apart from these sensuous pleasures, there is also the pleasure of hearing what they have to say. I listen avidly to what is said about people I know or have heard of and about new plays and restaurants and changes and fashions. However, neither the subject nor my interest in it is inexhaustible; and after that, it is my turn. What about India? Now they want to hear, but I don't want to say. I feel myself growing sullen. I don't want to talk about India. There is nothing I can tell them. There is nothing they would understand. However, I do begin to talk, and after a time even to talk with passion. But everything I say is wrong. I listen to myself with horror; they too listen with horror. I want to stop and reverse, but I can't. I want to cry out, this is not what I mean! You are listening to me in entirely the wrong context! But there is no way of explaining the context. It would take too long, and anyway what is the point? It's such a small, personal thing. I fall silent. I have nothing more to say. I turn my face and want them to go away.

So I am back again alone in my room with the blinds drawn and the air-conditioner on. Sometimes, when I think of my life, it seems to have contracted to this one point and to be concentrated in this one room, and it is always a very hot, very long afternoon when the air-conditioner has failed. I cannot describe the *oppression* of such afternoons. It is a physical oppression—heat pressing down on me and pressing in the walls and the ceiling and congealing together with time that has stood still and will never move again. And it is not only those two—heat and time—that are laying their weight on me but behind them, or held within them, there is something more, which I can only describe as the whole of India. This is hyperbole, but I need hyperbole to express my feelings about those countless afternoons spent over what now seem to me countless years in a country for which I was not born. India swallows me up and now it seems to me that I am no longer in my room but in the white-hot city streets under a white-hot sky; people cannot live in such heat, so everything is deserted—no, not quite, for here comes a smiling leper in a cart being pushed by another leper; there is also the carcass of a dog and vultures have swooped down on it. The river has dried up and stretches in miles of flat cracked earth; it is not possible to make out where the river ceases and the land begins, for this too is as flat, as cracked, as dry as the riverbed and stretches on forever. Until we come to a jungle in which wild beasts live, and then there are ravines and here live outlaws with the hearts of wild beasts. Sometimes they make raids into the villages and they rob and burn and mutilate and kill for sport. More mountains and these are very, very high, and now it is no longer hot but terribly cold, we are in snow and ice and here is Mount Kailash on which sits Siva the Destroyer wearing a necklace of human skulls. Down in the plains they are worshiping him. I can see them from here—they are doing something strange— what is it? I draw nearer. Now I can see. They are killing a boy. They hack him to pieces and now they bury the pieces into the

19

foundations dug for a new bridge. There is a priest with them who is quite naked except for ash smeared all over him; he is reciting some holy verses over the foundations, to bless and propitiate.

I am using these exaggerated images in order to give some idea of how intolerable India—the idea, the sensation of it—can become. A point is reached where one must escape, and if one can't do so physically, then some other way must be found. And I think it is not only Europeans but Indians too who feel themselves compelled to seek refuge from their often unbearable environment. Here perhaps less than anywhere else is it possible to believe that this world, this life, is all there is for us, and the temptation to write it off and substitute something more satisfying becomes overwhelming. This brings up the question whether religion is such a potent force in India because life is so terrible, or is it the other way around—is life so terrible because, with the eyes of the spirit turned elsewhere, there is no incentive to improve its quality? Whichever it is, the fact remains that the eyes of the spirit *are* turned elsewhere, and it really is true that God seems more present in India than in other places. Every morning I wake up at 3 A.M. to the sound of someone pouring out his spirit in devotional song; and then at dawn the temple bells ring, and again at dusk, and conch shells are blown, and there is the smell of incense and of the slightly overblown flowers that are placed at the feet of smiling, pink-cheeked idols. I read in the papers that the Lord Krishna has been reborn as the son of a weaver woman in a village somewhere in Madhya Pradesh. On the banks of the river there are figures in meditation and one of them may turn out to be the teller in your bank who cashed your check just a few days ago; now he is in the lotus pose and his eyes are turned up and he is in ecstasy. There are ashrams full of little old half-starved widows who skip and dance about, they giggle and play hide-and-seek because they are Krishna's milkmaids. And over all this there is a sky of enormous proportions—so much larger than the earth on which you live, and often so incredibly beautiful, an unflawed unearthly blue by day, all shining with stars at night, that it is difficult to believe that something grand and wonderful beyond the bounds of human comprehension does not emanate from there.

I love listening to Indian devotional songs. They seem pure like water drawn from a well; and the emotions they express are both beautiful and easy to understand because the imagery employed is so human. The soul crying out for God is always shown as the beloved yearning for the lover in an easily recognizable way ("I wait for Him. Do you hear His step? He has come"). I feel soothed when I hear such songs and all my discontentment falls away. I see that everything I have been fretting about is of no importance at all because all that matters is this promise of eternal bliss in the Lover's arms. I become patient and good and feel that everything is good. Unfortunately this tranquil state does not last for long, and after a time it again seems to me that nothing is good and neither am I. Once somebody said to me: "Just see, how sweet is the Indian soul that can see God in a cow!" But when I try to assume this sweetness, it turns sour: for, however much I may try to fool myself, whatever veils I may try, for the sake of peace of mind, to draw over my eyes, it is soon enough clear to me that the cow *is* a cow, and a very scrawny, underfed, diseased one at that. And then I feel that I want to keep this knowledge, however painful it is, and not exchange it for some other that may be true for an Indian but can never quite become that for me.

And here, it seems to me, I come to the heart of my problem. To live in India and be at peace, one must to a very considerable extent become Indian and adopt Indian attitudes, habits, beliefs, assume if possible an Indian personality. But how is this possible? And even if it were possible—without cheating oneself—would it be desirable? Should one want to try to become something other than what one is? I don't always say no to this question. Sometimes it seems to me how pleasant it would be to say yes and give in and wear a sari and be meek and accepting and see God in a cow. Other times it seems worthwhile to be defiant and European and—all right, be crushed by one's environment, but all the same have made some attempt to remain standing. Of course, this can't go on indefinitely and in the end I'm bound to lose—if only at the point where my ashes are immersed in the Ganges to the accompaniment of Vedic hymns, and then who will say that I have not truly merged with India?

I do sometimes go back to Europe. But after a time I get bored there and want to come back here. I also find it hard now to stand the European climate. I have got used to intense heat and seem to need it.

MY FIRST MARRIAGE

Last week Rahul went on a hunger strike. He didn't have to suffer long—his family got very frightened (he is the only son) and by the second day they were ready to do anything he wanted, even to let him marry me. So he had a big meal, and then he came to tell me of his achievement. He was so proud and happy that I too pretended to be happy. Now his father and Daddy are friends again, and they sit downstairs in the study and talk together about their university days in England. His mother too comes to the house, and yesterday his married sister Kamla paid me a visit. The last time I had met Kamla was when she told me all those things on their veranda, but neither of us seemed to have any recollection of that. Instead we had a very nice conversation about her husband's promotion and the annual flower show for which she had been asked to organize a raffle. Mama walks around the house looking pleased with herself and humming snatches of the national anthem (out of tune—she is completely unmusical). No one ever mentions M. any more.

It is two years now since he went away. I don't know where he is or what he is doing. Perhaps he is meditating somewhere in the Himalayas, or wandering by the banks of the Ganges with an orange robe and a begging bowl; or perhaps he is just living in another town, trying to start a newspaper or a school. Sometimes I ask myself: can there really have been such a man? But it is not a question to which I require any answer.

The first time I saw M., I was just going out to tennis with Rahul. I hardly glanced at him—he was just one of the people who came to see Daddy. But he returned many times, and I heard Daddy say: "That young man is a nuisance." "Of course," said Mama in a sarcastic way, "you can never say no to anyone." Daddy looked shy: it was true, he found it difficult to refuse people. He is the Director of Education, and because it is an important position, people are always coming, both to the house and to his office, to ask him to do something for them. Mostly there is nothing he can do, but because he is so nice and polite to them, they keep coming again. Then often Mama steps in.

One day, just as I was going out to Rahul's house, I heard her shouting outside the door of the study. "The Director is a busy man!" she was shouting. She had her back against the door and held her arms stretched out; M. stood in front of her, and his head was lowered. "Day after day you come and eat his life up!" she said.

I feel very embarrassed when I hear Mama shouting at people, so I went away quickly. But when I was walking down the road, he suddenly came behind me. He said, "Why are you walking so fast?"

I said nothing. I thought it was very rude of him to speak to me at all.

"You are running away," he said.

Then in spite of myself I had to laugh: "From what?"

"From the Real," he said, and he spoke so seriously that I was impressed and stood still in the middle of the road and looked at him.

He was not really young—not young like I am, or like Rahul. His hair was already going gray and he had lines around his eyes. But what eyes they were, how full of wisdom and experience! And he was looking at me with them. I can't describe how I felt suddenly.

He said he wanted Daddy to open a new department in the university. A department for moral training. He explained the scheme to me and we both stood still in the road. His eyes glowed. I understood at once; of course, not everything—I am not a brilliant person such as he—but I understood it was important and even grand. Here were many new ideas, which made life seem quite different. I began to see that I had been living wrongly because I had been brought up to think wrongly. Everything I thought important, and Daddy and Mama and Rahul and everyone, was not important: these were the frivolities of life we were caught up in. For the first time someone was explaining to me the nature of reality. I promised to help him and to speak to Daddy. I was excited and couldn't stop thinking of everything he had said and the way he had said it.

He often telephoned. I waited for his calls and was impatient and restless till they came. But I was also a little ashamed to talk to him because I could not tell him that I had succeeded. I spoke to Daddy many times. I said, "Education is no use without a firm moral basis."

"How philosophical my little girl is getting," Daddy said and smiled and was pleased that I was taking an interest in higher things.

Mama said, "Don't talk so much; it's not nice in a young girl."

When M. telephoned I could only say, "I'm trying."

"You are not trying!" he said; he spoke sternly to me. "You are thinking of your own pleasures only, of your tennis and games."

He was right—I often played tennis, and now that my examinations were finished, I spent a lot of time at the Club and went to the cinema and read novels. When he spoke to me, I realized all that was wrong; so that every time he telephoned I was thoughtful for many hours afterward and when Rahul came to fetch me for tennis, I said I had a headache.

But I tried to explain to Rahul. He listened carefully; Rahul listens carefully to everything I say. He becomes very serious, and his eyes, which are already very large, become even larger. He looks so sweet then, just as he did when he was a little boy. I remember Rahul as a little boy, for we always played together. His father and Daddy were great friends, almost like brothers. So Rahul and I grew up together, and later it was decided we would be married. Everyone was happy: I also, and Rahul. We were to be married quite soon, for we had both finished our college and Rahul's father had already got him a good job in a business firm, with very fine prospects.

"You see, Rahul, we live in nice houses and have nice clothes and good education and everything, and all the time we don't know what reality is."

Rahul frowned a bit, the way he used to do over his sums when they were difficult; but he nodded and looked at me with his big sweet eyes and was ready to listen to everything else I would tell him. Rahul has very smooth cheeks and they are a little bit pink because he is so healthy.

One day when M. telephoned he asked me to go and meet him. At first I tried to say no, but I knew I really wanted to go. He called me to a coffeehouse I had never been to before, and I felt shy when going in—there were many men and no girls at all. Everyone looked at me; some of them may have been students from the university and perhaps they knew me. It was noisy in there and full of smoke and smelled of fritters and chutney. The tablecloths were dirty and so were the bearers' uniforms. But he was there, waiting for me. I had often tried to recall his face but I never could: now I saw it and—of course, of course, I cried to myself, that was how it was, how could I forget.

Then I began to meet him every day. Sometimes we met in that coffeehouse, at other times in a little park where there was a broken swing and an old tomb and clerks came to eat their lunch out of tiffin carriers. It was the end of winter and the sky was pale blue with little white lines on it and the sun was just beginning to get hot again and there were scarlet creepers all over the tomb and green parrots flew about. When I went home, I would lie on the bed in my room and think. Rahul came and I said I had a headache. I hardly knew anything anyone was saying. I ate very little. Mama often came into my room and asked, "Where did you go today?" She was very sweet and gentle, the way she always is when she wants to find out something from you. I would tell her anything that came into my head—an old college friend had come from Poona, we had been to the cinema together—"Which cinema?" Mama said, still sweet and gentle and tidying the handkerchiefs in my drawer. I would even tell her the story of the film I had not seen. "Tomorrow I'm meeting her again." "No, tomorrow I want you to come with me to Meena auntie—"

It began to be difficult to get out of the house. Mama watched me every minute, and when she saw me ready to leave, she stood in the doorway: "Today you are coming with me."

"I told you, I have to meet—"

"You are coming with me!"

We were both angry and shouted. Daddy came out of the study. He told Mama, "She is not a child. . . ."

Then Mama started to shout at him and I ran out of the house and did not look back, though I could hear her calling me.

When I told M., he said, "You had better come with me." I also saw there was no other way. On Friday afternoons Mama goes to a committee meeting of the All-India Ladies' Council, so that was the best time. I bundled up all my clothes and jewels in a sheet and I walked out of the house. Faqir Chand, our butler, saw me, but he said nothing—probably he thought I was sending my clothes to the washerman. M. was waiting for me in a tonga by the post office and he helped me climb up and sit beside him; the tonga was a very old and shaky one, and the driver was also old and so was the horse. We went very slowly, first by the river, past the Fort and through all the bazaars, he and I sitting side by side at the back of the tonga with my bundle between us.

We had such a strange wedding. I laugh even now when I think of it. He had a friend who was a sign painter and had a workshop on the other side of the river. The workshop was really only a shed, but they made it very nice—they turned all the signboards to the wall and they hung my saris over them and over the saris they hung flower garlands. It looked really artistic. They also bought sweetmeats and nuts and put them on a long table that they had borrowed from a carpenter. Several friends of his came and quite a lot of people who lived in sheds and huts nearby. There was a priest and a fire was lit and we sat in front of it and the priest chanted the holy verses. I was feeling very hot because of the fire and of course my face was completely covered by the sari. It wasn't a proper wedding sari, but my own old red sari that I had last worn when Mama gave a tea party for the professors' wives in our drawing room, with cakes from Wenger's.

M. got very impatient, he kept telling the priest, "Now hurry hurry, we have heard all that before."

The priest was offended and said, "These are all holy words."

I couldn't help laughing under my sari, even though I was crying at the same time because I was thinking of Daddy and Rahul and Mama.

There was a quarrel—his friends also told him to keep quiet and let the priest say his verses in the proper manner, and he got angry and shouted, "Is it my marriage or yours?"

At last it was finished and we were married and everyone ate sweetmeats and nuts, even people who just wandered in from the road and whom no one knew.

We stayed a few days with his friend. There was a little room built out of planks just off the workshop and in that we all slept at night, rolled up in blankets. In the day, when the friend painted signs, we stayed in the room by ourselves, M. and I, and no one came in to disturb us. When he slept, I would look at him and look; I studied all the lines on his face. After I had looked my fill, I would shut my eyes and try and see his face in my mind, and when I opened them again, there he was really, his real face, and I cried out loud with joy.

After some days we went on a bus to Niripat. The journey was four hours long and the bus was crowded with farmers and laborers and many old women carrying little bundles. There was a strong smell of poor people who can't afford to change their clothes very often and of the food that the old women ate out of their bundles and the petrol from the bus. I began to feel a little sick. I often get carsick: when we used to drive up to Naini Tal for the summer holidays, Daddy always had to stop the car several times so that I could go out and take fresh air; and Mama would give me lemon drops to suck and rub my temples with eau de cologne.

In Niripat we stayed with M.'s cousin, who had a little brick house just outside the town. They were a big family, and the women lived in one side of the house, in a little set of dark rooms with only metal trunks and beds in them, and the men on the other side. But I ran all over the house; I was singing and laughing all the time. In the evenings I sat with the men and listened to them talking about religion and philosophy and their business (they had a grinding mill); and during the day I helped the women with their household work. M. and I went out for walks and sometimes we went swimming in a pond. The women of the house teased me a lot because I liked M. so much. "But look at him," they said, "he is so dark; and see! his hair is going gray like an old man's." Or, "He is just a loafer—it is only talking with him and never any work." I pretended to be annoyed with them (of course, I knew they were only joking) and that made them laugh more than ever. One of them said, "Now it is very fine, but just wait, in the end her state will be the same as Savitri's."

"Savitri?" I said.

So that was how I first heard about Savitri and the children. At first I was unhappy, but M. explained everything. He had been married very young and to a simple girl from a village. After some years he left her. She understood it was necessary for him to leave her because he had a task to fulfill in the world in which she could not help him. She went back to her parents, with the children. She was happy now, because she saw it was her duty to stay at home and look after the children and lead the good, simple, self-sacrificing life of a mother. He talked of her with affection: she was patient and good. I too learned to love her. I thought of her in the village, with the children, quietly doing her household tasks; early in the mornings and in the evenings she said her prayers. So her life passed. He had gone to see her a few times and she had welcomed him and been glad; but when he went away again, she never tried to keep him. I thought how it would be if he went away from me, but I could not even bear the idea. My heart hurt terribly and I stifled a cry. From that I saw how much nobler and more advanced Savitri was than I; and I hoped that, if the time ever came, I too could be strong like her. But not yet. Not yet. We sold my pearl brooch and sent money to her; he always sent money to her when he had it. Once he said of her: "She is a candle burning in a window of the world," and that was how I always thought of her—as a candle burning for him with a humble flame.

I had not yet written to Daddy and Mama, but I wrote to Rahul. I wrote, "Everything is for the best, Rahul. I often think about you. Please tell everyone that I am all right and happy." M. and I went to the post office together to buy a stamp and post the letter. On the way back he said, "You must write to your father also. He must listen to our ideas." How proud I was when he said *our* ideas.

Daddy and Mama came to Niripat. Daddy sent me a letter in which it said they were waiting for me at the Victoria Hotel. M. took me there, and then went away; he said I must talk to them and explain everything. The Victoria Hotel is the only hotel in Niripat and it is not very grand—it is certainly not the sort of hotel in which Mama is used to staying. In front there is the Victoria Restaurant, where meals can be had at a reduced rate on a monthly basis; there is an open passage at the side that leads to the hotel rooms. Some of the guests had pulled their beds out into the passage and were sitting on them: I noticed a very fat man in a dhoti and an undervest saying his prayers. But Daddy and Mama were inside their room.

It was a very small room with two big beds in it and a table with a blue cotton tablecloth in the middle. Mama was lying on one of the beds; she was crying, and when I came in, she cried more. Daddy and I embraced each other, but Mama turned her face away and pressed her eyes with her handkerchief and the tears rolled right down into her blouse. It made me impatient to see her like that: every mother must part with her daughter sometime, so what was there to cry about? I squeezed Daddy's hands, to show him how happy I was, but then he too turned his face away from me and he coughed. Here we were meeting after so many days, and they were both behaving in a ridiculous manner. I spoke to them quite sharply: "Every individual being must choose his own life and I have chosen mine."

"Don't, darling," Daddy said as if something were hurting him.

Mama suddenly shouted, "You are my shame and disgrace!"

"Quietly, quietly," Daddy said.

I felt like shouting back at her, but I controlled myself; I had not come there to quarrel with her, even if she had come to quarrel with me. I was a wiser person now than I had been. So I only said: "There are aspects of life which you will never grasp."

A little servant boy came in with tea on a tray. Mama sat up on the bed—she is always very keen on her tea—but after a while she sank back again and said in a fainting sort of voice, "There is something dirty in the milk." I had a look and there were only bits of straw, from the cowshed, which I fished out easily with a teaspoon.

Daddy gave a big sigh and said, "You had better let me speak with the young man."

So then I was happy again: I knew that when Daddy really spoke to him and got to know him, he would soon realize what sort of a person M. was and everything would be all right.

And everything was all right. It was true, Daddy couldn't start the department of moral training for him, as we had hoped, because the university didn't have enough funds for a new department; and also, Daddy said, he couldn't get him an academic post because M. didn't have the necessary qualifications. (How stupid are these rules and regulations! Here was a wonderful gifted person like M., with great ideas and wide experience of life, who had so much to pass on; yet he had to take a backward place to some poor little M.A. or Ph.D. who knows nothing of life at all except what he has read in other people's books.) So all Daddy could do was get him a post as secretary to one of the college principals; and I think it was very nice of M. to accept it, because it was not the sort of post a person such as he had a right to expect. But he was always like that: he knew nothing of petty pride and never stood on his dignity, unlike many other people who have really no dignity at all to stand on.

I was sorry to leave Niripat, where I had been so happy with everyone, and to go home again. But of course it was different now, because M. was with me. We had the big guest room at the back of the house and at night we made our beds out on the lawn. Sometimes I thought how funny it was—only a few weeks ago Mama had tried to turn him out of the house and here he was back in the best guest room. It is true that the wheel of fate has many unexpected revolutions. I think he quite liked living in the house, though I was afraid at first he would feel stifled with so many servants and all that furniture and carpets and clocks and Mama's china dinner-services. But he was too great in soul to be bothered by these trivial things; he transcended them and led his life and thought his thoughts in the same way as he would have done if he had been living in some little hut in the jungle.

If only Mama had had a different character. But she is too sunk in her own social station and habits to be able to look out and appreciate anything higher. She thinks if a person has not been abroad and doesn't wear suits and open doors for ladies, he is an inferior type of person. If M. had tried, I know he could have used a knife and fork quite as well as Mama or anyone, but why should he have tried? And there were other things like not making a noise when you drink your tea, which are just trivial little conventions we should all rise above. I often tried to explain this to Mama but I could never make her understand. So it became often quite embarrassing at meal times, with Mama looking at M. and pretending she couldn't eat her own food on account of the way he was eating his. M. of course never noticed, and I felt so ashamed of Mama that in the end I also refused to use any cutlery and ate with my hands. Daddy never said anything—in fact, Daddy said very little at all nowadays, and spent long hours in his office and went to a lot of meetings and, when he came home, he only sat in his study and did not come out to talk to us.

I often thought about Rahul. He had never answered my letter and when I tried to telephone, they said he was not at home. But I wanted very much to see him; there were so many things I had to tell him about. So one day I went to his house. The servants made me wait on the veranda and then Rahul's married sister Kamla came out. Kamla is a very ambitious person and she is always scheming for her husband's promotion (he is in the Ministry of Defense) so that she can take precedence over the other wives in his department. I was not surprised at the way she talked to me. I know a person like Kamla will always think only petty thoughts and doesn't understand that there is anything transcending the everyday life in which she is sunk up to her ears. So I let her say what she wanted and when she told me to go away, I went. When Mama found out that I had been to Rahul's house, she was furious. "All right, so you have lost

31

all pride for yourself, but for your family—at least think of us!" At the word pride I laughed out loud: Mama's ideas of pride were so different from mine and M.'s. But I was sorry that they wouldn't let me see Rahul.

M. went out every day, and I thought he went to his job in the university. But one day Daddy called me into his study and he said that M. had lost his job because he hadn't been going there for weeks. I had a little shock at first, but then I thought it is all right, whatever he wants to do is all right; and anyway, it hadn't been a suitable post for him in the first place. I told Daddy so.

Daddy played with his silver paper-knife and he didn't look at me at all; then he said, "You know he has been married before?" and still he didn't look at me.

I don't know how Daddy found out—I suppose he must have been making inquiries, it is the sort of thing people in our station of life always do about other people, we are so mistrustful—but I answered him quite calmly. I tried to explain to him about Savitri.

After a while Daddy said, "I only wanted you to know that your marriage is not legal and can be dissolved any time you want."

Then I told him that marriages are not made in the sight of the law but in the sight of God, and that in the sight of God both Savitri and I were married to M., she there and I here. Daddy turned his head away and looked out of the window.

M. told me that he wanted to start a school and that he could do so if Daddy got him a grant from the Ministry. I thought it was a very exciting idea and we talked a lot about it that night, as we lay together on our beds. He had many wonderful ideas about how a school should be run and said that the children should be taught to follow only their instincts, which would lead them to the highest Good. He talked so beautifully, like a prophet, a saint. I could hardly sleep all night, and first thing in the morning I talked to Daddy. Unfortunately Mama was listening at the door—she has a bad habit of doing that—and suddenly she came bursting in. "Why don't you leave your father alone?" she cried. "Isn't it enough that we give you both food and shelter?"

I said, "Mama please, I'm talking important business with Daddy."

She began to say all sorts of things about M. and why he had married me. Daddy tried to keep her quiet but she was beyond herself by that time, so I just covered my ears with my hands and ran out. She came after me, still shouting these horrible things.

There in the hall was M., and when I tried to run past him, he stopped me and took my hands from my ears and made me listen to everything Mama was saying. She got more and more furious, and then she went into one of her hysterical fits, in which she throws herself down and beats her head on the floor and tears at her clothes. Daddy tried to lift her up, but of course she is too heavy for him. She went on screaming and shouting at M.

M. said, "Go and get your things," so I went and wrapped everything up in the sheet again, his things and mine, and he slung the bundle over his shoulder and went out of the house, with me walking behind him.

I hoped we would go back to Niripat, but he wanted to stay in the city because he had several schemes in mind—there was the school, and he also had hopes of starting a newspaper in which he could print all his ideas. So he had to go around and see a lot of people, in ministries and so on. Sometimes he got quite discouraged because it was so difficult to make people understand. Then he looked tired and the lines on his face became very deep and I felt such love and pity for him. But he had great inner strength, and next day he always started on his rounds again, as fresh and hopeful as before.

We had no proper home at that time, but lived in several places. There was the sign painter, and another friend had a bookshop in one of the government markets with a little room at the back where we could stay with him; and once we found a model house that was left over from a low-cost housing exhibition, and we lived in that till workmen came to tear it down. There were plenty of places where we could stay for a few days or even weeks. In the evenings there were always many friends and all sat and discussed their ideas, and some of them recited poetry or played the flute, so that sometimes we didn't go to sleep at all. We never had any worries about money—M. said if one doesn't think about money, one doesn't need it, and how true that is. Daddy sent me a check every month, care of the friend who kept the bookshop, and we still had some of my jewelry, which we could sell whenever we wanted; so there was even money to send to Savitri and the children.

Once I met Rahul, quite by chance. That was at the time when we had just moved out of the exhibition house. M. had to go to one of the ministries to see an under-secretary, and I was taking our bundle to an orphanage, run by a friend of M.'s, where we were going to stay. I was waiting for a bus, holding the bundle; it wasn't heavy at all anymore, so there was no need to take a tonga. Rahul came out of a music shop with some records that he had just bought (he is very fond of dance records—how often we have danced together to his gramophone!). I called to him and when he didn't hear me, I went up to him. He lowered his eyes and wouldn't look at me and hardly greeted me.

"Rahul," I said in the stern voice I always use with him when I think he is misbehaving.

"Why did you do it?" he said. "My family are very angry with you and I'm also angry." He sulked, but he looked so sweet; he still had his pink cheeks.

"If you have your car, you can give me a lift," I said. Rahul is always a gentleman, and he even carried my bundle for me to his car.

It took us a long time to find the orphanage—it was right at the back of the Fatehpuri mosque somewhere—so there was plenty of time for me to talk to him. He listened quite quietly, driving the car through all that traffic. When at last we found the orphanage and I was ready to get out, he said, "Don't go yet." I stayed with him for a while, even though the car was parked very awkwardly in that crowded alleyway, and men with barrows swore at us because they could not get past.

Soon afterward a friend of M.'s who was in the railways got transferred, and as he lived in a house with a very low rent, it was a good opportunity for us and we took it over from him. There were two rooms and a little yard at the back, and upstairs two families were living. Daddy would send a check for the rent. I cooked for us and cleaned the house and talked with the families upstairs, while M. went out to see people about his ideas. But after a time he began to go out less and less, and he became depressed; he said the world had rejected him because he was not strong enough yet. Now it was his task to purify himself and make himself stronger. He stayed at home and meditated. A strange change came over him. Most of the time he sat in one of our rooms, in a corner of the floor by himself, and he wouldn't let me come in. Sometimes I heard him singing to himself and shouting—he made such strange noises, almost like an animal. For days he ate nothing at all and, when I tried to coax him, he upset the food I had brought and threw it on the floor. I tried to be patient and bear and understand everything.

34

His friends stopped coming and he hardly ever left that little room for two months. Then he started going out by himself—I never knew where and could not ask him. He had an expression on his face as if he were listening for something, so that one felt one couldn't disturb him. When he talked to me, he talked as if he were someone else and I were someone else. At night I slept in the yard at the back with the families from upstairs, who were always kind to me.

Then visitors began to come for him—not his old friends, but quite new people whom I had never seen before. They sat with him in the little room and I could hear him talking to them. At first only a few men used to come, but then more and more came, and women too. I also sat in the room sometimes and listened to him talk; he told strange stories about parrots and princes and tigers in the jungle, all of which had some deep meaning. When the people understood the deep meaning, they all exclaimed with pleasure and said God was speaking through his mouth.

Now they began to bring us gifts of food and money and clothes and even jewelry. M. never took any notice, and I just piled the things in the other room, which was soon very crowded. We ate the food and I also gave it to the families upstairs, but there was still plenty left over, and at night someone used to come from the beggars' home to take it away. I sent a lot of money to Savitri. The house was always full of people now, and they spilled over into the yard and out into the street. More and more women came—most of them were old but there were some young ones too, and the young ones were even more fervent and religious than the old ones. There was one plump and pretty young widow, who was always dressed very nicely and came every day. She said she was going mad with love of God and needed words of solace and comfort from M. She touched his feet and implored him to relieve her, and when he took no notice of her, she shook him and tugged at his clothes, so that he became quite angry.

Mama often came to see me. In the beginning she was very disgusted with the house and the way we lived and everything, but afterward, when she saw how many people came and all the things they brought and how they respected M., she kept quiet on that subject. Now she only said, "Who knows what is to become of it all?" Mama is not really a religious person, but she has a lot of superstitions. When holy men come begging to her house, she always gives them something—not because of their holiness, but because she is afraid they will curse her and bring the evil eye on us all. She no longer said anything bad about M., and when she talked about him, she didn't say, "that one" as she used to, but always "He." Once or twice she went and sat with the other people in the little room in which he was, and when she came out, she looked so grave and thoughtful that I had to laugh.

Rahul also visited me. At first he was stiff and sulky, as if he were doing me a favor by coming; but then he began to talk, all about how lonely he was and how his family were trying to persuade him to marry girls he didn't like. I felt sorry for him—I knew it is always difficult for him to make friends and he has never really had anyone except me. I let him talk, and he kept coming again and again. There was a little space with a roof of asbestos sheet over it in the yard where I did my cooking, and it was here that Rahul and I sat. It was not a very private place because of all the people in the yard, waiting to see M., but Rahul soon got used to it and talked just as he would have done if we had been sitting in Mama's drawing room. He was very melancholy, and when he had finished telling me about how lonely he was, he only sat and looked at me with big sad eyes. So I let him help me with the cooking—at first he only sifted the rice and lentils, but after a time I let him do some real cooking and he enjoyed it terribly. He would make all sorts of things—fritters and potato cakes and horseradish pancakes—and they were really delicious. We ate some ourselves and the rest we sent to the beggars' home.

There were always a few young men who stayed at night and slept outside the door of the room where M. was. I often heard him get up in the night and walk up and down; and sometimes he shouted at the young men sleeping outside his door, "Go home!" and he kicked them with his foot, he was so impatient and angry with them. He was often angry nowadays. I heard him shouting at people and scolding them for coming to pester him. When he scolded them, they said he was right to do so, because they were bad, sinful people; but they did not go away and, on the contrary, even more came.

One night I felt someone shaking me to wake up. I opened my eyes and it was M. I jumped up at once and we went out into the street together and sat on a doorstep. Here and there people were sleeping on the sidewalk or on the platforms of shuttered shops. It was very dark and quiet. Only sometimes someone coughed in his sleep or there was a watchman's cry and the tap of his stick. M. said, "Soon I shall have to go away."

Then I knew that the time I had always feared was near.

He said, "It will be best for you to go home again." He spoke very practically, and with gentleness and great concern for me.

But I didn't want to think about what I was going to do. For the moment I wanted it to be only now—always night and people always sleeping and he and I sitting together like this on the doorstep for ever and ever.

The plump young widow still came every day and every day in a different sari, and she made such scenes that in the end M. forbade her to come any more. So she hung about outside in the yard for a few days, and then she started peeping into his room and after that she crept in behind the others and sat quietly at the back; till finally she showed herself to him quite openly and even began to make scenes again. "Have pity!" she cried. "God is eating me up!" At last he quite lost his temper with her. He took off his slipper and began to beat her with it and when she ran away, screaming and clutching her sari about her, he ran after her, brandishing his slipper. They were a funny sight. He pursued her right out into the street, and then he turned back and began to chase all the other people out of the house. He scattered them right and left, beating at them with his slipper, and cursing and scolding. Everyone ran away very fast—even Rahul, who had been cooking potato cakes, made off in a great fright. When they had all gone, M. returned to his room and locked the door behind him. He looked hot and angry.

And next day he was gone. People came as usual that day but when they realized he was no longer there, they went away again and also took their gifts back with them. That night the men from the beggars' home were disappointed. I stayed on by myself, it didn't matter to me where I was. Sometimes I sat in one of the rooms, sometimes I walked up and down. The families from upstairs tried to make me eat and sleep, but I heard nothing of what they said. I don't remember much about that time. Later Daddy came to take me away. For the last time I tied my things up in a sheet and I went with him.

I think sometimes of Savitri, and I wonder whether I too am like her now—a candle burning for him in a window of the world. I am patient and inwardly calm and lead the life that has been appointed for me. I play tennis again and I go out to tea and garden parties

37

with Mama, and Rahul and I often dance to the gramophone. Probably I shall marry Rahul quite soon. I laugh and talk just as much as I used to and Mama says I am too frivolous, but Daddy smiles and encourages me. Mama has had a lot of new pieces of jewelry made for me to replace the ones I sold; she and I keep on quarreling as before.

I still try and see his face in my mind, and I never succeed. But I know—and that is how I can go on living the way I do, and even enjoy my life and be glad—that one day I shall succeed and I shall see that face as it really is. But whose face it is I shall see in that hour of happiness—and indeed, whose face it is I look for with such longing—is not quite clear to me.

THE WIDOW

Durga lived downstairs in the house she owned. There was a small central courtyard and many little rooms opening out from it. All her husband's relatives, and her own, wanted to come and live with her; they saw that it would be very comfortable, and anyway, why pay rent elsewhere when there was that whole house? But she resisted them all. She wouldn't even allow them to live in the upstairs part, but let it out to strangers and took rent and was a landlady. She had learned a lot since she had become a widow and a property owner. No one, not even her elder relatives, could talk her into anything.

Her husband would have been pleased to see her like that. He hated relatives anyway, on principle; and he hated weak women who let themselves be managed and talked into things. That was what he had always taught her: stand on your own, have a mind, be strong. And he had left her everything so that she could be. When he had drafted his will, he had cackled with delight, thinking of all his relatives and how angry they would be. His one anxiety had been that she would not be able to stand up to them and that she would give everything over into their hands; so that his last energies had been poured into training her, teaching her, making her strong.

She had grown fond of him in those last years—so much so that, if it hadn't been for the money and independent position with which he left her, she would have been sad at losing him. That was a great change from what she had felt at the beginning of her marriage when, God forgive her, she had prayed every day for him to die. As she had pointed out in her prayers, he was old and she was young; it was not right. She had hated everyone in those days—not only her husband, but her family too, who had married her to him. She

/Out of India/

would not speak to anyone. All day she sat in a little room, unbathed, unkempt, like a woman in mourning. The servant left food for her on a tray and tried to coax her to eat, but she wouldn't—not till she was very hungry indeed and then she ate grudgingly, cursing each mouthful for keeping her alive.

But the old man was kind to her. He was a strange old man. He did not seem to expect anything of her at all, except only that she should be there in his house. Sometimes he brought saris and bangles for her, and though at first she pretended she did not want them, afterward she was pleased and tried them on and admired herself. She often wondered why he should be so kind to her. He wasn't to anyone else. In fact, he was known as a mean, spiteful old man, who had made his money (in grain) unscrupulously, pressed his creditors hard, and maliciously refused to support his needy relatives. But with her he was always gentle and even generous, and after a while they got on very well together.

So when he was dead, she almost missed him, and it was only when she reminded herself of other things about him—his old-man smell, and his dried legs, when she had massaged them, with the useless rag of manhood flopping against the thigh—that she realized it was better he was gone. She was, after all, still young and healthy and hearty, and now with the money and property he had left her, she could lead the life she was entitled to. She kept two servants, got up when she wanted, and went to sleep when she wanted; she ate everything she liked and as much as she liked; when she felt like going out, she hired a tonga—and not just any tonga, but always a spruce one with shining red-leather seats and a well-groomed horse wearing jingling bells, so that people looked around at her as she was driven smartly through the streets.

It was a good life, and she grew plump and smooth with it. Nor did she lack for company: her own family and her husband's were always hovering around her and, now that she had them in the proper frame of mind, she quite enjoyed entertaining them. It had taken her some time to get them into that proper frame of mind. For in the beginning, when her husband had just died, they had taken it for granted that she was to be treated as the widow—that is, the cursed one who had committed the sin of outliving her husband and was consequently to be numbered among the outcasts. They had wanted—yes, indeed they had—to strip her of her silken colored clothes and of her golden ornaments. The more orthodox among

40

them had even wanted to shave her head, to reduce her diet to stale bread and lentils, and deprive her from ever again tasting the sweet things of life: to condemn her, in fact, to that perpetual mourning, perpetual expiation, that was the proper lot of widows. That was how they saw it and how their forefathers had always seen it; but not how she saw it at all.

There had been a struggle, of course, but not one of which the outcome was long in doubt. And now it was accepted that she should be mistress of what was hers and rule her household and wear her fine clothes and eat her fine foods; and out of her abundance she would toss crumbs to them, let them sit in her house and talk with them when she felt like talking, listen to their importunities for money and sometimes even perhaps—not out of pity or affection, but just as the whim took her—do them little favors and be praised and thanked for it. She was queen, and they knew it.

But even a queen's life does not bring perfect satisfaction always, and there were days and even weeks at a time when she felt she had not been dealt with as she had a right to expect. She could never say exactly what had been left out, but only that something *had* been left out and that somehow, somewhere, she had been shortchanged. And when this realization came over her, then she fell into a black mood and ate and slept more than ever—not for pleasure, but compulsively, sunk in sloth and greed because soft beds and foods were all that life had given to her. At such times she turned her relatives away from her house, and those who nevertheless wheedled their way in had to sit respectfully silent around her bed while she heaved and groaned like a sick woman.

There was one old aunt, known by everyone as Bhuaji, who always managed to wheedle her way in, whatever Durga's mood. She was a tough, shrewd old woman, small and frail in appearance and with a cast in one eye that made it seem as if she was constantly peeping around the next corner to see what advantage lay there. When Durga's black mood was on her, it was Bhuaji who presided at the bedside, saw to it that the others kept suitably mournful faces and, at every groan of Durga's, fell into loud exclamations of pity at her sufferings. When Durga finally got tired of all these faces gathered around her and, turning her back on them, told them to go away and never come back to be a torture and a burden on her, then it was again Bhuaji who saw to it that they left in haste and good order and suitably on compassionate tiptoe; and after locking the door behind them all, she would come back to sit with Durga and encourage her not only to groan but to weep as well and begin to unburden herself.

Only what was there of which she could unburden herself, much as, under Bhuaji's sympathetic encouragement, she longed to do so? She brought out broken sentences, broken complaints and accusations, but there was nothing she could quite lay her finger on. Bhuaji, always eager and ready to comfort with the right words, tried to lay it on for her, pointing out how cruelly fate had dealt with her in depriving her of what was every woman's right— namely, a husband and children. But no, no, Durga would cry, that was not it, that was not what she wanted: and she looked scornful, thinking of those women who did have husbands and children, her sisters and her cousins, thin, shabby, overworked, and overburdened, was there anything to envy in their lot? On the contrary, it was they who should and did envy Durga—she could read it in their eyes when they looked at her, who was so smooth and well-fed and had everything that they could never even dream for.

Then, gradually, Bhuaji began to talk to her of God. Durga knew about God, of course. One had to worship Him in the temple and also perform certain rites such as bathing in the river when there was an eclipse and give food to the holy men and observe fast-days. One did all these things so that no harm would befall, and everybody did them and had always done them: that was God. But Bhuaji talked differently. She talked about Him as if He were a person whom one could get to know, like someone who would come and visit in the house and sit and talk and drink tea. She spoke of Him mostly as Krishna, sometimes as the baby Krishna and sometimes as the lover Krishna. She had many stories to tell about Krishna, all the old stories that Durga knew well, for she had heard them since she was a child; but Bhuaji told them as if they were new and had happened only yesterday and in the neighborhood. And Durga sat up on her bed and laughed: "No, really, he did that?" "Yes yes, really—he stole the butter and licked it with his fingers and he teased the young girls and pulled their hair and kissed them—oh, he was such a naughty boy!" And Durga rocked herself to and fro with her hands clasped before her face, laughing in delight—"How naughty!" she cried. "What a bad bad boy, bless his heart!"

But when they came to the lover Krishna, then she sat quite still and looked very attentive, with her mouth a little open and her eyes fixed on Bhuaji's face. She didn't say much, just listened; only sometimes she would ask in a low voice, "He was very handsome?" "Oh very," said Bhuaji, and she described him all over again—lotus eyes and brows like strung bows and a throat like a conch. Durga couldn't form much of a picture from that, but never mind, she made her own, formed it secretly in her mind as she sat there listening to Bhuaji, and grew more and more thoughtful, more and more silent.

Bhuaji went on to tell her about Krishna's devotees and the rich rewards granted to those whose hearts were open to receive him. As Durga avidly listened, she narrated the life of Maya Devi, who had retired from the world and built herself a little hut on the banks of the Ganges: there to pass her days with the baby Krishna, whom she had made her child and to whom she talked all day as to a real child, and played with him and cooked for him, bathed his image and dressed it and put it to sleep at night and woke it up with a kiss in the morning. And then there was Pushpa Devi, for whom so many advantageous offers had come but who rejected them all because she said she was wedded already, to Krishna, and he alone was her lord and her lover; she lived with him in spirit, and sometimes in the nights her family would hear her screams of joy as she lay with him in their marital rite and gave him her soul.

Durga bought two little brass images of Krishna—one of him playing the flute, the other as a baby crawling on all fours. She gave them special prominence on her little prayer table and paid her devotions to him many times a day, always waiting for him to come alive for her and be all that Bhuaji promised he would be. Sometimes—when she was alone at night or lay on her bed in the hot, silent afternoons, her thoughts dwelling on Krishna—she felt strange new stirrings within her that were almost like illness, with a tugging in the bowels and a melting in the thighs. And she trembled and wondered whether this was Krishna descending on her, as Bhuaji promised he would, showing her his passion, creeping into her—ah! great God that he was—like a child or a lover, into her womb and into her breasts.

She became dreamy and withdrawn, so that her relatives, quick to note this change, felt freer to come and go as they pleased and sit around in her house and drink tea with a lot of milk and sugar in it. Bhuaji, indeed, was there almost all the time. She had even brought

43

a bundle of clothes and often stayed all day and all night, only scurrying off to have a quick look at her own household, with her own old husband in it, and coming back within the hour. Durga suspected that, on these home excursions of hers, Bhuaji went well provided with little stocks of rice and lentils and whatever other provisions she could filch from the kitchen store. But Durga hardly cared and was, at any rate, in no frame of mind to make a scene. And when they asked for money, Bhuaji or the other relatives, as often as not she gave—quite absentmindedly, taking out her keys to unlock the steel almira in which she kept her cashbox, while they eagerly, greedily, watched her.

At such moments she often thought of her husband and of what he would say if he could see her being so yielding with these relatives. She could almost imagine him getting angry—hear his shrill old man's voice and see him shaking his fist so that the sleeve of his kurta flapped and showed his plucked, dried arm trembling inside. But she did not care for his anger; it was her life, her money, she sullenly answered him, and she could let herself be exploited if she wished. Why should he, a dead old man, dictate his wishes to her, who was alive and healthy and a devotee of Krishna's? She found herself thinking of her husband with dislike. It was as if she bore him some grudge, though she did not know what for.

The relatives sat in the house and got bolder and bolder, until they were giving their own orders to the servants and complaining about the quality of the tea.

It was about this time that the tenants who had rented the place upstairs gave notice—an event that brought great excitement into the lives of the relatives, who spent many happy hours apportioning the vacant flat out among themselves (Bhuaji, of course, was going to move her old husband into one room, and she left the others to fight for the remaining space). But here suddenly Durga showed herself quite firm again: tenants meant rent, and she had no intentions, not even to spite her husband, of sacrificing a regular monthly income. So only a few days after the old tenants moved out, and the relatives were still hotly disputing among themselves as to how the place was to be apportioned, a new family of tenants moved in, consisting of one Mr. Puri (a municipal tax inspector) with his wife, two daughters, and a son. Their belongings were carried upstairs to loud, remonstrative cries from the relatives; to which Durga turned a deaf ear—even to the plaints of Bhuaji, who had already brought her old husband and her household chattels along and now had to take them back again.

Durga had been worshiping her two images for so long now, but nothing of what Bhuaji had promised seemed to be happening to them. And less and less was happening to her. She tried so hard, lying on her bed and thinking of Krishna and straining to reproduce that wave of love she had experienced; but it did not return or, if it did, came only as a weak echo of what it had been. She was unsatisfied and felt that much had been promised and little given. Once, after she had prayed for a long time before the two images, she turned away and suddenly kicked at the leg of a chair and hurt her toe. And sometimes, in the middle of doing something—sorting the laundry or folding a sari—she would suddenly throw it aside with an impatient gesture and walk away frowning.

She spent a lot of time sitting on a string cot in her courtyard, not doing anything nor thinking anything in particular, just sitting there, feeling heavy and too fat and wondering what there was in life that one should go on living it. When her relatives came to visit her, she as often as not told them to go away, even Bhuaji; she did not feel like talking or listening to any of them. But now there was a new person to stake a claim to her attention. The courtyard was overlooked by a veranda that ran the length of the flat upstairs. On this veranda Mrs. Puri, her new tenant, would frequently appear, leaning her arms on the balustrade and shouting down in friendly conversation. Durga did not encourage her and answered as dryly as politeness permitted; but Mrs. Puri was a friendly woman and persisted, appearing twice and three times a day to comment to Durga on the state of the weather. After a while she even began to exercise the prerogative of a neighbor and to ask for little loans—one day she had run out of lentils, a second out of flour, a third out of sugar. In return, when she cooked a special dish or made pickle, she would send some down for Durga, thus establishing a neighborly traffic that Durga had not wished for but was too lethargic to discourage.

Then one day Mrs. Puri sent some ginger pickle down with her son. He appeared hesitantly in the courtyard, holding his glass jar carefully between two hands. Durga was lying drowsily on her cot; her eyes were shut and perhaps she was even half asleep. The boy stood and looked down at her, knowing what to do, lightly coughing to draw her attention. Her eyes opened and stared up at him. He was perhaps seventeen years old, a boy with large black eyes and broad shoulders and cheeks already dark with growth. Durga lay and stared up at him, seeing nothing but his young face looming above her. He looked back at her, uncertain, tried to smile, and blushed. Then at last she sat up and adjusted the sari which had slipped down from her breasts. His eyes modestly lowered, he held the jar of pickle out to her as if in appeal.

"Your mother sent?"

He nodded briefly and, placing the jar on the floor by her cot, turned to go rather quickly. Just as he was about to disappear through the door leading out from the courtyard, she called him back, and he stopped and stood facing her, waiting. It was some time before she spoke, and then all she could think to say was "Please thank your mother." He disappeared before she could call him back again.

Durga had become rather slovenly in her habits lately, but that evening she dressed herself up in one of her better saris and went to call on Mrs. Puri upstairs. A visit from the landlady was considered of some importance, so Mrs. Puri, who had been soaking raw mangoes, left this work, wiped her hands on the end of her sari and settled Durga in the sitting room. The sitting room was not very grand; it had only a cane table in it and some cane stools and a few cheap bazaar pictures on the whitewashed walls. Durga sat in the only chair in the room, a velvet armchair that had the velvet rubbed bare in many places and smelled of old, damp clothes.

Mrs. Puri's two daughters sat on the floor, stitching a quilt together out of many old pieces. They were plain girls with heavy features and bad complexions. Mr. Puri evidently was out—and his wife soon dwelled on that subject: every night, she said, he was sitting at some friend's house, goodness knows what they did, sitting like that, what could they have so much to talk about? And wasting money in smoking cigarettes and chewing betel, while she sat at home with her daughters, poor girls, and wasn't it high time good husbands were found for them? But what did Mr. Puri care—he had thought only for his own enjoyment, his family was nothing to him. And Govind the same. . . .

"Govind?"

"My son. He too—only cinema for him and laughing with friends."

She had much to complain about and evidently did not often

have someone whom she could complain to; so she made the most of Durga. The two plain daughters listened placidly, stitching their quilt; only when their mother referred to the urgent necessity of finding husbands for them—as she did at frequent intervals and as a sort of capping couplet to each particular complaint—did they begin to wriggle and exchange sly glances and titter behind their hands.

It took Durga some time before she could disengage herself; and when she finally did, Mrs. Puri accompanied her to the stairs, carrying her burden of complaint right over into her farewell and even pursuing Durga with it as she picked her way down the steep, narrow stone stairs. And just as she had reached the bottom of them, Govind appeared to walk up them, and his mother shouted down to him, "Is this a time to come home for your meal?"

Durga passed him in the very tight space between the doorway and the first step. She was so close to him that she could feel his warmth and hear his breath. Mrs. Puri shouted down the stairs: "Running here and there all day like a loafer!" Durga could see his eyes gleaming in the dark and he could see hers; for a moment they looked at each other. Durga said in a low voice, "Your mother is angry with you," and then he was already halfway up the stairs.

Later, slowly unwinding herself from her sari and staring at herself in the mirror as she did so, she thought about her husband. And again, and stronger than ever, she had that feeling of dislike against him, that grudge against the useless dead old man. It was eighteen or nineteen years now since they had married her to him: and if he had been capable, wouldn't she have had a son like Govind now, a strong, healthy, handsome boy with big shoulders and his beard just growing? She smiled at the thought, full of tenderness, and forgetting her husband, thought instead how it would be if Govind were her son. She would not treat him like his mother did—would never reproach him, shout at him down the stairs—but, on the contrary, encourage him in all his pleasures so that, first thing when he came home, he would call to her—"Mama!"—and they would sit together affectionately, more like brother and sister, or even two friends, than like mother and son, while he told her everything that had happened to him during the day.

She stepped closer to the mirror—her sari lying carelessly where it had fallen around her feet—and looked at herself, drawing her hand over her skin. Yes, she was still soft and smooth and who could see the tiny little lines, no more than shadows, that lay around her eyes and the corners of her mouth? And how fine her eyes still were, how large and black and how they shone. And her hair too—she unwound it from its pins and it dropped down slowly, heavy and black and sleek with oil, and not one gray hair in it.

As she stood there, looking at herself in nothing but her short blouse and her waist petticoat, with her hair down, suddenly another image appeared behind her in the mirror: an old woman, gray and shabby and squinting and with an ingratiating smile on her face. "I am not disturbing?" Bhuaji said.

Durga bent down to pick up her sari. She began to fold it, but Bhuaji took it from her and did it far more deftly, the tip of her tongue eagerly protruding from her mouth.

"Why did you come?" Durga said, watching her. Bhuaji made no reply, but went on folding the sari, and when she had finished, she smoothed it ostentatiously from both sides. Durga lay down on the bed. As a matter of fact, she found she was quite glad that Bhuaji had come to see her.

She asked, "How long is it since they married me?"

"Let me see," Bhuaji said. She squatted by the side of the bed and began to massage Durga's legs. "It is fifteen years, sixteen ... "

"No, eighteen."

Bhuaji nodded in agreement, her lips mumbling as she worked something out in her head, her hands still skillfully massaging.

"Eighteen years," Durga said reflectively. "I could have been—"

"Yes, a grandmother by now," said Bhuaji, smiling widely with all her empty gums.

Durga suddenly pushed those soothing massaging hands away and sat upright. "Leave me alone! Why do you come here, who called you?"

Instead of sitting in her courtyard, Durga was now often to be found pacing up and down by the door that led to the staircase. When Govind came down, she always had a word for him. At first he was shy with her and left her as quickly as possible; sometimes he waited for her to go away before he came down or went up. But she was patient with him. She understood and even sympathized with his shyness: he was young, awkward perhaps, like a child, and didn't know how much good she meant him. But she persevered; she would ask him questions like: "You go often to the cinema?" or "What are you studying?" to prove to him how interested she was in him, interested like a mother or a favorite aunt, and ready to talk on any topic with him.

And slowly he responded. Instead of dashing away, he began to stand still at the bottom of the steps and to answer her questions; at first in monosyllables but soon, when his interest was stirred, at greater length; and finally at such great length that it seemed pointless to go on standing there in that dark cramped space when he could go into her house and sit there with her and drink almond sherbet. He kept on talking and told her everything: who were his friends, who his favorite film stars, his ambition to go abroad, to become an aircraft engineer. She listened and watched him while he spoke; she watched and watched him, her eyes fixed on his face. She became very familiar with his face, yet always it was new to her. When he smiled, two little creases appeared in his cheeks. His teeth were large and white, his hair sprang from a point on his forehead. Everything about him was young and fresh and strong—even his smell, which was that of a young animal full of sap and sperm.

She loved to do little things for him. At first only to ply him with almond sherbet and sweetmeats, of which he could take great quantities; later to give him money—beginning with small amounts, a rupee here and there, but then going on to five- and even ten-rupee notes. He wanted money so badly and his parents gave him so little. It was wrong to keep a boy short of money when he needed a lot: for treating his friends, for his surreptitious cigarettes, for T-shirts and jeans such as he saw other boys wearing.

It became so that he got into the habit of asking her for whatever he wanted. How could she refuse? On the contrary, she was glad and proud to give—if only to see the look of happiness on his face, his eyes shining at the thought of what he was going to buy, his smile, which brought little creases into his cheeks. At such moments she was warm and sick with mother's love, she longed to cradle his head and stroke his hair. He was her son, her child.

That was exactly what his mother told her: "He is your son also, your child." Mrs. Puri was glad to see Durga take such an interest in the boy. She taught him to say thank you for everything that Durga gave him and to call her auntie. She made pickle very often and sent it down in jars. She also came down herself and talked to Durga for hours on end about her family problems. So much was needed, and where was it all to come from? Mr. Puri's salary was small—175 rupees a month plus dearness allowance—and he spent a lot on betel and cigarettes and other pleasures. And what was to become of her poor children? Such good children they were, as anyone who took an interest in them was bound to find out. They needed a helping hand in life, that was all. Her boy, and her two girls who ought to have been married a year ago. She sent the girls down quite often, but Durga always sent them quickly back up again.

Toward the beginning of each month, when the rent was due, Govind came down every day with pickle and after a while Mrs. Puri would follow him. Dabbing with her sari in the corner of her eye, she would give an exact account of her monthly expenditure, what were her debts and what she had in hand, so that Durga could see for herself how impossible it was to impose any demand for rent on such an overburdened budget. And though Durga at first tried to ignore these plaints, this became more and more difficult, and in the end she always had to say that she would not mind waiting a few days longer. After which Mrs. Puri dried her eyes and the subject of rent was not mentioned again between them till the first week of the following month, when the whole procedure was repeated. In this way several months' rent accumulated—a fact that, had it been brought to their notice, would have surprised Durga's previous tenants, who had not found her by any means so lenient a landlady.

The relatives were much alarmed at this growing friendship with the Puris, which seemed to them both ominous and unnatural. What need had Durga to befriend strangers when there were all her own relatives, to whom she was bound in blood and duty? They became very indignant with her, but had to keep a check on their tongues; for Durga was short-tempered with them these days and, if they touched on subjects or showed moods not to her liking, was quicker than ever to show them the door. But something obviously had to be said and it was Bhuaji who took it upon herself to say it.

She began by praising Govind. A good boy, she said, that she could see at a glance, respectful and well mannered, just the sort of boy whom one ought to encourage and help on in life. She had nothing at all against Govind. But his mother now, and his sisters— Bhuaji, looking sideways at Durga, sadly shook her head. Alas, she knew women like that only too well, she had come across too many of them to be taken in by their soft speech. Greedy and shameless, that was what they were, self-seeking and unscrupulous, with their one aim to fasten upon and wring whatever advantage they could out of noble-hearted people like Durga. It was they, said Bhuaji, coming closer and whispering behind her hand as if afraid Mrs. Puri would hear from upstairs, who incited the boy to come down and ask for money and new clothes—just as a feeler and to see how far they could go. Let Durga wait and in a short time she would see: saris they would ask for, not ten-rupee notes but hundred-rupee ones, household furniture, a radio, a costly carpet; and they would not rest till they had possessed themselves not only of the upstairs part of the house but of the downstairs part as well. . . .

Just then Govind passed the door and Durga called out to him. When he came, she asked him, "Where are you going?" and then she stroked the shirt he was wearing, saying, "I think it is time you had another new bush shirt."

"A silk one," he said, which made Durga smile and reply in a soft, promising voice, "We will see," while poor Bhuaji stood by and could say nothing, only squint and painfully smile.

One day Bhuaji went upstairs. She said to Mrs. Puri: "Don't let your boy go downstairs so much. She is a healthy woman, and young in her thoughts." Mrs. Puri chose to take offense: she said her boy was a good boy, and Durga was like another mother to him. Bhuaji squinted and laid her finger by the side of her nose, as one who could tell more if she but chose. This made Mrs. Puri very angry and she began to shout about how much evil thought there was in the world today so that even pure actions were misinterpreted and made impure. Her two daughters, though they did not know what it was all about, also looked indignant. Mrs. Puri said she was proud of her son's friendship with Durga. It showed he was better than all those other boys who thought of nothing but their own pleasures and never cared to listen to the wisdom they could learn from their elders. And she looked from her veranda down into the courtyard, where Govind sat with Durga and was trying to persuade her to buy him a motor scooter. Bhuaji also looked down, and she bit her lip so that no angry word could escape her.

Durga loved to have Govind sitting with her like that. She had no intention of buying him a motor scooter, which would take more money than she cared to disburse, but she loved to hear him talk about it. His eyes gleamed and his hair tumbled into his face as he told her about the beautiful motor scooter possessed by his friend Ram, which had many shiny fittings and a seat at the back on which he gave rides to his friends. He leaned forward and came closer in his eagerness to impart his passion to her. He was completely carried

away—"It does forty miles per hour, as good as any motor car!"—
and looked splendid, full of strength and energy. Durga laid her
hand on his knee and he didn't notice. "I have something for you
inside," she said in a low hoarse voice.

He followed her into the room and stood behind her while she
fumbled with her keys at her steel almira. Her hand was shaking
rather, so that she could not turn the key easily. When she did, she
took something from under a pile of clothes and held it out to him.
"For you," she said. It was a penknife. He was disappointed, he
lowered his eyes and said, "It is nice," in a sullen, indifferent voice.
But then at once he looked up again and he wetted his lips with his
tongue and said, "Only twelve hundred rupees, just slightly used, it
is a chance in a million"—looking past her into the almira where he
knew there was a little safe in which she kept her cash. But already
she was locking it and fastening the key back to the string at her
waist. He suddenly reached out and held her hand with the key in
it—"Twelve hundred rupees," he said in a whisper as low and
hoarse as hers had been before. And when she felt him so close to
her, so eager, so young, so passionate, and his hand actually holding
hers, she shivered all over her body and her heart leaped up in her
and next thing she was sobbing. "If you knew," she cried, "how
empty my life has been, how lonely!" and the tears flowed down her
face. He let go her hand and stepped backward, and then backward
again as she followed him; till he was brought up short by her bed,
which he could feel pressing against the back of his knees, as he
stood, pinned, between it and her.

She was talking fast, about how alone she was and there was no
one to care for. Yet she was young still, she told him—she invited
him to look, look down into her face, wasn't it a young face still, and
full and plump? And the rest of her too, all full and plump, and
when she was dressed nicely in one of her best saris with a low-cut
blouse, then who would know that she wasn't a young girl or at least
a young woman in the very prime of her life? And she was good too,
generous and good and ready to do everything, give everything for
those she loved. Only who was there whom she could love with all
the fervor of which her heart was capable? In her excitement she
pushed against him so that he fell backward and sat down abruptly
on her bed. At once she was sitting next to him, very close, her hand
on his—if he knew, she said, what store of love there was in her, ready
and bursting and brimming in her! Then it was his turn to cry, he

said, "I want a motor scooter, that's all," in a hurt, grieved voice, trembling with tears like a child's.

That was the last time he came down to see her. Afterward he would hardly talk to her at all—even when she lay in wait for him by the stairs, he would brush hurriedly past her, silent and with averted face. Once she called after him, "Come in, we will talk about the motor scooter!" but all she got by way of reply was, "It is sold already," tossed over his shoulder as he ran upstairs. She was in despair and wept often and bitterly; there was a pain right in her heart, such as she had never experienced before. She longed to die and yet at the same time she felt herself most burningly alive. She visited Mrs. Puri several times and stayed for some hours; during which Mrs. Puri, as usual, talked a lot, and in the usual strain, and kept pointing out how her children were Durga's too, while the two daughters simpered. Evidently she knew nothing of what had happened, and assumed that everything was as it had been.

But, so Durga soon learned, Mrs. Puri knew very well that everything was not as it had been. Not only did she know, but it was she herself who had brought about the change. It was she who, out of evil and spite, had stopped Govind from coming downstairs and had forbidden him ever to speak to Durga again. All this Durga learned from Bhuaji one hot afternoon as she lay tossing on her bed, alternately talking, weeping, and falling into silent fits of despair. She had no more secrets from Bhuaji. She needed someone before whom she could unburden herself, and who more fit for that purpose than the ever available, ever sympathetic Bhuaji? So she lay on her bed and cried: "A son, that is all I want, a son!" And Bhuaji was soothing and understood perfectly. Of course Durga wanted a son; it was only natural, for had not God set maternal feelings to flow sweetly in every woman's breast? And now, said Bhuaji angrily, to have that God-given flow stopped in its course by the machinations of a mean-hearted, jealous, selfish woman—and so it all came out. It was a revelation to Durga. Her tears ceased and she sat up on her bed. She imagined Govind suffering under the restraint laid upon him and yearning for Durga and all her kindness as bitterly as she yearned for him. There was sorrow upstairs and sorrow downstairs. She sat very upright on the bed. After a while she turned her face toward Bhuaji, and her lips were tight and her eyes flashed. She said, "We will see whose son he is."

She waited for him by the stairs. He came late that night, but still she went on waiting. She was patient and almost calm. She could hear sounds from upstairs—a clatter of buckets, water running, Mrs. Puri scolding her daughters. At the sound of that voice, hatred swelled in Durga so that she was tempted to leave her post and run upstairs to confront her enemy. But she checked herself and remained standing downstairs, calm and resolute and waiting. She would not be angry. This was not the time for anger.

She heard him before she saw him. He was humming a little tune to himself. Probably he had been to see a film with friends and now he was singing a lyric from it. He sounded happy, light-hearted. She peeped out from the dark doorway and saw him clearly just under the lamppost outside the house. He was wearing an orange T-shirt that she had given him and that clung closely to him so that all his broad chest and his nipples were outlined; his black jeans too fitted as a glove over his plump young buttocks. She edged herself as close as she could against the wall. When he entered the doorway, she whispered his name. He stopped singing at once. She talked fast, in a low urgent voice: "Come with me—what do your parents ever do for you?"

He shuffled his feet and looked down at them in the dark.

"With me you will have everything—a motor scooter—"

"It is sold."

"A new one, a brand-new one! And also you can study to be an aircraft engineer, anything you wish—"

"Is that you, son?" Mrs. Puri called from upstairs.

Durga held fast to his arm: "Don't answer," she whispered.

"Govind! Is that boy come home at last?" And the two plain sisters echoed: "Govind!"

"I can do so much for you," Durga whispered. "And what can they do?"

"Coming, Ma!" he called.

"Everything I have is for you—"

"You and your father both the same! All night we have to wait for you to come and eat your food!"

Durga said, "I have no one, no one." She was stroking his arm, which was smooth and muscular and matted with long silky hair.

Mrs. Puri appeared at the top of the stairs: "Just let me catch that boy, I will twist his ears for him!"

"You hear her, how she speaks to you?" whispered Durga with a

54

flicker of triumph. But Govind wrenched his arm free and bounded up the stairs toward his mother.

It did not take Bhuaji long after that to persuade Durga to get rid of her tenants. There were all those months of rent unpaid, and besides, who wanted such evil-natured people in the house? Bhuaji's son-in-law had connections with the police, and it was soon arranged: a constable stood downstairs while the Puris' belongings—the velvet armchair, an earthenware water pot, two weeping daughters carrying bedding—slowly descended. Durga did not see them. She was sitting inside before the little prayer table on which stood her two Krishnas. She was unbathed and in an old crumpled sari and with her hair undone. Her relatives sat outside in the courtyard with their belongings scattered around them, ready to move in upstairs. Bhuaji's old husband sat on his little bundle and had a nap in the sun.

"Only pray," Bhuaji whispered into Durga's ear. "With prayer He will surely come to you." Durga's eyes were shut; perhaps she was asleep. "As a son and as a lover," Bhuaji whispered. The relatives talked gaily among themselves outside; they were in a good, almost a festive mood.

It seemed Durga was not asleep after all, for suddenly she got up and unlocked her steel almira. She took out everything—her silk saris, her jewelry, her cashbox. From time to time she smiled to herself. She was thinking of her husband and of his anger, his impotent anger, at thus seeing everything given away at last. The more she thought of him, the more vigorously she emptied her almira. Her arms worked with a will, flinging everything away in abandon, her hair fell into her face, perspiration trickled down her neck in runnels. Her treasure lay scattered in heaps and mounds all over the floor and Bhuaji squinted at it in avid surmise.

Durga said, "Take it away. It is for you and for them—" and she jerked her head toward the courtyard where the relatives twittered like birds. Bhuaji was already squatting on the floor, sorting everything, stroking it with her hands in love and wonder. As she did so, she murmured approvingly to Durga: "That is the way—to give up everything. Only if we give up everything will He come to us." And she went on murmuring, while stroking the fine silks and running hard gold necklaces through her fingers: "As a son and as a lover," she murmured, over and over again, but absently.

The relatives were glad that Durga had at last come around and accepted her lot as a widow. They were glad for her sake. There was no other way for widows but to lead humble, bare lives; it was for their own good. For if they were allowed to feed themselves on the pleasures of the world, then they fed their own passions too, and that which should have died in them with the deaths of their husbands would fester and boil and overflow into sinful channels. Oh yes, said the relatives, wise and knowing, nodding their heads, our ancestors knew what they were doing when they laid down these rigid rules for widows; and though nowadays perhaps, in these modern times, one could be a little more lenient—for instance, no one insisted that Durga should shave her head—still, on the whole, the closer one followed the old traditions, the safer and better it was.

THE INTERVIEW

I am always very careful of my appearance, so you could not say that I spent much more time than usual over myself that morning. It is true, I trimmed and oiled my moustache, but then I often do that; I always like it to look very neat, like Raj Kapoor's, the film star's. But I knew my sister-in-law and my wife were watching me. My sister-in-law was smiling, and she had one hand on her hip; my wife only looked anxious. I knew she was anxious. All night she had been whispering to me. She had whispered, "Get this job and take me away to live somewhere alone, only you and I and our children." I had answered, "Yes," because I wanted to go to sleep. I don't know where and why she has taken this notion that we should go and live alone.

When I had finished combing my hair, I sat on the floor and my sister-in-law brought me my food on a tray. It may sound strange that my sister-in-law should serve me, and not my wife, but it is so in our house. It used to be my mother who brought me my food, even after I was married; she would never allow my wife to do this for me, though my wife wanted to very much. Then, when my mother got so old, my sister-in-law began to serve me. I know that my wife feels deeply hurt by this, but she doesn't dare to say anything. My mother doesn't notice many things anymore, otherwise she certainly would not allow my sister-in-law to bring me my food; she has always been very jealous of this privilege herself, though she never cared who served my brother. Now she has become so old that she can hardly see anything, and most of the time she sits in the corner by the family trunks and folds and strokes her pieces of cloth. For years now she has been collecting pieces of cloth. Some of them are very old and dirty, but she doesn't care, she loves them all equally. Nobody is allowed to touch them. Once there was a great quarrel, because my wife had taken one of them to make a dress for our child. My mother shouted at her—it was terrible to hear her: but then, she has never liked my wife—and my wife was very much afraid and cried and tried to excuse herself. I hit her across the face, not very hard and not because I wanted to, but only to satisfy my mother. The old woman kept quiet then and went back to folding and stroking her pieces of cloth.

All the time I was eating, I could feel my sister-in-law looking at me and smiling. It made me uncomfortable. I thought she might be smiling because she knew I wouldn't get the job for which I had to go and be interviewed. I also knew I wouldn't get it, but I didn't like her to smile like that. It was as if she were saying, "You see, you will always have to be dependent on us." It is clearly my brother's duty to keep me and my family until I can get work and contribute my own earnings to the family household. There is no need for her to smile about it. But it is true that I am more dependent on her now than on anyone else. Since my mother has got so old, my sister-in-law has become more and more the most important person in the house, so that she even keeps the keys and the household stores. At first I didn't like this. As long as my mother managed the household, I was sure of getting many extra tidbits. But now I find that my sister-in-law is also very kind to me—much more kind than she is to her husband. It is not for him that she saves the tidbits, nor for her children, but for me; and when she gives them to me, she never says anything and I never say anything, but she smiles and then I feel confused and rather embarrassed. My wife has noticed what she does for me.

I have found that women are usually kind to me. I think they realize that I am a rather sensitive person and that therefore I must be treated very gently. My mother has always treated me very gently. I am her youngest child, and I am fifteen years younger than my brother who is next to me (she did have several children in between us, but they all died). Right from the time when I was a tiny baby, she understood that I needed greater care and tenderness than other children. She always made me sleep close beside her in the night, and in the day I usually sat with her and my grandmother and my widowed aunt, who were also very fond of me. When I got bigger, my father sometimes wanted to take me to help in his stall (he had a little grocer's stall, where he sold lentils and rice and cheap ciga-

rettes and colored drinks in bottles) but my mother and grandmother and aunt never liked to let me go. Once he did take me with
him, and he made me pour some lentils out of paper bags into a tin.
I rather liked pouring the lentils—they made such a nice noise as
they landed in the tin—but suddenly my mother came and was very
angry with my father for making me do this work. She took me
home at once, and when she told my grandmother and aunt what
had happened, they stroked me and kissed me and then they gave
me a hot fritter to eat. The fact is, right from childhood I have been
a person who needs a lot of peace and rest, and my food too has to be
rather more delicate than that of other people. I have often tried to
explain this to my wife, but as she is not very intelligent, she doesn't
seem to understand.

Now my wife was watching me while I ate. She was squatting on
the floor, washing our youngest baby; the baby's head was in her
lap, and all one could see of it was the back of its legs and its naked
bottom. My wife did not watch me as openly as my sister-in-law did;
only from time to time she raised her eyes to me, I could feel it, and
they were very worried and troubled. She too was thinking about
the job for which I was going to be interviewed, but she was anxious
that I should get it. "We will go and live somewhere alone," she had
said. Why did she say it? When she knows that it is not possible and
never will be.

And even if it were possible, I would not like it. I can't live away
from my mother; and I don't think I would like to live away from
my sister-in-law. I often look at her and it makes me happy. Even
though she is not young anymore, she is still beautiful. She is tall,
with big hips and big breasts and eyes that flash; she often gets
angry, and when she is angry, she is the most beautiful of all. Then
her eyes are like fire and she shows all her teeth, which are very
strong and white, and her head is proud with the black hair flying
loose. My wife is not beautiful at all. I was very disappointed in her
when they first married me to her. Now I have got used to her and I
even like her, because she is so good and quiet and never troubles me
at all. I don't think anybody else in our house likes her. My sister-in-
law always calls her "that beauty," but she does not mean it; and she
makes her do all the most difficult household tasks, and often she
shouts at her and even beats her. This is not right; my wife has never
done anything to her—on the contrary, she always treats her with
respect. But I cannot interfere in their quarrels.

Then I was ready to go, though I didn't want to go. I knew only too well what would happen at the interview. My mother blessed me, and my sister-in-law looked at me over her shoulder and her great eyes flashed with laughter. I didn't look at my wife, who still sat squatting on the floor, but I knew she was pleading with me to get the job like she had pleaded in the night. As I walked down the stairs, the daughter of the carpenter, who lives in one of the rooms on the lower floor, came out of her door and she walked up the stairs as I walked down, and she passed very close beside me, with her eyes lowered but her arm just touching my sleeve. She always waits for me to come out and then she passes me on the stairs. We have never spoken together. She is a very young girl, her breasts are only just forming; her blouse has short sleeves and her arms are beautiful, long and slender. I think soon she is to be married, I have heard my sister-in-law say so. My sister-in-law laughed when she told me, she said, "It is high time" and then she said something coarse. Perhaps she has noticed that the girl waits for me to pass on the stairs.

No, I did not want to go to the interview. I had been to so many during the last few months, and always the same things happened. I know I have to work, in order to earn money and give it to my mother or my sister-in-law for the household, but there is no pleasure for me in the work. Last time I had work, it was in an insurance office and all day they made me sit at a desk and write figures. What pleasure could there be for me in that? I am a very thoughtful person, and I like always to sit and think my own thoughts; but while I thought my own thoughts in the office, I sometimes made mistakes over the figures and then my superiors were very angry with me. I was always afraid of their anger, and I begged their forgiveness and admitted that I was much at fault. When they forgave me, I was no longer afraid and I continued doing my work and thinking my thoughts. But the last time they would not forgive me again, though I begged and begged and cried what a faulty, bad man I was and what good men they were, and how they were my mother and my father and how I looked only to them for my life and the lives of my children. But when they still said I must go, I saw that the work there was really finished and I stopped crying. I went into the washroom and combed my hair and folded my soap in my towel, and then I took my money from the accountant without a word and I left the office with my eyes lowered. But I was no longer afraid, because what is finished is finished, and my brother still had work and probably one day I would get another job.

Ever since then my brother has been trying to get me into government service. He himself is a clerk in government service and enjoys many advantages: every five years he gets an increase of ten rupees in his salary and he has ten days sick leave in the year and when he retires he will get a pension. It would be good for me also to have such a job; but it is difficult to get, because first there is an interview at which important people sit at a desk and ask many questions. I am afraid of them, and I cannot understand properly what they are saying, so I answer what I think they want me to answer. But it seems that my answers are not after all the right ones, because up till now they have not given me a job.

On my way to this interview, I thought how much nicer it would be to go to the cinema instead. If I had had ten annas, perhaps I would have gone; it was just time for the morning show. The young clerks and the students would be collecting in a queue outside the cinema now. They would be standing and not talking much, holding their ten annas and waiting for the box office to open. I enjoy these morning shows, perhaps because the people who come to them are all young men like myself, all silent and rather sad. I am often sad; it would even be right to say that I am sad most of the time. But when the film begins, I am happy. I love to see the beautiful women, dressed in golden clothes with heavy earrings and necklaces and bracelets covering their arms, and their handsome lovers who are all the things I would like to be. And when they sing their love songs, so full of deep feelings, the tears sometimes come into my eyes; but not because I am sad, no, on the contrary, because I am so happy. After the film is over, I never go home straightaway, but I walk around the streets and think about how wonderful life could be.

When I arrived at the place where the interview was, I had to walk down many corridors and ask directions from many peons before I could find the right room. The peons were all rude to me, because they knew what I had come for. They lounged on benches outside the offices, and when I asked them, they looked me up and down before answering, and sometimes they made jokes about me with one another. I was very polite to them, for even though they were only peons, they had uniforms and jobs and belonged here, and they knew the right way whereas I did not. At last I came to the room where I had to wait. Many others were already sitting there, on chairs that were drawn up all around the room against the wall. No one was talking. I also sat on a chair, and after a while an official

came in with a list and he asked if anyone else had come. I got up
and he asked my name, and then he looked down the list and made
a tick with a pencil. He said to me very sternly, "Why are you late?"
I begged pardon and told him the bus in which I had come had had
an accident. He said, "When you are called for interview, you have
to be here exactly on time, otherwise your name is crossed off the
list." I begged pardon again and asked him very humbly please not
to cross me off this time. I knew that all the others were listening,
though none of them looked at us. He was very stern with me and
even scornful, but in the end he said, "Wait here, and when your
name is called, you must go in at once."

I did not count the number of people waiting in the room, but
there were many. Perhaps there was one job free, perhaps two or
three. I knew that all the others were very worried and anxious to
get the job, so I became worried and anxious too. The walls of the
room were painted green halfway up and white above that and were
quite bare. There was a fan turning from the ceiling, but it was not
turning fast enough to give much breeze. Behind the big door the
interview was going on; one by one we would all be called in behind
this closed door.

I began to worry desperately. It always happens like this. When I
come to an interview, I don't want the job at all, but when I see all
the others waiting and worrying, I want it terribly. Yet at the same
time I know that I don't want it. It would only be the same thing
over again: writing figures and making mistakes and then being
afraid when they found out. And there would be a superior officer to
whom I would have to be very deferential, and every time I saw him
or heard his voice I would begin to be afraid that he had found out
something against me. For weeks and months I would sit and write
figures, getting wearier of it and wearier, so that more and more I
would be thinking my own thoughts. Then the mistakes would
come, and my superior officer would be angry and I afraid.

My brother never makes mistakes. For years he has been sitting
in the same office, writing figures and being deferential to his superior officer; he concentrates very hard on his work, and so he doesn't
make mistakes. But all the same he is afraid; that is why he concentrates so hard—because he is afraid that he will make a mistake and
they will be angry with him and take away his job. He is afraid of
this all the time. And he is right: what would become of us all if he
also lost his job? It is not the same with me. I think I am afraid to
lose my job only because that is a thing of which one is expected to

be afraid. When I have actually lost it, I am really relieved. But I am very different from my brother; even in appearance I am very different. It is true, he is fifteen years older than I am, but even when he was my age, he never looked like I do. My appearance has always attracted others, and up to the time I was married, my mother used to stroke my hair and my face and say many tender things to me. Once, when I was walking on my way to school through the bazaar, a man called to me, very softly, and when I came he gave me a ripe mango, and then he took me into a dark passage that led to a disused mosque, and he touched me under my clothes and he said, "You are so nice, so nice." He was very kind to me. I love wearing fine clothes, very thin white muslin kurtas that have been freshly washed and starched and are embroidered at the shoulders. Sometimes I also use scent, a fine khas smell; my hair oil also smells of khas. Some years ago, when the carpenter's daughter was still a small child and did not yet wait for me on the stairs, there was a girl living in the tailor's shop opposite our house and she used to follow me when I went out. But it is my brother who is married to a beautiful wife, and my wife is not beautiful at all. He is not happy with his wife; when she talks to him, she talks in a hard scornful way; and it is not for him that she saves the best food, but for me, even though I have not brought money home for many months.

The big closed door opened and the man who had been in there for interview came out. We all looked at him, but he walked out in a great hurry, with a preoccupied expression on his face; probably he was going over in his mind all that had been said at the interview. I could feel the anxiety in the other men getting stronger, so mine got stronger too. The official with the list came and we all looked at him. He read out another name and the man whose name was called jumped up from his chair; he did not notice that his dhoti had got caught on a nail in the chair and he wondered why he could not go farther. When he realized what had happened, he tried to disentangle himself, but his fingers shook so much that he could not get the dhoti off the nail. The official watched him and said, "Hurry, now, do you think the gentlemen will wait for you for as long as you please?" Then the man also dropped the umbrella he was carrying and now he was trying both to disentangle the dhoti and to pick up the umbrella. When he could not get the dhoti loose, he became so desperate that he tore at the cloth and ripped it free. It was a pity to see the dhoti torn because it was a new one, which he was probably wearing for the first time and had put on specially for the interview.

He clasped his umbrella to his chest and walked in a great hurry to the interviewing room, with his dhoti hanging about his legs and his face swollen with embarrassment and confusion.

We all sat and waited. The fan, which seemed to be a very old one, made a creaking noise. One man kept cracking his finger joints—*tik*, we heard, *tik* (it made my own finger joints long to be cracked too). All the rest of us kept very still. From time to time the official with the list came in, he walked around the room very slowly, tapping his list, and then we all looked down at our feet and the man who had been cracking his finger joints stopped doing it. A faint and muffled sound of voices came from behind the closed door. Sometimes a voice was raised, but even then I could not make out what was being said, though I strained very hard.

The last time I had an interview, it was very unpleasant for me. One of the people who was interviewing took a dislike to me and shouted at me very loudly. He was a large fat man and he wore an English suit; his teeth were quite yellow, and when he became angry and shouted, he showed them all, and even though I was very upset, I couldn't help looking at them and wondering how they had become so yellow. I don't know why he was angry. He shouted: "Good God, man, can't you understand what's said to you?" It was true, I could not understand, but I had been trying so hard to answer well. What more did he expect of me? Probably there was something in my appearance that he did not like. It happens that way sometimes—they take a dislike to you, and then of course there is nothing you can do.

When I thought of the man with the yellow teeth, I became more anxious than ever. I need great calm in my life. Whenever anything worries me too much, I have to cast the thought of it off immediately, otherwise there is a danger that I may become very ill. All my limbs were itching so that it was difficult for me to sit still, and I could feel blood rushing into my brain. It was this room that was doing me so much harm: all the other men waiting, anxious and silent, and the noise from the fan and the official with the list walking around, tapping his list or striking it against his thigh, and the big closed door behind which the interview was going on. I felt great need to get up and go away. I didn't *want* the job. I wasn't even thinking about it anymore—I was thinking only about how to avoid having to sit here and wait.

Now the door opened again and the man with the torn new dhoti came out. He was biting his lip and scratching the back of his neck, and he too walked straight out without looking at us at all. The big door was left slightly open for a moment, and I could see a man's arm in a white shirtsleeve and part of the back of his head. His shirt was very white and of good material, and his ears stood away from his head so that one could see how his spectacles fitted into the backs of his ears. I realized at once that this man would be my enemy and that he would make things very difficult for me and perhaps even shout at me. Then I knew it was no use for me to stay there. The official with the list came back and great panic seized me that he would read out my name. I got up quickly, murmuring, "Please excuse me—bathroom," and went out. The official with the list called after me, "Hey mister, where are you going?" so I lowered my head and walked faster. I would have started to run, but that might have caused suspicion, so I just walked as fast as I could, down the long corridors and right out of the building. There at last I was able to stop and take a deep breath, and I felt much better.

I stood still for only a little while, then I moved on, though not in any particular direction. There were many clerks and peons moving around in the street, hurrying from one office building to another and carrying files and papers. Everyone seemed to have something to do. I was glad when I had moved out of this block and on to the open space where people like myself, who had nothing to do, sat under the trees or in any other patch of shade they could find. But I couldn't sit there; it was too close to the office blocks, and any moment someone might come and say to me, "Why did you go away?" So I walked farther. I was feeling quite light-hearted; it was such a relief for me not to have to be interviewed.

I came to a row of eating stalls, and I sat down on a wooden bench outside one of them, which was called the Paris Hotel, and asked for tea. I felt badly in need of tea, and since I intended to walk part of the way home, I was in a position to pay for it. There were two Sikhs sitting at the end of my bench who were eating with great appetite, dipping their hands very rapidly into brass bowls. In between eating they exchanged remarks with the proprietor of the Paris Hotel, who sat high up inside his stall, stirring in a big brass pot in which he was cooking the day's food. He was chewing a betel leaf, and from time to time he spat out the red betel juice far over the cooking pot and on to the ground between the wooden benches and tables.

I sat quietly at my end of the bench and drank my tea. The food smelled very good, and it made me realize that I was hungry. I decided that if I walked all the way home, I could afford a little cake (I am very fond of sweet things). The cake was not new, but it had a beautiful piece of bright-green peel inside it. On reaching home I would lie down at once to sleep and not wake up again till tomorrow morning. That way no one would be able to ask me any questions. I would not look at my wife at all, so I would be able to avoid her eyes. I would not look at my sister-in-law either; but she would be smiling, that I knew already—leaning against the wall with her hand on her hip, looking at me and smiling. She would know that I had run away, but she would not say anything.

Let her know! What does it matter? It is true I have no job and no immediate prospect of getting one. It is true that I am dependent on my brother. Everybody knows that. There is no shame in it: there are many people without jobs. And she has been so kind to me up till now, there is no reason why she should not continue to be kind to me. Though I know she is not by nature a kind woman; she speaks mostly with a very harsh tongue and her actions also are harsh. Only to me she has been kind.

The Sikhs at the end of the bench had finished eating. They licked their fingers and belched deeply, the way one does after a good meal. They started to laugh and joke with the proprietor. I sat quiet and alone at my end of the bench. Of course they did not laugh and joke with me. They knew that I was superior to them, for whereas they work with their hands, I am a lettered man who does not have to sweat for a living but sits on a chair in an office and writes figures and can speak in English. My brother is very proud of his superiority, and he has great contempt for carpenters and mechanics and such people who work with their hands. I am also proud of being a lettered man, but when I listened to the Sikhs laughing and joking, the thought came to me that perhaps their life was happier than mine. It was a thought that had come to me before. There is the carpenter who lives downstairs in our house, the one whose daughter waits for me on the stairs, and though he is poor, there is always great eating in his house and many people come and I hear them laughing and singing and even dancing. The carpenter is a big strong man and he always looks happy, never anxious and sick with worry the way my brother does. He doesn't wear shoes and clean white clothes like my brother and I do, nor does he speak any English, but all the same he is happy. Even though his work is inferior, I don't think he gets as weary of it as I do of mine, and he has no superior officer to make him afraid.

Then I thought again about my sister-in-law and I thought that if I were kind to her, she would continue to be kind to me. I became quite excited when I thought of being kind to her. I would know then how her big breasts felt under the blouse, how warm they were and how soft. And I would know about the inside of her mouth with the big strong teeth. Her tongue and palate are very pink, like the pink satin blouse she wears on festive occasions, and I had often wondered whether they felt as soft as the blouse too. Her eyes would be shut and perhaps there would be tears on the lashes; and she would be making warm animal sounds and her big body too would be warm like an animal's. I became very excited when I thought of it; but when the excitement had passed, I was sad. Because then I thought of my wife, who is thin and not beautiful and there is no excitement in her body. But she does whatever I want and always tries to please me. I remembered her whispering to me in the night, "Take me away, let us go and live somewhere alone, only you and I and our children." That can never be, and so always she will have to be unhappy.

I was very sad when I thought of her being unhappy; because it is not only she who is unhappy but I also and many others. Everywhere there is unhappiness. I thought of the man whose new dhoti had been torn and who would now have to go home and sew it carefully so that the tear would not be seen. I thought of all the other men sitting and waiting to be interviewed, all but one or two of whom would not get the job for which they had come to be interviewed, and so again they would have to go to another interview and another and another, to sit and wait and be anxious. And my brother who has a job, but is frightened that he will lose it; and my mother so old that she can only sit on the floor and stroke her pieces of cloth; and my sister-in-law who does not care for her husband; and the carpenter's daughter who is to be married and perhaps she also will not be happy. Yet life could be so different. When I go to the cinema and hear the beautiful songs they sing, I know how different it could be; and also sometimes when I sit alone and think my thoughts, then I have a feeling that everything could be so beautiful. But now my tea was finished and also my cake, and I wished I had not bought them, because it was a long way to walk home and I was tired.

A SPIRITUAL CALL

The river, broad, swift, swollen, was at this season too dangerous to cross in a boat. One had to walk across the bridge, which was holy and thronged with pilgrims chanting salutations as they crossed. On the other side of the bridge began a cluster of tiny temples, all of them made spruce with silver tinsel, peacock fans, gilt ornaments, and pink paint. The gods inside them were also painted pink—pink cheeks and rosebud lips—and the plump priests who looked after them were immaculately bathed and their skulls were newly shaven and naked except for their one tuft of hair. Worshipers were constantly passing in and out to leave their offerings and obeisances, while the rest houses, which alternated with the temples, were equally well populated, though they offered no amenities beyond a dark, bare room of whitewashed brick. But here anyone was welcome to spread their bedding on the floor and put the children to sleep and light the cooking fires and stir in their cooking vessels, and all the time be very merry and make friends with strangers: for coming like this, here to this holy place in quest of grace, lightened the heart and made it loving to all the world.

Beyond the temples and rest houses came a wood with a path through it; on either side of the path were trees and shrubs and sadhus doing penance. Some of the sadhus were stark naked, some wore animal skins, all had long, matted hair and beards and were immobile, so that it was easy to believe they had been sitting there for centuries, as rooted and moss-grown as the trees and as impervious as they to snakes and any wild animals there might be prowling around. Besides the sadhus, there were beggars, and these were not in the least still or immobile but very lively indeed, especially if someone happened to pass by: then they would set up voluble claims to alms, holding up their palms and pointing out any sores or other disfigurements that might have laid them victim.

Over everything towered the mountains, receding far up into the blue sky to unknown heights of holiness, steppe upon steppe of them, and dissolving from sight at last amid mysterious white veils that may have been mist or snow or, who knew, the emanation of a promised Presence.

It was all, in short, too good to be true; a dream, though better than anything, Daphne felt, she could have dreamed of. The coolie, naked except for a loincloth, walked in front of her and carried her baggage on his head; he was her guide and protector, who cleared a path for her through the crowd of pilgrims, warded off the beggars, and knew exactly where she wanted to go. It was quite a long walk, but Daphne was too entranced to mind; nor did she for one moment doubt that she was being led along the right way. And sure enough, her messenger, like some angel sent direct, brought her at last into the presence she had desired for many weeks now, and when she was there and saw him again, so great was her relief and her happiness that she burst into tears.

"Welcome!" he said to her, and did ever eyes and smile swell the word with such meaning? And then he said, to her tears, "Now what is this? What nonsense?"

"I'm silly," she said, wiping away at her eyes but unable to check a further gush of tears.

"Yes, very silly," he said, and turned to the others around him: "Isn't she? A silly goose?" and all smiled at her, with him, all of them tender, friendly, saying welcome.

One or two of them she recognized, the cheerful, bearded, athletic young men in orange robes who were his permanent disciples and who had been with him in London. She did not know any of the others. They included quite a number of non-Indians, and these she guessed to be people like herself who had followed him out here to undergo an intensive course of spiritual regeneration. In addition there were many casual visitors constantly passing in and out of the room, devotees come to have a sight of him who sat for a while and then got up and went away while others took their place. Daphne was used to seeing him thus in the midst of crowds. It had been the same in London, where he had been constantly surrounded—by women mostly, rich women in smart hats who bustled around him and besieged him with requests uttered in shrill voices; and he so patient, unruffled, eating ice cream in someone's drawing room, and smiling on them all equally.

Nevertheless it had seemed to Daphne that his smile had in some way been special for her. There was no reason why she should think so, yet she had been convinced of it. When he looked at her, when he spoke to her (though he said nothing that he did not say to others), she felt chosen. She was not by nature a fanciful girl; on the contrary, she had always been known as straightforward and sensible, good at sickbeds, had done history at Oxford, wore tasteful, unobtrusive, English clothes. Yet after she had met Swamiji, she knew without a word being spoken that he meant her to follow him back to India. It was not an easy path. She was fond of traveling in a way, and always spent her summer vacation in France or Italy, and twice she had gone to Greece: but she had never contemplated anything much farther than that. She was quite happy in London—had her few friends, her quite interesting job with a secretarial agency—and though perhaps, if opportunity had knocked that way, she would not have minded a year or two doing some sort of interesting job in America or on the continent, it was not, one would have said, in her nature to go off on a spiritual quest to India.

Everyone was indeed amazed; she herself was, but she knew it was inevitable. No one tried to stand in her way, although of course her mother—a wonderfully energetic lady of middle years prominent on several welfare committees—pointed out quite a few of the drawbacks to her enterprise. But there was nothing she could say that Daphne had not already said to herself: so that the mother, who was tolerant in the best English way and believed in people being allowed to make their own mistakes, had not spoken any further but instead confined herself to bringing forward several aged relatives who had served in India as administrators during the Raj and were thus suited to give Daphne advice on at least such basic questions as to what clothes to take and what diseases to guard against.

Everyone, whatever their private thoughts, had been too tactful outright to warn Daphne of disaster. But if they had done, how triumphantly she could, after some weeks' stay, have contradicted them! She was supremely happy in the ashram. It was not a very grand place—Swamiji had rented it for a few months for himself and his followers, and it consisted merely of three rows of rooms grouped around a courtyard. The courtyard was triangular in shape, and the apex was formed by Swamiji's room, which was of course much bigger than all the others and led to a veranda with a view out over the river. The other rooms were all small and ugly, inadequately lit by skylights set so high up on the walls that no one could ever get at them to clean them; the only pieces of furniture were cheap string cots, some of which had the string rotting away. The meals were horrible—unclean, badly cooked, and irregular—and the cooks kept running away and had to be replaced at short notice. There were many flies, which were especially noticeable at mealtimes when they settled in droves on the food and on the lips of people eating it. Daphne rose, with ease, above all this; and she lived only in the beautiful moments engendered by the love they all bore to Swamiji, by the hours of meditation to which he exhorted them, the harmonious rhythm of their selfless days, and the surrounding atmosphere of this place holy for centuries and where God was presumed to be always near.

The door to Swamiji's room was kept open day and night, and people came and went. He was always the same: cheerful and serene. He sat on the floor, on a mattress covered with a cream-colored silk cloth, and the robe he wore loosely wrapped around himself was of the same silk, and both of them were immaculate. His beard and shoulder-length hair shone in well-oiled waves, and at his feet there lay a heap of flowers among which his fingers often toyed, picking up petals and smelling them and then rubbing them to and fro. He was not a handsome man—he was short and not well built, his features were blunt, his eyes rather small—yet there was an aura of beauty about him that may have been partly due to the flowers and the spotless, creamy, costly silk, but mostly of course to the radiance of his personality.

He was often laughing. The world seemed a gay place to him, and his enthusiasm for it infected those around him so that they also often laughed. They were very jolly together. They had many private jokes and teased each other about their little weaknesses (one person's inability to get out of bed in the mornings, another's exploits as a fly-swatter, Swamiji's fondness for sweets). Often they sat together and just gossiped, like any group of friends, Swamiji himself taking a lively lead; any more serious talk they had was interspersed among the gossip, casually almost, and in the same tone. They were always relaxed about their quest, never overintense: taking their cue from Swamiji himself, they spoke of things spiritual in the most matter-of-fact way—and why not: weren't they matter-of-fact? the most matter-of-fact things of all?—and hid their basic seriousness under a light, almost flippant manner.

Daphne felt completely at ease with everyone. In England, she had been rather a shy girl, had tended to be awkward with strangers and, at parties or any other such gathering, had always had difficulty in joining in. But not here. It was as if an extra layer of skin, which hitherto had kept her apart from others, had dropped from off her heart, and she felt close and affectionate toward everyone. They were a varied assortment of people, of many different nationalities: a thin boy from Sweden called Klas, two dumpy little Scottish schoolteachers, from Germany a large blond beauty in her thirties called Helga. Helga was the one Daphne shared a room with. Those dark, poky little rooms made proximity very close, and though under different circumstances Daphne might have had difficulty in adjusting to Helga, here she found it easy to be friendly with her.

Helga was, in any case, too unreserved a person herself to allow reserve to anyone else; especially not to anyone she was sharing a room with. She was loud and explicit about everything she did, expressing the most fleeting of her thoughts in words and allowing no action, however trivial, to pass without comment. Every morning on waking she would report on the quality of the sleep she had enjoyed, and thence carry on a continuous stream of commentary as she went about her tasks ("I think I need a new toothbrush." "These flies—I shall go mad!"). In the morning it was—not a rule, the ashram had no rules, but it was an understanding that everyone should do a stretch of meditation. Somehow Helga quite often missed it, either because she got up too late, or took too long to dress, or something prevented her; and then, as soon as she went into Swamiji's room, she would make a loud confession of her omission. "Swamiji, I have been a naughty girl again today!" she would announce in her Wagnerian voice. Swamiji smiled, enjoying her misdemeanor as much as she did, and teased her, so that she would throw her hands before her face and squeal in delight, "Swamiji, you're not to, please, please, you are not to be horrid to me!"

Swamiji had a very simple and beautiful message to the world. It was only this: meditate; look into yourself and so, by looking, cleanse yourself; harmony and happiness will inevitably follow. This philosophy, simple as its end-product appeared to be, he had forged after many, many solitary years of thought and penance in some icy Himalayan retreat. Now he had come down into the world of men to deliver his message, planning to return to his mountain solitude as soon as his task here was achieved. It might, however, take longer than he had reckoned on, for men were stubborn and tended to be blind to Truth. But he would wait, patiently, and toil till his work was done. Certainly, it was evident that the world urgently needed his message, especially the Western world where both inner and outer harmony were in a state of complete disruption. Hence his frequent travels abroad, to England and other countries, and next he was planning a big trip to America, to California, where a group of would-be disciples eagerly awaited him. His method was to go to these places, make contacts, give lectures and informal talks, and then return with a number of disciples whom he had selected for more intensive training. He had, of course, his little nucleus of permanent disciples—those silent, bearded young men in orange robes who accompanied him everywhere and looked after his simple needs—but the people he brought with him from abroad, such as Daphne and Helga and the others, were expected to stay with him for only a limited time. During that time he trained them in methods of meditation and generally untangled their tangled souls, so that they could return home, made healthy and whole, and disseminate his teaching among their respective countrymen. In this way, the Word would spread to all corners of the earth, and to accelerate the process, he was also writing a book, called *Vital Principle of Living,* to be published in the first place in English and then to be translated into all the languages of the world.

Daphne was fortunate enough to be chosen as his secretary in this undertaking. Hitherto, she had observed, his method of writing had been very strange, not to say wonderful: he would sit there on his silken couch, surrounded by people, talk with them, laugh with them, and at the same time he would be covering, effortlessly and in a large flowing hand, sheets of paper with his writing. When he chose her as his secretary, he presented these sheets to her and told her to rewrite them in any way she wanted. "My English is very poor, I know," he said, which made Helga exclaim, "Swamiji! Your English! Poor? Oh if I could only speak one tiniest bit as well, how conceited I would become!" And it was true, he did speak well: very fluently in his soft voice and with a lilting Indian accent; it was a pleasure to hear him. Daphne sometimes wondered where he could

74

have learned to speak so well. Surely not in his mountain cave? She did not know, no one knew, where he had been or what he had done before that.

Strangely enough, when she got down to looking through his papers, she found that he had not been unduly modest. He did not write English well. When he spoke, he was clear and precise, but when he wrote, his sentences were turgid, often naïve, grammatically incorrect. And his spelling was decidedly shaky. In spite of herself, Daphne's Oxford-trained mind rose at once, as she read, in judgment; and her feelings, in face of this judgment, were ones of embarrassment, even shame for Swamiji. Yet a moment later, as she raised her burning cheeks from his incriminating manuscript, she realized that it was not for him she need be ashamed but for herself. How narrow was her mind, how tight and snug it sat in the strait-jacket her education had provided for it! Her sole, pitiful criterion was conventional form, whereas what she was coming into contact with here was something so infinitely above conventional form that it could never be contained in it. And that was precisely why he had chosen her: so that she could express him (whose glory it was to be inexpressible) in words accessible to minds that lived in the same narrow confines as her own. Her limitation, she realized in all humility, had been her only recommendation.

She worked hard, and he was pleased with her and made her work harder. All day she sat by his side and took down the words that he dictated to her in between talking to his disciples and to his other numerous visitors; at night she would sit by the dim bulb in the little room she shared with Helga to write up these notes and put them into shape. Helga would be fast asleep, but if she opened her eyes for a moment, she would grumble about the light disturbing her. "Just one minute," Daphne would plead, but by that time Helga had tossed her big body to its other side and, if she was still grumbling, it was only in her sleep. Very often Daphne herself did not get to sleep before three or four in the morning, and then she would be too tired to get up early enough for her meditation.

She could not take this failure as lightly as Helga took her own. When Helga boasted to Swamiji, "Today I've been naughty again," Daphne would hang her head and keep silent, unable to confess. Once, though, Helga told on her—not in malice, but rather in an excess of good humor. Having just owned up to her own fault and been playfully scolded for it by Swamiji, she was brimming with fun and her eyes danced as she looked around for further amusement; they came to rest on Daphne, and suddenly she shot out her finger to point: "There's another one just as bad!" and when she saw Daphne blush and turn away, rallied her gaily, "No pretending, I saw you lie snug in bed, old lazybones!"

Daphne felt awkward and embarrassed and wondered what Swamiji would say: whatever it was, she dreaded it, for unlike Helga she took no pride in her shortcomings nor did she have a taste for being teased. And, of course, Swamiji knew it. Without even glancing at Daphne, he went on talking to Helga: "If you manage to do your morning meditation three days running," he told her, "I shall give you a good conduct prize." "Swamiji! A prize! Oh lucky lucky girl I am!"

But the next time they were alone together—not really alone, of course, only comparatively so: there were just a few visitors and they sat at a respectful distance and were content with looking at and being near him—as Daphne sat cross-legged on the floor, taking dictation from him, her notebook perched on her knee, he interrupted his fluent flow of wisdom to say to her in a lower voice: "You know that private meditation is the—how shall I say?—the foundation, the cornerstone of our whole system?"

After a short pause, she brought out, "It was only that I was—" she had been about to say "tired," but checked herself in time: feeling how ridiculous it would be for her to bring forward her tiredness, the fact that she had sat up working till the early hours of the morning, to him who was busy from earliest morning till latest night, talking to people and helping them and writing his book and a hundred and one things, without ever showing any sign of fatigue but always fresh and bright as a bridegroom. So she checked herself and said, "I was lazy, that's all," and waited, pencil poised, hoping for a resumed dictation.

"Look at me," he said instead.

She was too surprised to do so at first, so he repeated it in a soft voice of command, and she turned her head, blushing scarlet, and lifted her eyes—and found herself looking into his. Her heart beat up high and she was full of sensations. She would have liked to look away again, but he compelled her not to.

"What's the matter?" he said softly. He took a petal from the pile of flowers lying at his feet and held it up to his nose. "Why are you like that?" he asked. She remained silent, looking into his face.

Now he was crushing the petal between his fingers, and the smell of it, pungent, oversweet, rose into the air. "You must relax. You must trust and love. Give," he said and he smiled at her and his eyes brimmed with love. "Give yourself. Be generous." He held her for a moment longer, and then allowed her at last to look away from him; and at once he continued his dictation which she endeavored to take down, though her hands were trembling.

After that she was no longer sure of herself. She was an honest girl and had no desire to cheat herself, any more than she would have desired to cheat anyone else. She felt now that she was here under false pretenses, and that her state of elation was due not, as she had thought, to a mystic communion with some great force outside herself, but rather to her proximity to Swamiji, for whom her feelings were very much more personal than she had hitherto allowed herself to suspect. Yet even after she admitted this, the elation persisted. There was no getting away from the fact that she was happy to be there, to be near him, working with him, constantly with him: that in itself was satisfaction so entire that it filled and rounded and illumined her days. She felt herself to be like a fruit hanging on a bough, ripening in his sunshine and rich with juices from within. And so it was, not only with her, but with everyone else there too. All had come seeking something outside of themselves and their daily preoccupations, and all had found it in or through him. Daphne noticed how their faces lit up the moment they came into his presence—she noticed it with Klas, a very fair, rather unattractive boy with thin lips and thin hair and pink-rimmed eyes; and the two Scottish schoolteachers, dumpy, dowdy little women who, before meeting Swamiji, had long since given up any expectations they might ever have had—all of them bloomed under his smile, his caressing gaze, his constant good humor. "Life," he once dictated to Daphne, "is a fountain of joy from which the lips must learn to drink with relish as is also taught by our sages from the olden times." (She rewrote this later.) He was the fountain of joy from which they all drank with relish.

She was working too hard, and though she would never have admitted it, he was quick to notice. One day, though she sat there ready with notebook and pencil, he said, "Off with you for a walk." Her protests were in vain. Not only did he insist, but he even instructed her for how long she was to walk and in what direction. "And when you come back," he said, "I want to see roses in your

cheeks." So dutifully she walked and where he had told her to: this
was away from the populated areas, from the throng of pilgrims and
sadhus, out into a little wilderness where there was nothing except
rocky ledges and shrubs and, here and there, small piles of faded
bricks where once some building scheme had been begun and soon
abandoned. But she did not look around her much; she was only
concerned with reckoning the time he had told her to walk, and then
getting back quickly to the ashram, to his room, to sit beside him
and take down his dictation. As soon as she came in, he looked at
her, critically: "Hm, not enough roses yet, I think," he commented,
and ordered her to take an hour-long walk in that same direction
every day.

On the third day she met him on the way. He had evidently just
had his bath, for his hair hung in wet ringlets and his robe was slung
around him hastily, leaving one shoulder bare. He always had his
bath in the river, briskly pouring water over himself out of a brass
vessel, while two of his disciples stood by on the steps with his towel.
They were coming behind him now as he—nimbler, sprightlier than
they—clambered around ledges and stones and prickly bushes. He
waved enthusiastically to Daphne and called to her: "You see, I also
am enjoying fresh air and exercise!"

She waited for him to catch up with her. He was radiant: he
smiled, his eyes shone, drops of water glistened on his hair and
beard. "Beautiful," he said, and his eyes swept over the landscape,
over the rocky plateau on which they stood—the holy town huddled
on one side, the sky, immense and blue, melting at one edge into the
mountains and at another into the river. "Beautiful, beautiful," he
repeated and shook his head and she looked with him, and it was,
everything was, the whole earth, shining and beautiful.

"Did you know we are building an ashram?" he asked her.

"Where?"

"Just here."

He gave a short sweep of the hand, and she looked around her,
puzzled. It did not seem possible for anything to grow in this spot
except thistles and shrubs: and as if to prove the point, just a little
way off was an abandoned site around which were scattered a few
sad, forgotten bricks.

"A tiptop, up-to-date ashram," he was saying, "with air-conditioned meditation cells and a central dining hall. Of course it will be
costly, but in America I shall collect a good deal of funds. There are

many rich American ladies who are interested in our movement."
He tilted his head upward and softly swept back his hair with his
hand, first one side and then the other, in a peculiarly vain and
womanly movement.

She was embarrassed and did not wish to see him like that, so she
looked away into the distance and saw the two young men who had
accompanied him running off toward the ashram; they looked like
two young colts, skipping and gamboling and playfully tripping
each other up. Their joyful young voices, receding into the distance,
were the only sounds, otherwise it was silent all round, so that one
could quite clearly hear the clap of birds' wings as they flew up from
the earth into the balmy, sparkling upper air.

"I have many warm invitations from America," Swamiji said.
"From California especially. Do you know it? No? There is a Mrs.
Fisher, Mrs. Gay Fisher, her husband was in shoe business. She often
writes to me. She has a very spacious home that she will kindly put
at our disposal and also many connections and a large acquaintance
among other ladies interested in our movement. She is very anxious
for my visit. Why do you make such a face?"

Daphne gave a quick, false laugh and said, "What face?"

"Like you are making. Look at me—why do you always look
away as if you are ashamed?" He put his hand under her chin and
turned her face toward himself. "Daphne," he said, tenderly; and
then, "It is a pretty name."

Suddenly, in her embarrassment, she was telling him the story of
Daphne: all about Apollo and the laurel tree, and he seemed interested, nodding to her story, and now he was making her walk
along with him, the two of them all alone and he leaning lightly on
her arm. He was slightly shorter than she was.

"So," he said, when she had finished, "Daphne was afraid of love
... I think you are rightly named, what do you say? Because I
think—yes, I think this Daphne also is afraid of love."

He pinched her arm, mischievously, but seeing her battle with
stormy feelings, he tactfully changed the subject. Again his eyes
shone, again he waved his hand around: "Such a lovely spot for our
ashram, isn't it? Here our foreign friends—from America, like yourself from U.K., Switzerland, Germany, all the countries of the
world—here their troubled minds will find peace and slowly they
will travel along the path of inner harmony. How beautiful it will
be! How inspiring! A new world! Only one thing troubles me,

Daphne, and on this question now I want advice from your cool and rational mind."

Daphne made a modest disclaiming gesture. She felt not in the least cool or rational, on the contrary, she knew herself to have become a creature tossed by passion and wild thoughts.

But "No modesty, please," he said to her disclaimer. "Who knows that mind of yours better, you or I? Hm? Exactly. So don't be cheeky." At which she had to smile: on top of everything else, how nice he was, how terribly, terribly nice. "Now can I ask my question? You see, what is troubling me is, should we have a communal kitchen or should there be a little cooking place attached to each meditation cell? One moment: there are pros and cons to be considered. Listen."

He took her arm, familiar and friendly, and they walked. Daphne listened, but there were many other thoughts rushing in and out of her head. She was very conscious of his hand holding her arm, and she kept that arm quite still. Above all, she was happy and wanted this to go on forever, he and she walking alone in that deserted place, over shrubs and bricks, the river glistening on one side and the mountains on the other, and above them the sky where the birds with slow, outstretched wings were the only patterns on that unmarred blue.

Not only did it not go on forever, but it had to stop quite soon. Running from the direction of the ashram, stumbling, waving, calling, came a lone, familiar figure: "Yoo-hoo!" shouted Helga. "Wait for me!"

She was out of breath when she caught up with them. Strands of blond hair had straggled into her face, perspiration trickled down her neck into the collar of her pale cerise blouse with mother-of-pearl buttons: her blue eyes glittered like ice as they looked searchingly from Swamiji to Daphne and back. She looked large and menacing.

"Why are you walking like two lovebirds?"

"Because that is what we are," Swamiji said. One arm was still hooked into Daphne's and now he hooked the other into Helga's. "We are talking about kitchens. Let's hear what you have to advise us."

"Who cares for me?" said Helga, pouting. "I'm just silly old Helga."

"Stop thinking about yourself and listen to the problem we are faced with."

Now there were three of them walking, and Daphne was no longer quite so happy. She didn't mind Helga's presence, but she knew that Helga minded hers. Helga's resentment wafted right across Swamiji, and once or twice she looked over his head (which she could do quite easily) to throw an angry blue glance at Daphne. Daphne looked back at her to ask, what have I done? Swamiji walked between them, talking and smiling and holding an arm of each.

That night there was an unpleasant scene. As usual, Daphne was sitting writing up her notes while Helga lay in bed and from time to time called out, "Turn off the light" before turning around and going back to sleep again. Only tonight she didn't go back to sleep. Instead she suddenly sat bolt upright and said, "The light is disturbing me."

"I won't be a minute," Daphne said, desperately writing, for she simply had to finish, otherwise tomorrow's avalanche of notes would be on top of her—Swamiji was so quick, so abundant in his dictation—and she would never be able to catch up.

"Turn it off!" Helga suddenly shouted, and Daphne left off writing and turned around to look at her. From the high thatched roof of their little room, directly over Helga's bed, dangled a long cord with a bulb at the end: it illumined Helga sitting up in bed in her lemon-yellow nylon nightie, which left her large marble shoulders bare; above them loomed her head covered in curlers, which made her look awesome like Medusa, while her face, flecked with pats of cream, also bore a very furious and frightening expression.

"Always making up to Swamiji," she was saying in a loud, contemptuous way. "All night you have to sit here and disturb me so tomorrow he will say, 'You have done so much work, good girl, wonderful girl, Daphne.' Pah. It is disgusting to see you flirting with him all the time."

"I don't know what you're talking about," Daphne said in a trembly voice.

"Don't know what you're talking about," Helga repeated, making a horrible mimicking face and attempting to reproduce Daphne's accent but drowning it completely in her German one. "I hate hypocrites. Of course everyone knows you English are all hypocrites, it is a well-known fact all over the world."

"You're being terribly unfair, Helga."

"Turn off the light! Other people want to sleep, even if you are busy being Miss Goody-goody!"

"In a minute," Daphne said, sounding calm and continuing with her task.

Helga screamed with rage: "Turn it off! Turn it off!" She bounced up and down in her bed with her fists balled. Daphne took no notice whatsoever but went on writing. Helga tossed herself face down into her pillow and pounded it and sobbed and raged from out of there. When Daphne had finished writing, she turned off the light and, undressing in the dark, lay down in her lumpy bed next to Helga, who by that time was asleep, still face downward and her fists clenched and dirty tear marks down her cheeks.

Next morning Helga was up and dressed early, but contrary to her usual custom, she was very quiet and tiptoed around so as not to disturb her roommate. When Daphne finally woke up, Helga greeted her cheerfully and asked whether she had had a good sleep, and then she told her how she had watched poor Klas stepping into a pat of fresh cow dung on his way to meditation. Helga thought this was very funny, she laughed loudly at it and encouraged Daphne to laugh too by giving her shoulder a hearty push. Then she went off to get breakfast for the two of them, and, after they had had it, and stepped outside the room to cross over to Swamiji's, she suddenly put her arm around Daphne and whispered into her ear: "You won't tell him anything? No? Daphnelein?" And to seal their friendship, their conspiracy, she planted a big, wet kiss on Daphne's neck and said, "There. Now it is all well again."

Swamiji was receiving daily letters from America, and he was very merry nowadays and there was a sense of bustle and departure about him. The current meditation course, for which Daphne and Helga and all of them had enrolled, was coming to an end, and soon they would be expected to go home again so that they might radiate their newly acquired spiritual health from there. But when they talked among themselves, none of them seemed in any hurry to go back. The two Scottish schoolteachers were planning a tour of India to see the Taj Mahal and the Ajanta caves and other such places of interest, while Klas wanted to go up to Almora to investigate a spiritual brotherhood he had heard of there. Swamiji encouraged them—"It is such fun to travel," he said, and obviously he was gleefully looking forward to his own travels, receiving and answering all those airmail letters and studying airline folders, and one of the young men who attended on him had already been sent to Delhi to make preliminary arrangements.

Daphne had no plans. She didn't even think of going home; it was inconceivable to her that she could go or be anywhere where he was not. The Scottish schoolteachers urged her to join them on their tour, and she halfheartedly agreed, knowing though that she would not go. Helga questioned her continuously as to what she intended to do, and when she said she didn't know, came forward with suggestions of her own. These always included both of them; Helga had somehow taken it for granted that their destinies were now inseparable. She would sit on the side of Daphne's bed and say in a sweet, soft voice, "Shall we go to Khajurao? To Cochin? Would you like to visit Ceylon?" and at the same time she would be coaxing and stroking Daphne's pillow as if she were thereby coaxing and stroking Daphne herself.

All the time Daphne was waiting for him to speak. In London she had been so sure of what he meant her to do, without his ever having to say anything; now she had to wait for him to declare himself. Did he want her to accompany him to America; did he want her to stay behind in India; was she to go home? London, though it held her mother, her father, her job, her friends, all her memories, was dim and remote to her; she could not imagine herself returning there. But if that was what he intended her to do, then she would; propelled not by any will of her own, but by his. And this was somehow a great happiness to her: that she, who had always been so self-reliant in her judgments and actions, should now have succeeded in surrendering not only her trained, English mind but everything else as well—her will, herself, all she was—only to him.

His dictation still continued every day; evidently this was going to be a massive work, for though she had already written out hundreds of foolscap pages, the end was not yet in sight. Beyond this daily dictation, he had nothing special to say to her; she still went on her evening walk, but he did not again come to meet her. In any case, this walk of hers was now never taken alone but always in the company of Helga, whose arm firmly linked hers. Helga saw to it that they did everything together these days: ate, slept, sat with Swamiji, even meditated. She did not trust her alone for a moment, so even if Swamiji had wanted to say anything private to Daphne, Helga would always be there to listen to it.

Daphne wasn't sure whether it was deep night or very early in the morning when one of the bearded young men came to call her. Helga, innocently asleep, was breathing in and out. Daphne followed the messenger across the courtyard. Everything was sleeping in a sort of gray half-light, and the sky too was gray with some dulled, faint stars in it. Across the river a small, wakeful band of devotees was chanting and praying; they were quite a long way off and yet the sound was very clear in the surrounding silence. There was no light in Swamiji's room, nor was he in it; her guide led her through the room and out of an opposite door that led to the adjoining veranda, overlooking the river. Here Swamiji sat on a mat, eating a meal by the light of a kerosene lamp. "Ah, Daphne," he said, beckoning her to sit opposite him on the mat. "There you are at last."

The bearded youth had withdrawn. Now there were only the two of them. It was so strange. The kerosene lamp stood just next to Swamiji and threw its light over him and over his tray of food. He ate with pleasure and with great speed, his hand darting in and out of the various little bowls of rice, vegetable, lentils, and curds. He also ate very neatly, so that only the very tips of the fingers of his right hand were stained by the food and nothing dropped into his beard. It struck Daphne that this was the first time that she had seen him eat a full meal: during the course of his busy day, he seemed content to nibble at nuts and at his favorite sweetmeats, and now and again drink a tumbler of milk brought to him by one of his young men.

"Can I talk to you?" he asked her. "You won't turn into a laurel tree?"

He pushed aside his tray and dabbled his hand in a finger bowl and then wiped it on a towel. "I think it would be nice," he said, "if you come with me to America."

She said, "I'd like to come."

"Good."

He folded the towel neatly and then pressed it flat with his hand. For a time neither of them said anything. The chanting came from across the river; the kerosene lamp cast huge shadows.

"We shall have to finish our book," he said. "In America we shall have plenty of leisure and comfort for this purpose ... Mrs. Gay Fisher has made all arrangements."

He bent down to adjust the flame of the lamp and now the light fell directly on his face. At that moment Daphne saw very clearly that he was not a good-looking man, nor was there anything noble in his features: on the contrary, they were short, blunt, and common, and his expression, as he smiled to himself in anticipation of America, had something disagreeable in it. But the next moment he had straightened up again, and now his face opposite her was full of shadows and so wise, calm, and beautiful, that she had to look away for a moment, for sheer rapture.

"We shall be staying in her home," he said. "It is a very large mansion with swimming pool and all amenities—wait, I will show you." Out of the folds of his gown he drew an envelope, which he had evidently kept ready for her and out of which he extracted some color photographs.

"This is her mansion. It is in Greek style. See how gracious these tall pillars, so majestic. It was built in 1940 by the late Mr. Fisher." He raised the lamp and brought it near the photograph to enable her to see better. "And this," he said, handing her another photograph, "is Mrs. Gay Fisher herself."

He looked up and saw that light had dawned, so he lowered the wick of the lamp and extinguished the flame. Thus it was by the frail light of earliest dawn that Daphne had her first sight of Mrs. Gay Fisher.

"She writes with great impatience," he said. "She wants us to come at once, straightaway, woof like that, on a magic carpet if possible." He smiled, tolerant, amused: "She is of a warm, impulsive nature."

The picture showed a woman in her fifties in a pastel two-piece and thick ankles above dainty shoes. She wore a three-rope pearl necklace and was smiling prettily, her head a little to one side, her hands demurely clasped before her. Her hair was red.

"The climate in California is said to be very beneficial," Swamiji said. "And wonderful fruits are available. Not to speak of ice cream," he twinkled, referring to his well-known weakness. "Please try and look a little bit happy, Daphne, or I shall think that you don't want to come with me at all."

"I want to," she said. "I do."

He collected his photographs from her and put them carefully back into the envelope. There was still chanting on the other side of the river. The river looked a misty silver now and so did the sky and the air and the mountains as slowly, minute by minute, day emerged from out of its veils. The first bird woke up and gave a chirp of pleasure and surprise that everything was still there.

"Go along now," he said. "Go and meditate." He put out his

hand and placed it for a moment on her head. She felt small, weak, and entirely dependent on him. "Go, go," he said, pretending impatience, but when she went, he called: "Wait!" She stopped and turned back. "Wake up that sleepy Helga," he said. "I want to talk to her." Then he added: "She's coming with us too." "To America?" she said, and in such a way that he looked at her and asked, "What's wrong?" She shook her head. "Then be quick," he said.

A few days later he sent her a present of a sari. It was of plain mill cloth, white with a thin red border. She put it away but when, later, he saw her in her usual skirt and blouse, he asked her where it was. She understood then that from now on that was what he wanted her to wear, as a distinguishing mark, a uniform almost, the way his bearded young attendants always wore orange robes. She put it on just before her evening walk; it took her a long time to get it on, and when she had, she felt awkward and uncomfortable. She knew she did not look right, her bosom was too flat, her hips too narrow, nor had she learned how to walk in it, and she kept stumbling. But she knew she would have to get used to it, so she persevered; it seemed a very little obstacle to overcome.

Instead of going on her usual route, she turned today in the opposite direction and walked toward the town. First she had to pass all the other ashrams, then she had to go through the little wood where the sadhus did penance, and the beggars stretched pitiful arms toward her and showed her their sores. In these surroundings, it did not seem to matter greatly, not even to herself, what she wore and how she wore it; and when she had crossed the wood, and had got to the temples and bazaars, it still did not matter, for although there were crowds of people, none of them had any time to care for Daphne. The temple bells rang and people bought garlands and incense and sweetmeats to give to their favorite gods. Daphne crossed the holy bridge and, as she did so, folded her hands in homage to the holy river. Once or twice she tripped over her sari, but she didn't mind, she just hitched it up a bit higher. When she came to the end of the bridge, she turned and walked back over it, again folding her hands and even saying, *"Jai Ganga-ji,"* only silently to herself and not out loud like everyone else. Then she saw Helga coming toward her, also dressed in a white sari with a red border; Helga waved to her over the heads of people and when they came together, she turned and walked back with Daphne, her arm affectionately around her shoulder. Helga was wearing her sari all wrong, it was too short for her and her feet coming out at the end were enormous. She looked ridiculous, but no one cared; Daphne didn't either. She was glad to be with Helga, and she thought probably she would be glad to be with Mrs. Gay Fisher as well. She was completely happy to be going to California, and anywhere else he might want her to accompany him.

PASSION

Apart from the fact that they had both been in India for about a year and both had well-paid jobs with British cultural organizations, Christine and Betsy had very little in common. Nevertheless they shared a flat. Their friends—Christine's friends especially, Betsy didn't have all that many—were surprised when they first decided on this step and wondered how it would ever work out; but in fact it worked very well, perhaps just because they were so different, and led different lives, and so never got in each other's way.

The mantelpiece in their flat was always full of invitations, and they were almost all Christine's. She was tall, slim, and good-looking. She had a number of Indian boyfriends, who would call for her at the flat in the evenings in order to take her out in their cars. Sometimes she wasn't quite ready and she would trill from out of the bathroom that she wouldn't be a second; Betsy in the meantime invited them to make themselves comfortable in the sitting room and have a drink. Sometimes they had several before Christine finally appeared, and then they jumped smartly to their feet while she, laughing and breathless and tying a gauze scarf around her hair, flippantly apologized for keeping them waiting.

Her favorite escort was a tall, handsome officer of the President's bodyguard called Captain Manohar Singh ("Manny" to his friends). Betsy too was glad when it was Manny who was taking Christine out, and the longer he was kept waiting the better Betsy liked it. She felt good sitting next to the handsome Manny on the sofa and talking to him. She talked to him about India—Indian philosophy or music, or about the current political situation—while he drank one whiskey after the other and sat at his ease with his large legs apart and a good-natured, listening expression on his face. Betsy sometimes had reason to believe that he wasn't really listening, for he never made any kind of remark that could be construed as a comment on what she was telling him. Indeed, he hardly said anything at all, and when he did, it was something completely unexpected like, "Boy, did we have a party last night! Wow!" But for Betsy it was really enough to be allowed to talk to him and look at him at such close quarters to her heart's content. Manny was a Sikh, and he had an exquisitely barbered, shining black beard and wore a dark-blue turban; his eyes were not dark but surprisingly light-colored, a pellucid gray shining like a lake between the heavy fringe of his black lashes.

Once Manny kissed Betsy. It was entirely unexpected. They were sitting on the sofa and Betsy was telling him about her preference for the Kangra school of painting over that of Basohli, when suddenly he jumped on her. Really, there was no other word for it—he *jumped,* took a leap from where he was sitting and snatched her into his arms. She gave a short cry of shock, but next moment his lips were pressed weightily on hers, his tongue—strong, pulsing, muscled like some animal alive in its own right—pushed its way into her mouth; beneath his silk shirt she could feel his chest and his ribs as strong as steel. Waves of rapture passed over her like a fainting fit. But it seemed he was more collected than she was. As suddenly as he had seized her, he pushed her away, hastily adjusted his turban and got to his feet as Christine came breezing in, wafting scent and shouting "Darling!" "Darling!" he answered with his great boom of a laugh. "Again you are late, ho-ho, darling!" He was quite unembarrassed, while Betsy was left sitting stunned on the sofa with her hair disheveled and her skirt slipped high up on her thighs.

With few friends and few entertainments, Betsy had very little to do in her spare time and spent most of it reading. She often went to the American library and became well known to the local staff there. One member of the staff was particularly assiduous in finding the books she wanted and keeping back those she had asked for. He was a slim, shy young Indian who, like a thousand other clerks, was always dressed in a clean but rather old white shirt and Western-style trousers. In the evenings, when she took a taxi home from the office, Betsy often saw him standing in a bus queue. The queue was always immensely long, and many of the buses that passed were crowded and did not even stop. He looked very patient standing there, holding a small, worn brass tiffin carrier in his hand. Once it was raining, and she saw him trying to protect himself by placing the tiffin carrier on his head. She stopped her taxi and offered him a lift; he got in without a word.

"Where can I drop you?" she asked.

"Where you are going."

"But that may be miles out of your way."

"It is all right."

That was all she could get out of him: "It is all right." For the rest, he sat straight and silent on the edge of the seat, holding his arms close to his sides; he was very wet and exuded vapors of dampness and discomfort. When the taxi stopped at her house and she got out, he got out with her, without a word. "Do you live near here?" she asked; she felt quite guilty about him by this time. "It is all right," he said, and stood and waited. Perhaps he was waiting to be asked up, but Betsy couldn't do that because Christine was having people in. She fumbled in her bag for her keys and, in the process, feeling nervous and hurried, dropped many things on the pavement. He stooped to pick them up, and she cried out in alarm, "No, don't bother!" She crouched down with him on the pavement, and they both scrabbled for her things and got wet in the rain. When she had found her keys, she stuffed everything back into her bag and tucked it bulging under her arm and ran inside, leaving him standing. She had a bad conscience about him for hours afterward.

A few days later she passed him again at the bus stand. Feeling embarrassed, she looked quickly the other way, but he had seen her, and without a moment's hesitation he ran into the road and signaled her taxi to a halt; he waved both arms like a person in distress. But he wasn't in distress at all, he only wanted a ride with her. Again he came to her door and stood there, waiting expectantly. When she asked him up, he agreed at once. He sat down on a chair and looked around him with undisguised curiosity, up and down the walls, across the ceiling, at all the furniture. Betsy said, "Would you like a drink?" Now that she had brought him here, she didn't know what to do with him.

When she had mixed him his drink, he held the glass as if it were some strange object and then he asked: "It is alcohol?"

"Oh dear." She bit her lip and stared at him in consternation. "Don't you drink? I'm so sorry—"

But he took a big gulp and, after coughing a bit, another; then he finished the glass. She looked at him apprehensively. "It doesn't taste very nice," he said.

"No, if you're not used to it. It never occurred to me that you might not—everybody seems to drink such a lot. I mean, all the people one meets—" She stopped herself, for she realized she was saying he was not the sort of person one met. She sought desperately for something to say to cancel this out. But he did not seem to have noticed. He was smiling: "It is a funny taste."

"Would you like some more?"

"Yes."

This time too he drank it down very quickly, as if it were water or tea. She would have liked to warn him but was afraid of hurting his feelings. When he had finished, he was smiling again; he seemed happy.

"Once we drank beer," he said. "It was at my friend's sister's wedding. We hid behind the cowshed, but afterward one of the uncles found the empty bottle, and how angry everyone was with us!" He giggled. Betsy realized to her dismay that he was drunk. "We were very mischievous boys. I could tell you other stories also ... It is a nice place here. Who else lives here? There are many rooms?" He got up and began to walk around the room as if he owned it. He picked up objects and asked their price, and peeped into cupboard doors. "I think you must be getting a lot of salary. How much? More than one thousand rupees? More? How much more? Tell me, please. Only for my information."

Suddenly and without any warning he was sick all over the off-white rug. He stood there and retched, and held his stomach and groaned. Betsy laid her hand on his forehead. "Don't worry," she said. "It doesn't matter." She had to turn her head away, but she felt terribly sorry for him.

And afterward she blamed herself severely. She disliked herself for having mismanaged the not overwhelmingly difficult task of inviting an unsophisticated young man up to her flat and making him welcome. She longed to make amends, to invite him again and see to it that the occasion went off with dignity on both sides. Yet at the same time she felt that she could not bear to have him here again, indeed ever to see him again; and what she would really have liked to do was to forget the whole incident and the person who had caused it.

A day or two later she heard an altercation at the door. Angry voices were raised, and then her servant came in. "He says he wants to see you," said the servant accusingly. The young librarian had followed him into the room, looking indignant and like a man determined to stand on his rights.

"Your servant was rude to me," he said as soon as they were alone. He waved aside her explanation and apologies. "I am not very much used to being treated rudely by servants."

"Betsy!" called Christine from inside her bedroom. "Has Manny come?"

"Not yet!"

"Who is that?" asked the young man sternly, but before Betsy could explain, Christine stood in the doorway. She was wearing a pink flowered wrap that she held shut with one hand. "Hallo," she told the young man.

Betsy said, "This is—" and realized she didn't know her visitor's name. He was too stunned by Christine's appearance to help her out.

"I'm Christine," Christine said. She waited politely for him to introduce himself, but when he didn't, she smiled at him in her friendly way and disappeared again inside. She could be heard, a moment later, singing in her bath. The young man remained staring at the spot where she had stood.

Betsy explained, "We share this flat." She smiled: "I don't even know your name, how silly."

"Har Gopal. She is English also?"

"Oh yes. She works for the British Council." For want of anything better to say, she began to tell him about Christine's job. But he did not listen. He looked rather distraught, glancing now around the room, now at the spot where Christine had stood. Betsy noticed how refined his face was, with a delicately chiseled nose and sad eyes. Every now and again he brought his hand up to his open collar, pressing the two ends together over his throat as if wanting thereby to improve his appearance; it was a movement at once modest and self-protective. Betsy found herself feeling very tender toward this young man.

Then Manny came to fetch Christine. He was in uniform and all his buttons shone and so did his beautiful, brown, hard-leather boots. He strode up and down the room, waiting for Christine, immensely tall and exuding a smell of whisky and eau de cologne. His eyes had merely swept for a second over the top of Har Gopal's head—it did not need more than that for him to sum up a fellow countryman. With Betsy he was, as usual, absently affable. He had never, after the event, given a sign that he remembered having kissed her. Probably he didn't remember. He strode about the room, thinking of other things, and only became alert when Christine entered. She was no longer in her negligée but in a primrose-yellow dress, and golden sandals with high heels that made her even taller than she was. The room seemed very small with these two in it, and when they had gone, it seemed very empty.

Har Gopal spoke bitterly: "Are they your friends? I don't like that Sikh. I know his type very well." When she made no comment, he spoke harshly to her, as if she had dared to contradict him: "I tell you I have seen hundreds like him. What do you know about it?" Neither of them in the least questioned his right to speak to her in this manner.

"I am B.A. Kurukshetra University," he said next. "Yes, now you are surprised. You thought I was just anyone, isn't it? B.A. in history and philosophy. And my wife is a matriculate. Come here." He beckoned to her with his slender, fine-boned hand, displaying a surprising authority, and she went.

He jumped on her in the same sudden way Manny had done. Betsy thought, do all Indian men make love like this? In spite of his frail appearance, Har Gopal was strong. Not with Manny's massive body strength, but he had a sort of sharp, incisive, relentless quality that rode down opposition. He went straight ahead without question, not skillful but resolute, steely. He commanded respect.

Betsy was in love with Har Gopal. If she hadn't been, the situation might have become embarrassing. He came every day to the flat, and when any of Christine's friends was there, he sat in a corner like a poor relation and looked at them with burning, hungry eyes. Afterward he was angry with Betsy and blamed her for any lack of respect he felt had been shown to him. Christine was always very nice and tactful with him, and in return he went to some pains to make serious conversation with her. He would tell her about the unemployment problem in Uttar Pradesh, or the number of light aircraft manufactured by the Hindustan aircraft factory per year. She would appear to be listening and would say "No really?" and "How fascinating!" in between, without irony. She might be doing her nails, daubing on the varnish with exquisite little brush strokes, and he would look on in fascination. He loved seeing her do her nails.

Sometimes he asked Betsy why she didn't paint hers, and he clicked his tongue in disapproval when she held them out to him, clipped very short and one or two of them bitten down at the end of her short, squarish fingers.

But she took a lot of trouble for him. She brushed and brushed her hair till it shone, and then she slipped a red band around it. She wore white frilly blouses and short skirts and white ballet shoes and a gold locket around her neck. She loved going out for walks with him and would tuck her hand proudly under his arm. He allowed her to keep it there and walked by her side in a stately manner, with his head held stiffly. Many people looked at them. They were both about the same height, both short, but he was thin and she was rather stocky with very muscular legs. Once or twice they met people he knew—some friend or neighbor—and he would stop to exchange a few words in a rather formal, self-conscious way, and though her hand remained tucked under his arm, he made no attempt to introduce her. But if they met anyone she knew, some fellow countrymen from her office or the High Commission, she made a point of introducing Har Gopal at once, flaunting him and clinging to him in such a way that her acquaintances became embarrassed and looked away and parted from her as quickly as possible. But Har Gopal always behaved correctly and said "Very happy to meet you," and shook hands all around the way he knew foreigners did.

Betsy confided a lot in Christine. She needed to have someone to talk to about Har Gopal. "I know it's ridiculous, ridiculous," she said and buried her head in her arms, overwhelmed with laughter and happiness. "He's all wrong—of course he is—*and* he's married, *and* three children." She hid her face again and her shoulders shook laughing. She tried to but could never quite explain to Christine what it was she loved so much about Har Gopal. His finely drawn features, yes, his dark, dreaming eyes, his sadness, his sensitivity: and also—but how could she tell Christine this?—she loved the shabby clothes he wore, his badly cut cotton trousers and his frequently washed shirt with his thin wrists coming out of the buttoned cuffs. She was positively proud of the fact that he looked so much like everybody else—like hundreds and thousands of other Indian clerks going to offices every morning on the bus and coming home again with their empty tiffin carriers in the evenings: people who worked for small salaries and supported their families and worried. She frowned with the effort of trying to express all this to Christine and said finally that well, she supposed she loved him for being so typically Indian.

Christine laughed: "But that's why I like Manny too."

Betsy had to admit that Manny too was typically Indian—but in a very different way. Manny was the India one read about in childhood, colored with tigers, sunsets, and princes; but Har Gopal was *real*, he was everyday, urban, suffering India that people in the West didn't know about.

Har Gopal often asked her: "Do you talk about me with Christine?" He wanted to know everything that they said. When she teased and wouldn't tell, he twisted her wrist or squeezed her muscles till she screamed. He loved practicing these boyhood tortures on her; it was the only way he knew of being playful, for that was how he had played with his friends at school and college. He had never had a woman friend before. But he had had many male friends, and they had had grand times together. He often told Betsy about his friends, and it always put him in a good mood. He had a serious, even melancholy nature, but when he recollected his student days, he became gay and laughed at all the mad pranks they had played together. One of his friends, Chandu, had been a great joker, and how he had teased the masters at school! No one could do anything to him, because his father was an important man in town. Another friend had had the ability to chew up newspapers and even razor blades. They were all crazy about the cinema and went to see the same film over and over again till they knew the lyrics and dialogues by heart. He could still recite great chunks of old films and he did so for Betsy, and he sang the songs for her. She loved his voice, which was sweet and girlish, and the soft expression that came into his eyes when he sang; but he said no no, his voice was nothing, she should have heard Mohan, then she would have known what good singing was. They had all thought that Mohan would surely go into films and become a playback singer, but instead he had got a job in the life insurance corporation. There had been so many friends, and they had all been so close and had thought their friendship was eternal; but now Har Gopal didn't even know where most of them were. Everyone was married, like himself, and had their own worries and no more time for their friends. But he still thought about them often and wished for the old days back again, or at least to have one friend left with him in whom to confide his thoughts and have a good time together.

"Well you've got me now," said Betsy, putting her arm around his neck, tender and comradely.

But he could not feel about her the way he did about his friends. He was, she knew, less fond of her. She excited him, and he was proud to have her, but he did not really, she often suspected, *like* her. All the loving came from her side, and he accepted it as his due but made no attempt to return it. There was something lordly, almost tyrannical in his attitude to her. When he lounged at his ease in her room, all his shyness and shabbiness—that *depressed* quality that was so evident in him when he stood with his tiffin carrier at the bus-stop—left him completely, and he became what, as a Brahmin, he perhaps was by nature: an aristocrat for whom the goods and riches of this world were created and whose right it was to be served by others. Betsy was the one who served, and the goods and riches were the things she gave him for which he had developed a taste: English biscuits, raspberry syrup (he never again drank alcohol), tinned peaches.

He kept some clothes in her room, and when he came to her straight from the office, as he usually did, he would take off his trousers and carefully fold them and then put on his dhoti. He dressed and undressed with delicate precaution, so as never to be seen naked by any human eye, not even his own. Although his lovemaking left nothing to be desired, he never lost his reticence: his manner was always controlled and fastidious, and never for a moment was there any abandon in it. Betsy, on the other hand, was all abandon. She would fling off her clothes, leaving them just where they dropped, and walk around the room naked. Very often she forgot to lock the door, so that the servant or Christine or anyone who came to the flat could have walked in at any time. She didn't care. Her attitude shocked and at the same time pleased him. In the beginning he could only watch her undressing with his face averted and his eyes half lowered, ashamed of himself and of her, but as time went on, he looked at her boldly and with a strange smile that was perhaps partly appreciation and partly, she sometimes suspected, contempt.

He never spoke to her about his family. She wanted to know so much about them, but he always completely evaded her questions. If she insisted too much, he became annoyed and refused to speak to her at all and perhaps even went home earlier than usual. So she dared not ask much. But it tortured her to have all this area of his life concealed from her with a deliberateness that suggested she was not worthy to approach it. Why should he feel that way? He was *proud* of her—she knew he was—otherwise would he parade through the town with her on his arm and greet people he met on the way with such a superior air?

Sometimes, when she found he was relaxed and in a good mood, she tried to coax him into talking: "Is your wife taller than me? Shorter? The same? Say!" But at once his good mood would disappear and he turned away from her, frowning. Once she asked him half jokingly, "What's the matter? You don't think I'm good enough to hear about your family?" But at that he took on such a strange, closed expression that she realized she had stumbled on something near the truth. But she wouldn't at first believe it; she even laughed at it and said, "My God, what am I—a fallen woman or something?" Still he made no answer, but the expression on his face did not change nor did he make any attempt to contradict or deny. She laughed again, more harshly, even though by now she felt far from laughing. It was ridiculous, something out of Victorian melodrama, but still it was true, it was the way he saw her. She felt so humiliated that she could speak nothing further and tears flowed silently from her eyes: but even as they rolled down her cheeks and her heart heaved with pain at the thought of her humiliation, at the same time—so bizarre were her feelings for him—this very humiliation actually increased, exacerbated her passion for him.

One day she went secretly to see the place where he lived. She found blocks of tenements set out side by side and surrounded by an area of wasteland on which had sprung up a dusty little bazaar and a shanty colony of thatched huts. As soon as she got out of her taxi, she found herself the center of a group of children who laughed and marveled at her strangeness and followed her closely. She looked around her for a time, then plucked up courage and walked through the doorway that led into the compound of the first block of buildings. It was as lively here as in any street. Children played, and there were some men repairing string beds and a number of itinerant vegetable sellers and a fish seller, all of whom were bargaining with women who suspiciously untied their bundles of money from the end of their saris and complained to one another about dishonest traders; other women called down from the windows that opened in tiers and rows from the tall buildings. Betsy, with her little cluster of attendant children, looked around her and did not know what to do next. Suddenly she wondered what would happen if he were to come now out of one of those dark doorways and find her standing there.

She could almost see the expression of panic and fury that would instantly transform his face, and at the thought of it, she began to panic a little herself and to wish she had not come.

But then it was too late to retreat. A round little man in an English-style suit came running up to her, calling in an excited voice, "Yes, please, yes, please! You have come to see Mr. Har Gopal?" Betsy did not recognize him, but guessed at once that he must be someone whom they had met and Har Gopal had talked to on one of their evening walks.

"This way, please," said the little man, pushing aside all the children and leading her out of the compound. To curious bystanders he explained importantly, "For Har Gopal in C Block." He strutted in front while the children surged after him and Betsy found herself swept along in the procession. Behind her the women nudged and talked. The little man led her along the street and then turned into the next compound, waving a plump hand over his shoulder at her and calling, "This way, please!"

Then she saw that the little procession had brought her back to the street where her taxi was waiting. Murmuring apologies that no one heard, she suddenly climbed into it and sat down, and the driver skillfully flicked away the children who at once surrounded the car. Betsy did not dare look out of the window as she was driven away, and she even put her handkerchief up to her face as if she hoped thereby neither to see nor be seen.

The next time Har Gopal came to the flat he did not talk to her at all but straightaway took his dhoti and a pair of slippers and bottle of hair oil he kept in her bedroom and, grimly determined, wrapped them up in a bundle. "What are you doing?" she cried out in distress. He did not answer but made for the door. She clung to him to prevent him. She begged him to stay.

"Let me go, please," he said, but standing quite still and making no effort to release himself.

"It's only that I wanted to *see* where you were."

"You came to spy on me. Yes, and now you will laugh at me with your friends because my house is poor and I am poor." Suddenly he shrieked: "I don't care! You can laugh, what do I care!"

"Please don't," she said and clung to him tighter, but he shook her off and shouted at her, "And my position? That's nothing to you what people will say that you come openly to my home—" He sank down to sit on the edge of her bed and covered his eyes with his hands in grief and shame. And Betsy sank down beside him, and she too covered her eyes. What followed was a loud scene, echoing all over the flat, in which he spoke a lot about his position in the world and she lacerated herself with accusations regarding her own selfishness and insensitivity; and when this had gone on for a long time, and she had again and again begged his forgiveness, they were at last reconciled, and she dissolved in tears of gratitude while he was proud and gracious with her.

Then it was time for him to go home, and on his way out, they had to pass through the sitting room where Christine sat playing ludo with Manny. Those two must have heard every word of what had passed in the other room. Christine delicately kept her eyes fixed on the ludo board, and Manny hummed a tune to himself. Har Gopal's face took on a tight expression, and his thin body seemed to shrink as he walked through the room; he looked as he did waiting at the bus stop. Only Betsy was entirely free from embarrassment as she ushered her lover out of the flat.

That night Christine knocked timidly on Betsy's door. Betsy was lying stark naked on her rumpled bed, reading the Katha-Upanishad. She was wearing her reading glasses and thoughtfully twisting a lock of hair around her finger. She didn't seem to be a bit shy to be found naked. Her breasts were very much heavier than one would have expected from seeing her dressed. "Yes, come in," she said and shut her book with her finger inside to hold the page. "I'm sorry, we made an awful lot of noise today, didn't we?" she said cheerfully.

Christine sat on the edge of a chair. She was wearing a flowered wrap and looked crisp and fresh and a contrast to Betsy's room, which was rather untidy.

"I know it's none of my business," said Christine, talking very quickly so as to get it over with, "but I do think you ought to be a bit more careful."

Betsy laughed and said, "I wish I were the sort of person who *could* be careful."

"Everyone's talking you know, Betsy, in the office and everywhere. I mean, good heavens, not that anyone cares about your having an Indian boyfriend—don't we all?—but he's so . . . *different* from the other Indians we all know."

"You mean he's poor."

"It's not that," Christine said miserably. "But he's—I don't know, odd. And there's something unhealthy about it all—of course it's absolutely terrible of me to be saying all this and do tell me to shut up if you want to."

There was a moment's pause. Then Betsy said, "It *is* unhealthy." She tried to sound detached and dispassionate, but could not keep it up for long. "I suppose all passion is unhealthy. Sometimes I tell you I feel *insane*—and what's more—what's terrible: I revel in it! I glory in it!" She rolled over onto her side to face Christine, and her big breasts fell to that side and her eyes shone behind her flesh-colored glasses.

Christine was not the only person who tried to warn Betsy. One day her office chief invited her to lunch at his house, and in the kindest manner possible, full of embarrassment and apologies, told her that unless she behaved in what he called a more conventional way he would have to have her sent home. Betsy understood that he had to tell her this and that he was right, but she had no intention of changing. Instead she began to make plans what to do if she were really posted back home. Of course, she would resign immediately; she would stay and get a job locally. She was vague as to what kind of job and did not stop much to wonder whether anyone would employ her; but she knew that, whatever she did, her salary would only be a fraction of what it was now and she would have to change her whole way of life. She didn't mind that; in fact, she rather looked forward to it. She would have to move out of the flat and go somewhere much cheaper. She thought of herself in some small room in a crowded locality; to get to her, one would have to cross a courtyard and climb up a very dark, very narrow winding staircase. She would be the only European living in the house. Every day Har Gopal would come to visit her. Actually Betsy couldn't cook, but now she had visions of herself squatting over a little bucket of coal and preparing a meal for him and serving him just like an Indian wife. She might take to wearing a sari. Perhaps she would have a baby, a boy, who would grow up dark and delicate like Har Gopal.

She neglected her work in the office and was distant with her colleagues. She realized vaguely that something was going on around her and that perhaps steps were being taken against her, but she did not bother to find out what they were. Christine told her that she would be moving out of their joint flat soon; she made up some polite lies that the flat was getting too expensive for her and that she had found another smaller one elsewhere, but Betsy cut her short and said it didn't matter, that she herself would be moving out too, very soon. She already saw herself in her small room in the house with the winding staircase.

She even began to make inquiries about the rents to be paid for such places, and about how much money would be needed for the simple, Indian-style life she intended to adopt. All her thoughts were concentrated on this problem. Once, finding herself alone with Manny who was waiting for Christine to get ready, she even asked him, very seriously, "Supposing you only eat dal and rice twice a day—how much would that come to a week?"

"Only dal and rice!" exclaimed Manny humorously. "And what about a peg of whiskey?"

"I'm being serious, Manny," Betsy said impatiently, but it was impossible to make him be serious with her. Ever since she had started her affair with Har Gopal, Manny's attitude to her had become strange and ambivalent: on the one hand, he was rather more brusque, and even rude with her than he had been before; on the other, he indulged in sudden spurts of familiarity that extended to, whenever they found themselves alone in a room, pinching her in intimate places.

He did this now, and at the same time he joked with her: "My two-three pegs a day I must have, otherwise I'm like my car without petrol. Hm? Han?" He encouraged her to laugh with him and drew her close, and his beard nuzzled against her cheek. She struggled to get free, but that made him hold her all the more tightly. She stared into his face, and she saw his light-colored eyes and his red, moist, healthy mouth smiling inside his black beard. She let out a cry. He released her immediately and even gave her a push to get her farther away from him. Christine, zipping her dress, came in and said, "Whatever's the matter?"

"It is Betsy," said Manny. "She thought she saw a snake." He laughed uproariously.

Betsy did not speak to Har Gopal about her future plans. She was afraid. She knew that the idea of anyone giving up a job, an assured livelihood, was not one he would ever be able to understand. He himself was very timid about his own job and took good care never to give cause for complaint to his superiors. Not only was he very polite, even deferential, to them in their presence, but he also spoke of them in tones of the highest respect when they were not there and had no chance of ever knowing what he was saying about them. Once, when Betsy spoke with lighthearted disdain of one or two of the top people in her own organization, he rebuked her for

doing so, and when she laughed at the rebuke, he frowned and became annoyed with her and said that she had no respect in her nature. The very least, he said, that one owed one's superiors was
respect; and quite apart from that, one should be careful what one
said about them because who knew what might not get back to
them. But how *could* anything get back to them, asked Betsy,
amused, when there was no one there but he and she, and surely he
wasn't going to go and tell on her, was he? He refused to smile at the
idea but only said that in these matters one could never be careful
enough. His eyes even roved solemnly for a moment around the
room—her bedroom—as if he feared someone might be lurking
somewhere listening.

One Sunday afternoon he was reclining on her bed in his rather
lordly way, wearing his vest and dhoti, his feet crossed comfortably
at the ankle; he had his arms folded behind his head and was staring
into space with melancholy eyes. He looked noble and sensitive and
gave the impression of being sunk in deep philosophic thought. This
impression, however, was false, for when he finally broke his silence
it was to say nothing more significant than, "Just see, I have had this
blister for two days. It is very painful." He plaintively held up his
finger to her.

She burst out laughing and, overcome with tenderness for him,
threw herself on his reclining figure. "Oh, you're so sweet, so *sweet!*"
she cried, and crushed him as tight as she could as if she hoped
thereby to relieve her overwhelming feelings. He cried out and
struggled to get free—unsuccessfully, till she released him of her own
accord. He smoothed down his hair with one hand and his dhoti
with the other and said indignantly, "How rough you are."

She laughed again and settled herself happily on the floor, leaning her head against the edge of the bed on which he lay. She felt
exquisitely comfortable and domestic and knew that this was the
way she wanted her life to go on forever. And then she blurted it
out, about giving up her job and staying in India so as to be always
near him.

Har Gopal was appalled. He quite genuinely thought she was
mad. He argued with her, pointed out that even if she managed to
get some kind of job in India, which was in itself unlikely, she would
never be able to live on the salary she would be paid. But Betsy said
no, she wanted to live on it; she was tired of living the way she did
here, as a foreigner, as a privileged person.

"I want to live in India like an Indian," she said, "like everyone else, like you. Exactly like you," and she seized his fine, frail hand and kissed it.

He drew it away from her. "You don't know anything," he said. "If you had to live in a place where there is never enough water and the neighbors quarrel and you clean and clean but still the cockroaches come—"

"I don't care," Betsy said.

"Yes, it is so easy to talk," he said bitterly. He got up from the bed and began to get dressed, though it was not yet his usual time for departure.

"I want to give up everything for you," Betsy said. "To lay my whole life at your feet and say: here, take it." She shut her eyes, carried away by the passion with which she spoke.

He uttered a short sound of impatience and turned his back on her. He began to comb his hair in the mirror. She came up behind him and put her arms round his waist and laid her cheek caressingly against his back. He continued to comb his hair very carefully; he was always careful of his appearance before going out into the street.

"I'm not sacrificing anything," she said. "Don't think that. Good heavens, what do you think I care for my job, or this flat, or money, or anything?"

He could hold himself no longer: "No, you don't care! You are like that. You have everything in life and you throw it all away. Aren't you ashamed? There are others who would give God knows what to have something, to live nicely, but for them—no, there's nothing, not even in their dreams . . ." His voice failed him, and he could not go on. It was as if all the frustrations of his life had risen up and formed a hard ball in his chest and left him unable to speak. He waved his hand in her direction, dismissing her, not wanting her, and turned to the door.

"Don't go," she pleaded and held on to his arm. He attempted to free himself but she held on tightly. Suddenly he became vicious. He thumped his fist on the hand holding on to his arm and cursed her in Hindi: *"Hath mat lagao, besharm kahin ki!"* He left the room, with her running after him.

Christine and Manny were having drinks in the sitting room. Manny put down his glass and got up and strode over to Har Gopal. He seized him by the front of his shirt and shook him to and fro, and Har Gopal allowed this to be done without offering resistance. His face was frozen with fright while his body was being shaken, and the oiled, stiff hair on his head flopped up and down.

"Let him go, Manny," Christine said in a low, embarrassed voice.

Manny gave one last shake and then flung him toward the door. Har Gopal fell down but he picked himself up again and patiently dusted off his knees and hands. Without looking back at anyone, he walked down the stairs, slowly and with dignity. Betsy followed him.

When he reached the bottom of the stairs, he told her in a tone of cold command, "Get my things."

"What things?"

"My things. My dhoti and my slippers, and don't forget my bottle of hair oil."

He stood very straight and thin and proud. But suddenly he sat down on the bottom stair. He hid his face in his arms and his shoulders shook with sobbing. She sat down next to him; she held him and murmured to him, words of the sweetest comfort.

After a while he raised his face, which was smeared with tears. He cut across her murmuring and said, "You must leave this place. I don't want you to stay with these people one day more."

Betsy said that they would look for a place for her together; somewhere very cheap, very Indian. She glanced at him to note his reaction, but he gave no sign of having heard her and remained staring gloomily in front of him. She allowed herself to believe that his silence meant assent. At this her heart leaped in joy and her mind shone with visions of the new life that was about to begin for her.

THE MAN
WITH THE DOG

I think of myself sometimes as I was in the early days, and I see myself moving around my husband's house the way I used to do: freshly bathed, flowers in my hair, I go from room to room and look in corners to see that everything is clean. I walk proudly. I know myself to be loved and respected as one who faithfully fulfills all her duties in life—toward God, parents, husband, children, servants, and the poor. When I pass the prayer room, I join my hands and bow my head and sweet reverence flows in me from top to toe. I know my prayers to be pleasing and acceptable.

Perhaps it is because they remember me as I was in those days that my children get so angry with me every time they see me now. They are all grown up now and scattered in many parts of India. When they need me, or when my longing for them becomes too strong, I go and visit one or other of them. What happiness! They crowd round me, I kiss them and hug them and cry, I laugh with joy at everything my little grandchildren say and do, we talk all night there is so much to tell. As the days pass, however, we touch on other topics that are not so pleasant, or even if we don't touch on them, they are there and we think of them, and our happiness becomes clouded. I feel guilty and, worse, I begin to feel restless, and the more restless I am the more guilty I feel. I want to go home, though I dare not admit it to them. At the same time I want to stay, I don't ever ever want to leave them—my darling beloved children and grandchildren for whom what happiness it would be to lay down my life! But I have to go, the restlessness is burning me up, and I begin to tell them lies. I say that some urgent matter has come up and I have to consult my lawyer. Of course, they know it is lies, and they argue with me and quarrel and say things that children should not have to say to their mother; so that when at last I have my way and my bags are packed, our grief is more than only that of parting. All the way home, tears stream down my cheeks and my feelings are in turmoil, as the train carries me farther and farther away from them, although it is carrying me toward that which I have been hungering and burning for all the time I was with them.

Yes, I, an old woman, a grandmother many times over—I hunger and burn! And for whom? For an old man. And having said that, I feel like throwing my hands before my face and laughing out loud, although of course it may happen, as it often does to me nowadays, that my laughter will change into sobs and then back again as I think of him, of that old man whom I love so much. And how he would hate it, to be called an old man! Again I laugh when I think of his face if he could hear me call him that. The furthest he has got is to think of himself as middle-aged. Only the other day I heard him say to one of his lady friends, "Yes, now that we're all middle-aged, we have to take things a bit more slowly"; and he stroked his hand over his hair, which he combs very carefully so that the bald patches don't show, and looked sad because he was middle-aged.

I think of the first time I ever saw him. I remember everything exactly. I had been to Spitzer's to buy some little Swiss cakes, and Ram Lal, who was already my chauffeur in those days, had started the car and was just taking it out of its parking space when he drove straight into the rear bumper of a car that was backing into the adjacent space. This car was not very grand, but the Sahib who got out of it was. He wore a beautifully tailored suit with creases in the trousers and a silk tie and a hat on his head; under his arm he carried a very hairy little dog, which was barking furiously. The Sahib too was barking furiously, his face had gone red all over and he shouted abuses at Ram Lal in English. He didn't see me for a while, but when he did he suddenly stopped shouting, almost in the middle of a word. He looked at me as I sat in the back of the Packard in my turquoise sari and a cape made out of an embroidered Kashmiri shawl; even the dog stopped barking. I knew that look well. It was one that men had given me from the time I was fifteen right till—yes, even till I was over forty. It was a look that always filled me with annoyance but also (now that I am so old I can admit it) pride and pleasure. Then, a few seconds later, still looking at me in the same way but by this time with a little smile as well, he raised his hat to me; his hair was blond and thin. I inclined my head, settled my cape around my shoulders, and told Ram Lal to drive on.

In those days I was very pleasure-loving. Children were all quite big, three of them were already in college and the two younger ones at their boarding schools. When they were small and my dear husband was still with us, we lived mostly in the hills or on our estate near X (which now belongs to my eldest son, Shammi); these were quiet, dull places where my dear husband could do all his reading, invite his friends, and listen to music. Our town house was let out in those years, and when we came to see his lawyer or consult some special doctor, we had to stay in a hotel. But after I was left alone and the children were bigger, I kept the town house for myself, because I liked living in town best. I spent a lot of time shopping and bought many costly saris that I did not need; at least twice a week I visited a cinema and I even learned to play cards! I was invited to many tea parties, dinners, and other functions.

It was at one of these that I met him again. We recognized each other at once, and he looked at me in the same way as before, and soon we were making conversation. Now that we are what we are to each other and have been so for all these years, it is difficult for me to look back and see him as I did at the beginning—as a stranger with a stranger's face and a stranger's name. What interested me in him the most at the beginning was, I think, that he was a foreigner; at the time I hadn't met many foreigners, and I was fascinated by so many things about him that seemed strange and wonderful to me. I liked the elegant way he dressed, and the lively way in which he spoke, and his thin fair hair, and the way his face would go red. I was also fascinated by the way he talked to me and to the other ladies: so different from our Indian men who are always a little shy with us and clumsy, and even if they like to talk with us, they don't want anyone to see that they like it. But he didn't care who saw—he would sit on a little stool by the side of the lady with whom he was talking, and he would look up at her and smile and make conversation in a very lively manner, and sometimes, in talking, he would lay his hand on her arm. He was also extra polite with us, he drew back the chair for us when we wanted to sit down or get up, and he would open the door for us, and he lit the cigarettes of those ladies who smoked, and all sorts of other little services that our Indian men would be ashamed of and think beneath their dignity. But the way he did it all, it was full of dignity. And one other thing, when he greeted a lady and wanted her to know that he thought highly of her, he would kiss her hand, and this too was beautiful, although the first time he did it to me I had a shock like electricity going down my spine and I wanted to snatch away my hand from him and wipe it clean on my sari. But afterward I got used to it and I liked it.

His name is Boekelman, he is a Dutchman, and when I first met him he had already been in India for many years. He had come out to do business here, in ivory, and was caught by the war and couldn't get back; and when the war was over, he no longer wanted to go back. He did not earn a big fortune, but it was enough for him. He lived in a hotel suite that he had furnished with his own carpets and pictures, he ate well, he drank well, he had his circle of friends, and a little hairy dog called Susi. At home in Holland all he had left were two aunts and a wife, from whom he was divorced and whom he did not even like to think about (her name was Annemarie, but he always spoke of her as "Once bitten, twice shy"). So India was home for him, although he had not learned any Hindi except *achchha,* which means all right and *pani,* which means water, and he did not know any Indians. All his friends were foreigners; his lady friends also.

Many things have changed now from what they were when I first knew him. He no longer opens the door for me to go in or out, nor does he kiss my hand; he still does it for other ladies, but no longer for me. That's all right, I don't want it, it is not needed. We live in the same house now, for he has given up his hotel room and has moved into a suite of rooms in my house. He pays rent for this, which I don't want but can't refuse, because he insists; and anyway, perhaps it doesn't matter, because it isn't very much money (he has calculated the rent not on the basis of what would have to be paid today but on what it was worth when the house was first built, almost forty years ago). In return, he wishes to have those rooms kept quite separate and that everyone should knock before they go in; he also sometimes gives parties in there for his European friends, to which he may or may not invite me. If he invites me, he will do it like this: "One or two people are dropping in this evening, I wonder if you would care to join us?" Of course I have known long before this about the party, because he has told the cook to get something ready, and the cook has come to me to ask what should be made, and I have given full instructions; if something very special is needed, I make it myself. After he has invited me and I have accepted, the next thing he asks me, "What will you wear?" and he looks at me very critically. He always says women must be elegant, and that was why he first liked me, because in those days I was very careful about my appearance, I bought many new saris and had blouses made to match them, and I went to a beauty parlor and had facial massage and other things. But now all that has vanished, I no longer care about what I look like.

It is strange how often in one lifetime one changes and changes again, even an ordinary person like myself. When I look back, I see myself first as the young girl in my father's house, impatient, waiting for things to happen; then as the calm wife and mother, fulfilling all my many duties; and then again, when children are bigger and my dear husband, many years older than myself, has moved far away from me and I am more his daughter than his wife—then again I am different. In those years we mostly lived in the hills, and I would go for long walks by myself, for hours and hours, sometimes with great happiness to be there among those great green mountains in sun and mist. But sometimes also I was full of misery and longed for something as great and beautiful as those mountains to fill my own life, which seemed, in those years, very empty. But when my dear husband left us forever, I came down from the mountains and then began that fashionable town-life of which I have already spoken. But that too has finished. Now I get up in the mornings, I drink my tea, I walk around the garden with a peaceful heart; I pick a handful of blossoms; and these I lay at the feet of Vishnu in my prayer room. Without taking my bath or changing out of the old cotton sari in which I have spent the night, I sit for many hours on the veranda, doing nothing, only looking out at the flowers and the birds. My thoughts come and go.

At about twelve o'clock Boekelman is ready and comes out of his room. He always likes to sleep late, and after that it always takes him at least one or two hours to get ready. His face is pink and shaved, his clothes are freshly pressed, he smells of shaving lotion and eau de cologne and all the other things he applies out of the rows of bottles on his bathroom shelf. In one hand he has his rolled English umbrella, with the other he holds Susi on a red-leather lead. He is ready to go out. He looks at me, and I can see he is annoyed at the way I am sitting there, rumpled and unbathed. If he is not in a hurry to go, he may stop and talk with me for a while, usually to complain about something; he is never in a very good mood at this time of day. Sometimes he will say the washerman did not press his shirts well, another time that his coffee this morning was stone cold; or he could not sleep all night because of noise coming from the servant quarters; or that a telephone message was not delivered to him promptly enough, or that it looked as if someone had tampered with his mail. I answer him shortly, or sometimes not at all, only go on looking out into the garden; and this always makes him angry, his face becomes very red and his voice begins to shake a little though he tries to control it: "Surely it is not too much to ask," he says, "to have such messages delivered to me clearly and at the right time?" As he speaks, he stabs tiny holes into the ground with his umbrella to emphasize what he is saying. I watch him doing this, and then I say, "Don't ruin my garden." He stares at me in surprise for a moment, after which he deliberately makes another hole with his umbrella and goes on talking: "It so happened it was an extremely urgent message—" I don't let him get far. I'm out of my chair and I shout at him, "You are ruining my garden," and then I go on shouting about other things, and I advance toward him and he begins to retreat backward. "This is ridiculous," he says, and some other things as well, but he can't be heard because I am shouting so loud and the dog too has begun to bark. He walks faster now in order to get out of the gate more quickly, pulling the dog along with him; I follow them, I'm very excited by this time and no longer know what I'm saying. The gardener, who is cutting the hedge, pretends not to hear or see anything but concentrates on his work. At last he is out in the street with the dog, and they walk down it very fast, with the dog turning around to bark and he pulling it along, while I stand at the gate and pursue them with my angry shouts till they have disappeared from sight.

That is the end of my peace and contemplation. Now I am very upset, I walk up and down the garden and through the house, talking to myself and sometimes striking my two fists together. I think bad things about him and talk to him in my thoughts, and likewise in my thoughts he is answering me and these answers make me even more angry. If some servant comes and speaks to me at this time, I get angry with him too and shout so loud that he runs away, and the whole house is very quiet and everyone keeps out of my way. But slowly my feelings begin to change. My anger burns itself out, and I am left with the ashes of remorse. I remember all my promises to myself, all my resolutions never to give way to my bad temper again;

I remember my beautiful morning hours, when I felt so full of peace, so close to the birds and trees and sunlight and other innocent things. And with that memory tears spring into my eyes, and I lie down sorrowfully on my bed. Lakshmi, my old woman servant who has been with me nearly forty years, comes in with a cup of tea for me. I sit up and drink it, the tears still on my face and more tears rolling down into my cup. Lakshmi begins to smooth my hair, which has come undone in the excitement, and while she is doing this I talk to her in broken words about my own folly and bad character. She clicks her tongue, contradicts me, praises me, and that makes me suddenly angry again, so that I snatch the comb out of her hand, I throw it against the wall and drive her out of the room.

So the day passes, now in sorrow now in anger, and all the time I am waiting only for him to come home again. As the hour draws near, I begin to get ready. I have my bath, comb my hair, wear a new sari. I even apply a little scent. I begin to be very busy around the house, because I don't want it to be seen how much I am waiting for him. When I hear his footsteps, I am busier than ever and pretend not to hear them. He stands inside the door and raps his umbrella against it and calls out in a loud voice: "Is it safe to come in? Has the fury abated?" I try not to smile, but in spite of myself my mouth corners twitch.

After we have had a quarrel and have forgiven each other, we are always very gay together. These are our best times. We walk around the garden, my arm in his, he smoking a cigar and I chewing a betel leaf; he tells me some funny stories and makes me laugh so much that sometimes I have to stand still and hold my sides and gasp for air, while begging him to stop. Nobody ever sees us like this, in this mood; if they did, they would not wonder, as they all do, why we are living together. Yes, everyone asks this question, I know it very well, not only my people but his too—all his foreign friends who think he is miserable with me and that we do nothing but quarrel and that I am too stupid to be good company for him. Let them see us like this only once, then they would know; or afterward, when he allows me to come into his rooms and stay there with him the whole night.

It is quite different in his rooms from the rest of the house. The rest of the house doesn't have very much furniture in it, only some of our old things—some carved Kashmiri screens and little carved tables with mother-of-pearl tops. There are chairs and a few sofas, but I always feel most comfortable on the large mattress on the floor that is covered with an embroidered cloth and many bolsters and cushions; here I recline for hours, very comfortably, playing patience or cutting betel nuts with my little silver shears. But in his rooms there is a lot of furniture, and a radiogram and a cabinet for his records and another for his bottles of liquor. There are carpets and many pictures—some paintings of European countryside and one old oil painting of a pink and white lady with a fan and in old-fashioned dress. There is also a framed pencil sketch of Boekelman himself, which was made by a friend of his, a chemist from Vienna who was said to have been a very good artist but died from heatstroke one very bad Delhi summer. Hanging on the walls or standing on the mantelpiece or on little tables all over the room are a number of photographs, and these I like to look at even better than the paintings, because they are all of him as a boy or as oh! such a handsome young man, and of his parents and the hotel they owned and all lived in, in a place called Zandvoort. There are other photographs in a big album, which he sometimes allows me to look at. In this album there are also a few pictures of his wife ("Once bitten, twice shy"), which I'm very interested in; but he never lets me look at the album for long, because he is afraid I might spoil it, and he takes it away from me and puts it back in the drawer where it belongs. He is neat and careful with all his things and gets very angry when they are disarranged by the servants during dusting; yet he also insists on very thorough dusting, and woe to the whole household if he finds some corner has been forgotten. So, although there are so many things, it is always tidy in his rooms, and it would be a pleasure to go in there if it were not for Susi.

He has always had a dog, and it has always been the same very small, very hairy kind, and it has always been called Susi. This is the second Susi I have known. The first died of very old age and this Susi too is getting quite old now. Unfortunately dogs have a nasty smell when they get old, and since Susi lives in Boekelman's rooms all the time, the rooms also have this smell although they are so thoroughly cleaned every day. When you enter the first thing you notice is this smell, and it always fills me with a moment's disgust, because I don't like dogs and certainly would never allow one inside a room. But for B. dogs are like his children. How he fondles this smelly Susi with her long hair, he bathes her with his own hands and brushes her and at night she sleeps on his bed. It is horrible. So when

114

he lets me stay in his room in the night, Susi is always there with us, and she is the only thing that prevents me from being perfectly happy then. I think Susi also doesn't like it that I'm there. She looks at me from the end of the bed with her running eyes, and I can see that she doesn't like it. I feel like kicking her off the bed and out of the room and out of the house: but because that isn't possible I try and pretend she is not there. In any case, I don't have any time for her, because I am so busy looking at B. He is usually asleep before me, and then I sit up in bed beside him and look and look my eyes out at him. I can't describe how I feel. I have been a married woman, but I have never known such joy as I have in being there alone with him in bed and looking at him: at this old man who has taken his front teeth out so that his upper lip sags over his gums, his skin is grey and loose, he makes ugly sounds out of his mouth and nose as he sleeps. It is rapture for me to be there with him.

No one else ever sees him like this. All those friends he has, all his European lady friends—they only see him dressed up and with his front teeth in. And although they have known him all these years, longer than I have, they don't really know anything about him. Only the outer part is theirs, the shell, but what is within, the essence, that is known only to me. But they wouldn't understand that, for what do they know of outer part and inner, of the shell and of the essence! It is all one to them. For them it is only life in this world and a good time and food and drink, even though they are old women like me and should not have their thoughts on these things.

I have tried hard to like these friends of his, but it is not possible for me. They are very different from anyone else I know. They have all of them been in India for many, many years—twenty-five, thirty—but I know they would much rather be somewhere else. They only stay here because they feel too old to go anywhere else and start a new life. They came here for different reasons—some because they were married to Indians, some to do business, others as refugees and because they couldn't get a visa for anywhere else. None of them has ever tried to learn any Hindi or to get to know anything about our India. They have some Indian "friends," but these are all very rich and important people—like maharanis and cabinet ministers, they don't trouble with ordinary people at all. But really they are only friends with one another, and they always like each other's company best. That doesn't mean they don't quarrel together, they do it all the time, and sometimes some of them are not on speaking terms for months or even years; and whenever two of them are together, they are sure to be saying something bad about a third. Perhaps they are really more like family than friends, the way they both love and hate each other and are closely tied together whether they like it or not; and none of them has any other family, so they are really dependent on each other. That's why they are always celebrating one another's birthday the way a family does, and they are always together on their big days like Christmas or New Year. If one of them is sick, the others are there at once with grapes and flowers, and sit all day and half the night around the sickbed, even if they have not been on speaking terms.

I know that Boekelman has been very close with some of the women, and there are a few of them who are still fond of him and would like to start all over again with him. But he has had enough of them—at least in that way, although of course he is still on very friendly terms with them and meets them every day almost. When he and I are alone together, he speaks of them very disrespectfully and makes fun of them and tells me things about them that no woman would like anyone to know. He makes me laugh, and I feel proud, triumphant, that he should be saying all this to me. But he never likes me to say anything about them, he gets very angry if I do and starts shouting that I have no right to talk, I don't know them and don't know all they have suffered; so I keep quiet, although often I feel very annoyed with them and would like to speak my mind.

The times I feel most annoyed is when there is a party in Boekelman's rooms and I'm invited there with them. They all have a good time, they eat and drink, tell jokes, sometimes they quarrel; they laugh a lot and kiss each other more than is necessary. No one takes much notice of me, but I don't mind that, I'm used to it with them; anyway, I'm busy most of the time running in and out of the kitchen to see to the preparations. I am glad I have something to do because otherwise I would be very bored only sitting there. What they say doesn't interest me, and their jokes don't make me laugh. Most of the time I don't understand what they are talking about, even when they are speaking in English—which is not always, for sometimes they speak in other languages such as French or German. But I always know, in whatever language they are speaking, when they start saying things about India. Sooner or later they always come to this subject, and then their faces change, they look mean and bitter like people who feel they have been cheated by some shopkeeper and it is too late to return the goods. Now it becomes very difficult for me to keep calm. How I hate to hear them talking in this way, saying that India is dirty and everyone is dishonest; but because they are my guests, they are in my house, I have to keep hold of myself and sit there with my arms folded. I must keep my eyes lowered, so that no one should see how they are blazing with fire. Once they have started on this subject, it always takes them a long time to stop, and the more they talk the more bitter they become, the expression on their faces becomes more and more unpleasant. I suffer, and yet I begin to see that they too are suffering, all the terrible things they are saying are not only against India but against themselves too—because they are here and have nowhere else to go—and against the fate that has brought them here and left them here, so far from where they belong and everything they hold dear.

Boekelman often talks about India in this way, but I have got used to it with him. I know very well that whenever something is not quite right—for instance, when a button is missing from his shirt, or it is a very hot day in summer—at once he will start saying how bad everything is in India. Well, with him I just laugh and take no notice. But once my eldest son, Shammi, overheard him and was so angry with him, as angry as I get with B.'s friends when I hear them talking in this way. It happened some years ago—it is painful for me to recall this occasion. . . .

Shammi was staying with me for a few days. He was alone that time, though often he used to come with his whole family, his wife, Monica, and my three darling grandchildren. Shammi is in the army—he was still a major then, though now he is a lieutenant colonel—which is a career he has wanted since he was a small boy and which he loves passionately. At the cadet school he was chosen as the best cadet of the year, for there was no one whose buttons shone so bright or who saluted so smartly as my Shammi. He is a very serious boy. He loves talking to me about his regiment and about tank warfare and 11·1 bore rifles and other such things, and I love listening to him. I don't really understand what he is saying, but I love his eager voice and the way he looks when he talks—just as he looked when he was a small boy and told me about his cricket. Anyway, this is what we were doing that morning, Shammi and I, sitting on the veranda, he talking and I looking sometimes at him and sometimes out into the garden, where everything was green and cool and birds bathed themselves in a pool of water that had oozed out of the hose pipe and sunk into the lawn.

This peace was broken by Boekelman. It started off with his shouting at the servant, very loudly and rudely, as he always does; nobody minds this, I don't mind it, the servant doesn't mind it, we are so used to it and we know it never lasts very long; in any case, the servant doesn't understand what is said for it is always in English, or even some other language that none of us understands, and afterward, if he has shouted very loudly, Boekelman always gives the servant a little tip or one of his old shirts or pair of old shoes. But Shammi was very surprised for he had never heard him shout and abuse in this way (B. was always very careful how he behaved when any of the children were there). Shammi tried to continue talking to me about his regiment, but B. was shouting so loud that it was difficult to pretend not to hear him.

But it might still have been all right and nothing would have been said and Shammi and I could have pretended to each other that nothing had been heard if Boekelman had not suddenly come rushing out on to the veranda. He held his shaving brush in one hand, and half his face was covered in shaving lather and on the other half there was a spot of blood where he had cut himself; he was in his undervest and trousers, and the trousers had braces dangling behind like two tails. He had completely lost control of himself, I could see at once, and he didn't care what he said or before whom. He was so excited that he could hardly talk and he shook his shaving brush in the direction of the servant, who had followed him and stood helplessly watching him from the doorway. "These people!" he screamed. "Monkeys! Animals!" I didn't know what had happened but could guess that it was something quite trivial, such as the servant removing a razor blade before it was worn out. "Hundreds, thousands of times I tell them!" B. screamed, shaking his brush. "The whole country is like that! Idiots! Fools! Not fit to govern themselves!"

Shammi jumped up. His fists were clenched, his eyes blazed. Quickly I put my hand on his arm; I could feel him holding himself back, his whole body shaking with the effort. Boekelman did not notice anything but went on shouting, "Damn rotten backward country!" I kept my hand on Shammi's arm, though I could see he had himself under control now and was standing very straight and at attention, as if on parade, with his eyes fixed above Boekelman's head.

"Go in now," I told B., trying to sound as if nothing very bad was happening; "at least finish your shaving." Boekelman opened his mouth to shout some more abuses, this time probably at me, but then he caught sight of Shammi's face and he remained with his mouth open. "Go in," I said to him again, but it was Shammi who went in and left us, turning suddenly on his heel and marching away with his strong footsteps. The screen door banged hard behind him on its spring hinges. Boekelman stood and looked after him, his mouth still open and the soap caking on his cheek. I went up close to him and shook my fist under his nose. "Fool!" I said to him in Hindi and with such violence that he took a step backward in fear. I didn't glance at him again but turned away and swiftly followed Shammi into the house.

Shammi was packing his bag. He wouldn't talk to me and kept his head averted from me while he took neat piles of clothes out of the drawer and packed them neatly into his bag. He has always been a very orderly boy. I sat on his bed and watched him. If he had said something, if he had been angry, it would have been easier; but he was quite silent, and I knew that under his shirt his heart was beating fast. When he was small and something had happened to him, he would never cry, but when I held him close to me and put my hand under his shirt I used to feel his heart beating wildly inside his child's body, like a bird in a frail cage. And now too I longed to do this, to lay my hand on his chest and soothe his suffering. Only now he was grown up, a big major with a wife and children, who had no need of his foolish mother anymore. And worse, much worse, now it was not something from outside that was the cause of his suffering, but I, I myself! When I thought of that, I could not restrain myself—a sob broke from me and I cried out "Son!" and next moment, before I knew myself what I was doing, I was down on the ground, holding his feet and bathing them with my tears to beg his forgiveness.

He tried to raise me, but I am a strong, heavy woman and I clung obstinately to his feet; so he too got down on the floor and in his effort to raise me took me in his arms. Then I broke into a storm of tears and hid my face against his chest, overcome with shame and remorse and yet also with happiness that he was so near to me and holding me so tenderly. We stayed like this for some time. At last I raised my head, and I saw tears on his lashes, like silver drops of dew. And these tender drops on his long lashes like a girl's, which always seem so strange in his soldier's face—these drops were such a burning reproach to me that at this moment I decided I must do what he wanted desperately, he and all my other children, and what I knew he had been silently asking of me since the day he came. I took the end of my sari and with it wiped the tears from his eyes and as I did this I said, "It's all right, son. I will tell him to go." And to reassure him, because he was silent and perhaps didn't believe me, I said, "Don't worry at all, I will tell him myself," in a firm, promising voice.

Shammi went home the next day. We did not mention the subject any more, but when he left he knew that I would not break my promise. And indeed that very day I went to Boekelman's room and told him that he must leave. It was a very quiet scene. I spoke calmly, looking not at B. but over his head, and he answered me calmly, saying very well, he would go. He asked only that I should give him time to find alternative accommodation, and of course to this I agreed readily, and we even had a quiet little discussion about what type of place he should look for. We spoke like two acquaintances, and everything seemed very nice till I noticed that, although his voice was quite firm and he was talking so reasonably, his hands were slightly trembling. Then my feelings changed, and I had quickly to leave the room in order not to give way to them.

From now on he got up earlier than usual in the mornings and went out to look for a place to rent. He would raise his hat to me as he passed me sitting on the veranda, and sometimes we would have a little talk together, mainly about the weather, before he passed on, raising his hat again and with Susi on the lead walking behind him, her tail in the air. The first few days he seemed very cheerful, but after about a week I could see he was tired of going out so early and never finding anything, and Susi too seemed tired and her tail was no longer so high. I hardened my heart against them. I could guess what was happening—how he went from place to place and found everywhere that rents were very high and the accommodation very small compared with the large rooms he had had in my house all these years for almost nothing. Let him learn, I thought to myself and said nothing except "Good morning" and "The weather is changing fast, soon it will be winter" as I watched him going with slower and slower footsteps day after day out of the gate.

At last one day he confessed to me that, in spite of all his efforts, he had not yet succeeded in finding anything suitable. He had some hard things to say about rapacious landlords. I listened patiently but did not offer to extend his stay. My silence prompted him to stand on his pride and say that I need not worry, that very shortly he would definitely be vacating the rooms. And indeed only two days later he informed me that although he had not yet found any suitable place, he did not want to inconvenience me any further and had therefore made an alternative arrangement, which would enable him to leave in a day or two. Of course I should have answered only "Very well" and inclined my head in a stately manner, but like a fool instead I asked, "What alternative arrangement?" This gave him the opportunity to be stately with me; he looked at me in silence for a moment and then gave a little bow and, raising his hat, proceeded toward the gate with Susi. I bit my lip in anger. I would have liked to run after him and shout as in the old days, but instead I had to sit there by myself and brood. All day I brooded what alternative arrangement he could have made. Perhaps he was going to a hotel, but I didn't think so, because hotels nowadays are very costly, and although he is not poor, the older he gets the less he likes to spend.

In the evening his friend Lina came to see him. There was a lot of noise from his rooms and also some thumping, as of suitcases being taken down; Lina shouted and laughed at the top of her voice, as she always does. I crept halfway down the stairs and tried to hear what they were saying. I was very agitated. As soon as she had gone, I walked into his room—without knocking, which was against his strict orders—and at once demanded, standing facing him with my hands at my waist, "You are not moving in with *Lina?*" Some of his pictures had already been removed from the walls and his rugs rolled up; his suitcases stood open and ready.

Although I was very heated, he remained calm. "Why not Lina?" he asked, and looked at me in a mocking way.

I made a sound of contempt. Words failed me. To think of him living with Lina, in her two furnished rooms that were already overcrowded with her own things and always untidy! And Lina herself, also always untidy, her hair blond when she remembered to dye it, her swollen ankles, and her loud voice and laugh! She had first come to India in the 1930s to marry an Indian, a boy from a very good family, but he left her quite soon—of course, how could a boy like that put up with her ways? She is very free with men, even now though she is old and ugly, and I know she has liked B. for a long time. I was quite determined on one thing; never would I allow him to move to her place, even if it meant keeping him here in the house with me for some time longer.

But when I told him that where was the hurry, he could wait till he found a good place of his own, then he said thank you, he had made his arrangements, and as I could see with my own eyes he had already begun to pack up his things; and after he had said that, he turned away and began to open and shut various drawers and take out clothes, just to show me how busy he was with packing. He had his back to me, and I stood looking at it and longed to thump it.

The next day too Lina came to the house and again I heard her talking and laughing very loudly, and there was some banging about as if they were moving the suitcases. She left very late at night, but even after she had gone I could not sleep and tossed this side and that on my bed. I no longer thought of Shammi but only of B. Hours passed, one o'clock, two o'clock, three, still I could not sleep. I walked up and down my bedroom, then I opened the door and walked up and down the landing. After a while it seemed to me I could hear sounds from downstairs, so I crept halfway down the stairs to listen. There was some movement in his room, and then he coughed also, a very weak cough, and he cleared his throat as if it were hurting him. I put my ear to the door of his room; I held my breath, but I could not hear anything further. Very slowly I opened the door. He was sitting in a chair with his head down and his arms hanging loose between his legs, like a sick person. The room was in disorder, with the rugs rolled up and the suitcases half packed, and there were glasses and an empty bottle, as if he and Lina had been having a party. There was also the stale smoke of her cigarettes; she never stops smoking and then throws the stubs, red with lipstick, anywhere she likes.

He looked up for a moment at the sound of the door opening, but when he saw it was I he looked down again without saying anything. I tiptoed over to his armchair and sat at his feet on the floor. My hand slowly and soothingly stroked his leg, and he allowed me to do this and did not stir. He stared in front of him with dull eyes; he had his teeth out and looked an old, old man. There was no need for us to say anything, to ask questions and give answers. I knew what he was thinking as he stared in front of him in this way, and I too thought of the same thing. I thought of him gone away from here and living with Lina, or alone with his dog in some rented room; no contact with India or Indians, no words to communicate with except *achchha* (all right) and *pani* (water); no one to care for him as he grew older and older, and perhaps sick, and his only companions people just like himself—as old, as lonely, as disappointed, and as far from home.

He sighed, and I said, "Is your indigestion troubling you?" although I knew it was something worse than only indigestion. But he said yes, and added, "It was the spinach you made them cook for my supper. How often do I have to tell you I can't digest spinach at night." After a while he allowed me to help him into bed. When I had covered him and settled his pillows the way he liked them, I threw myself on the bed and begged, "Please don't leave me."

"I've made my arrangements," he said in a firm voice. Susi, at the end of the bed, looked at me with her running eyes and wagged her tail as if she were asking for something.

"Stay," I pleaded with him. "Please stay."

There was a pause. At last he said, as if he were doing me a big favor, "Well, we'll see"; and added, "Get off my bed now, you're crushing my legs—don't you know what a big heavy lump you are?"

None of my children ever comes to stay with me now. I know they are sad and disappointed with me. They want me to be what an old widowed mother should be, devoted entirely to prayer and self-sacrifice; I too know it is the only state fitting to this last stage of life that I have now reached. But that great all-devouring love that I should have for God, I have for B. Sometimes I think: perhaps this is the path for weak women like me? Perhaps B. is a substitute for God whom I should be loving, the way the little brass image of Vishnu in my prayer room is a substitute for that great god himself? These are stupid thoughts that sometimes come to me when I am lying next to B. on his bed and looking at him and feeling so full of peace and joy that I wonder how I came to be so, when I am living against all right rules and the wishes of my children. How do I deserve the great happiness that I find in that old man? It is a riddle.

AN EXPERIENCE
OF INDIA

Today Ramu left. He came to ask for money and I gave him as much as I could. He counted it and asked for more, but I didn't have it to give him. He said some insulting things, which I pretended not to hear. Really I couldn't blame him. I knew he was anxious and afraid, not having another job to go to. But I also couldn't help contrasting the way he spoke now with what he had been like in the past: so polite always, and eager to please, and always smiling, saying "Yes sir," "Yes madam please." He used to look very different too, very spruce in his white uniform and his white canvas shoes. When guests came, he put on a special white coat he had made us buy him. He was always happy when there were guests—serving, mixing drinks, emptying ashtrays—and I think he was disappointed that more didn't come. The Ford Foundation people next door had a round of buffet suppers and Sunday brunches, and perhaps Ramu suffered in status before their servants because we didn't have much of that. Actually, coming to think of it, perhaps he suffered in status anyhow because we weren't like the others. I mean, I wasn't. I didn't look like a proper memsahib or dress like one—I wore Indian clothes right from the start—or ever behave like one. I think perhaps Ramu didn't care for that. I think servants want their employers to be conventional and put up a good front so that other people's servants can respect them. Some of the nasty things Ramu told me this morning were about how everyone said I was just someone from a very low sweeper caste in my own country and how sorry they were for him that he had to serve such a person.

He also said it was no wonder Sahib had run away from me. Henry didn't actually run away, but it's true that things had changed between us. I suppose India made us see how fundamentally different we were from each other. Though when we first came, we both came we thought with the same ideas. We were both happy that Henry's paper had sent him out to India. We both thought it was a marvelous opportunity not only for him professionally but for both of us spiritually. Here was our escape from that Western materialism with which we were both so terribly fed up. But once he got here and the first enthusiasm had worn off, Henry seemed not to mind going back to just the sort of life we'd run away from. He even didn't seem to care about meeting Indians anymore, though in the beginning he had made a great point of doing so; now it seemed to him all right to go only to parties given by other foreign correspondents and sit around there and eat and drink and talk just the way they would at home. After a while, I couldn't stand going with him anymore, so we'd have a fight and then he'd go off by himself. That was a relief. I didn't want to be with any of those people and talk about inane things in their tastefully appointed air-conditioned apartments.

I had come to India to *be* in India. I wanted to be changed. Henry didn't—he wanted a change, that's all, but not to be changed. After a while because of that he was a stranger to me and I felt I was alone, the way I'm really alone now. Henry had to travel a lot around the country to write his pieces, and in the beginning I used to go with him. But I didn't like the way he traveled, always by plane and staying in expensive hotels and drinking in the bar with the other correspondents. So I would leave him and go off by myself. I traveled the way everyone travels in India, just with a bundle and a roll of bedding that I could spread out anywhere and go to sleep. I went in third-class railway carriages and in those old lumbering buses that go from one small dusty town to another and are loaded with too many people inside and with too much scruffy baggage on top. At the end of my journeys, I emerged soaked in perspiration, soot, and dirt. I ate anything anywhere and always like everyone else with my fingers (I became good at that)—thick, half-raw chapatis from wayside stalls and little messes of lentils and vegetables served on a leaf, all the food the poor eat; sometimes if I didn't have anything, other people would share with me from out of their bundles. Henry, who had the usual phobia about bugs, said I would kill myself eating that way. But nothing ever happened. Once, in a desert fort in Rajasthan, I got very thirsty and asked the old caretaker to pull some water out of an ancient disused well for me. It was brown and sort of foul-smelling, and maybe there was a corpse in the well, who knows. But I was thirsty so I drank it, and still nothing happened.

People always speak to you in India, in buses and trains and on the streets, they want to know all about you and ask you a lot of personal questions. I didn't speak much Hindi, but somehow we always managed, and I didn't mind answering all those questions when I could. Women quite often used to touch me, run their hands over my skin just to feel what it was like I suppose, and they specially liked to touch my hair which is long and blond. Sometimes I had several of them lifting up strands of it at the same time, one pulling this way and another that way and they would exchange excited comments and laugh and scream a lot; but in a nice way, so I couldn't help but laugh and scream with them. And people in India are so hospitable. They're always saying "Please come and stay in my house," perfect strangers that happen to be sitting near you on the train. Sometimes, if I didn't have any plans or if it sounded as if they might be living in an interesting place, I'd say "All right thanks," and I'd go along with them. I had some interesting adventures that way.

I might as well say straight off that many of these adventures were sexual. Indian men are very, very keen to sleep with foreign girls. Of course men in other countries are also keen to sleep with girls, but there's something specially frenzied about Indian men when they approach you. Frenzied and at the same time shy. You'd think that with all those ancient traditions they have—like the Kama Sutra, and the sculptures showing couples in every kind of position—you'd think that with all that behind them they'd be very highly skilled, but they're not. Just the opposite. Middle-aged men get as excited as a fifteen-year-old boy, and then of course they can't wait, they *jump*, and before you know where you are, in a great rush, it's all over. And when it's over, it's over, there's nothing left. Then they're only concerned with getting away as soon as possible before anyone can find them out (they're always scared of being found out). There's no tenderness, no interest at all in the other person as a person; only the same kind of curiosity that there is on the buses and the same sort of questions are asked, like are you married, any children, why no children, do you like wearing our Indian dress ... There's one question though that's not asked on the buses but that always inevitably comes up during sex, so that you learn to wait for it: always, at the moment of mounting excitement, they ask "How many men have you slept with?" and it's repeated over and over: "How many? How many?" and then they shout "Aren't you ashamed?" and "Bitch!"—always that one word, which seems to excite them more than any other, to call you that is the height of their lovemaking, it's the last frenzy, the final outrage: "Bitch!" Sometimes I couldn't stop myself but had to burst out laughing.

I didn't like sleeping with all these people, but I felt I had to. I felt I was doing good, though I don't know why, I couldn't explain it to myself. Only one of all those men ever spoke to me: I mean the way people having sex together are supposed to speak, coming near each other not only physically but also wanting to show each other what's deep inside them. He was a middle-aged man, a fellow passenger on a bus, and we got talking at one of the stops the bus made at a wayside tea stall. When he found I was on my way to X and didn't have anywhere to stay, he said, as so many have said before him, "Please come and stay in my house." And I said, as I had often said before, "All right." Only when we got there he didn't take me to his house but to a hotel. It was a very poky place in the bazaar and we had to grope our way up a steep smelly stone staircase and then there was a tiny room with just one string cot and an earthenware water jug in it. He made a joke about there being only one bed. I was too tired to care much about anything. I only wanted to get it over with quickly and go to sleep. But afterward I found it wasn't possible to go to sleep because there was a lot of noise coming up from the street where all the shops were still open though it was nearly midnight. People seemed to be having a good time and there was even a phonograph playing some cracked old love song. My companion also couldn't get to sleep: he left the bed and sat down on the floor by the window and smoked one cigarette after the other. His face was lit up by the light coming in from the street outside and I saw he was looking sort of thoughtful and sad, sitting there smoking. He had rather a good face, strong bones but quite a feminine mouth and of course those feminine suffering eyes that most Indians have.

I went and sat next to him. The window was an arch reaching down to the floor so that I could see out into the bazaar. It was quite gay down there with all the lights; the phonograph was playing from the cold-drink shop and a lot of people were standing around there having highly colored pop drinks out of bottles; next to it was a shop with pink and blue brassieres strung up on a pole. On top of the shops were wrought-iron balconies on which sat girls dressed up in tatty georgette and waving peacock fans to keep themselves cool. Sometimes men looked up to talk and laugh with them and they talked and laughed back. I realized we were in the brothel area; probably the hotel we were in was a brothel too.

I asked "Why did you bring me here?"

He answered "Why did you come?"

That was a·good question. He was right. But I wasn't sorry I came. Why should I be? I said "It's all right. I like it."

He said "She likes it," and he laughed. A bit later he started talking: about how he had just been to visit his daughter who had been married a few months before. She wasn't happy in her in-laws' house, and when he said good-bye to her she clung to him and begged him to take her home. The more he reasoned with her, the more she cried, the more she clung to him. In the end he had had to use force to free himself from her so that he could get away and not miss his bus. He felt very sorry for her, but what else was there for him to do. If he took her away, her in-laws might refuse to have her back again and then her life would be ruined. And she would get used to it, they always did; for some it took longer and was harder, but they all got used to it in the end. His wife too had cried a lot during the first year of marriage.

I asked him whether he thought it was good to arrange marriages that way, and he looked at me and asked how else would you do it. I said something about love and it made him laugh and he said that was only for the films. I didn't want to defend my point of view; in fact, I felt rather childish and as if he knew a lot more about things than I did. He began to get amorous again, and this time it was much better because he wasn't so frenzied and I liked him better by now too. Afterward he told me how when he was first married, he and his wife had shared a room with the whole family (parents and younger brothers and sisters), and whatever they wanted to do, they had to do very quickly and quietly for fear of anyone waking up. I had a strange sensation then, as if I wanted to strip off all my clothes and parade up and down the room naked. I thought of all the men's eyes that follow one in the street, and for the first time it struck me that the expression in them was like that in the eyes of prisoners looking through their bars at the world outside; and then I thought maybe I'm that world outside for them—the way I go here and there and talk and laugh with everyone and do what I like—maybe I'm the river and trees they can't have where they are. Oh, I felt so sorry, I wanted to do so much. And to make a start, I flung myself on my companion and kissed and hugged him hard, I lay on top of him, I smothered him, I spread my hair over his face because I wanted to make him forget everything that wasn't me—this room, his daughter, his wife, the women in georgette sitting on the balconies—I wanted everything to be new for him and as beautiful as I could make it. He liked it for a while but got tired quite quickly, probably because he wasn't all that young anymore.

It was shortly after this encounter that I met Ahmed. He was eighteen years old and a musician. His family had been musicians as long as anyone could remember and the alley they lived in was full of other musicians, so that when you walked down it, it was like walking through a magic forest all lit up with music and sounds. Only there wasn't anything magic about the place itself, which was very cramped and dirty; the houses were so old that, whenever there were heavy rains, one or two of them came tumbling down. I was never inside Ahmed's house or met his family—they'd have died of shock if they had got to know about me—but I knew they were very poor and scraped a living by playing at weddings and functions. Ahmed never had any money, just sometimes if he was lucky he had a few coins to buy his betel with. But he was cheerful and happy and enjoyed everything that came his way. He was married, but his wife was too young to stay with him and after the ceremony she had been sent back to live with her father who was a musician in another town.

When I first met Ahmed, I was staying in a hostel attached to a temple that was free of charge for pilgrims; but afterward he and I wanted a place for us to go to, so I wired Henry to send me some more money. Henry sent me the money, together with a long complaining letter that I didn't read all the way through, and I took a room in a hotel. It was on the outskirts of town, which was mostly wasteland except for a few houses and some of these had never been finished. Our hotel wasn't finished either because the proprietor had run out of money, and now it probably never would be for the place had turned out to be a poor proposition; it was too far out of town and no one ever came to stay there. But it suited us fine. We had this one room, painted bright pink and quite bare except for two pieces of furniture—a bed and a dressing table, both of them very shiny and new. Ahmed loved it, he had never stayed in such a grand room before; he bounced up and down on the bed, which had a mattress, and stood looking at himself from all sides in the mirror of the dressing table.

I never in all my life was happy with anyone the way I was with Ahmed. I'm not saying I never had a good time at home; I did. I had a lot of friends before I married Henry and we had parties and danced and drank and I enjoyed it. But it wasn't like with Ahmed because no one was ever as *carefree* as he was, as light and easy and just ready to play and live. At home we always had our problems, personal ones of course, but on top of those there were universal problems—social, and economic, and moral, we really cared about what was happening in the world around us and in our own minds, we felt a responsibility toward being here alive at this point in time and wanted to do our best. Ahmed had no thoughts like that at all; there wasn't a shadow on him. He had his personal problems from time to time, and when he had them, he was very downcast and sometimes he even cried. But they weren't anything really very serious—usually some family quarrel, or his father was angry with him—and they passed away, blew away like a breeze over a lake and left him sunny and sparkling again. He enjoyed everything so much: not only our room, and the bed and the dressing table, and making love, but so many other things like drinking Coca-Cola and spraying scent and combing my hair and my combing his; and he made up games for us to play like indoor cricket with a slipper for a bat and one of Henry's letters rolled up for a ball. He taught me how to crack his toes, which is such a great Indian delicacy, and yelled with pleasure when I got it right; but when he did it to me, I yelled with pain so he stopped at once and was terribly sorry. He was very considerate and tender. No one I've ever known was sensitive to my feelings as he was. It was like an instinct with him, as if he could feel right down into my heart and know what was going on there; and without ever having to ask anything or my ever having to explain anything, he could sense each change of mood and adapt himself to it and feel with it. Henry would always have to ask me "Now what's up? What's the matter with you?" and when we were still all right with each other, he would make a sincere effort to understand. But Ahmed never had to make an effort, and maybe if he'd had to he wouldn't have succeeded because it wasn't ever with his mind that he understood anything, it was always with his feelings. Perhaps that was so because he was a musician and in music everything is beyond words and explanations anyway; and from what he told me about Indian music, I could see it was very, very subtle, there are effects that you can hardly perceive they're so subtle and your sensibilities have to be kept tuned all the time to the finest, finest point; and perhaps because of that the whole of Ahmed was always at that point and he could play me and listen to me as if I were his sarod.

After some time we ran out of money and Henry wouldn't send any more, so we had to think what to do. I certainly couldn't bear to part with Ahmed, and in the end I suggested he'd better come back to Delhi with me and we'd try and straighten things out with Henry. Ahmed was terribly excited by the idea; he'd never been to Delhi and was wild to go. Only it meant he had to run away from home because his family would never have allowed him to go, so one night he stole out of the house with his sarod and his little bundle of clothes and met me at the railway station. We reached Delhi the next night, tired and dirty and covered with soot the way you always get in trains here. When we arrived home, Henry was giving a party; not a big party, just a small informal group sitting around chatting. I'll never forget the expression on everyone's faces when Ahmed and I came staggering in with our bundles and bedding. My blouse had got torn in the train all the way down the side, and I didn't have a safety pin so it kept flapping open and unfortunately I didn't have anything underneath. Henry's guests were all looking very nice, the men in smart bush shirts and their wives in little silk cocktail dresses; and although after the first shock they all behaved very well and carried on as if nothing unusual had happened, still it was an awkward situation for everyone concerned.

Ahmed never really got over it. I can see now how awful it must have been for him, coming into that room full of strange white people and all of them turning around to stare at us. And the room itself must have been a shock to him; he can never have seen anything like it. Actually, it was quite a shock to me too. I'd forgotten that that was the way Henry and I lived. When we first came, we had gone to a lot of trouble doing up the apartment, buying furniture and pictures and stuff, and had succeeded in making it look just like the apartment we have at home except for some elegant Indian touches. To Ahmed it was all very strange. He stayed there with us for some time, and he couldn't get used to it. I think it bothered him to have so many *things* around, rugs and lamps and objets d'art; he couldn't see why they had to be there. Now that I had traveled and lived the way I had, I couldn't see why either; as a matter of fact I felt as if these things were a hindrance and cluttered up not only your room but your mind and your soul as well, hanging on them like weights.

We had some quite bad scenes in the apartment during those days. I told Henry that I was in love with Ahmed, and naturally that upset him, though what upset him most was the fact that he had to keep us both in the apartment. I also realized that this was an undesirable situation, but I couldn't see any way out of it because where else could Ahmed and I go? We didn't have any money, only Henry had, so we had to stay with him. He kept saying that he would turn both of us out into the streets but I knew he wouldn't. He wasn't the type to do a violent thing like that, and besides he himself was so frightened of the streets that he'd have died to think of anyone connected with him being out there. I wouldn't have minded all that much if he *had* turned us out: it was warm enough to sleep in the open and people always give you food if you don't have any. I would have preferred it really because it was so unpleasant with Henry; but I knew Ahmed would never have been able to stand it. He was quite a pampered boy, and though his family were poor, they looked after and protected each other very carefully; he never had to miss a meal or go dressed in anything but fine muslin clothes, nicely washed and starched by female relatives.

Ahmed bitterly repented having come. He was very miserable, feeling so uncomfortable in the apartment and with Henry making rows all the time. Ramu, the servant, didn't improve anything by the way he behaved, absolutely refusing to serve Ahmed and never losing an opportunity to make him feel inferior. Everything went out of Ahmed; he crumpled up as if he were a paper flower. He didn't want to play his sarod and he didn't want to make love to me, he just sat around with his head and his hands hanging down, and there were times when I saw tears rolling down his face and he didn't even bother to wipe them off. Although he was so unhappy in the apartment, he never left it and so he never saw any of the places he had been so eager to come to Delhi for, like the Juma Masjid and Nizamuddin's tomb. Most of the time he was thinking about his family. He wrote long letters to them in Urdu, which I posted, telling them where he was and imploring their pardon for running away; and long letters came back again and he read and read them, soaking them in tears and kisses. One night he got so bad he jumped out of bed and, rushing into Henry's bedroom, fell to his knees by the side of Henry's bed and begged to be sent back home again. And Henry, sitting up in bed in his pajamas, said all right, in rather a lordly way I thought. So next day I took Ahmed to the station and put him on the train, and through the bars of the railway carriage he kissed my hands and looked into my eyes with all his old ardor and tenderness, so at the last moment I wanted to go with him but it was too late and the train pulled away out of the station and all that was left to me of Ahmed was a memory, very beautiful and delicate like a flavor or a perfume or one of those melodies he played on his sarod.

I became very depressed. I didn't feel like going traveling anymore but stayed home with Henry and went with him to his diplomatic and other parties. He was quite glad to have me go with him again; he liked having someone in the car on the way home to talk to about all the people who'd been at the party and compare their chances of future success with his own. I didn't mind going with him; there wasn't anything else I wanted to do. I felt as if I'd failed at something. It wasn't only Ahmed. I didn't really miss him all that much and was glad to think of him back with his family in that alley full of music where he was happy. For myself I didn't know what to do next, though I felt that something still awaited me. Our apartment led to an open terrace and I often went up there to look at the view, which was marvelous. The house we lived in and all the ones around were white and pink and very modern, with picture windows and little lawns in front, but from up here you could look beyond them to the city and the big mosque and the fort. In between there were stretches of wasteland, empty and barren except for an occasional crumbly old tomb growing there. What always impressed me the most was the sky because it was so immensely big and so unchanging in color, and it made everything underneath it—all the buildings, even the great fort, the whole city, not to speak of all the people living in it—seem terribly small and trivial and passing somehow. But at the same time as it made me feel small, it also made me feel immense and eternal. I don't know, I can't explain, perhaps because it was itself like that and this thought—that there *was* something like that—made me feel that I had a part in it, I too was part of being immense and eternal. It was all very vague really and nothing I could ever speak about to anyone; but because of it I thought well maybe there is something more for me here after all. That was a relief because it meant I wouldn't have to go home and be the way I was before and nothing different or gained. For all the time, ever since I'd come and even before, I'd had this idea that there was something in India for me to *gain,* and even though for the time being I'd failed, I could try longer and at last perhaps I would succeed.

I'd met people on and off who had come here on a spiritual quest, but it wasn't the sort of thing I wanted for myself. I thought anything I wanted to find, I could find by myself traveling around the way I had done. But now that this had failed, I became interested in the other thing. I began to go to a few prayer meetings and I liked the atmosphere very much. The meeting was usually conducted by a swami in a saffron robe who had renôunced the world, and he gave an address about love and God and everyone sang hymns also about love and God. The people who came to these meetings were mostly middle-aged and quite poor. I had already met many like them on my travels, for they were the sort of people who sat waiting on station platforms and bus depots, absolutely patient and uncomplaining even when conductors and other officials pushed them around. They were gentle people and very clean though there was always some slight smell about them as of people who find it difficult to keep clean because they live in crowded and unsanitary places where there isn't much running water and the drainage system isn't good. I loved the expression that came into their faces when they sang hymns. I wanted to be like them, so I began to dress in plain white saris and I tied up my hair in a plain knot and the only ornament I wore was a string of beads not for decoration but to say the names of God on. I became a vegetarian and did my best to cast out all the undesirable human passions, such as anger and lust. When Henry was in an irritable or quarrelsome mood, I never answered him back but was very kind and patient with him. However, far from having a good effect, this seemed to make him worse. Altogether he didn't like the new personality I was trying to achieve but sneered a lot at the way I dressed and looked and the simple food I ate. Actually, I didn't enjoy this food very much and found it quite a trial eating nothing but boiled rice and lentils with him sitting opposite me having his cutlets and chops.

The peace and satisfaction that I saw on the faces of the other hymn singers didn't come to me. As a matter of fact, I grew rather bored. There didn't seem much to be learned from singing hymns and eating vegetables. Fortunately just about this time someone took me to see a holy woman who lived on the roof of an old over-crowded house near the river. People treated her like a holy woman but she didn't set up to be one. She didn't set up to be anything really, but only stayed in her room on the roof and talked to people who came to see her. She liked telling stories and she could hold ev-eryone spellbound listening to her, even though she was only telling the old mythological stories they had known all their lives long, about Krishna, and the Pandavas, and Rama and Sita. But she got terribly excited while she was telling them, as if it wasn't something that had happened millions of years ago but as if it was all real and going on exactly now. Once she was telling about Krishna's mother who made him open his mouth to see whether he had stolen and was eating up her butter. What did she see then, inside his mouth?

"Worlds!" the holy woman cried. "Not just this world, not just one world with its mountains and rivers and seas, no, but world upon world, all spinning in one great eternal cycle in this child's mouth, moon upon moon, sun upon sun!"

She clapped her hands and laughed and laughed, and then she burst out singing in her thin old voice some hymn all about how great God was and how lucky for her that she was his beloved. She was dancing with joy in front of all the people. And she was just a little shriveled old woman, very ugly with her teeth gone and a growth on her chin: but the way she carried on it was as if she had all the looks and glamour anyone ever had in the world and was in love a million times over. I thought, well whatever it was she had, obviously it was the one thing worth having and I had better try for it.

I went to stay with a guru in a holy city. He had a house on the river in which he lived with his disciples. They lived in a nice way: they meditated a lot and went out for boat rides on the river and in the evenings they all sat around in the guru's room and had a good time. There were quite a few foreigners among the disciples, and it was the guru's greatest wish to go abroad and spread his message there and bring back more disciples. When he heard that Henry was a journalist, he became specially interested in me. He talked to me about the importance of introducing the leaven of Indian spiritual-ity into the lump of Western materialism. To achieve this end, his own presence in the West was urgently required, and to ensure the widest dissemination of his message he would also need the full support of the mass media. He said that since we live in the modern age, we must avail ourselves of all its resources. He was very keen for me to bring Henry into the ashram, and when I was vague in my answers—I certainly didn't want Henry here nor would he in the least want to come—he became very pressing and even quite annoyed and kept returning to the subject.

He didn't seem a very spiritual type of person to me. He was a hefty man with big shoulders and a big head. He wore his hair long but his jaw was clean-shaven and stuck out very large and prominent and gave him a powerful look like a bull. All he ever wore was a saffron robe and this left a good part of his body bare so that it could be seen at once how strong his legs and shoulders were. He had huge eyes, which he used constantly and apparently to tremendous effect, fixing people with them and penetrating them with a steady beam. He used them on me when he wanted Henry to come, but they never did anything to me. But the other disciples were very strongly affected by them. There was one girl, Jean, who said they were like the sun, so strong that if she tried to look back at them something terrible would happen to her like being blinded or burned up completely.

Jean had made herself everything an Indian guru expects his disciples to be. She was absolutely humble and submissive. She touched the guru's feet when she came into or went out of his presence, she ran eagerly on any errand he sent her on. She said she gloried in being nothing in herself and living only by his will. And she looked like nothing too, sort of drained of everything she might once have been. At home her cheeks were probably pink but now she was quite white, waxen, and her hair too was completely faded and colorless. She always wore a plain white cotton sari and that made her look paler than ever, and thinner too, it seemed to bring out the fact that she had no hips and was utterly flat-chested. But she was happy—at least she said she was—she said she had never known such happiness and hadn't thought it was possible for human beings to feel like that. And when she said that, there was a sort of sparkle in her pale eyes, and at such moments I envied her because she seemed to have found what I was looking for. But at the same time I wondered whether she really had found what she thought she had, or whether it wasn't something else and she was cheating herself, and one day she'd wake up to that fact and then she'd feel terrible.

She was shocked by my attitude to the guru—not touching his feet or anything, and talking back to him as if he were just an ordinary person. Sometimes I thought perhaps there was something wrong with me because everyone else, all the other disciples and people from outside too who came to see him, they all treated him with this great reverence and their faces lit up in his presence as if there really was something special. Only I couldn't see it. But all the same I was quite happy there—not because of him, but because I liked the atmosphere of the place and the way they all lived. Everyone seemed very contented and as if they were living for something high and beautiful. I thought perhaps if I waited and was patient, I'd also come to be like that. I tried to meditate the way they all did, sitting cross-legged in one spot and concentrating on the holy word that had been given to me. I wasn't ever very successful and kept thinking of other things. But there were times when I went up to sit on the roof and looked out over the river, the way it stretched so calm and broad to the opposite bank and the boats going up and down it and the light changing and being reflected back on the water: and then, though I wasn't trying to meditate or come to any higher thoughts, I did feel very peaceful and was glad to be there.

The guru was patient with me for a long time, explaining about the importance of his mission and how Henry ought to come here and write about it for his paper. But as the days passed and Henry didn't show up, his attitude changed and he began to ask me questions. Why hadn't Henry come? Hadn't I written to him? Wasn't I going to write to him? Didn't I think what was being done in the ashram would interest him? Didn't I agree that it deserved to be brought to the notice of the world and that to this end no stone should be left unturned? While he said all this, he fixed me with his great eyes and I squirmed—not because of the way he was looking at me, but because I was embarrassed and didn't know what to answer. Then he became very gentle and said never mind, he didn't want to force me, that was not his way, he wanted people slowly to turn toward him of their own accord, to open up to him as a flower opens up and unfurls its petals and its leaves to the sun. But next day he would start again, asking the same questions, urging me, forcing me, and when this had gone on for some time and we weren't getting anywhere, he even got angry once or twice and shouted at me that I was obstinate and closed and had fenced in my heart with seven hoops of iron. When he shouted, everyone in the ashram trembled and afterward they looked at me in a strange way. But an hour later the guru always had me called back to his room and then he was very gentle with me again and made me sit near him and insisted that it should be I who handed him his glass of milk in preference to one of the others, all of whom were a lot keener to be selected for this honor than I was.

Jean often came to talk to me. At night I spread my bedding in a tiny cubbyhole that was a disused storeroom, and just as I was falling asleep, she would come in and lie down beside me and talk to me very softly and intimately. I didn't like it much, to have her so close to me and whispering in a voice that wasn't more than a breath and which I could feel, slightly warm, on my neck; sometimes she touched me, putting her hand on mine ever so gently so that she hardly was touching me but all the same I could feel that her hand was a bit moist and it gave me an unpleasant sensation down my spine. She spoke about the beauty of surrender, of not having a will and not having thoughts of your own. She said she too had been like me once, stubborn and ego-centered, but now she had learned the joy of yielding, and if she could only give me some inkling of the infinite bliss to be tasted in this process—here her breath would give out for a moment and she couldn't speak for ecstasy. I would take the opportunity to pretend to fall asleep, even snoring a bit to make it more convincing; after calling my name a few times in the hope of waking me up again, she crept away disappointed. But next night she'd be back again, and during the day too she would attach herself to me as much as possible and continue talking in the same way.

It got so that even when she wasn't there, I could still hear her voice and feel her breath on my neck. I no longer enjoyed anything, not even going on the river or looking out over it from the top of the house. Although they hadn't bothered me before, I kept thinking of the funeral pyres burning on the bank, and it seemed to me that the smoke they gave out was spreading all over the sky and the river and covering them with a dirty yellowish haze. I realized that nothing good could come to me from this place now. But when I told the guru that I was leaving, he got into a great fury. His head and neck swelled out and his eyes became two coal-black demons rolling around in rage. In a voice like drums and cymbals, he *forbade* me to go. I didn't say anything but I made up my mind to leave next morning. I went to pack my things. The whole ashram was silent and stricken, no one dared speak. No one dared come near me either till late at night when Jean came as usual to lie next to me. She lay there completely still and crying to herself. I didn't know she was crying at first because she didn't make a sound, but slowly her tears seeped into her side of the pillow and a sensation of dampness came creeping over to my side of it. I pretended not to notice anything.

Suddenly the guru stood in the doorway. The room faced an open courtyard and this was full of moonlight that illumined him and made him look enormous and eerie. Jean and I sat up. I felt scared, my heart beat fast. After looking at us in silence for a while, he ordered Jean to go away. She got up to do so at once. I said "No, stay," and clung to her hand but she disengaged herself from me and, touching the guru's feet in reverence, she went away. She seemed to dissolve in the moonlight outside, leaving no trace. The guru sat beside me on my bedding spread on the floor. He said I was under a delusion, that I didn't really want to leave; my inmost nature was craving to stay by him—he knew, he could hear it calling out to him. But because I was afraid, I was attempting to smother this craving and to run away. "Look how you're trembling," he said. "See how afraid you are." It was true, I was trembling and cowering against the wall as far away from him as I could get. Only it was impossible to get very far because he was so huge and seemed to spread and fill the tiny closet. I could feel him close against me, and his pungent male smell, spiced with garlic, overpowered me.

"You're right to be afraid," he said: because it was his intention, he said, to batter and beat me, to smash my ego till it broke and flew apart into a million pieces and was scattered into the dust. Yes, it would be a painful process and I would often cry out and plead for mercy, but in the end—ah, with what joy I would step out of the prison of my own self, remade and reborn! I would fling myself to the ground and bathe his feet in tears of gratitude. Then I would be truly his. As he spoke, I became more and more afraid because I felt, so huge and close and strong he was, that perhaps he really had the power to do to me all that he said and that in the end he would make me like Jean.

I now lay completely flattened against the wall, and he had moved up and was squashing me against it. One great hand traveled up and down my stomach, but its activity seemed apart from the rest of him and from what he was saying. His voice became lower and lower, more and more intense. He said he would teach me to obey, to submit myself completely, that would be the first step and a very necessary one. For he knew what we were like, all of us who came from Western countries: we were self-willed, obstinate, *licentious.* On the last word his voice cracked with emotion, his hand went further and deeper. *Licentious,* he repeated, and then, rolling himself across the bed so that he now lay completely pressed against me, he asked "How many men have you slept with?" He took my hand and made me hold him: how huge and hot he was! He pushed hard against me. "How many? Answer me!" he commanded, urgent and dangerous. But I was no longer afraid: now he was not an unknown quantity nor was the situation any longer new or strange. "Answer me, answer me!" he cried, riding on top of me, and then he cried "Bitch!" and I laughed in relief.

I quite liked being back in Delhi with Henry. I had lots of baths in our marble bathroom, soaking in the tub for hours and making myself smell nice with bath salts. I stopped wearing Indian clothes and took out all the dresses I'd brought with me. We entertained quite a bit, and Ramu scurried around in his white coat, emptying ashtrays. It wasn't a bad time. I stayed around all day in the apartment with the air-conditioner on and the curtains drawn to keep out the glare. At night we drove over to other people's apartments for buffet suppers of boiled ham and potato salad; we sat around drinking in their living rooms, which were done up more or less like ours, and talked about things like the price of whiskey, what was the best hill station to go to in the summer, and servants. This last subject often led to other related ones like how unreliable Indians were and how it was impossible ever to get anything done. Usually this subject was treated in a humorous way, with lots of funny anecdotes to illustrate, but occasionally someone got quite passionate; this happened usually if they were a bit drunk, and then they went off into a long thing about how dirty India was and backward, riddled with vile superstitions—evil, they said—corrupt—corrupting.

Henry never spoke like that—maybe because he never got drunk enough—but I know he didn't disagree with it. He disliked the place very much and was in fact thinking of asking for an assignment elsewhere. When I asked where, he said the cleanest place he could think of. He asked how would I like to go to Geneva. I knew I wouldn't like it one bit, but I said all right. I didn't really care where I was. I didn't care much about anything these days. The only positive feeling I had was for Henry. He was so sweet and good to me. I had a lot of bad dreams nowadays and was afraid of sleeping alone, so he let me come into his bed even though he dislikes having his sheets disarranged and I always kick and toss about a lot. I lay close beside him, clinging to him, and for the first time I was glad that he had never been all that keen on sex. On Sundays we stayed in bed all day reading the papers and Ramu brought us nice English meals on trays. Sometimes we put on a record and danced together in our pajamas. I kissed Henry's cheeks, which were always smooth—he didn't need to shave very often—and sometimes his lips, which tasted of toothpaste.

Then I got jaundice. It's funny, all that time I spent traveling about and eating anything anywhere, nothing happened to me, and now that I was living such a clean life with boiled food and boiled water, I got sick. Henry was horrified. He immediately segregated all his and my things, and anything that I touched had to be sterilized a hundred times over. He was forever running into the kitchen to check up whether Ramu was doing this properly. He said jaundice was the most catching thing there was, and though he went in for a whole course of precautionary inoculations that had to be specially flown in from the States, he still remained in a very nervous state. He tried to be sympathetic to me, but couldn't help sounding reproachful most of the time. He had sealed himself off so carefully, and now I had let this in. I knew how he felt, but I was too ill and miserable to care. I don't remember ever feeling so *ill*. I didn't have any high temperature or anything, but all the time there was this terrible nausea. First my eyes went yellow, then the rest of me as if I'd been dyed in the color of nausea, inside and out. The whole world went yellow and sick. I couldn't bear anything: any noise, any person near me, worst of all any smell. They couldn't cook in the kitchen anymore because the smell of cooking made me scream. Henry had to live on boiled eggs and bread. I begged him not to let Ramu into my bedroom for, although Ramu always wore nicely laundered clothes, he gave out a smell of perspiration that was both sweetish and foul and filled me with disgust. I was convinced that under his clean shirt he wore a cotton vest, black with sweat and dirt, which he never took off but slept in at night in the one-room servant quarter where he lived crowded together with all his family in a dense smell of cheap food and bad drains and unclean bodies.

I knew these smells so well—I thought of them as the smells of India, and had never minded them; but now I couldn't get rid of them, they were like some evil flood soaking through the walls of my air-conditioned bedroom. And other things I hadn't minded, had hardly bothered to think about, now came back to me in a terrible way so that waking and sleeping I saw them. What I remembered most often was the disused well in the Rajasthan fort out of which I had drunk water. I was sure now that there had been a corpse at the bottom of it, and I saw this corpse with the flesh swollen and blown but the eyes intact: they were huge like the guru's eyes and they stared, glazed and jellied, into the darkness of the well. And worse than seeing this corpse, I could taste it in the water that I had drunk—that I was still drinking—yes, it was now, at this very moment, that I was raising my cupped hands to my mouth and feeling the dank water lap around my tongue. I screamed out loud at the taste of the dead man and I called to Henry and clutched his hand and begged him to get us sent to Geneva quickly, quickly. He disengaged his hand—he didn't like me to touch him at this time—but he promised. Then I grew calmer, I shut my eyes and tried to think of Geneva and of washing out my mouth with Swiss milk.

I got better, but I was very weak. When I looked at myself in the mirror, I started to cry. My face had a yellow tint, my hair was limp and faded; I didn't look old but I didn't look young anymore either. There was no flesh left, and no color. I was drained, hollowed out. I was wearing a white nightdress and that increased the impression. Actually, I reminded myself of Jean. I thought, so this is what it does to you (I didn't quite know at that time what I meant by it—jaundice in my case, a guru in hers; but it seemed to come to the same). When Henry told me that his new assignment had come through, I burst into tears again; only now it was with relief. I said let's go now, let's go quickly. I became quite hysterical so Henry said all right; he too was impatient to get away before any more of those bugs he dreaded so much caught up with us. The only thing that bothered him was that the rent had been paid for three months and the landlord refused to refund. Henry had a fight with him about it but the landlord won. Henry was furious but I said never mind, let's just get away and forget all about all of them. We packed up some of our belongings and sold the rest; the last few days we lived in an empty apartment with only a couple of kitchen chairs and a bed. Ramu was very worried about finding a new job.

Just before we were to leave for the airport and were waiting for the car to pick us up, I went on the terrace. I don't know why I did that, there was no reason. There was nothing I wanted to say good-bye to, and no last glimpses I wanted to catch. My thoughts were all concentrated on the coming journey and whether to take airsickness pills or not. The sky from up on the terrace looked as immense as ever, the city as small. It was evening and the light was just fading and the sky wasn't any definite color now: it was sort of translucent like a pearl but not an earthly pearl. I thought of the story the little saintly old woman had told about Krishna's mother and how she saw the sun and the moon and world upon world in his mouth. I liked that phrase so much—world upon world—I imagined them spinning around each other like glass spheres in eternity and every-thing as shining and translucent as the sky I saw above me. I went down and told Henry I wasn't going with him. When he realized—and this took some time—that I was serious, he knew I was mad. At first he was very patient and gentle with me, then he got in a frenzy. The car had already arrived to take us. Henry yelled at me, he grabbed my arm and began to pull me to the door. I resisted with all my strength and sat down on one of the kitchen chairs. Henry con-tinued to pull and now he was pulling me along with the chair as if on a sleigh. I clung to it as hard as I could but I felt terribly weak and was afraid I would let myself be pulled away. I begged him to leave me. I cried and wept with fear—fear that he would take me, fear that he would leave me.

Ramu came to my aid. He said it's all right Sahib, I'll look after her. He told Henry that I was too weak to travel after my illness but later, when I was better, he would take me to the airport and put me on a plane. Henry hesitated. It was getting very late, and if he didn't go, he too would miss the plane. Ramu assured him that all would be well and Henry need not worry at all. At last Henry took my papers and ticket out of his inner pocket. He gave me instructions how I was to go to the air company and make a new booking. He hesitated a moment longer—how sweet he looked all dressed up in a suit and tie ready for traveling, just like the day we got married—but the car was hooting furiously downstairs and he had to go. I held on hard to the chair. I was afraid if I didn't I might get up and run after him. So I clung to the chair, trembling and crying. Ramu was quite happily dusting the remaining chair. He said we would have to get some more furniture. I think he was glad that I had stayed and he still had somewhere to work and live and didn't have to go tramping around looking for another place. He had quite a big family to support.

I sold the ticket Henry left with me but I didn't buy any new furniture with it. I stayed in the empty rooms by myself and very rarely went out. When Ramu cooked anything for me, I ate it, but sometimes he forgot or didn't have time because he was busy looking for another job. I didn't like living like that but I didn't know what else to do. I was afraid to go out: everything I had once liked so much—people, places, crowds, smells—I now feared and hated. I would go running back to be by myself in the empty apartment. I felt people looked at me in a strange way in the streets; and perhaps I was strange now from the way I was living and not caring about what I looked like anymore; I think I talked aloud to myself sometimes—once or twice I heard myself doing it. I spent a lot of the money I got from the air ticket on books. I went to the bookshops and came hurrying back carrying armfuls of them. Many of them I never read, and even those I did read, I didn't understand very much. I hadn't had much experience in reading these sort of books—like the Upanishads and the Vedanta Sutras—but I liked the sound of the words and I liked the feeling they gave out. It was as if I were all by myself on an immensely high plateau breathing in great lungfuls of very sharp, pure air. Sometimes the landlord came to see what I was doing. He went around all the rooms, peering suspiciously into corners, testing the fittings. He kept asking how much longer I was going to stay; I said till the three months' rent was up. He brought prospective tenants to see the apartment, but when they saw me squatting on the floor in the empty rooms, sometimes with a bowl of half-eaten food that Ramu had neglected to clear away, they got nervous and went away again rather quickly. After a time the electricity got cut off because I hadn't paid the bill. It was very hot without the fan and I filled the tub with cold water and sat in it all day. But then the water got cut off too. The landlord came up twice, three times a day now. He said if I didn't clear out the day the rent was finished he would call the police to evict me. I said it's all right, don't worry, I shall go. Like the landlord, I too was counting the days still left to me. I was afraid what would happen to me.

Today the landlord evicted Ramu out of the servant quarter. That was when Ramu came up to ask for money and said all those things. Afterward I went up on the terrace to watch him leave. It was such a sad procession. Each member of the family carried some part of their wretched household stock, none of which looked worth taking. Ramu had a bed with tattered strings balanced on his head. In two days' time I too will have to go with my bundle and my bedding. I've done this so often before—traveled here and there without any real destination—and been so happy doing it; but now it's different. That time I had a great sense of freedom and adventure. Now I feel compelled, that I *have* to do this whether I want to or not. And partly I don't want to, I feel afraid. Yet it's still like an adventure, and that's why besides being afraid I'm also excited, and most of the time I don't know why my heart is beating fast, is it in fear or in excitement, wondering what will happen to me now that I'm going traveling again.

THE HOUSEWIFE

$\mathcal{S}$he had her music lesson very early in the morning before anyone else was awake. She had it up on the roof of the house so no one was disturbed. By the time the others were up, she had already cooked the morning meal and was supervising the cleaning of the house. She spent the rest of the day in seeing to the family and doing whatever had to be done, so no one could say that her music in any way interfered with her household duties. Her husband certainly had no complaints. He wasn't interested in her singing but indulged her in it because he knew it gave her pleasure. When his old aunt, Phuphiji, who lived with them, hinted that it wasn't seemly for a housewife, a matron like Shakuntala, to take singing lessons, he ignored her. He was good at ignoring female relatives, he had had a lot of practice at it. But he never ignored Shakuntala. They had been married for twenty-five years and he loved her more year by year.

It wasn't because of anything Phuphiji said but because of him, who said nothing, that Shakuntala sometimes felt guilty. And because of her daughter and her little grandson. She loved all of them, but she could not deny to herself that her singing meant even more to her than her feelings as wife and mother and grandmother. She was unable to explain this, she tried not to think of it. But it was true that with her music she lived in a region where she felt most truly, most deeply herself. No, not herself, something more and higher than that. By contrast with her singing, the rest of her day, indeed of her life, seemed insignificant. She felt this to be wrong but there was no point in trying to struggle against it. Without her hour's practice in the morning, she was as if deprived of food and water and air.

One day her teacher did not come. She went on the roof and

practiced by herself but it was not the same thing. By herself she felt weak and faltering. She *was* weak and faltering, but when he was there it didn't matter so much because he had such strength. Later, when her husband had gone to his place of work (he was a building contractor) and she had arranged everything for the day's meals and left Phuphiji entertaining some friends from the neighborhood with tea, she went to find out what had happened. She took her servant boy with her to show her the way, for although she often sent messages to her teacher's house, she had not been there before. The house was old and in a narrow old alley. There was some sort of workshop downstairs and she had to step over straw and bits of packing cases; on the first floor was a music school consisting of a long room in which several people sat on the floor playing on drums. Her teacher lived on the second story. He had only one room and everything was in great disorder. There was practically no furniture but a great many discarded clothes were hung up on hooks and on a line strung across the room. A bedraggled, cross woman sat on the floor, turning the handle of a sewing machine. The teacher himself lay on a mat in a corner, tossing and groaning; when Shakuntala, full of concern, bent over him, he opened his eyes and said "I'm going now." He wore a red cloth tied around his brow and this gave him a rather gruesome appearance.

Shakuntala tried to rally him, but the more she did so, the sicker he became. "No," he insisted, "I'm going." Then he added, "I'm not afraid to die."

His wife, turning the handle of her sewing machine, snorted derisively. This did rally him; he gathered sufficient strength to prop himself up on one elbow. "There's no food," he said to Shakuntala, making pathetic gestures toward his mouth to show how he lacked sustenance to put into it. "She doesn't know how to cook for a sick person."

His wife stopped sewing in order to laugh heartily. "Soup!" she laughed. "That's what he's asking for. Where has he ever tasted soup? In his father's house? They thought themselves lucky if they could get a bit of dal with their dry bread. *Soup,*" she repeated in a shaking voice, her amusement abruptly changing into anger.

Shakuntala, who had not anticipated being caught in a domestic quarrel, was embarrassed. But she also felt sorry for the teacher. She did not believe him to be very ill but she saw he was very uncomfortable. The room was hot, and dense with various smells, and full of flies; there was thumping from the workshop downstairs, drums and some thin stringed instruments from the music school, and inside the room the angry whirring of the sewing machine. In spite of the heat, the sick man was covered with a sheet under which he tossed and turned—not with pain, Shakuntala saw, but with irritation.

After that her own home seemed so sweet and orderly to her. They had recently built a new bungalow with shiny woodwork and pink and green terrazzo floors. Their drawing room was furnished with a blue rexine-covered sofa set. She wished she could have brought her teacher here to nurse him; she could have made him so comfortable. All day she was restless, thinking of that. And as always when Shakuntala was restless and her mind turned away from her household affairs, Phuphiji noticed and pursued her through the house and insisted on drawing her attention to various deficiencies, such as the month's sugar supply running out too quickly or a cooking vessel not having been scoured to shine as it should. Shakuntala had lived with Phuphiji long enough to remain calm and answer her calmly, but Phuphiji had also lived with Shakuntala long enough to know that these answers were desultory and that Shakuntala's thoughts remained fixed elsewhere. She continued to follow her, to circle her, to fix her with her bright old eyes.

Later in the day Shakuntala's daughter, Manju, came with little Baba. Of course Shakuntala was happy to see them and played with and kissed Baba as usual; but, like Phuphiji, Manju noticed her mother's distraction. Manju became querulous and had many complaints. She said she had a headache every morning, and Baba sometimes was very naughty and woke them all up in the night and wanted to play. For all this she required her mother's sympathy, and Shakuntala gave it but Manju noticed that she couldn't give it with all her heart, and that made her more querulous. And Phuphiji joined in, encouraging Manju, pitying her, drawing the subject out more and more and all the time keeping her eyes on Shakuntala to make sure she participated as keenly as she was in duty bound to. Between them, they drove Shakuntala quite crazy; and the worst of it was that she was on their side, she knew that she ought to be absorbed in their problems and blamed herself because she wasn't.

It was a relief to her when her husband came home, for he was the one person who was always satisfied with her. Unlike the others, he wasn't interested in her secret thoughts. For him it was enough that she dressed up nicely before his arrival home and oiled her hair and adorned it with a wreath of jasmine. She was in her early forties but plump and fresh. She loved jewelry and always wore great quantities of it, even in the house. Her arms were full of bangles, she had a diamond nose ring and a gold necklace around her smooth, soft neck. Her husband liked to see all that; and he liked her to stand beside him to serve him his meal, and then to lie next to him on the bed while he slept. That night he fell asleep as usual after eating large helpings of food. He slept fast and sound, breathing loudly, for he was a big man with a lot of weight on him. Sometimes he tossed himself from one side to the other with a grunt. Then Shakuntala gently patted him as if to soothe him; she wanted him to be always entirely comfortable and recognized it to be her mission in life to see that he was. When she fell asleep herself, she slept badly and was disturbed by garbled dreams.

But the next morning the teacher was there again. He wasn't ill at all anymore, and when she inquired after his health, he shrugged as if he had forgotten there had ever been anything wrong with it. She sang so well that day that even he was satisfied—at least he didn't make the sour face he usually wore while listening to her. As she sang, her irritation and anxiety dissolved and she felt entirely clear and happy. The sky was translucent with dawn and birds woke up and twittered like fresh gurgling water. No one else was up in the whole neighborhood, only she and the teacher and the birds. She sang and sang, her voice rose high and so did her heart; sometimes she laughed with enjoyment and saw that in response the shadow of a smile flitted over the teacher's features as well. Then she laughed again and her voice rose—with what ease—to even greater feats. And the joy that filled her at her own achievement and the peace that entered into her with that pure clear dawn, these sensations stayed with her for the rest of the day. She polished all the mirrors and brass fittings with her own hands, and afterward she cooked sweet vermicelli for her husband, which was his favorite dish. Phuphiji, at once aware of her change of mood, was suspicious and followed her around as she had done the previous day and looked at her in the same suspicious way; but today Shakuntala didn't mind, in fact she even laughed at Phuphiji within herself.

Her teacher always went away after the early morning lesson, but about this time, after his illness, he began to visit her in the afternoons as well. Shakuntala was glad. Now that she had seen his home, she realized what a relief it must be to him to have a clean and peaceful room to sit in; and she did her best to make him comfortable and served him with tea and little fried delicacies. But he was never keen on these refreshments and often did not touch anything she set before him, simply letting his eyes glance over it with the expression of distaste that was so characteristic of him. Phuphiji was amazed. She thought he was being excessively and unwarrantably honored by having these treats placed before him and could not understand why he did not fall upon them as eagerly as she expected him to. She looked from them to him and back again. Tantalized beyond endurance, she even pushed the dishes toward him, saying "Eat, eat," as if he were some bizarre animal whose feeding habits she wished to observe. He treated her in the same way as he did the refreshments, ignoring her after a swift contemptuous glance in her direction. But she was fascinated by him. Whenever he came, she hurried and placed herself in a strategic position in order to look her fill into his face. Sometimes as she gazed she shook her head in wonder and murmured to herself and even gave herself incredulous little laughs. He wasn't bothered by her in the least. He sat there for as long as he felt like it, often in complete silence, and then departed, still in silence.

Occasionally, however, he talked. His conversation was as arbitrary as his silence; he needed no stimulus to start him off and always ended as abruptly as he had begun. Shakuntala loved listening to him, everything he said was of interest to her. She was especially fascinated when he talked about his own teacher who had been a very great and famous and temperamental musician. He often spoke of him, for a good many years of his life and certainly the most formative part of it had been spent under the old man's tutelage. All the disciples had lived with their guru and his family in an old house in Benaras. There had been strict discipline as far as the hours of practice were concerned and all were expected to get up before dawn and spend most of their day in improving their technique; but in between their way of life was entirely without constraint. They ate when they liked, slept when they liked, chewed opium in their betel, loved and formed friendships. When the old man was invited to perform at private or public concerts in other parts of India, most of the disciples traveled with him. They all crammed together into a railway carriage, and when they got to their destination, they stayed together in the quarters allotted to them. Sometimes these were a dingy room in a rest house, other times they were ornate chambers in some maharaja's palace. They were equally happy wherever it was, sleeping on the floor around the great bed on which their guru snored, and eating their fill of the rich meals provided for them. They were up all night listening to and performing in concerts that never ended before dawn. They were most of them quite unattached and had no ties apart from those they had formed with their guru. Some of them—such as Shakuntala's teacher—had run away from their parents to be with their guru, others had left their wives and children for his sake. He was a very hard master. He often beat his disciples, and they had to serve him as his servants, doing the most menial tasks for him; he never lifted a finger for himself and got into a terrible rage if some little comfort of his had been neglected. Once Shakuntala's teacher had forgotten to light his hookah, and for this fault was chased all around the house and at last out into the street, where he had to stay for three days, sitting on the doorstep like a beggar and being fed on scraps till he was forgiven and admitted inside again. Phuphiji was shocked to hear of such treatment and called the guru by many harsh names; but to Shakuntala, as to her teacher, it did not seem so deplorable—on the contrary, she thought it a reasonable price to pay for the privilege of being near so great and blessed a man.

Whenever a famous musician came to the town to give a performance, Shakuntala did her best to attend. It was not easy for her because she had no one willingly to go with her. She didn't want to trouble her husband. He cared nothing for music and, in any case, would have found it an ordeal to sit upright on a chair for so many hours. Once or twice she asked Phuphiji to be her chaperone. Phuphiji was quite glad; she always enjoyed an outing. At first she was interested in everything, she looked around eagerly, craning her neck this way and that. But when the concert started and went on, she became restless. She yawned and slid about on the chair to show how uncomfortable she was; she asked often how much longer they would have to stay, and then she said "Let's go," and when Shakuntala tried to soothe and detain her, she became plaintive and said her back was hurting unbearably. So they always had to come home early, just as the best part of the concert was beginning. And it wasn't much better when Shakuntala took her daughter with her, for although Manju didn't complain the way Phuphiji did, she was obviously bored and made a suffering face. It was usually necessary to take Baba along too, and if they were lucky, he fell asleep quite soon, but if they weren't, he made a lot of disturbance and kicked and struggled and finally he would begin to cry so that there was nothing for it, they had to leave. Shakuntala always tried to put a good face on it and hide her disappointment, but later, when she was at home and in bed beside her husband who had been asleep these many hours, then her thoughts kept reverting to the concert. She wondered what raga was being sung now—"Raga Yaman," serene and sublime, "Raga Kalawati," full of sweet yearning?—and saw the brightly lit stage on which the musicians sat: the singer in the middle, the accompanists grouped all around, the disciples forming an outer ring, and all of them caught up in a mood of exaltation inspired by the music. Their heads slowly swayed, they exchanged looks and smiles, their hearts were open and sweet sensations flowed in them like honey. And thinking of this, alone in the silent bedroom beside her sleeping husband, she turned her face and buried it deep into her pillow as if she hoped thereby to bury her feelings of bitter disappointment.

One morning her teacher surprised her. It was at the end of their lesson when she had sung as usual and he had listened to her with his usual pained face. But before he went, he suddenly said it was time she sang before an audience. She was so astonished, she couldn't answer for a while, and when she could, it was only to say "I didn't know." She meant she didn't know he thought she was good enough for that. He seemed to understand and it annoyed him. He said "Why do you think I come here," and got up to go downstairs. She followed him but he didn't turn back and didn't speak to her again, he was so irritated with her. And she longed for him to say more, to tell her *why* he came, for once to hear from him that she had talent: but he left the house and turned down the street and she looked after him. He was tall, lean, and rather shabby, and walked like a person who is not in a hurry and has no particular destination. She didn't know where he went after he left her or how he spent his time; she guessed, however, that he didn't spend much of it at his home. When he had turned the corner she went back into the house. She was triumphant that day with joy. She even had visions of the marquee where the concerts took place and saw herself sitting on the stage, in the center of a group of musicians. There would only be a thin and scattered audience—most people didn't bother to come till later when it was time for the important musician to start—nor would they be paying much attention, the way audiences don't pay much attention to the preliminaries before the big fight. But she would be there, singing, and not only for herself and her teacher. Yes, that was beautiful too, she loved it, but there had to be something more, she knew that; she had to give another dimension to her singing by performing before strangers. Now she realized she longed to do so. But she also knew it was not to be thought of. She was a housewife from a fine, respectable, middle-class family—people like her didn't sing in public. It would be an outrage, to her husband, to Phuphiji, to Manju's husband, and Manju's in-laws. Even little Baba would be shocked, he wouldn't know what to think if he saw his granny singing before a lot of strangers.

That day she had another surprise. Her husband came home with a packet, which he threw in her direction, saying laconically "Take." She opened it and, when she saw the contents, a lightning flash of pleasure passed through her. It was a pair of earrings, 24-caret gold set with rubies and pearls. Her husband watched her hooking them into her ears, pleased with her and pleased with his purchase. He explained to her how he had got them cheaply, as a bargain, from a fellow contractor who was in difficulties and had been forced to sell his wife's jewelry. Shakuntala locked them away carefully in her steel safe in which she kept all her other ornaments. Next day she took them out again and wore them and looked at herself this side and that. While she was doing this, Phuphiji came in and, seeing the earrings, let out a cry. "Hai, hai!" she cried, and came up and touched them as they dangled from Shakuntala's ears. Shakuntala took them off and locked them up again with the other things, though not before Phuphiji's eyes had devoured them in every detail. "He brought for you?" Phuphiji inquired and Shakuntala nodded briefly and turned the key of the safe and fastened the bunch back to the string at her waist. Suddenly Phuphiji was sitting on the bed, weeping. She wept over the good fortune of some and the ill fortune of others who had been left widows at an early age and had no one to care for them. When Shakuntala had nothing to say to comfort her, she comforted herself and, wiping the corners of her eyes with the end of her sari, said it was fate, there was nothing to be done about it. It was the way things were ordained in this particular life—though next time, who knew, everything might come out quite differently; wheels always came full circle and those that were kings and queens now might, at the next turn, find themselves nothing more than ants or some other form of lowly insect. This thought cheered her, and she went out and sat on the veranda and called to the servant boy for a glass of hot tea.

Over the next few days, Shakuntala kept taking out her new earrings. She also took out some of her other pieces and admired them and put them on before the mirror. She loved gold and precious stones and fine workmanship; she also loved to see these things sparkling on herself and the effect they made against her skin and set off all her good points. She preened herself before the mirror and smiled like a girl. One afternoon, when she had spent some time in this pleasant way, she came out and found her teacher sitting on the blue sofa in the drawing room. Phuphiji had as usual taken up her place near him. She was staring at him and he was yawning widely. They looked like two people who had been sitting there for a long time with nothing to say to each other. Shakuntala went out into the kitchen and quickly got some refreshments ready. Phuphiji followed her. "What's the use?" she said. "He won't eat, his stomach is not accustomed to these things." But that day he did eat, very quickly and ravenously, like a man who has had nothing for some time. Shakuntala, watching him, saw that there was something wolflike about him when he ate like that; she also noticed that he looked more haggard and unkempt than usual. And just before leaving, when he was already by the door, he asked her for an advance of salary. He asked quite casually and without embarrassment; it was she who was embarrassed. She went into the bedroom to take out her money. Phuphiji followed and whispered urgently "He asked for money? don't give him." Shakuntala ignored her. She went out and gave it to him and he put it in his pocket without counting and walked away without saying anything further.

Next morning, however, after she had finished singing, he said that it was good she had given him that money, it had come in very useful. She didn't ask anything, out of delicacy, but he volunteered the information that there was some "domestic upset." He said this with a shrug and a laugh, not out of bravado but really, obviously, because it didn't matter to him. Then also she realized that his whole domestic setup—his dirty room, his quarrelsome wife—which had so unpleasantly affected her, that too didn't matter to him and her pity was misplaced. On the contrary, today as she watched him walk away down the street, in his shabby gray-white clothes and his downtrodden slippers, she envied him. She thought how he went where he liked and did what he liked. Her own circumstances were so different. All that day Phuphiji was after her, she nagged at her, she kept asking how much money she had given him, why had she given him, had her husband been told that this money had been given? At last Shakuntala went into her bedroom and bolted the door from inside. It was a very hot day, and the room was closed and humid and mosquitoes buzzed inside with stinging noises. Partly out of boredom, partly in the hope of cheering herself up, she unlocked her jewelry again; but now it failed to give her pleasure. It was just things, metal.

Someone rattled at the door, she shouted, "No, no!" But it was Manju. She unbolted the door and opened it just sufficiently to let Manju in; Phuphiji hovered behind but Shakuntala quickly shut her out. Manju saw her mother's jewelry spread out on the bed. She at once detected the new earrings and picked them up and asked where they had come from. "Put them on," Shakuntala invited her, and Manju lost no time in doing so. She looked in the mirror and liked herself very much in them. She went back to the bed and played with the other ornaments. One day they would all be hers but that day was still far off. She looked wistful and Shakuntala guessed what she was thinking and it made her want to pile everything into Manju's lap right now and say "Take it." And indeed when Manju, sighing a bit, put up her hand to take the earrings off again, Shakuntala suddenly said "You can keep them." Manju was astonished, she tried to protest, she said "Papa will be angry"; but her mother insisted. Then Manju returned to the mirror, she admired herself more than ever and a pleased smile of proprietorship lit up her somewhat glum features. Shakuntala stood behind her at the mirror. She too smiled with pleasure, though she could see that the earrings didn't suit Manju as well as they suited herself. This made her kiss her all the more tenderly. She was glad to see Manju happy with the gift.

For herself, nothing nowadays seemed to make her happy. Not even her early morning singing. Yet she was making good progress. It was one of those periods when she was beginning to master something that had up till then defeated her: now she saw that it lay within her power, a little more effort and she would be there and then she could begin to set her sights on the next impossible step.

But, in spite of this triumph, she was dissatisfied and she knew her teacher was too. Once or twice he had again broached the subject of her singing in public; each time she had had to put him off, by silence, by a sad smile. He knew her reasons, of course, but did not sympathize with them. Once he even told her, then what is the use? And she knew he was right—what *was* the use—if it was all to be locked up here in the house and no one to hear, no one to care, no other heart to be touched and respond. And all around her the birds tumbled about in the bright air and sang out lustily, pouring themselves out without stint. She fell into despondency at herself, but her teacher was angry. He said what did she expect, that he came here to waste his time on training *housewives?* Then she began to be afraid that he would stop coming, and every morning she got up and went on the roof with her heart beating in fear; and how it leaped in relief when he did come—cross usually, and sour, and displeased with her, but he was there, he hadn't yet given her up.

He didn't come so often in the afternoons anymore, and when he did come, he stayed for a shorter time. It seemed he was bored and restless there. Now his glance of disdain fell not only on the refreshments but on all the shiny furniture and the calendars and the pictures on the wall. And most of all on Phuphiji. Her presence, which he had before accepted with such equanimity, now irritated him intensely. He made no attempt to hide this, but Phuphiji did not care: she kept right on sitting there, and when any comment occurred to her she made it. His visit usually ended in his jumping up and hurrying away, muttering to himself. Once, when he had got outside the door, he said to Shakuntala "You should burn her, that's the only thing old women are good for, burning." Shakuntala's mouth corners twitched with amusement, but he was not in a joking mood. Next morning he asked her for another loan and she was glad to give it. He frequently asked her for money now. He ceased to make the excuse that it was an advance on salary, he just asked for the money and then pocketed it as if it were his right. He never counted it, the transaction was too trifling for him to bother that much about it.

It was not in the least trifling to Phuphiji. Although Shakuntala tried to keep these loans secret, it was not easy—indeed not possible—to keep anything that went on in the house secret from Phuphiji. She kept asking questions about the teacher's salary and whether he had taken any advance and, if so, how much; and when Shakuntala said she didn't remember, Phuphiji reproached her, she said that was not the way to deal with her husband's money. Once she caught them at it. She had hidden herself behind the water butt in the courtyard and came pouncing out just as Shakuntala untied a bundle of notes and passed them to the teacher. Oh, asked Phuphiji, she was paying him his salary? That was strange, she said, it wasn't the first of the month, it wasn't anywhere near the first, it was somewhere about the middle of the month and surely that wasn't the time for paying anyone's salary? Before she could get any further, the teacher had taken out the money and flung it at her feet. Phuphiji jumped back a step or two as if it were some dangerous explosive. "Look at that," she cried, "see how he behaves!" But Shakuntala swooped down on the notes and picked them up and ran after him. He was already halfway down the street and didn't turn around. She had to implore him to stop. When he did, she thrust the money into his hand and he took it and stuffed it carelessly into his pocket and then continued his progress down the street.

Phuphiji would have dearly liked to complain to Shakuntala's husband, but she dared not. Indeed, she could not, for Shakuntala's husband never listened to her; if she wanted anything from him, she always had to approach him through Shakuntala. All she could do now was hover around him while he sat and ate his food. She shook out cushions that didn't need shaking, she waved away flies that weren't there, and talked to herself darkly in soliloquy. When she became too obtrusive, he turned to Shakuntala and asked "What's she say? What does the old woman want?" Then Phuphiji left off and went to sit outside, squatting on the floor with her knees hunched up and her head supported on her fist like a woman in mourning. Sometimes she used the supporting fist to strike her brow.

But she was more successful with Manju. She managed, by hints rather than by direct narration, to convey a sense of unease, even danger, to Manju. She mentioned no figures but gave the impression that large sums of money were changing hands and that the teacher and all his family were being kept in luxury on money supplied by Shakuntala. "I hear they are buying a television set," Phuphiji whispered. "Can you imagine people like that, who never had five rupees to their name? A television set! Where do they get it from?" And Manju drew back from Phuphiji's face thrust close into hers, in shock and fright. Shakuntala came in and found them like that. "What's the matter?" she asked, looking from one to the other. "We're just having a talk," Phuphiji said.

Another day Phuphiji hinted that it was not only money that was going out of the house but other things too.

"What?" Manju, who was not very quick, asked her.

"Very precious things," Phuphiji said.

Manju faltered: "Not—?"

Phuphiji nodded and sighed.

"Her *jewelry?*" Manju asked, hand on heart.

Phuphiji stared into space.

"Oh, God," Manju said. She caught up little Baba and held him in a close embrace as if to protect him against unscrupulous people out to rob him of his inheritance. Baba began to cry. Manju cried with him, and so did Phuphiji, two hard little tears dropping from her as if squeezed from eyes of stone.

"It's true, she's in a strange mood," Manju said. She told Phuphiji how her mother had given her the new earrings: for no reason at all, had just waved her hand and said casually "Take them." That was not the way to give away jewelry, no not even to your own daughter. It showed a person was strange. And who knew, if she was in that kind of mood, what she would do next—was perhaps already doing—perhaps she was already telling other people "Take them" in that same casual way, waving her hand negligently over all that was most precious to a woman and a family. The thought struck horror into Phuphiji and Manju, and when Shakuntala came in, they both looked up at her as if she were someone remote from and dangerous to them.

Shakuntala hardly noticed them. Her thoughts were day and night elsewhere, and she longed only to be sitting on the roof practicing her singing while her teacher listened to her. But nowadays he seemed to be bored with her. He tended to stay for shorter periods, he yawned and became restless and left her before she had finished. When he left her like that, she ceased to sing but continued to sit on the roof by herself; she breathed heavily as if in pain, and indeed her sense of unfulfillment was like pain and stayed with her for the rest of the day. The worst was when he did not turn up at all. This was happening more and more frequently. Days passed and she didn't see him and didn't sing; then he came again—she would step up on the roof in the morning, almost without hope, and there he would be. He had no explanation to offer for his absence, nor did she ask for one. She began straightaway to sing, grateful and happy. She was also grateful and happy when he asked her for money; it seemed such a small thing to do for him. Phuphiji noticed everything—his absences, her loans. She said nothing to Shakuntala but watched her. Manju came often and the two of them sat together and Phuphiji whispered into Manju's ear and Manju cried and looked with red, reproachful eyes at her mother.

One evening Manju and Phuphiji were both present while Shakuntala was serving her husband his meal. When he had finished and was dabbling his hand in the finger bowl held for him by his wife, Phuphiji suddenly got up and, stepping close to Shakuntala, stood on tiptoe to look at her ears. She peered and squinted as if she couldn't see very well: she with eyes as sharp as little needles! "Are they new?" she asked.

"He gave them to me when Manju was born," Shakuntala replied quite calmly and even smiled a bit at the transparency of Phuphiji's tactics.

"Ah," said Phuphiji and paused. Her nose itched, she scratched it by pressing the palm of her hand against it and rubbing it around and around. When she had finished and emerged with her nose very red and tears in her eyes from this exertion, she said, "But he gave you some new ones?"

"Yes," Shakuntala said.

"I haven't seen them," Phuphiji said. She turned to Manju: "Have you?"

Manju was silent. Shakuntala could feel that she was very tense, and so was Phuphiji. Both of them were anxious as to the outcome of this scene. But Shakuntala found herself to be completely indifferent.

Phuphiji turned to Shakuntala's husband: "Have you seen them?" she asked. "Where are they? Those new earrings you gave her?"

Shakuntala knew that Phuphiji and Manju were both waiting for her to speak so that they could deny what she was going to say. But she said nothing and only handed the towel to her husband to dry his hands. She didn't want Manju to have to say or do anything that would make her feel very bad afterward.

"Why don't you ask her?" Phuphiji said. "Go on, ask her: where are those new earrings I gave you? Ask. Let's hear what she has to say."

For one second her husband looked at Shakuntala; his eyes were like those of an old bear emerging from his winter sleep. But the next moment he had flung down the towel and stamped on it in rage. He shouted at Phuphiji and abused her. He said he didn't come home to be pestered and needled by a pack of women, that's not what he expected after his hard day's work. He also shouted at Manju and asked her why sit on his back, let her go home and sit on her husband's back, what else had she been married off for at enormous expense? Manju burst into tears, but that was nothing new and no one tried to comfort her, not even Phuphiji, who busied herself with clearing away the dirty dishes, patient and resigned in defeat.

That night passed slowly for Shakuntala. She lay beside her husband and was full of restless thoughts. But when morning came and her teacher again failed to show up, then she did not hesitate any longer. She went straight to his house. She walked through his courtyard where they were hammering pieces of plywood together, up the stairs, past the music school, and up to his door. It had a big padlock on it. She was put out, but only for a moment. She went down to the music school. Several thin men in poor clothes sat on the floor testing out drums and tuning stringed instruments; they looked at her curiously, and even more curiously when she asked for him. They shrugged at each other and laughed. "God knows," they said. "Ever since she went, he's here and there." "Who went?" Shakuntala asked. They looked at her again and wondered. "His wife," one of them said at last. Shakuntala was silent and so were they. She didn't know what else to ask. She turned and went down the stairs. One of them followed and looked down at her from the landing. As if in afterthought he called: "He sits around in the restaurants!" She walked through the courtyard where they stopped hammering and also looked after her with curiosity.

Shakuntala had lived in the town all her life, but she was only familiar with certain restricted areas of it. There were others that she knew of, had seen and of necessity passed through on her way to somewhere else, but which remained mysterious and out of bounds to her. One of these was the street where the singing and dancing girls lived, and another was the street where the restaurants were. The two were connected, and to get to the restaurants Shakuntala had first to pass through the other street. This was lined with shops selling colored brassieres, scents, and filigree necklaces, and on top of the shops were balconies on which the girls sat. Downstairs stood little clusters of men with betel-stained mouths; they looked at Shakuntala and some of them made sweet sounds as she passed. Here and there from upstairs came the sound of ankle bells and a few bars tapped out for practice on a drum. The street of the restaurants was much quieter. No sounds came out from behind the closed doors of the restaurants. They were called "Bombay House," "Shalimar," "Monna Lisa," "Taj Mahal." Shakuntala hesitated only before the first one and even then only for a moment before pushing open the door. They were mostly alike from inside with a lot of peeling plaster-of-Paris decorations and a smell of fried food, tobacco, and perfumed oil. The clientele was alike too. There was no woman among them, and Shakuntala's presence attracted attention. There was some laughter and, despite her age, also the sweet sounds she had heard from the men in the streets.

She found him in the third one she entered (Bombay House). He was one of a group lounging against the wall on a red-leather bench behind a table cluttered with plates and glasses. He was drumming one hand rhythmically on the table and swaying and dipping his head in time to a tune playing inside it. When Shakuntala stepped up to the table, the other men sitting with him were astonished; their jaws stopped chewing betel and dropped open. Only he went on swaying and drumming to the tune in his mind. He let her stand there for a while, then he said to the others "She's my pupil. I teach her singing." He added "She's a housewife," and sniggered. No one else said anything nor moved. She noticed that his eyes were heavy and with a faraway blissful look in them.

He got up and, tossing some money on the table, left the restaurant. She followed him, back the same way she had come past the restaurants and through the street of the singing and dancing girls. He walked in front all the time. He was still singing the same tune to himself and was still at the introductory stage, letting the raga develop slowly and spaciously. His hand made accompanying gestures in the air. He also waved this hand at people who greeted him on the way and sometimes to the girls when they called down to him from the balconies. He seemed to be a well-known figure. Walking behind him, Shakuntala remembered the many times she had stood in the doorway of her house watching him as he walked, slowly and casually like someone with all time at his disposal, away from her down the street; only now she did not have to turn back into her house, no she was following him and going where he was going. The tune he was singing began in her mind too and she smiled to it and let it unfold itself in all its glory.

He led the way back to his house and they walked up the stairs, and first the men in the courtyard and then the men in the music school looked after them. He unfastened the big padlock on his door. Inside everything was as before when she had visited him in his sickness, except that the sewing machine was gone and the air was denser because no one had opened the window for a long time. His bedding, consisting of a mat and tumbled sheet, was as he must have left it in the morning. He wasted no time but at once came close to her and fumbled at her clothes and at his own. He was about the same age as her husband but lean, hard, and eager; as he came on top of her, she saw his drugged eyes so full of bliss and he was still smiling at the tune he was playing to himself. And this tune continued to play in her too. He entered her at the moment when, the structure of the raga having been expounded, the combination of notes was being played up and down, backward and forward, very fast. There was no going back from here, she knew. But who would want to go back, who would exchange this blessed state for any other?

ROSE PETALS

He loves being a cabinet minister, he thinks it's wonderful. His bearer comes to wake him with tea early in the morning, and he gets up and starts getting dressed, ready to see the stream of callers who have already begun to gather downstairs. He thinks I'm still asleep but I'm awake and know what he is doing. Sometimes I peep at him as he moves around our bedroom. How fat and old he has become; and he makes an important face even when he is alone like this and thinks no one is watching him. He frowns and thinks of all his great affairs. Perhaps he is rehearsing a speech in Parliament. I see his lips move and sometimes he shakes his head and makes a gesture as if he were talking to someone. He struggles into his cotton tights; he still has not quite got used to these Indian clothes but he wears nothing else now. There was a time when only suits made in London were good enough for him. Now they hang in the closet, and no one ever wears them.

I don't get up till several hours later, when he has left the house. I don't like to get up early, and anyway there is nothing to do. I lie in bed with the curtains drawn. They are golden-yellow in color, like honey, and so is the carpet, and the cushions and everything; because of this the light in the room is also honey-colored. After a while Mina comes in. She sits on the bed and talks to me. She is fully dressed and very clean and tidy. She usually has breakfast with her father; she pours the tea for him and any guests there might be and takes an interest in what is being said. She too likes it that her father is a cabinet minister. She wants to be helpful to him in his work and reads all the newspapers and is very well up in current affairs. She intends to go back to college and take a course in political science and economics. We discuss this while she is sitting on my bed. She holds my hand in hers and plays with it. Her hand is broader than mine, and she cuts her nails short and does not use any varnish or anything. I look up into her face. It is so young and earnest; she frowns a little bit the way her father does when he is talking of something serious. I love her so much that I have to shut my eyes. I say "Kiss me, darling." She bends down to do so. She smells of Palmolive soap.

By the time I get up, Mina too has left the house. She has many interests and activities. I'm alone in the house now with the servants. I get up from my bed and walk over to the dressing table to see myself in the mirror there. I always do this first thing when I get up. It is a habit that has remained with me from the past when I was very interested in my appearance and took so much pleasure in looking in the mirror that I would jump eagerly out of bed to see myself. Now this pleasure has gone. If I don't look too closely and with the curtains drawn and the room all honey-colored, I don't appear so very different from what I used to be. But sometimes I'm in a mischievous mood with myself. I stretch out my hand and lift the yellow silk curtain. The light comes streaming in straight on to the mirror, and now yes I can see that I do look very different from the way I used to.

Biju comes every day. Often he is already sitting there when I come down. He is reading the papers, but only the cinema and restaurant advertisements and perhaps the local news if there has been a murder or some interesting social engagement. He usually stays all day. He has nowhere to go and nothing to do. Every day he asks "And how is the Minister?" Every day he makes fun of him. I enjoy that, and I also make fun of him with Biju. They are cousins but they have always been very different. Biju likes a nice life, no work, good food and drinking. The Minister also likes good food and drinking, but he can't sit like Biju in a house with a woman all day. He always has to be doing something or he becomes restless and his temper is spoiled. Biju's temper is never spoiled, although sometimes he is melancholy; then he recites sad poetry or plays sad music on the gramophone.

Quite often we have a lunch or dinner party in the house. Of course it is always the Minister's party and the guests are all his. There are usually one or two cabinet ministers, an ambassador, a few newspaper editors—people like that. Biju likes to stay for these parties, I don't know why, they are not very interesting. He moves around the room talking to everyone. Biju looks distinguished—he is tall and well built, and though the top of his head is mostly bald he keeps long sideburns; he is always well dressed in an English suit, just like the Minister used to wear before taking to Indian clothes. The guests are impressed with Biju and talk to him as if he were as clever and important as they themselves are. They never guess that he is not because he speaks in a very grand English accent and is ready to talk on any subject they like.

Mina also enjoys her father's parties and she mingles with the guests and listens to the intelligent conversation. But I don't enjoy them at all. I talk to the wives, but it is tiring for me to talk with strangers about things that are not interesting to me; very soon I slip away, hoping they will think that I have to supervise the servants in the kitchen. Actually, I don't enter the kitchen at all—there is no need because our cooks have been with us a long time; instead I lie down on a sofa somewhere or sit in the garden where no one can find me. Only Biju does find me sooner or later, and then he stays with me and talks to me about the guests. He imitates the accent of a foreign ambassador or shows how one of the cabinet ministers cracks nuts and spits out the shells. He makes me laugh, and I like being there with him in the garden, which is so quiet with the birds all asleep in the trees and the moon shining down with a silver light. I wish we didn't have to go back. But I know that if I stay away too long, the Minister will miss me and get annoyed and send Mina to look for me. And when she has found us, she too will be annoyed— she will stand there and look at us severely as if we were two children that were not to be trusted.

Mina is often annoyed with us. She lectures us. Sometimes she comes home earlier than usual and finds me lying on a sofa and Biju by my side with a drink in one hand and cigar in the other. She says "Is this all you ever do?"

Biju says "What else *is* there to do?"

"Aren't you awful." But she can't concentrate on us just now. She is very hungry and is wondering what to eat. I ring for the bearer and order refreshments to be brought for Mina on a tray. She sits with us while she is eating. After a while she feels fit enough to speak to us again. She asks "Don't you want to do something constructive?"

Biju thinks about this for a while. He examines the tip of his cigar while he is thinking; then he says "No."

"Well you ought to. Everybody ought to. There's such a lot to do! In every conceivable field." She licks crumbs off the ends of her fingers—I murmur automatically "Darling, use the napkin"—and when she has got them clean she uses them to tick off with: "Social. Educational. Cultural—that reminds me: are you coming to the play?"

"What play?"

"I've been telling you for *weeks.*"

"Oh, yes of course," I say. "I remember." I don't really, but I know vaguely that her friends are always putting on advanced plays translated from French or German or Romanian. Mina has no acting talent herself but she takes great interest in these activities. She often attends rehearsals, and as the time of the performance draws near, she is busy selling tickets and persuading shopkeepers to allow her to stick posters in their windows.

"This is really going to be something special. It's a difficult play but terribly interesting, and Bobo Oberoi is just great as God the Father. What talent he has, that boy, oh." She sighs with admiration, but next moment she has recollected something and is looking suspiciously at Biju and me: "You're welcome to buy tickets of course, and I'm certainly going to sell you some, but I hope you'll behave better than last time."

Biju looks guilty. It's true he didn't behave very well last time. It was a long play, and again a difficult one. Biju got restless—he sighed and crossed his long legs now one way and now another and kept asking me how much longer it was going to be. At last he decided to go out and smoke and pushed his way down the row so that everybody had either to get up or to squeeze in their legs to let him pass, while he said "Excuse me" in a loud voice and people in rows behind said "Sh."

"Why don't they put on one of these nice musical plays?" Biju asks now, as Mina eats the last biscuit from her tray and washes it down with her glass of milk. She doesn't answer him, but looks exasperated. *"My Fair Lady,"* Biju presses on. *"Funny Girl."* The expression on Mina's face becomes more exasperated, and I tell him to be quiet.

"If you'd only make an *effort,*" Mina says, doing her best to be patient and in a voice that is almost pleading. "To move with the times. To understand the modern mind."

I try to excuse us: "We're too old, darling."

"It's nothing to do with age. It's an attitude, that's all. Now look at Daddy."

"Ah," says Biju.

"He's the same age as you are."

"Two years older," Biju says.

"So you see."

Biju raises his glass as if he were drinking to someone, and as he does so, his face becomes so solemn and respectful that it is difficult for me not to laugh.

The Minister is very keen to "move with the times." It has always been one of his favorite sayings. Even when he was young and long before he entered politics, he was never satisfied doing what everyone else did—looking after the estates, hunting and other sports, entertaining guests—no, it was not enough for him. When we were first married, he used to give me long lectures like Mina does now—about the changing times and building up India and everyone putting their shoulder to the wheel—he would talk to me for a long time on this subject, getting all the time more and more excited and enthusiastic; only I did not listen too carefully because, as with Mina, I was so happy only looking at him while he talked that it didn't matter to me what he said. How handsome he was in those days! His eyes sparkled, and he was tall and strong and always appeared to be in a great hurry as if difficult tasks awaited him. When he went up any stairs it was two, three steps at a time, doors banged behind him, his voice was loud and urgent like a king in battle even when he was only calling to the servant for his shoes. He used to get very impatient with me because he said I was slow and lazy like an elephant, and if he was walking behind me, he would prod my hips (which were always rather heavy) and say "Get moving." In those days he wanted me to do everything with him. At one time he had imported a new fertilizer that was going to do magic, and together we would walk through the fields to see its effect (which was not good: it partially killed the maize crop). Another time we traveled to Japan to study their system of hotel management because he thought of converting one of our houses into a hotel. Then he had an idea that he would like to start a factory for manufacturing steel tubing, and we went to Russia to observe the process of manufacture. Wherever we went, he drew up a heavy program for us that I found very tiring; but since he himself never needed any rest, he couldn't understand why I should. He began to feel that I was a hindrance to him on these tours, and as the years went by, he became less eager to take me with him.

Fortunately, just at that time Biju came back from abroad, and he began to spend a lot of time with me so I did not feel too lonely. It was said in the family that Biju had been abroad all these years to study, but of course it was well known that he had not done much studying. Even at that age he was very lazy and did not like to do anything except enjoy himself and have a good time. In the beginning, when he first came back, he used to go to Bombay quite often, to meet with friends and dance and go to the races, but later he did not care so much for these amusements and came to stay on his land, which was near to ours, or—during the summer when we went up to Simla—he also took a house there. Everyone was keen for him to get married, and his aunts were always finding suitable girls for him. But he didn't like any of them. He says it is because of me that he didn't marry, but that's only his excuse. It is just that he was too lazy to take up any burdens.

It is not easy to be a minister's wife. People ask me to do all sorts of things that I don't like to do. They ask me to sit on welfare committees and give away prizes at cultural shows. I want to say no, but the Minister says it's my duty, so I go. But I do it very badly. All the other ladies are used to sitting on committees and they make speeches and know exactly what is wanted. Sometimes they get very heated, especially when they have to elect one another onto subcommittees. They all want to be on as many committees and subcommittees as possible. Not for any selfish reasons but because they feel it is necessary for the good of India. Each proves to the other point by point how necessary it is and they hotly debate with one another. Sometimes they turn to me to ask my opinion, but I don't have any opinion, I don't know what it is they are discussing. Then they turn away from me again and go on talking to each other, and although they are polite to me, I know they don't have a high opinion of me and think I'm not worthy to be a minister's wife. I wish Mina could be there instead of me. She would be able to talk like they do, and they would respect her.

When I have to give a speech anywhere, it is always Mina who writes it for me. She writes a beautiful speech and then she makes me rehearse it. She is very thorough and strict with me. "No!" she cries, "Not 'today each of us carries a burden of responsibility,' but 'each of us carries a burden of *responsibility*'!" I start again and say it the way she wants me to say it, and as many times as she wants me to till at last she is satisfied. She is never entirely satisfied: at the end of each rehearsal, she sighs and looks at me with doubtful eyes. And she is right to be doubtful because, when the time comes to make the speech, I forget all about our rehearsal and just read it off as quickly as possible. When I come home, she asks me how did it go, and I tell her that everyone praised the speech and said it was full of beautiful words and thoughts.

But once she was with me. It was a school's sports day, and it was really quite nice, not like some of the other functions I have had to attend. We all sat on chairs in the school grounds and enjoyed the winter sunshine. Mina and I sat in the front row with the headmistress and the school governors and some other people who had been introduced to us, but I could not remember who they were. The girls did mass PT, and rhythmic exercises, and they ran various races. They were accompanied by the school band, and one of the teachers announced each item over the microphone which, however, was not in good order so that the announcement could not be heard very well. From time to time the headmistress explained something to me, and I nodded and smiled, although—because of the noise from the loudspeaker and the band—I could not hear what she said. The sun was warm on my face, and I half shut my eyes, and the girls were a pretty colored blur. Mina nudged me and whispered "Mummy, are you falling asleep?" so I opened my eyes again quickly and clapped loudly at the conclusion of an item and turned to smile at the headmistress who smiled back to me.

When it was time for my speech, I got up quite happily and read it from the paper Mina had got ready for me. The microphone crackled very loudly so I don't think my speech could be heard distinctly, but no one seemed to mind. I didn't mind either. Then I gave away the prizes, and it was all over and we could go home. I was cheerful and relieved, as I always am when one of these functions is finished, but as soon as we were alone in the car together, Mina began to reproach me for the way I had delivered the speech. She was upset not because I had spoiled her speech—that didn't matter, she said—but because I hadn't cared about it: I hadn't cared about the whole function; I was not serious. "You even fell asleep," she accused me.

"No no, the sun was in my eyes, so I shut them."

"Why are you like that? You and Uncle Biju. Nothing is serious for you. Life is just a game."

I was silent. I was sorry that she was so disappointed in me. We rode along in silence. My head was turned away from her. I looked out of the window but saw nothing. From time to time a sigh escaped my lips. Then, after a while, she laid her hand on mine. I pressed it, and she came closer and put her head on my shoulder. How sweetly she forgave me, how affectionately she clung to me. I laid my lips against her hair and kissed it again and again.

Is life only a game for Biju and me? I don't know. It's true, we laugh a lot together and have jokes that Mina says are childish. The Minister also gets impatient with us, although we are always careful not to laugh too much when he is there. He himself is of course very serious. The important face with which I see him get up in the morning remains with him till he goes to bed at night. But, in spite of all the great affairs with which his day is filled, once he is in bed he falls asleep at once and his face next to me on the pillow is peaceful like a child's. I toss and turn for many hours, and although I try not to, I usually have to take one of my pills. Biju also has to sleep with pills. And he has terrible nightmares. Often his servant has to rush into his bedroom because he hears him screaming with fear and he shakes him by the shoulder and shouts "Sahib, Sahib!" till Biju wakes up. Terrible things happen in Biju's dreams: he falls down mountainsides, tigers jump through his window, he is publicly hanged on a gallows. When his servant shakes him awake, he is trembling all over and wet with perspiration. But he is glad to be awake and alive.

Nothing like that ever happens in the Minister's dreams. He has no dreams. When he goes to sleep at night, there is a complete blank till he wakes up again in the morning and starts to do important things. He always says that he has a great number of worries—his whole life he tells me is one big worry, and sometimes he feels as if he has to carry all the problems of the government and the country on his own shoulders—but all the same he sleeps so soundly. He never seems to be troubled by the sort of thoughts that come to me. Probably he doesn't have time for them. I see him look into the mirror but he appears to do so with pleasure, pulling down his coat and smoothing his hair and turning this way and that to see himself sideways. He smiles at what he sees, he likes it. I wonder—doesn't he remember what he was? How can he like that fat old man that now looks back at him?

It is strange that when you're young you don't think that it can ever happen to you that you'll get old. Or perhaps you do think about it but you don't really believe it, not in your heart of hearts. I remember once we were talking about it, many years ago, Biju and I. We were staying in a house we have by a lake. We never used this house much because it was built as a shooting lodge and none of us cared for hunting and shooting. In fact, the Minister had definitely renounced them on what he called humanitarian grounds, and he was always telling people about these grounds and had even printed a pamphlet about them; only it had been done very badly by the local printers and had so many spelling mistakes in it that the Minister felt ashamed and didn't want it distributed. That time we were staying in the shooting lodge because he had come on an inspection tour. These inspection tours were another favorite idea of his. He always came on them without any advance notice so as to keep the people who looked after the properties alert all the year round. Sometimes he took a whole party of guests with him, but that time it was only he and I and Biju, who had come with us because he thought he would be bored alone at home.

The Minister—of course he wasn't a minister at that time—was busy going over the house, running his finger along ledges for dust and inspecting dinner services that hadn't been in use for twenty years, while Biju and I rested after our journey in the small red sitting room. This room had many ornaments in it that my father-in-law, who frequently traveled to Europe, had brought back with him. There were views of Venice in golden frames on the walls, and an ormolu clock on the mantelpiece, and next to it a lacquered musical box that intrigued Biju very much. He kept playing it over and again. The house was built on a lake and the light from the water filled the room and was reflected from the glass of the pictures of Venice so that the walls appeared to be swaying and rippling as if waves were passing over them. The music box played a very sweet sad tinkling little tune, and Biju didn't seem to get tired of it and I didn't either; indeed, the fact that it was being played over and over again somehow made it even sweeter and sadder so that all sorts of thoughts and feelings rose in the heart. We were drinking orange squash.

Biju said "How do you think it'll be when we're old?"

This question was perhaps sudden but I understood how it had come into his head at that particular moment. I said "Same as now."

"We'll always be sitting like this?"

"Why not."

At that time it wasn't possible for me to think of Biju as old. He was very slim and had a mop of hair and wore a trim little moustache. He was a wonderful dancer and knew all the latest steps. When he heard a snatch of dance music on the radio, at once his feet tapped up and down.

He wound the music box again, and the sad little tune played. The thought of being together like this forever—always in some beautiful room with a view from its long windows of water or a lawn; or hot summer nights in a garden full of scents and overlaid with moonlight so white that it looked like snow—the thought of it was sad and yet also quite nice. I couldn't really think of us as old: only the same as we were now with, at the most, white hair.

"What about the Revolution?" I asked.

Biju laughed: "No, then we won't be here at all." He put his head sideways and showed a rope going around his neck: "Up on a lamppost."

The Revolution was one of our jokes. I don't know whether we really thought it would come. I think often we felt it ought to come, but when we talked about it, it was only to laugh and joke. The Minister did sometimes talk about it seriously, but he didn't believe in it. He said India would always remain a parliamentary democracy because that was the best mode of government. Once all three of us were driving in a car when we were held up by some policemen. They were very polite and apologized and asked us please to take another road because some slum houses were being demolished on this one. Our chauffeur tried to reverse but the gear was stuck and for a while we couldn't move. Out of our car window we could see a squad of demolition workers knocking down the hovels made of old tins and sticks and rags, and the people who lived in the hovels picking up what they could from among the debris. They didn't look angry, just sad, except for one old woman who was shaking her fist and shouting something that we couldn't hear. She ran around and got in the way of the workers till someone gave her a push and she fell over. When she got up, she was holding her knee and limping but she had stopped shouting and she too began to dig among the debris. The Minister was getting very impatient with the car not starting, and he was busy giving instructions to the chauffeur. When at last we managed to get away, he talked all the time about the car and that it was a faulty model—all the models of that year were—cars were like vintages he said, some years were good, some not so good. I don't think Biju was paying any more attention than I was. He didn't say anything that time, but later in the day he was making a lot of jokes about the Revolution and how we would all be strung up on lampposts or perhaps, if we were lucky, sent to work in the salt mines. The Minister said "What salt mines? At least get your facts straight."

But to go back to that time in the shooting lodge. After finishing his inspection tour, the Minister came striding into the room and asked "What are you doing?" and when we told him we were talking about our old age, he said "Ah," as if he thought it might be a good subject for discussion. He liked people to have discussions and got impatient with Biju and me because we never had any.

"When I think of my old age," he said, "I think mainly: what will I have achieved? That means, what sort of person will I be? Because a person can only be judged by his achievements." He walked up and down the room, playing an imaginary game of tennis: he served imaginary balls hard across an imaginary net, stretching up so that his chest swelled out. "I hope I'll have done something," he said as he served. "I intend to. I intend to be a very busy person. Not only when I'm young but when I'm old too." He kept on serving and with such energy that he got a bit out of breath. "Right-till-the-end," he said, slamming a particularly hard ball.

"Out," Biju said.

The Minister turned on him with indignation. "Absolutely in," he said. "And turn off that damn noise, it's getting on my nerves." Biju shut the music box.

"I'll tell you something else," said the Minister. "The point about old age is not to be afraid of it. To meet it head-on. As a challenge that, like everything else, has to be faced and won. The king of Sweden played tennis at the age of *ninety*. I intend to be like that."

How pleased he would have been at that time if he had known that he was going to be a cabinet minister. Things have not really turned out very different from the way we thought they would. The

Minister is busy, and Biju and I are not. We sit in the room and look out into the garden, or sit in the garden and enjoy the trees and flowers. But being old does not mean only white hair. As a matter of fact, we neither of us have all that much white hair (Miss Yvonne takes care of mine, and Biju has lost most of his anyway). We still talk the way we used to, and laugh and joke, but—no, it is not true that life is a game for us. When we were young, we even enjoyed being sad—like when we listened to the music box—and now even when we're laughing, I don't know that we really *are* laughing. Only it is not possible for us to be serious the way the Minister is, and Mina.

Everyone nowadays is serious—all the people who come to the house, and the ladies on committees—they are forever having discussions and talking about important problems. The Minister of course likes it very much, and he hardly ever stops talking. He gives long interviews to the press and addresses meetings and talks on the radio, and he is always what he calls "threshing out his ideas" with the people who come to see him and those who come to our parties and with Mina and with Mina's friends. He especially enjoys talking to Mina's friends, and no wonder because they hang on every word he says, and although they argue quite a lot with him, they do so in a very respectful way. He gets carried away talking to them and forgets the time so that his secretary has to come and remind him; then he jumps up with a shout of surprise and humorously scolds them for keeping him from his duties; and they all laugh and say "Thank you, sir," and Mina kisses his cheek and is terribly proud of him.

The Minister says it is good to be with young people and listen to their ideas. He says it keeps the mind flexible and conditions it to deal with the problems of tomorrow as well as those of today. Biju too would like to talk to Mina's friends. I see him go into the room in which they are all sitting. Before he goes in, he pats his tie, and smoothes his hair to look extra smart. But as a matter of fact he looks rather too smart. He is wearing an English suit and has a handkerchief scented with eau de cologne arranged artistically in his top pocket. He seems taller than everyone else in the room. He begins to make conversation. He says "Any of you seen the new film at the Odeon?" in his clipped, very English accent that always impresses the people at the Minister's parties. But these young people are not impressed. They even look puzzled as if they have not understood what he said, and he repeats his question. They are polite young people and they answer him politely. But no one is at ease. Biju also is embarrassed; he clears his throat and flicks his handkerchief out of his pocket and holds it against his nose for a moment as if to sniff the eau de cologne. But he doesn't want to go away, he wants to go on talking. He begins to tell them some long story. Perhaps it is about the film, perhaps it is about a similar film he has once seen, perhaps it is some incident from his past life. It goes on for a long time. Sometimes Biju laughs in the middle and he is disappointed when no one laughs with him. He flicks out his handkerchief again and sniffs it. His story doesn't come to an end; it has no end; he simply trails off and says "Yes." The young people patiently wait to see if he wants to say anything more. He looks as if he does want to say more, but before he can do so, Mina says "Oh Uncle, I think I hear Mummy calling you." Biju seems as relieved as everyone else to have an excuse to go away.

Once Mina and her friends rolled up the carpet in the drawing room and danced to records. The doors of the drawing room were wide open and the light and music came out into the garden where Biju and I were. We sat on a stone bench by the fountain and looked at them. They were stamping and shaking from side to side in what I suppose were the latest dances. We stayed and watched them for a long time. Biju was very interested, he craned forward and sometimes he said "Did you see that?" and sometimes he gave a short laugh as if he didn't believe what he saw. I was only interested in looking at Mina. She was stamping and shaking like all the rest, and she had taken off her shoes and flung her veil over her shoulders so that it danced behind her. She laughed and turned and sometimes flung up her arms into the air.

Biju said "Care to dance?" and when I shook my head, he jumped up from the bench and began to dance by himself. He tried to do it the way they were doing inside. He couldn't get it right, but he kept on trying. He wanted me to try too, but I wouldn't. "Come on," he said, partly to me, partly to himself, as he tried to get his feet and his hips to make the right movements. He was getting out of breath but he wouldn't give up. I was worried that he might strain his heart, but I didn't say anything because he never likes to be reminded of his heart. Suddenly he said "There, now see!" and indeed when I looked he was doing it absolutely right, just like they were doing inside. Only he looked more graceful than they did because probably he was a better dancer. He was enjoying himself; he

177

laughed and spun round on his heel several times and how he shook
and glided—around the rim of the fountain, on the grass, up and
down the path; he had really got into the rhythm of it now and
wouldn't stop though I could see he was getting more and more out
of breath. Sometimes he danced in the light that came out of the
drawing room, sometimes he moved over into the dark and was illumined only by faint moonlight. But suddenly there was a third light,
a great harsh beam that came from the Minister's car bringing him
home from a late-night meeting. I hoped Biju would stop now but,
on the contrary, he went on dancing right there in the driveway and
only jumped out of the way before the advancing car at the last possible moment, and then he continued on the grass, at the same time
saluting the Minister as he passed in the backseat of the car. The
Minister pretended not to see but seemed preoccupied with
thoughts of the highest importance.

Sometimes Biju doesn't come for several days to the house. I
don't miss him at all—on the contrary, I'm quite glad. I do all sorts
of little things that I wouldn't do if he were there. For instance, I
stick photographs of Mina into an album, or I tidy some drawers in
the Minister's cupboard. I wait for them both to come home. Mina
is there first. She talks to me about what she has been doing all day
and about her friends. I do her hair in various attractive styles. She
looks so nice, but when I have finished, she takes it all down again
and plaits it back into a plain pigtail. I ask her whether she wouldn't
like to get married but she laughs and says what for. I'm partly relieved but partly also worried because she is nearly twenty-two now.
At one time she wanted to be a doctor but kept getting headaches on
account of the hard studying she had to do, so she left it. I was glad.
I never liked the idea of her becoming a doctor and having to work
so hard and seeing so much suffering. The Minister was keen on it
because he said the country needed a lot of doctors, but now he says
what it needs even more is economists. So Mina often talks to me
about becoming an economist.

On those days when Biju is not there, I seem to see more of the
Minister. If he is late, I wait up for him to come. He is full of whatever he has been doing—whether attending a meeting or a dinner or
some other function—and convinced that it was an event of great
importance to the nation. Perhaps it was, I don't know. He tells me
about it, and then it is like it was in the old days: I don't listen carefully but I'm glad to have him there. He still speaks with the same

178

enthusiasm and moves with the same energy while he is speaking, often bumping into things in his impatience. He continues to talk when we go up to bed and while he is undressing, but then he gets into bed and is suddenly fast asleep, almost in the middle of a sentence. I leave the light on for a while to look at him; I like to see him sleeping so peacefully, it makes me feel safe and comfortable.

When I get up next morning, I'm half hoping that Biju will not come that day either; but if there is no sign of him by afternoon, I get restless. I wonder what has happened. I telephone to his house, but his old servant is not much used to the telephone and it is difficult to understand or make him understand anything. In the end I have to go to Biju's house and see for myself. Usually there is nothing wrong with him and it is only one of his strange moods when he doesn't feel like getting out of bed or doing anything. After I have been with him for some time, he feels better and gets up and comes home with me. I'm glad to get him out of his house. It is not a cheerful place and he takes no care of it and his servant is too old to be able to keep it nicely. It is a rented house, which he has taken only so that he can live in Delhi and be near us. It has cement floors, and broken-down servant quarters at the back, and no one ever looks after the garden so that when entering the gate one has to be careful not to get scratched by the thorny bushes that have grown all over the path.

Once I found him ill. He had a pain in his back and had not got up but kept lying there, not even allowing his bed to be made. It looked very crumpled and untidy and so did he, and this was strange and sad because when he is up he is always so very careful of himself. Now he was unshaven and his pajama jacket was open, showing tangled gray hair growing on his chest. He looked at me with frightened eyes. I called the doctor, and then Biju was taken away to a nursing home, and he had to stay there for several weeks because they discovered he had a weak heart.

When he came out of the nursing home, the Minister wanted him to give up his house and come and live with us. But he wouldn't. It is strange about Biju: he has always gone where we have gone, but he has always taken a place on his own. He says that if he didn't live away from us, then where would he go every day and what would he do? I don't like to think of him alone at night in that house with only the old servant and with his violent dreams and his weak heart. The Minister too doesn't like it. Ever since he has heard about Biju's heart, he has been worried. And not only about Biju. He thinks of himself too, for he and Biju are about the same age, and he is afraid that anything that was wrong with Biju could be wrong with him too. In the days after Biju was taken to the nursing home, the Minister began not to feel well. He even woke up at nights and wanted me to put my hand on his heart. It felt perfectly all right to me, but he said no, it was beating too fast, and he was annoyed with me for not agreeing. He was convinced now that he too had a weak heart, so we called in the doctor and a cardiogram was taken and it was discovered that his heart was as healthy and sound as that of a fifteen-year-old boy. Then he was satisfied, and didn't have any more palpitations, and indeed forgot all about his heart.

I had an old aunt who was very religious. She was always saying her prayers and went to the temple to make her offerings. I was not religious at all. I never thought there is anything other than what there is every day. I didn't speak of these matters, and I don't speak of them today. I never like anyone to mention them to me. But my old aunt was always mentioning them, she could speak of nothing else. She said that even if I did not feel prayerful, I should at least go through the form of prayer, and if I only repeated the prescribed prayers every day, then slowly something would waken in my heart. But I wouldn't listen to her, and behind her back I laughed at her with Biju. He also did not believe in these things. Neither did the Minister, but whereas Biju and I only laughed and did not care about it much, the Minister made a great issue out of it and said a lot about religion retarding the progress of the people. He even told my aunt that for herself she could do what she liked, but he did not care for her to bring these superstitions into his house. She was shocked by all he said, and after that she never liked to stay with us, and when she did she avoided him as much as she could. She didn't avoid Biju and me, but continued to try to make us religious. One thing she said I have always remembered and sometimes I think about it. She said that yes, now it was easy for us not to care about religion, but later when our youth had gone, and our looks, and everything that gave us so much pleasure now had lost its savor, then what would we do, where would we turn?

Sometimes I too, like Biju, don't feel like getting up. Then I stay in bed with the curtains drawn all day. Mina comes in and is very concerned about me. She moves about the room and pulls at the curtains and rearranges things on my bedside table and settles my pillows and does everything she can to make me comfortable. She fully intends to stay with me all day, but after a while she gets restless. There are so many things for her to do and places to go to. She begins to telephone her friends and tells them that she can't meet them today because she is looking after her mother. I pretend to be very drowsy and ask why doesn't she go out while I'm asleep, it would be much better. At first she absolutely refuses, but after a while she says if I'm quite sure, and I urge her to go till at last she agrees. She gives me many hurried instructions as to rest and diet, and in saying good-bye she gathers me in her arms and embraces me so hard that I almost cry out. She leaves in a great hurry as if there were a lot of lost time to be made up. Then Biju comes in to sit with me. He reads the newspaper to himself, and when there is anything specially interesting he reads it aloud to me. He stays the whole day. Sometimes he dozes off in his chair, sometimes he lays cards out for patience. He is not at all bored or restless, but seems quite happy to stay not only for one day but for many more. I don't mind having him there; it is not very different from being by myself alone.

But when the Minister comes in, it is a great disturbance. "Why is it so dark in here?" he says and roughly pulls apart the curtains, dispelling the soothing honey-colored light in which Biju and I have been all day like two fish in an aquarium. We both have to shut our eyes against the light coming in from the windows. My head begins to hurt; I suffer. "But what's the matter with you?" the Minister asks. He wants to call the doctor. He says when people are ill, naturally one calls a doctor. Biju asks "What will *he* do?" and this annoys the Minister. He gives Biju a lecture on modern science, and Biju defends himself by saying that not everything can be cured by science. As usual when they talk together for any length of time, the Minister gets more and more irritated with Biju. I can understand why. All the Minister's arguments are very sensible but Biju's aren't one bit sensible—in fact, after a while he stops answering altogether and instead begins to tear up the newspaper he has been reading and makes paper darts out of it. I watch him launching these darts. He looks very innocent while he is doing this, like a boy; he smiles to himself and his tie flutters over his shoulder. When people have a weak heart they can die quite suddenly, one has to expect it. I think of my old aunt asking where will you turn to? I look at the Minister. He too has begun to take an interest in Biju's paper darts. He picks one up and throws it into the air with a great swing of his body like a discus thrower; but it falls down on the carpet very lamely. He tries again and then again, always attempting this great sportsman's swing though not very successfully because he is so fat and heavy. It gives me pleasure to watch him; it also gives me pleasure to think of his strong heart like a fifteen-year-old boy's. There is a Persian poem. It says human life is like the petals that fall from the rose and lie soft and withering by the side of the vase. Whenever I think of this poem, I think of Biju and myself. But it is not possible to think of the Minister and Mina as rose petals. No, they are something much stronger. I'm glad! They are what I have to turn to, and it is enough for me. I need nothing more. My aunt was wrong.

TWO MORE UNDER
THE INDIAN SUN

Elizabeth had gone to spend the afternoon with Margaret. They were both English, but Margaret was a much older woman and they were also very different in character. But they were both in love with India, and it was this fact that drew them together. They sat on the veranda, and Margaret wrote letters and Elizabeth addressed the envelopes. Margaret always had letters to write; she led a busy life and was involved with several organizations of a charitable or spiritual nature. Her interests were centered in such matters, and Elizabeth was glad to be allowed to help her.

There were usually guests staying in Margaret's house. Sometimes they were complete strangers to her when they first arrived, but they tended to stay weeks, even months, at a time—holy men from the Himalayas, village welfare workers, organizers of conferences on spiritual welfare. She had one constant visitor throughout the winter, an elderly government officer who, on his retirement from service, had taken to a spiritual life and gone to live in the mountains at Almora. He did not, however, very much care for the winter cold up there, so at that season he came down to Delhi to stay with Margaret, who was always pleased to have him. He had a soothing effect on her—indeed, on anyone with whom he came into contact, for he had cast anger and all other bitter passions out of his heart and was consequently always smiling and serene. Everyone affectionately called him Babaji.

He sat now with the two ladies on the veranda, gently rocking himself to and fro in a rocking chair, enjoying the winter sunshine and the flowers in the garden and everything about him. His companions, however, were less serene. Margaret, in fact, was beginning to get angry with Elizabeth. This happened quite frequently, for Margaret tended to be quickly irritated, and especially with a meek and conciliatory person like Elizabeth.

"It's very selfish of you," Margaret said now.

Elizabeth flinched. Like many very unselfish people, she was always accusing herself of undue selfishness, so that whenever this accusation was made by someone else it touched her closely. But because it was not in her power to do what Margaret wanted, she compressed her lips and kept silent. She was pale with this effort at obstinacy.

"It's your duty to go," Margaret said. "I don't have much time for people who shirk their duty."

"I'm sorry, Margaret," Elizabeth said, utterly miserable, utterly ashamed. The worst of it, almost, was that she really wanted to go; there was nothing she would have enjoyed more. What she was required to do was take a party of little Tibetan orphans on a holiday treat to Agra and show them the Taj Mahal. Elizabeth loved children, she loved little trips and treats, and she loved the Taj Mahal. But she couldn't go, nor could she say why.

Of course Margaret very easily guessed why, and it irritated her more than ever. To challenge her friend, she said bluntly, "Your Raju can do without you for those few days. Good heavens, you're not a honeymoon couple, are you? You've been married long enough. Five years."

"Four," Elizabeth said in a humble voice.

"Four, then. I can hardly be expected to keep count of each wonderful day. Do you want me to speak to him?"

"Oh no."

"I will, you know. It's nothing to me. I won't mince my words." She gave a short, harsh laugh, challenging anyone to stop her from speaking out when occasion demanded. Indeed, at the thought of anyone doing so, her face grew red under her crop of gray hair, and a pulse throbbed in visible anger in her tough, tanned neck.

Elizabeth glanced imploringly toward Babaji. But he was rocking and smiling and looking with tender love at two birds pecking at something on the lawn.

"There are times when I can't help feeling you're afraid of him," Margaret said. She ignored Elizabeth's little disclaiming cry of horror. "There's no trust between you, no understanding. And married life is nothing if it's not based on the twin rocks of trust and understanding."

Babaji liked this phrase so much that he repeated it to himself several times, his lips moving soundlessly and his head nodding with approval.

"In everything I did," Margaret said, "Arthur was with me. He had complete faith in me. And in those days— Well." She chuckled. "A wife like me wasn't altogether a joke."

Her late husband had been a high-up British official, and in those British days he and Margaret had been expected to conform to some very strict social rules. But the idea of Margaret conforming to any rules, let alone those! Her friends nowadays often had a good laugh at it with her, and she had many stories to tell of how she had shocked and defied her fellow countrymen.

"It was people like you," Babaji said, "who first extended the hand of friendship to us."

"It wasn't a question of friendship, Babaji. It was a question of love."

"Ah!" he exclaimed.

"As soon as I came here—and I was only a chit of a girl, Arthur and I had been married just two months—yes, as soon as I set foot on Indian soil, I knew this was the place I belonged. It's funny isn't it? I don't suppose there's any rational explanation for it. But then, when was India ever the place for rational explanations."

Babaji said with gentle certainty, "In your last birth, you were one of us. You were an Indian."

"Yes, lots of people have told me that. Mind you, in the beginning it was quite a job to make them see it. Naturally, they were suspicious—can you blame them? It wasn't like today. I envy you girls married to Indians. You have a very easy time of it."

Elizabeth thought of the first time she had been taken to stay with Raju's family. She had met and married Raju in England, where he had gone for a year on a Commonwealth scholarship, and then had returned with him to Delhi; so it was some time before she met his family, who lived about two hundred miles out of Delhi, on the outskirts of a small town called Ankhpur. They all lived together in an ugly brick house, which was divided into two parts—one for the men of the family, the other for the women. Elizabeth, of course, had stayed in the women's quarters. She couldn't speak any Hindi and they spoke very little English, but they had not had much trouble communicating with her. They managed to make it clear at once that they thought her too ugly and too old for Raju (who was indeed some five years her junior), but also that they did not hold this against her and were ready to accept her, with all her shortcomings, as the will of God. They got a lot of amusement out of her, and she enjoyed being with them. They dressed and undressed her in new saris, and she smiled good-naturedly while they stood around her clapping their hands in wonder and doubling up with laughter. Various fertility ceremonies had been performed over her, and before she left she had been given her share of the family jewelry.

"Elizabeth," Margaret said, "if you're going to be so slow, I'd rather do them myself."

"Just these two left," Elizabeth said, bending more eagerly over the envelopes she was addressing.

"For all your marriage," Margaret said, "sometimes I wonder how much you do understand about this country. You live such a closed-in life."

"I'll just take these inside," Elizabeth said, picking up the envelopes and letters. She wanted to get away, not because she minded being told about her own wrong way of life but because she was afraid Margaret might start talking about Raju again.

It was cold inside, away from the sun. Margaret's house was old and massive, with thick stone walls, skylights instead of windows, and immensely high ceilings. It was designed to keep out the heat in summer, but it also sealed in the cold in winter and became like some cavernous underground fortress frozen through with the cold of earth and stone. A stale smell of rice, curry, and mango chutney was chilled into the air.

Elizabeth put the letters on Margaret's work table, which was in the drawing room. Besides the drawing room, there was a dining room, but every other room was a bedroom, each with its dressing room and bathroom attached. Sometimes Margaret had to put as many as three or four visitors into each bedroom, and on one occasion—this was when she had helped to organize a conference on Meditation as the Modern Curative—the drawing and dining rooms too had been converted into dormitories, with string cots and bedrolls laid out end to end. Margaret was not only an energetic and active person involved in many causes but she was also the soul of generosity, ever ready to throw open her house to any friend or acquaintance in need of shelter. She had thrown it open to Elizabeth and Raju three years ago, when they had had to vacate their rooms almost overnight because the landlord said he needed the accommodation for his relatives. Margaret had given them a whole suite—a bedroom and dressing room and bathroom—to themselves and they had had all their meals with her in the big dining room, where the table was always ready laid with white crockery plates, face down so as not to catch the dust, and a thick white tablecloth that got rather stained toward the end of the week. At first, Raju had been very grateful and had praised their hostess to the skies for her kind and generous character. But as the weeks wore on, and every day, day after day, two or three times a day, they sat with Margaret and whatever other guests she had around the table, eating alternately lentils and rice or string beans with boiled potatoes and beetroot salad, with Margaret always in her chair at the head of the table talking inexhaustibly about her activities and ideas—about Indian spirituality and the Mutiny and village uplift and the industrial revolution—Raju, who had a lot of ideas of his own and rather liked to talk, began to get restive. "But Madam, Madam," he would frequently say, half rising in his chair in his impatience to interrupt her, only to have to sit down again, unsatisfied, and continue with his dinner, because Margaret was too busy with her own ideas to have time to take in his.

Once he could not restrain himself. Margaret was talking about—Elizabeth had even forgotten what it was—was it the first Indian National Congress? At any rate, she said something that stirred Raju to such disagreement that this time he did not restrict himself to the hesitant appeal of "Madam" but said out loud for everyone to hear, "Nonsense, she is only talking nonsense." There was a moment's silence; then Margaret, sensible woman that she was, shut her eyes as a sign that she would not hear and would not see, and, repeating the sentence he had interrupted more firmly than before, continued her discourse on an even keel. It was the other two or three people sitting with them around the table—a Buddhist monk with a large shaved skull, a welfare worker, and a disciple of the Gandhian way of life wearing nothing but the homespun loincloth in which the Mahatma himself had always been so simply clad—it was they who had looked at Raju, and very, very gently one of them had clicked his tongue.

Raju had felt angry and humiliated, and afterward, when they were alone in their bedroom, he had quarreled about it with Elizabeth. In his excitement, he raised his voice higher than he would have if he had remembered that they were in someone else's house, and the noise of this must have disturbed Margaret, who suddenly stood in the doorway, looking at them. Unfortunately, it was just at the moment when Raju, in his anger and frustration, was pulling his wife's hair, and they both stood frozen in this attitude and stared back at Margaret. The next instant, of course, they had collected themselves, and Raju let go of Elizabeth's hair, and she pretended as best she could that all that was happening was that he was helping her comb it. But such a feeble subterfuge would not do before Margaret's penetrating eye, which she kept fixed on Raju, in total silence, for two disconcerting minutes; then she said, "We don't treat English girls that way," and withdrew, leaving the door open behind her as a warning that they were under observation. Raju shut it with a vicious kick. If they had had anywhere else to go, he would have moved out that instant.

Raju never came to see Margaret now. He was a proud person, who would never forget anything he considered a slight to his honor. Elizabeth always came on her own, as she had done today, to visit her friend. She sighed now as she arranged the letters on Margaret's work table; she was sad that this difference had arisen between her husband and her only friend, but she knew that there was nothing she could do about it. Raju was very obstinate. She shivered and rubbed the tops of her arms, goose-pimpled with the cold in that high, bleak room, and returned quickly to the veranda, which was flooded and warm with afternoon sun.

Babaji and Margaret were having a discussion on the relative merits of the three ways toward realization. They spoke of the way of knowledge, the way of action, and that of love. Margaret maintained that it was a matter of temperament, and that while she could appreciate the beauty of the other two ways, for herself there was no path nor could there ever be but that of action. It was her nature.

"Of course it is," Babaji said. "And God bless you for it."

"Arthur used to tease me. He'd say, 'Margaret was born to right all the wrongs of the world in one go.' But I can't help it. It's not in me to sit still when I see things to be done."

"Babaji," said Elizabeth, laughing, "once I saw her—it was during the monsoon, and the river had flooded and the people on the bank were being evacuated. But it wasn't being done quickly enough for Margaret! She waded into the water and came back with

someone's tin trunk on her head. All the people shouted, 'Memsahib, Memsahib! What are you doing?' but she didn't take a bit of
notice. She waded right back in again and came out with two rolls of
bedding, one under each arm.

Elizabeth went pink with laughter, and with pleasure and pride,
at recalling this incident. Margaret pretended to be angry and gave
her a playful slap, but she could not help smiling, while Babaji
clasped his hands in joy and opened his mouth wide in silent, ec-
static laughter.

Margaret shook her head with a last fond smile. "Yes, but I've
got into the most dreadful scrapes with this nature of mine. If I'd
been born with an ounce more patience, I'd have been a pleasanter
person to deal with and life could have been a lot smoother all
round. Don't you think so?"

She looked at Elizabeth, who said, "I love you just the way you
are."

But a moment later, Elizabeth wished she had not said this.
"Yes," Margaret took her up, "that's the trouble with you. You love
everybody just the way they are." Of course she was referring to
Raju. Elizabeth twisted her hands in her lap. These hands were
large and bony and usually red, although she was otherwise a pale
and rather frail person.

The more anyone twisted and squirmed, the less inclined was
Margaret to let them off the hook. Not because this afforded her any
pleasure but because she felt that facts of character must be faced
just as resolutely as any other kinds of fact. "Don't think you're
doing anyone a favor," she said, "by being so indulgent toward their
faults. Quite on the contrary. And especially in marriage," she went
on unwaveringly. "It's not mutual pampering that makes a marriage but mutual trust."

"Trust and understanding," Babaji said.

Elizabeth knew that there was not much of these in her marriage. She wasn't even sure how much Raju earned in his job at the
municipality (he was an engineer in the sanitation department), and
there was one drawer in their bedroom whose contents she didn't
know, for he always kept it locked and the key with him.

"I'll lend you a wonderful book," Margaret said. "It's called
Truth in the Mind, and it's full of the most astounding insight. It's by
this marvelous man who founded an ashram in Shropshire. Shafi!"
she called suddenly for the servant, but of course he couldn't hear,

because the servants' quarters were right at the back, and the old man now spent most of his time there, sitting on a bed and having his legs massaged by a granddaughter.

"I'll call him," Elizabeth said, and got up eagerly.

She went back into the stone-cold house and out again at the other end. Here were the kitchen and the crowded servant quarters. Margaret could never bear to dismiss anyone, and even the servants who were no longer in her employ continued to enjoy her hospitality. Each servant had a great number of dependents, so this part of the house was a little colony of its own, with a throng of people outside the rows of peeling hutments, chatting or sleeping or quarreling or squatting on the ground to cook their meals and wash their children. Margaret enjoyed coming out there, mostly to advise and scold—but Elizabeth felt shy, and she kept her eyes lowered.

"Shafi," she said, "Memsahib is calling you."

The old man mumbled furiously. He did not like to have his rest disturbed and he did not like Elizabeth. In fact, he did not like any of the visitors. He was the oldest servant in the house—so old that he had been Arthur's bearer when Arthur was still a bachelor and serving in the districts, almost forty years ago.

Still grumbling, he followed Elizabeth back to the veranda.

"Tea, Shafi!" Margaret called out cheerfully when she saw them coming.

"Not time for tea yet," he said.

She laughed. She loved it when her servants answered her back; she felt it showed a sense of ease and equality and family irritability, which was only another side of family devotion. "What a cross old man you are," she said. "And just look at you—how dirty."

He looked down at himself. He was indeed very dirty. He was unshaven and unwashed, and from beneath the rusty remains of what had once been a uniform coat there peeped out a ragged assortment of gray vests and torn pullovers into which he had bundled himself for the winter.

"It's hard to believe," Margaret said, "that this old scarecrow is a terrible, terrible snob. You know why he doesn't like you, Elizabeth? Because you're married to an Indian."

Elizabeth smiled and blushed. She admired Margaret's forthrightness.

"He thinks you've let down the side. He's got very firm principles. As a matter of fact, he thinks I've let down the side too. All his life he's longed to work for a real memsahib, the sort that entertains other memsahibs to tea. Never forgave Arthur for bringing home little Margaret."

The old man's face began working strangely. His mouth and stubbled cheeks twitched, and then sounds started coming that rose and fell—now distinct, now only a mutter and a drone—like waves of the sea. He spoke partly in English and partly in Hindi, and it was some time before it could be made out that he was telling some story of the old days—a party at the Gymkhana Club for which he had been hired as an additional waiter. The sahib who had given the party, a Major Waterford, had paid him not only his wages but also a tip of two rupees. He elaborated on this for some time, dwelling on the virtues of Major Waterford and also of Mrs. Waterford, a very fine lady who had made her servants wear white gloves when they served at table.

"Very grand," said Margaret with an easy laugh. "You run along now and get our tea."

"There was a little Missie sahib too. She had two ayahs, and every year they were given four saris and one shawl for the winter."

"Tea, Shafi," Margaret said more firmly, so that the old man, who knew every inflection in his mistress's voice, saw it was time to be off.

"Arthur and I've spoiled him outrageously," Margaret said. "We spoiled all our servants."

"God will reward you," said Babaji.

"We could never think of them as servants, really. They were more our friends. I've learned such a lot from Indian servants. They're usually rogues, but underneath all that they have beautiful characters. They're very religious, and they have a lot of philosophy—you'd be surprised. We've had some fascinating conversations. You ought to keep a servant, Elizabeth—I've told you so often." When she saw Elizabeth was about to answer something, she said, "And don't say you can't afford it. Your Raju earns enough, I'm sure, and they're very cheap."

"We don't need one," Elizabeth said apologetically. There were just the two of them, and they lived in two small rooms. Sometimes Raju also took it into his head that they needed a servant, and once he had even gone to the extent of hiring an undernourished little boy from the hills. On the second day, however, the boy was discovered rifling the pockets of Raju's trousers while their owner was having his bath, so he was dismissed on the spot. To Elizabeth's relief, no attempt at replacing him was ever made.

"If you had one you could get around a bit more," Margaret said. "Instead of always having to dance attendance on your husband's mealtimes. I suppose that's why you don't want to take those poor little children to Agra?"

"It's not that I don't want to," Elizabeth said hopelessly.

"Quite apart from anything else, you ought to be longing to get around and see the country. What do you know, what will you ever know, if you stay in one place all the time?"

"One day you will come and visit me in Almora," Babaji said.

"Oh Babaji, I'd love to!" Elizabeth exclaimed.

"Beautiful," he said, spreading his hands to describe it all. "The mountains, trees, clouds . . ." Words failed him, and he could only spread his hands farther and smile into the distance, as if he saw a beautiful vision there.

Elizabeth smiled with him. She saw it too, although she had never been there: the mighty mountains, the grandeur and the peace, the abode of Shiva where he sat with the rivers flowing from his hair. She longed to go, and to so many other places she had heard and read about. But the only place away from Delhi where she had ever been was Ankhpur, to stay with Raju's family.

Margaret began to tell about all the places she had been to. She and Arthur had been posted from district to district, in many different parts of the country, but even that hadn't been enough for her. She had to see everything. She had no fears about traveling on her own, and had spent weeks tramping around in the mountains, with a shawl thrown over her shoulders and a stick held firmly in her hand. She had traveled many miles by any mode of transport available—train, bus, cycle, rickshaw, or even bullock cart—in order to see some little-known and almost inaccessible temple or cave or tomb. Once she had sprained her ankle and lain all alone for a week in a derelict rest house, deserted except for one decrepit old watchman, who had shared his meals with her.

"That's the way to get to know the country," she declared. Her cheeks were flushed with the pleasure of remembering everything she had done.

Elizabeth agreed with her. Yet although she herself had done none of these things, she did not feel that she was on that account cut off from all knowledge. There was much to be learned from living with Raju's family in Ankhpur, much to be learned from Raju himself. Yes, he was her India! She felt like laughing when this thought came to her. But it was true.

"Your trouble is," Margaret suddenly said, "you let Raju bully you. He's got something of that in his character—don't contradict. I've studied him. If you were to stand up to him more firmly, you'd both be happier."

Again Elizabeth wanted to laugh. She thought of the nice times she and Raju often had together. He had invented a game of cricket that they could play in their bedroom between the steel almirah and the opposite wall. They played it with a rubber ball and a hairbrush, and three steps made a run. Raju's favorite trick was to hit the ball under the bed, and while she lay flat on the floor groping for it he made run after run, exhorting her with mocking cries of "Hurry up! Where is it? Can't you find it?" His eyes glittered with the pleasure of winning; his shirt was off, and drops of perspiration trickled down his smooth, dark chest.

"You should want to do something for those poor children!" Margaret shouted.

"I do want to. You know I do."

"I don't know anything of the sort. All I see is you leading an utterly useless, selfish life. I'm disappointed in you, Elizabeth. When I first met you, I had such high hopes of you. I thought, Ah, here at last is a serious person. But you're not serious at all. You're as frivolous as any of those girls that come here and spend their days playing mah-jongg."

Elizabeth was ashamed. The worst of it was she really had once been a serious person. She had been a schoolteacher in England, and devoted to her work and her children, on whom she had spent far more time and care than was necessary in the line of duty. And, over and above that, she had put in several evenings a week visiting old people who had no one to look after them. But all that had come to an end once she met Raju.

"It's criminal to be in India and not be committed," Margaret went on. "There isn't much any single person can do, of course, but to do nothing at all—no, I wouldn't be able to sleep at nights."

And Elizabeth slept not only well but happily, blissfully! Sometimes she turned on the light just for the pleasure of looking at Raju lying beside her. He slept like a child, with the pillow bundled under his cheek and his mouth slightly open, as if he were smiling.

193

"But what are you laughing at!" Margaret shouted.

"I'm not, Margaret." She hastily composed her face. She hadn't been aware of it, but probably she had been smiling at the image of Raju asleep.

Margaret abruptly pushed back her chair. Her face was red and her hair disheveled, as if she had been in a fight. Elizabeth half rose in her chair, aghast at whatever it was she had done and eager to undo it.

"Don't follow me," Margaret said. "If you do, I know I'm going to behave badly and I'll feel terrible afterward. You can stay here or you can go home, but *don't follow me."*

She went inside the house, and the screen door banged after her. Elizabeth sank down into her chair and looked helplessly at Babaji.

He had remained as serene as ever. Gently he rocked himself in his chair. The winter afternoon was drawing to its close, and the sun, caught between two trees, was beginning to contract into one concentrated area of gold. Though the light was failing, the garden remained bright and gay with all its marigolds, its phlox, its pansies, and its sweet peas. Babaji enjoyed it all. He sat wrapped in his woolen shawl, with his feet warm in thick knitted socks and sandals.

"She is a hot-tempered lady," he said, smiling and forgiving. "But good, good."

"Oh, I know," Elizabeth said. "She's an angel. I feel so bad that I should have upset her. Do you think I ought to go after her?"

"A heart of gold," said Babaji.

"I know it." Elizabeth bit her lip in vexation at herself.

Shafi came out with the tea tray. Elizabeth removed some books to clear the little table for him, and Babaji said, "Ah," in pleasurable anticipation. But Shafi did not put the tray down.

"Where is she?" he said.

"It's all right, Shafi. She's just coming. Put it down, please."

The old man nodded and smiled in a cunning, superior way. He clutched his tray more tightly and turned back into the house. He had difficulty in walking, not only because he was old and infirm but also because the shoes he wore were too big for him and had no laces.

"Shafi!" Elizabeth called after him. "Babaji wants his tea!" But he did not even turn around. He walked straight up to Margaret's bedroom and kicked the door and shouted, "I've brought it!"

Elizabeth hurried after him. She felt nervous about going into

Margaret's bedroom after having been so explicitly forbidden to follow her. But Margaret only looked up briefly from where she was sitting on her bed, reading a letter, and said, "Oh, it's you," and "Shut the door." When he had put down the tea, Shafi went out again and the two of them were left alone.

Margaret's bedroom was quite different from the rest of the house. The other rooms were all bare and cold, with a minimum of furniture standing around on the stone floors; there were a few isolated pictures hung up here and there on the whitewashed walls, but nothing more intimate than portraits of Mahatma Gandhi and Sri Ramakrishna and a photograph of the inmates of Mother Teresa's Home. But Margaret's room was crammed with a lot of comfortable, solid old furniture, dominated by the big double bed in the center, which was covered with a white bedcover and a mosquito curtain on the top like a canopy. A log fire burned in the grate, and there were photographs everywhere—family photos of Arthur and Margaret, of Margaret as a little girl, and of her parents and her sister and her school and her friends. The stale smell of food pervading the rest of the house stopped short of this room, which was scented very pleasantly by woodsmoke and lavender water. There was an umbrella stand that held several alpenstocks, a tennis racquet, and a hockey stick.

"It's from my sister," Margaret said, indicating the letter she was reading. "She lives out in the country and they've been snowed under again. She's got a pub."

"How lovely."

"Yes, its a lovely place. She's always wanted me to come and run it with her. But I couldn't live in England anymore, I couldn't bear it."

"Yes, I know what you mean."

"What do you know? You've only been here a few years. Pour the tea, there's a dear."

"Babaji was wanting a cup."

"To hell with Babaji."

She took off her sandals and lay down on the bed, leaning against some fat pillows that she had propped against the headboard. Elizabeth had noticed before that Margaret was always more relaxed in her own room than anywhere else. Not all her visitors were allowed into this room—in fact, only a chosen few. Strangely enough, Raju had been one of these when he and Elizabeth had stayed in the house. But he had never properly appreciated the privilege; either he sat on the edge of a chair and made signs to Elizabeth to go or he wandered restlessly around the room looking at all the photographs or taking out the tennis racquet and executing imaginary services with it; till Margaret told him to sit down and not make them all nervous, and then he looked sulky and made even more overt signs to Elizabeth.

"I brought my sister out here once," Margaret said. "But she couldn't stand it. Couldn't stand anything—the climate, the water, the food. Everything made her ill. There are people like that. Of course, I'm just the opposite. You like it here too, don't you?"

"Very, very much."

"Yes, I can see you're happy."

Margaret looked at her so keenly that Elizabeth tried to turn away her face slightly. She did not want anyone to see too much of her tremendous happiness. She felt somewhat ashamed of herself for having it—not only because she knew she didn't deserve it but also because she did not consider herself quite the right person to have it. She had been over thirty when she met Raju and had not expected much more out of life than had up till then been given to her.

Margaret lit a cigarette. She never smoked except in her own room. She puffed slowly, luxuriously. Suddenly she said, "He doesn't like me, does he?"

"Who?"

" 'Who?' " she repeated impatiently. "Your Raju, of course."

Elizabeth flushed with embarrassment. "How you talk, Margaret," she murmured deprecatingly, not knowing what else to say.

"I know he doesn't," Margaret said. "I can always tell."

She sounded so sad that Elizabeth wished she could lie to her and say that no, Raju loved her just as everyone else did. But she could not bring herself to it. She thought of the way he usually spoke of Margaret. He called her by rude names and made coarse jokes about her, at which he laughed like a schoolboy and tried to make Elizabeth laugh with him; and the terrible thing was sometimes she did laugh, not because she wanted to or because what he said amused her but because it was he who urged her to, and she always found it difficult to refuse him anything. Now when she thought of this compliant laughter of hers she was filled with anguish, and she began unconsciously to wring her hands, the way she always did at such secretly appalling moments.

But Margaret was having thoughts of her own, and was smiling

196

to herself. She said. "You know what was my happiest time of all in India? About ten years ago, when I went to stay in Swami Vishwananda's ashram."

Elizabeth was intensely relieved at the change of subject, though somewhat puzzled by its abruptness.

"We bathed in the river and we walked in the mountains. It was a time of such freedom, such joy. I've never felt like that before or since. I didn't have a care in the world and I felt so—light. I can't describe it—as if my feet didn't touch the ground."

"Yes, yes!" Elizabeth said eagerly, for she thought she recognized the feeling.

"In the evening we all sat with Swamiji. We talked about everything under the sun. He laughed and joked with us, and sometimes he sang. I don't know what happened to me when he sang. The tears came pouring down my face, but I was so happy I thought my heart would melt away."

"Yes," Elizabeth said again.

"That's him over there." She nodded toward a small framed photograph on the dressing table. Elizabeth picked it up. He did not look different from the rest of India's holy men—naked to the waist, with long hair and burning eyes.

"Not that you can tell much from a photo," Margaret said. She held out her hand for it, and then she looked at it herself, with a very young expression on her face. "He was such fun to be with, always full of jokes and games. When I was with him, I used to feel—I don't know—like a flower or a bird." She laughed gaily, and Elizabeth with her.

"Does Raju make you feel like that?"

Elizabeth stopped laughing and looked down into her lap. She tried to make her face very serious so as not to give herself away.

"Indian men have such marvelous eyes," Margaret said. "When they look at you, you can't help feeling all young and nice. But of course your Raju thinks I'm just a fat, ugly old memsahib."

"Margaret, Margaret!"

Margaret stubbed out her cigarette and, propelling herself with her heavy legs, swung down from the bed. "And there's poor old Babaji waiting for his tea."

She poured it for him and went out with the cup. Elizabeth went after her. Babaji was just as they had left him, except that now the sun, melting away between the trees behind him, was even more intensely gold and provided a heavenly background, as if to a saint in a picture, as he sat there at peace in his rocking chair.

Margaret fussed over him. She stirred his tea and she arranged his shawl more securely over his shoulders. Then she said, "I've got an idea, Babaji." She hooked her foot around a stool and drew it close to his chair and sank down on it, one hand laid on his knee. "You and I'll take those children up to Agra. Would you like that? A little trip?" She looked up into his face and was eager and bright. "We'll have a grand time. We'll hire a bus and we'll have singing and games all the way. You'll love it." She squeezed his knee in anticipatory joy, and he smiled at her and his thin old hand came down on the top of her head in a gesture of affection or blessing.

BOMBAY

$\mathcal{S}$ometimes the Uncle did not visit his niece for several days. He stayed in his bare, unventilated lodging and fed himself with food from the bazaar. Once, after such an absence, there was a new servant in the niece's house, who refused to let him in. "Not at home!" the servant said, viewing the Uncle with the utmost suspicion. And indeed who could blame him; certainly not the Uncle himself.

But Nargis, the niece, the mistress of the house, was annoyed—not with the servant but with her uncle. In any case, she was usually annoyed with him when he reappeared after one of his absences. It was resentment partly at his having stayed away, partly at his having reappeared.

"Look at you," she said. "Like a beggar. And I suppose you have been eating that dirty bazaar food again. Or no food at all."

She rang the bell and gave orders to a servant, who soon returned with refreshments. The Uncle enjoyed them; sometimes he did enjoy things in that house, though only if he and she were alone together.

That could never be for long. Khorshed, one of her unmarried sisters-in-laws, was soon with them, greeting the Uncle with the formal courtesy—a stately inclination of the head—that she extended to everyone. Since he was family, she also smiled at him. She had yellow teeth and was yellow all over; her skin was like thin old paper stretched over her bones. She sat in one of the winged armchairs by the window—her usual place, which enabled her to keep an eye on the road and anything that might be going on there. She entertained them with an account of a charity ball she had witnessed at the Taj Mahal Hotel the day before. Soon she was joined by her sister Pilla, who took the opposite armchair in order to see the other end of the road. They always shared a view between them in this way. They had done the same the day before at the Taj Mahal Hotel. They themselves had not bought tickets—it had not been one of their charities—but had taken up a vantage point on the velvet bench on the first landing of the double staircase. Khorshed had watched the people who had come up from the right-hand wing, and Pilla those from the left. Now they described who had been there, supplementing each other's account and sometimes arguing whether it had been Lady Ginwala who had worn a tussore silk or Mrs. Homy Jussawala. They quarreled over it ever so gently.

Rusi came in much later. He had only just got up. He always got up very late; he couldn't sleep at night, and moved around the house and played his record player at top volume. When he came in—in his brocade dressing gown and with his hair tousled—everyone in the room became alert and intense, though they tried to hide it. His two aunts bade him good morning in sweet fluting voices; his mother inquired after his breakfast. He ignored them all. He sank into a chair, scowling heavily and supporting his forehead on his hand, as if weighted down by thoughts too lofty for anyone there to understand.

"Look, look," said Pilla to create a diversion, "here she is again!"

"Where!" cried Khorshed, helping her sister.

"There. In *another* new sari. Walking like a princess—and they owe rent and bills everywhere."

"Just see—a new parasol too, matching the sari."

Both shook their heads. The boy, Rusi, took his hand from his brow, and his scowling eyes swept around the room and rested on the Uncle.

"Oh, back again," he said. "Thought we'd got rid of you." He gave one of his short, mad laughs.

"Yes," said the Uncle, "here you see me again. I had no food at home, so I came. Because of this," he said, patting his thin stomach.

"All dogs are like that," Rusi said. "Where there is food to be got, there they run. Have you heard of Pavlov? Of course not. You people are all so ignorant."

"Tell us, darling," said Nargis, his mother.

"Please teach us, Rusi darling," the aunts begged eagerly.

He relapsed into silence. He sat hunched in the chair and, drawing his feet out of his slippers, held them up one by one and studied them, wriggling the toes. He did this with great concentration, so that no one dared speak for fear of disturbing him.

The Uncle now forced himself to look at him. Every time he came here, it seemed to him that the boy had deteriorated further. Rusi had a shambling, flabby body, and though he was barely twenty his hair was beginning to fall out in handfuls. He was dreadful. The Uncle, instead of feeling sorry for this sick boy, hated him more than any other human being on earth. Rusi looked up. Their eyes met; the Uncle looked away. Rusi gave another of his laughs and said, "When Pavlov rang a bell, saliva came out of the dog's mouth." He tittered and pointed at the Uncle. "We don't even have to ring a bell! Khorshed, Pilla—look at him! Not even a bell!"

The women laughed with him, and so did the Uncle, though only after he caught his niece's eye and had read the imploring look there. Then it was not so difficult for him to join in; in fact, he wanted to.

Everyone always thought of the Uncle as a bachelor, but he had once been married. His wife had been dull and of a faded color, and soon he sent her back to her parents and went to live with his brother and with Nargis, the brother's daughter. The brother's wife had also been dull and faded; she did not have to be sent away, but died, leaving the two brothers alone with the girl. These three had lived together very happily in a tiny house with a tiny garden that had three banana plants and a papaya tree in it. This was in an outlying suburb of Bombay, with a lot of respectable neighbors who did not quite know what to make of the household. It included an ancient woman servant, who was sometimes deaf, sometimes dumb, sometimes both. Whatever the truth of her disability, it prevented her from communicating with anyone outside the house and quite often with anyone in it. The two brothers didn't work much, though Nargis's father was a journalist and the Uncle a lawyer. They only went out to practice their respective professions when money ran very low. Then Nargis's father made the rounds of the newspaper offices, and the Uncle sat outside the courts to draw up documents and write legal letters. The rest of the time, they stayed at home and amused Nargis. They were both musical, and one sang while the other accompanied him on the harmonium. The whole household kept very odd hours, and sometimes when they got excited over their music they stayed up all night and slept through the day, keeping the shutters closed. Then the neighbors, wondering whether something untoward had happened, stood outside the little house and peered through the banana plants, until at last, toward evening, the shutters would be thrown open and a brother would appear at each window, fresh and rested and smiling at the little crowd gathered outside.

Both were passionate readers of Persian poetry and Victorian poetry and prose. They taught Nargis everything they could, and since she was in any case not a keen scholar, there was no necessity to send her to school. Altogether they kept her so much to themselves that no one realized she was growing up, till one day, there she was—a lush fruit, suddenly and perfectly ready. The two brothers carried on as if nothing had happened—singing, reading poetry, amusing her to the best of their ability. They bought her all sorts of nice clothes too, and whatever jewelry they could afford, so that it became necessary for them to go out to work rather more frequently than in the past. Nargis's father began to accept commissions to write biographies of prominent members of their own Parsi community. He wrote these in an ornate, fulsome style, heaping all the ringing superlatives he had gathered from his Victorian readings onto these shrewd traders in slippers and round hats. In this way, he was commissioned to write a biography of the founder of the great commercial house of Paniwala & Sons. The present head of the house took a keen interest in the project and helped with researches into the family archives. Once he got so excited over the discovery of a document that he had himself driven to the little house in the suburb. That was how he first saw Nargis, and how he kept coming back again even after the biography had been printed and distributed.

Nargis had no objections to marrying him. He wasn't really old—in his late thirties—though he was already perfectly bald, with his head and face the same pale yellow color. His hands were pale too, and plump like a woman's, with perfectly kept fingernails. He was a very kind man—very kind and gentle—with a soft voice and soft ways. He wanted to do everything for Nargis. She moved into the family mansion with him and his two sisters and with his servants and the treasures he had bought from antique dealers all over Europe. Positions were found in the house of Paniwala for Nargis's father and the Uncle, so that they no longer had to go out in order to work but only to collect their checks. Everyone should have been happy, and no one was. The little house in the suburb died the way a tree dies and all its leaves drop off and the birds fly away. It was the old woman who felt the blight first and had herself taken to hospital to die there. Next, Nargis's father lay down with an ailment that soon carried him off. Then the Uncle moved out of the house and into his quarters in the city.

Nargis had once visited him there, to persuade him to come and live in the family mansion. He wouldn't hear of it. He also said, "Who asked you to come here?" He was quite angry. Her arrival had thrown the whole house—indeed, the whole neighborhood—into commotion. A crowd gathered around her large car parked outside, and some lay waiting on the stairs, and children even opened the door of his room to peep in at the grand lady who had come. He bared his teeth at them and made blood-curdling noises.

"Come," Nargis pleaded. She looked around the room, which was quite squalid, though it had a patterned marble floor and colored-glass panes set in a fan above the door. The house had once been a respectable merchant's dwelling, but now, like the whole neighborhood, it was fast turning into a slum.

"You needn't talk with anyone," she promised. "Only with me."

"And Khorshed?" he asked. "And Pilla?" He opened his mouth wide to laugh. He got great amusement out of the two sisters.

"Only with me."

He gave an imitation of Khorshed and Pilla looking out of the window. Then he laughed at his joke. He jumped up and cackled and hopped up and down on one foot with amusement.

"You haven't come for four days," she accused him, above this.

He pretended not to hear, and went on laughing and hopping.

"What's wrong? Why not?" she persisted. "Don't you want to see me?"

"How is Paniwala?"

"He says bring Uncle. Get the big room upstairs ready. Send a car for him."

"Oh go away," he said, his laughter suddenly gone. "Leave me alone."

She wouldn't. Usually complaisant, even phlegmatic, she became quite obstinate. She sat on his rickety string bed and folded her hands in her lap. She said if he wasn't coming, then she was staying. She wouldn't move till he had promised that, even if he

203

wouldn't go and live in the house, he would visit there every day. Then at last she consented to be led back to her car. He went in front, clearing a way for her by poking his stick at all the sightseers.

He kept his promise for a while and went to the house every day. But he was always glad to come back home again. He walked up and down in the bazaar, looking at the stalls and the people, and then he sat outside the sweetmeat seller's and had tea and milk sweets and read out of his little volume of Sufi poetry. Sometimes he was so stirred that he read out loud for the benefit of the other customers and passersby, even though they couldn't understand Persian:

> "When you lay me in my grave,
> don't say, 'Farewell, farewell.'
> For the grave is a screen hiding the
> cheers and welcome of the
> people of Paradise.
> Which seed was cast but did not
> sprout?
> And why should it be otherwise for
> the seed of man?
> Which bucket went down but
> came not up full of water?"

Then it seemed to him that everything had become suffused in purity and brightness—yes, even this bazaar where people haggled and made money and passed away the time in idle, worldly pursuits. He walked slowly home and up the wooden stairs, which were so dark (he often reproached the landlady) that one could fall and break one's neck. He went past the common lavatory and the door of the paralytic landlady, which was left open so that she could look out. He sat by the open window in his room, looking at the bright stars above and the bright street below, and couldn't sleep for hours because of feeling so good.

In the Paniwala house, it always seemed to be mealtime. A great deal of food was cooked. Paniwala himself could only eat very bland boiled food, on account of his weak digestion. Khorshed had a taste for continental food masked in cheese sauces, while for Pilla a meal was not a meal if it was not rice with various curries of fish and meat and a great number of spicy side dishes. Servants passed around the table with dishes catering to all these various tastes. The sideboard that ran the length of the wall carried more dishes under silver covers, and there were pyramids of fruits, bought fresh every morning, that were so polished and immaculate that they appeared artificial. The meals lasted for hours. Plates kept getting changed and everyone chewed very slowly, and it got hotter and hotter, so that the Uncle, eating all he could, felt as if he were in a fever. The sisters talked endlessly, but their conversation seemed an activity indistinguishable from masticating. By the time the meal was over, the Uncle felt his mind and body bathed in perspiration, and in this state he had to retire with them into the drawing room, where sleep overtook everyone except Nargis and himself. The afternoon light that filtered through the slatted blinds made the room green and dim like an ocean bed; and uncle and niece sat staring at each other among the marble busts and potted plants, while the snores of the sleeping family lapped around them.

Once, as they sat like that, the Uncle saw tears oozing out of Nargis's eyes. It took him some time to realize they *were* tears—he stared at her as they dropped—and then he said in exasperation, "But what do you want?"

"Come and live here."

"No!" he cried like a drowning man.

All that had been a long time ago, before Rusi was born. After that event, although the Uncle continued to live in his slum house and the Paniwala family continued to eat their succession of meals, there was a change in both establishments. During one very heavy Bombay monsoon, an upper balcony of the Uncle's house collapsed and the whole tenement suffered a severe shock, so that the cracks on the staircase walls gaped wider and plaster fell in flakes from the ceilings. What remained of the colored windowpanes dropped out, and some were replaced with plain glass and some with cardboard and some were simply forgotten till more rain came. Also, in the same year as this heavy monsoon, the Uncle's skin began to discolor. This was not unexpected; leukoderma was a family disease and, indeed, very prevalent in the Parsi community. The Uncle first noticed the small telltale spot on his thumb. Of course, the affliction continued to spread and then the spots broke out all over him like mildew, so that within a few years he was completely discolored. It was neither a painful nor a dangerous disease, only disfiguring.

The change in the Paniwala family was both more positive and more far-reaching. Somehow no one had expected any offspring, so that when Rusi nevertheless appeared, everyone was too excited to notice that his head was rather big or that it took him a long time to sit up. He was three before he could walk. "Let him take his time," they all said, and his slowness became a virtue, like the growth of a very special flower that one must wait upon to unfold. Only the Uncle did not much like to look at him. Rusi was always the center around which the rest of the family was, quite literally, grouped. With his big head shaking, he tottered around on the carpet making guttural sounds, while they formed a smiling circle around him, encouraging him, calling his name, reciting long-forgotten baby rhymes, holding out loving fingers for him to steady himself on. They nodded at each other, and their soft, yellow, middle-aged faces beamed. And Nargis was one of them. The Uncle did not, as far as he could help it, look at the child; he looked at her. She had changed. Motherhood had ripened and extended her, and she was almost fat. But it suited her, and her eyes, which had once been tender and misty and shining as if through a veil, were now luminous with fulfillment. They never looked at the Uncle—only at her son.

The Uncle tried staying away. At first he thought he liked it. He sat for hours outside the sweetmeat seller's and read and talked to everyone who had time. He also talked to the people who lived in the tenement with him—especially with the paralytic landlady. She had as much time as he did. She had spent over twenty years lying on her bed, looking out of the open door at the people going up and down on the stairs. Sometimes he went in and sat with her and listened to her reflections on the transient stream of humanity flowing past her door. She was a student of palmistry and astrology and was always keen to tell his fortune. She grasped his discolored hand and studied it very earnestly and ignored his jokes about how the only fortune still left to him was the further fading of his pigmentation. She traced the lines of his palm and said she still saw a lot of beautiful living left. Then he turned the joke and said, "What about you?" Quite seriously, she stretched out her palm and interpreted its lines, and they too, it seemed, were as full of promise as a freshly sown field.

However long he stayed away now, Nargis never came to visit him or sent him any messages. If he wanted to see her, he had to present himself there. When he did, she rarely seemed pleased. His clothes were very shabby—he only possessed two shirts and two patched trousers, and never renewed them till they were past all wear—but whereas before Rusi's birth Nargis had taken his appearance entirely for granted, now she often asked him, "Why do you come like that? How do you think it looks?" He feigned surprise and looked down at himself with an innocent expression. She was not amused. Once she even lost her temper and shouted at him that if he did not have enough money to buy clothes, then please take it from her; she said she would be glad to give it to him. Of course, he did have enough, as she knew; his checks came in regularly. Suddenly she became more angry and pulled out some rupee notes and flung them at his feet and rushed out of the room. There was a moment's silence; everyone was surprised, for she was usually so calm. Then one of the sisters bent down to pick up the money, gently clicking her tongue as she did so.

"She is upset," she said.

"Yes, because of Rusi," said the other sister.

"He had a little tummy trouble last night."

"Naturally, she is upset."

"Naturally."

"A mother . . ."

"Of course."

They went on like that, like a purling, soothing stream. They did this partly to cover up for Nargis, and partly for him, so that he might have time to collect himself. Although he sat quite still and with his gaze lowered to the carpet, he was trembling from head to foot. After a time, ignoring the sisters, he got up to leave. He walked very slowly down the stairs and was about to let himself out when Nargis called to him. He looked up. She was leaning over the curved banister with Rusi, whom she was dancing up and down in her arms. "Ask Uncle to come up and play with us!" she told Rusi. "Say, 'Please, Uncle! Please, Uncle dear!'" For reply, Rusi opened his mouth wide and screamed. The Uncle did not look up again but continued his way toward the front door, which a servant was holding open for him. Nargis called down loudly, "Where are you going?"

At that the child was beside himself. His face went purple and his mouth was stretched open as wide as it would go, but no screams came out. This made him more frantic, and he caught his fingers in his mother's hair, pulling it out of its pins, and then flailed his hands against her breasts. He was only three years old but as strong as a demon. She fell to the floor with him on top of her. The Uncle ran up the stairs as fast as he could. He tried to help her up, tugging at her from under the child, who now began to flail his fists at the Uncle.

"Yes yes, I'm all right," Nargis said, to reassure them both. She managed to sit up; her hair was about her shoulders and there were scratches on her face. "Where are you going?" she asked the Uncle.

"I'm not going," he said. "I'm here. Can't you see?" he shouted, "I'm here! Here!" very loudly, in order to make himself heard above the child's screams.

As Rusi grew up, it was decided that he was too brilliant. He did too much thinking. His mother and aunts were disturbed to see him sitting scowling and hunched in an armchair, sunk in deep processes of thought. Occasionally he would emerge with some fragment dredged up from that profundity. "There will be a series of natural disasters due to the explosion of hitherto undiscovered minerals from under the earth's surface," he might say. He would fix his aunts with his brooding eyes and say, "You look out." Then they became very disturbed—not because of his prophecy but because they feared the damage so much mental activity might do his brain. They would try to bring him some distraction—share some exciting piece of news with him regarding a wedding or a tea party, or feed him some sweet thing that he liked. Sometimes he accepted their offering graciously, sometimes not. He was unpredictable, though very passionate in his likes and dislikes.

The person to whom Rusi took the deepest dislike was the Uncle. He baited him mercilessly and had all sorts of unpleasant names for him. The one he used most frequently was the Leper, on account of the Uncle's skin disease. Sometimes he said he could not bear to be in the house with him and that either the Uncle or he himself must leave. Then the Uncle would leave. Next time he came, Rusi might be quite friendly to him—it was impossible to tell. The Uncle tried not to mind either way, and the rest of the family did all they could to make it up to him. At least Paniwala and his sisters did; Nargis was more unpredictable. Sometimes, when Rusi had been very harsh, she would follow the Uncle to the door and be very nice to him, but other times she would encourage Rusi and clap her hands and laugh loudly in applause and then jeer when the Uncle got up to go away. On such occasions, the Uncle did not take the train or bus but walked all the way home through the city in the hope of tiring himself out. He never did, though, but lay awake half the night, saying to himself over and over, "Now enough, now enough." Then he thought of the landlady downstairs eagerly reading in his palm that great things were still in store for him. It made him laugh, for he was in his seventies now.

Rusi ordered a lot of books, though he did not do much reading. His aunts said he didn't have to, because he had it all in his head already. For the same reason, there was not much point in his going to school; he only quarreled with the teachers, who were very ignorant and not at all up to his standards. In all the schools he tried, everyone eventually agreed that it would be better for him to leave. Then came a succession of private tutors, but here too there was the same trouble—there was just no one who knew as much as he did. Those who did not leave quite soon of their own accord had to be told to go, because their inferior qualities made him take such a dislike to them. Once he got so angry with one of them that he stabbed him with a penknife. Although everyone was disturbed by this incident, still no one said anything beyond what they always said: the boy was too highly strung. It came, his aunts explained, from having too active a mind. They recommended more protein in his diet and some supplementary vitamin pills. Nargis listened to them eagerly and went out to buy the pills. The three women tried to coax him to take them, but he laughed in derision and told them how he had a method, evolved by himself, of storing extra energy in his body through his own mineral deposits. He had plans to patent this method and expected to make a large fortune out of it. The aunts shook their heads behind his back and tapped their foreheads to indicate that he had too much brilliance for his own good. When he looked at them, they changed their expression, to appear as interested and intelligent as possible. He said that they were a couple of foolish old women who understood nothing, so what was the use of talking to them; the only person in the house who might understand something of what he was saying was his father, who was going to put up the money for the project.

His father was not seen very much in the house nowadays. It seemed he was very busy in the office and spent almost all his time there. Weeks passed when the Uncle did not meet him at all. When he did, he found him more gentle than ever, but there was something furtive about him now and he did not like to meet anyone's eye. If he was present while Rusi was baiting the Uncle, he tried to remonstrate. He said, "Rusi, Rusi," but so softly that his son probably failed to hear him. After a while, he would get up and quietly leave the room and not come back. Once, though, when this happened, the Uncle found him waiting for him downstairs by the door. "One moment," Paniwala said and drew him into his study; he pressed the Uncle's hand as he did so. The Uncle wondered what he was going to say, and he waited and Paniwala also waited. A gold clock could be heard ticking in a very refined way.

When Paniwala at last did speak, it was on an unexpected subject. He informed the Uncle that the oil painting on the wall above his desk—it was of the Paniwala ancestor who had founded their fortune—was not done from life but had been copied from a photograph. Even the photograph was the only one of him known to be in existence; he had not been a man who could be induced to pose very often in a photographer's studio.

"He came to Bombay from a village near Surat," Paniwala said. "To the end of his days, what he relished most was the simple village food of chapati and pickle. He built this house with many bathrooms, but still he liked to take his bath in a bucket out in the garden, thereby also watering the plants."

Paniwala chuckled, and both of them looked up at the portrait, which showed a shriveled face with a big bony Parsi nose sticking out of it. Paniwala also had a big nose, but his was not bony; it was soft and fleshy. Altogether he looked very different from his ancestor, being very much softer and gentler in the contours of his face and in expression.

"He was a very strict man," Paniwala said. "With himself and also with others. Everyone had to work hard, no slacking allowed. My grandfather also got his discipline from him. Yes, in those days they were different men—a different breed of men." He passed his hands over his totally bald head. When he spoke again, it was to say, "Your expenses must have gone up; money is not what it was. I wonder if your check . . . You'll excuse me." He lowered his eyes.

The Uncle waved his hand in a gesture that could mean anything.

"You'll allow me," said Paniwala, terribly ashamed. "From the first of next month. Thank you. The little house where he was born, near Surat, is still there. It is so small you would not believe that the whole family lived there. There were nine children, and all grew up healthy and well. Later he brought his brothers and brothers-in-laws to Bombay, and everyone did well and they too had large families . . . You are going? No, you must take one of the cars—what are they all standing there for? Allow me." But the Uncle wanted to walk, so Paniwala escorted him to the door. He told him how his grandfather had always insisted on walking to the warehouse, even when he was very old and quite unsteady, so that the family had made arrangements for a carriage and an attendant to follow him secretly.

The two sisters also often spoke about their family—not about past generations but about the present one. They were always visiting relatives, many of whom were bedridden, and then they would come home and discuss the case. Sometimes they predicted an early end, but this rarely came to pass. The family tended to be very long-lived, and though crippled by a variety of diseases, the invalids lingered on for years and years. They stayed in their mahogany bedsteads and were fed and washed by servants. There was also an imbecile called Poor Falli, who had lived in the same Edwardian house for over fifty years, though confined to one room with bars on the windows; he was not dangerous, but his personal habits made it difficult for other people. The two sisters spoke about all these family matters quite openly now before the Uncle. It had not always been so. True, they had always been scrupulously polite to him—ignoring his shabby clothes, calling him by his first name, never omitting a greeting to him on entering or leaving a room—but he had remained an outsider. Nor had they forgotten the difference between his family and theirs. But as the years passed they regarded him more and more as one of themselves. This happened not all at once, but gradually, and only after Rusi's birth—an event, in the eyes of the sisters, that had finally drawn the two families together and made them as one.

The Uncle fell ill with fever. He lay in his room, tossing on his string bed, which had no sheets but only a cotton mat and a little pillow hard as a stone. Neighbors came in and, because he was shivering so much, covered him with a blanket and tried to make him drink milk and soup. He let them do whatever was necessary. His body felt as if it were being broken up bone by bone by someone wielding a stone hammer. He wondered whether he was going to die now. All the time he was smiling—not outwardly, for he groaned and cried out so much that the neighbors were very worried and sent messages to the Paniwala house, but inside himself. Sometimes he thought he was at the sweetmeat seller's, sometimes he saw himself back in the little house in the suburb with his brother and the old woman and Nargis ripening like a fruit in sunshine. It didn't matter in which of these places he fancied himself, for they were both wonderful, a foretaste of Paradise. He thought if he were really going to die now, he would never need to return to the Paniwala house at all. When he thought of this, tears welled into his eyes and flowed down his cheeks, so that the neighbors exclaimed in pity.

When Nargis came, he was better. The fever had abated and he lay exhausted. He had not died and yet he felt dead, as if everything were spent. Nargis wasted no time. She paid what was left of his rent and reimbursed the neighbors. They helped her pack up his things. He kept wanting to say no, but he didn't have the strength. Instead he wept again; only now the tears were cold and hard. The neighbors, not seeing the difference, told Nargis that he had been weeping like that all through his sickness, and when she heard this, she also wept. At last he was carried down the stairs, and as they passed the door of the paralytic landlady, she called out to him in triumph, "You see! It has come true what I said! It was all written in your hand."

Sometimes, as he lay in the large four-poster in the Paniwala bedroom, he looked at his hand and wondered which were the lines that had told the landlady about the new life awaiting him. It was very still and quiet in that room. He gazed at the painting on the opposite wall; it had been specially commissioned and showed a scene in the Paniwala counting house at the beginning of the century. The Paniwala founder sat at a desk high up on a dais, and his sons at other desks on a slightly lower dais, and they overlooked a hall full of clerks sitting cross-legged in rows and writing in ledgers. It had been done in dark, murky colors, to look like a Renaissance painting. When he was tired of it, he looked at the other wall, where there was a window and the top of a tree just showing against it. Nargis had engaged a servant for him, who made his bed and washed him and performed other personal functions. Khorshed and Pilla came in at least once a day and sat on either side of him and told him everything that was happening, in the family and in

212

Bombay society in general. Rusi also came in; he had been warned to be good to his uncle, and for quite some time he observed this injunction. But as the weeks and then the months passed and the Uncle still lay there, Rusi could not help himself and reverted to his former manner. He was especially gleeful if he happened to come in while the Uncle was being fed. This had to be done very carefully and with a specially curved spoon, and even then quite a lot went to waste and trickled down the Uncle's chin.

It was usually his servant who fed the Uncle, but sometimes Nargis did it herself. Although she was less satisfactory than the servant and got impatient quite quickly, the Uncle much preferred her to do it. Then he would linger over his food as long as possible. Then Rusi could stand there and say what he liked—the Uncle didn't care at all. He just looked into Nargis's face. She always sat with her back to the window and the tree. Even when she got annoyed with him—saying, "You are doing it on purpose,"when the food dropped on his chin—still he loved to have her sitting there. At such times it seemed to him that his landlady had been right and that his life was not over by any means.

ON BAIL

Although I get tired working in the shop all day, once I reach home I forget all about it. I change into an old cotton sari and tuck it around my waist and I sing as I cook. Sometimes he is at home but not often, and usually only if he is sick with a cold. What a fuss he makes then; I have to take his temperature many times and prepare hot drinks and crush pills in honey and altogether feel very sorry for him. That's the best time, especially since he forgets quite soon about being sick and wants to amuse himself and me. How we laugh then, what a fine time we have! He doesn't seem to miss his friends and coffeehouses and all those places one bit but is as happy to be at home with me as I am to be with him. Next evening, of course, he is off again, but I don't mind, for I know it's necessary—not only because he is a very sociable person but because it is for business contacts too.

I'm used to waiting up for him quite late, so I was not worried that night at all. When my cooking was finished, I sat at the table waiting for him. I love these hours; it is silent and peaceful and the clock ticks and I have many pleasant thoughts. I know that soon I will hear his step on the stairs, and the door will open and he will be there. I smile to myself, sitting there at the table with my head supported on my hand, full of drowsy thoughts. Sometimes I nod off and those thoughts turn into dreams on the same subject. But I always start up at the sound of his steps—only *his* steps, because that night Daddy was already in the room, calling my name, before I woke up. Then I jumped to my feet. I knew something terrible had happened.

When Daddy said that Rajee had been arrested, I sank down again onto my chair. I couldn't stand, I couldn't speak. Daddy thought it was with shock, but of course it was out of relief. I had imagined far worse. It took me some time to realize that this too was very bad. I knew Daddy thought it was the worst thing there could be. He was so badly affected that I had to make him lie down while I prepared tea for him. I also served him the meal I had cooked for Rajee and myself. Daddy ate both our portions. Now that he is old, he seems to need a great deal of food and is always ready to eat at any hour, whatever his state of mind may be.

But when he had finished this time, he became very upset again. He pushed away the dish and said, "Yes, yes, yes, I knew how it would be."

Of course, this was no time to start defending Rajee. In any case, I have long stopped doing so. I know it isn't so much Rajee that Daddy doesn't like but the fact that I'm married to him and have not become any of the grand things Daddy wanted.

"A case of cheating and impersonation," Daddy said now. "A criminal case."

I cried, "But where is he?"

"In jail! In prison! Jail!"

Daddy moaned, and so did I. I thought of Rajee sitting in a cell. I could see him sitting there and the expression on his face. I put my head down on the table and sobbed. I could not stop.

After a while Daddy began to pat my back. He didn't know what else to do; unlike Rajee, he has never been good at comforting people. I wiped my eyes and said as steadily as I could, "What about bail?"

That made Daddy excited again; he cried, "Five thousand rupees! Where should we take it from?"

No, we didn't have five thousand rupees. Daddy only had his pension, and Rajee and I only had my salary from the shop. Again I saw Rajee sitting there, but I quickly shut my eyes against this unbearable vision.

I made Daddy comfortable on our bed and told him I would be back soon. He wanted to know where I was going. He asked how I could go alone in the streets at this time of night, but he was too tired to protest much. I think he was already asleep when I left. I had to walk all the way through the empty streets. I wasn't frightened, although there had lately been some bad cases in the newspapers of women being attacked. I had other things to think about, and chief among them at the moment was how I could wake up

Sudha without waking the rest of her household. But this turned out to be no problem at all, because it was she who came to the door as soon as I knocked. I think she hadn't gone to sleep yet, although it was two o'clock in the morning. No one else stirred in the house.

When I told her, she had a dreadful shock. I think she had the same vision of him that I had. I put out my hand to touch her, but she pushed me away. The expression of pain on her face turned to one of anger. She said, "Why do you come here? What should I do?" Of course she knew what it was I wanted. She said, "I haven't got it." Then she shouted, "Do you know how long I haven't seen him! How many days!"

I looked around nervously, and she laughed. She said, "Don't worry. He wouldn't wake up if the house fell down." She was right; I could hear her husband snoring, with those fat sounds fat people make in their sleep. "Listen," she said. "It's the same every night. He eats his meal and then—" She imitated the snoring sounds. "And I can't sleep. I walk round the house, thinking. Does Rajee talk about me to you? What does he say?"

I didn't know what to answer. I had already suspected that Rajee did not like to be with her as much as before, but I didn't want to hurt her feelings. Also, this was not the time to talk about it. I had to have the money from her. I had to. There was no other way.

When I said nothing, her face became hard. She and I have known each other for a long time—we were at college together—but I have always been a bit afraid of her. She is a very passionate person. "Go!" she said to me now, and her voice was hard. "How dare you come here? Aren't you ashamed?"

"Where else can I go?"

We were silent. Her husband snored.

I said, "I had cooked fish curry for him tonight, he loves it so much. Do you think they gave him anything to eat there? You know how particular he is about his food."

She shrugged, like someone to whom this is of no concern. But I knew these were not her true feelings, so I continued. "Will he be able to sleep? I don't know if they give beds. Perhaps there are other people with him in the cell—bad characters. I've heard there are many people who share each cell, there is such overcrowding nowadays. And there are no facilities for them, only one bucket, and they take away their belts and shoelaces, because they are afraid that—"

"Be quiet!"

She went out of the room, stumbling over a footstool in her hurry. I could hear her in the bedroom, rattling keys and banging drawers. She took absolutely no care about making a noise, but the sounds from her husband went on undisturbed. I waited for her. I didn't like being here. The room was furnished with costly things, but they were not in good taste. I have always disliked coming here. The atmosphere is not good, probably because she and her husband don't like each other.

At last she came back. She didn't have cash, but she gave me some jewelry. She had wrapped it in a cloth, which she thrust into my hands. Then she said, "Go, go, go," but that was not necessary, for I was already on my way out.

Rajee came home the next evening. I wished we could have been alone, but Daddy and Sudha were also there. Rajee smiled at them, but they both averted their eyes from him and then his smile faded. He didn't know what to say. Neither did I.

Rajee is so good-humored and sociable that he hates it when the atmosphere is like that, and he feels he has to do something to cheer everyone up again. He rubbed his hands and said, "Nice to be home," in a cheerful, smiling voice.

Sudha shot him a burning look. Her eyes are already large enough, but they look even larger because of the kohl with which she outlines them.

"North, South, East, West, home is best," Rajee said.

"Fool! Idiot!" Sudha screamed.

There was a silence, in which we seemed to be listening to the echo of this scream. Then Rajee said, "Please let me explain."

"What is there to explain?" Daddy said. "Cheating, impersonation—"

"A mistake," Rajee said.

They were silent in a rather grim way, as if waiting to hear what he had to say. He cleared his throat a few times and spread his hands and began a long story. It was very involved and got more and more so as he went on. It was all about some man he had met in the coffeehouse who had seemed an honest, decent person but had turned out not to be so. It was he who had drawn Rajee into this deal, which also had turned out not to be as honest and decent as Rajee had thought. I didn't listen very carefully; I was watching the two others to see what impression he was making on them. Rajee too was watching them, and every now and again he stopped to scan their faces, and then he ran his tongue over his lips and went on talking faster. He didn't once look at me, though; he knew it didn't make any difference to me what he said, because I was on his side anyway.

Rajee is a very good talker, and I could see that Sudha and Daddy were wavering. But of course they weren't happy yet, and they continued to sit there with very glum faces. So then Rajee, sincerely anxious to cheer them up, said to me, "How about some tea? And a few biscuits, if you have any?" He smiled and winked at me, and I also smiled and went away to make the tea.

When I came back, Daddy was arguing with Rajee. Daddy was saying, "But is this the way to do business? In a coffeehouse, with strangers, is this the way to make a living?" Rajee was proving to him that it was. He told him all big deals were made this way. He gave him a lot of examples of fortunes that had been made just by two or three people meeting by chance—how apartment houses had been bought and sold, and a new sugar mill set up with all imported machinery by special government license. It was all a matter of luck and skill and being there at the right time. I knew all these stories, for Rajee had told them to me many times. He loves telling them and thinking about them; they are his inspiration in life. It is because of them, I think, that he gets up in such good humor every day and hums to himself while shaving and dresses up smartly and goes out with a shining, smiling face.

But Daddy remained glum. It is not in his nature to believe such stories. He is retired now, but all through his working life he never got up in good humor or ever went to his office with high expectations. All he ever expected was his salary, and afterward his pension, and that is all he ever got.

"Do you know about Verma Electricals, how they started—have you any idea?" Rajee said, flushed with excitement. But Daddy said, "It would be better to get some regular job."

Rajee smiled politely. He could have pointed out—only he didn't, because he is always very careful of people's feelings—that the entire salary that Daddy had earned throughout his thirty-five years of government service was less than Rajee can expect to make out of one of his deals.

Now Daddy started to get excited. His lips trembled and his hands fumbled about in the air. He said, "If you— Then she—

she—she—" He pointed at me with a shaking finger. We all knew what he meant. If Rajee got a job, then I wouldn't have to go to work in the shop.

I said, "I like it."

Daddy got more excited. He stammered and his hands waved frantically in the air as if they were searching for the words that wouldn't come to him. Rajee tried to soothe him. He kept saying, "Please, Daddy." He was afraid for his heart.

And, indeed, Daddy's hands suddenly left off fumbling in the air and clutched his side instead. He must have got one of his tremors. He started whimpering like a child. Rajee jumped up and kept saying, "Oh my goodness." He took Daddy's arm to lead him to our sofa and make him lie down there. Rajee said several times, "Now keep quite calm," but in fact it was he who was the most excited.

I got Daddy's pills and Sudha got water and Rajee ran for pillows. Daddy lay on the sofa, with his eyes shut. He looked quite exhausted, as if he didn't want to say or think anything more. Rajee kept fussing over him, but after a time there was nothing more to be done. Daddy was all right and fast asleep. Rajee said to me, "Sit with him." I took a cane stool and sat by the sofa holding Daddy's hand.

But I wasn't thinking of him, I was watching the other two. There was going to be a big scene between them, I knew. Rajee also knew it, and he was very uncomfortable. Sudha lounged in a chair in the middle of the room, with her legs stretched out before her under her sari. She was wearing a brilliant emerald silk sari and gold-and-diamond earrings. She seemed too large and too splendid for our little room. Everything in the room appeared very shabby—the old black oilcloth sofa with the white cotton stuffing bulging out where the material has split; the rickety little table with the cane unwinding like apple peel from the legs; last year's free calendar hanging from a nail on the wall, which hasn't been whitewashed for a long time. I only notice these things when she is here. She makes everything look shabby—me included. Only Rajee matches up to her. Even now, after a night in jail, he looked plump and prosperous, and he shone the way she did.

He was waiting for her to say something, but she only looked at him from under her big lids, half lowered over her big eyes. It seemed she was waiting for him to speak first. He started telling her about Daddy's heart—about the attack last year and how careful we have had to be since then and how we always keep his pills handy. Suddenly she interrupted him. She did this in a strange way—by clutching the top part of her sari and pulling it down from her breasts. She commanded, "Look!"

What was he to look at? At her big breasts that swelled from out of her low-cut blouse? Modestly—because of Daddy and me being in the room—he lowered his eyes, but she repeated, "Look, look," in an impatient voice. She struck her hand against her bared throat.

"Your necklace," he murmured uncomfortably.

She threw a savage look in my direction, so that I felt I had to defend myself. I said to Rajee, "Where else could I get it from? Five thousand!"

He shook his head, as if rebuking me. This infuriated her, and she began to shout at me. She cried, "Yes, you should have left him there in jail where he belongs!"

"Sh-h-h, sh-h-h," said Rajee, afraid she might wake up Daddy.

She lowered her voice but went on with the same fury. "It's the place where you belong. Because you are not only a cheat but a thief also. Can you deny it? Try. Say, 'No, I'm not a thief.' No? Then what about that time in my house?" She turned to me. "I never told you, but now I will show you what sort of a person you are married to."

I didn't look at her but stared straight in front of me.

"I'll make him tell you himself. Tell her!" she ordered him, but the next moment she was shouting, "The servant caught him! He called me, 'Quick, quick, come quick, Memsahib,' and when I went into the room, yes, there he was with his hand right inside my purse. Oh, how he looked then! I will never, never, never forget as long as I live his face at that moment!" She flung her hands before her face like someone who didn't want to see.

"I don't believe you," I said.

"Ask him!"

"I don't believe you."

Our clock ticked. It is a round battered old metal clock, and it ticks with a loud metal sound. Usually, when I am alone here sitting quietly at the table waiting for him, I like that sound; it is soothing and homely to me. But now, in the silence that had fallen between us, it was like a sick heart beating.

When Sudha spoke again, it was in quite a different voice. "It doesn't matter," she said. "I don't care at all." Then she said,

"Whatever you need, you think I wouldn't give? Would I ever say no to you? If you want, take these too. Here—" She put up her hands to her earrings. "No, take them. Take," she said as he held out his hand to restrain her, though she did not go any farther in unhooking them. "That's all nothing. I don't care one jot. I only care that you haven't come. For so long you haven't come to me. Every Tuesday afternoon, every Thursday, I got ready for you and I waited and waited— Why are you looking at her!" she cried, for Rajee had glanced nervously in my direction. "Who is she to grudge me those few hours with you, when she has taken everything else!"

She got up from where she had been sprawled in the chair. I didn't know what she was going to do. She looked capable of anything; the room seemed too small for all she seemed capable of doing. I think Rajee felt the same, and that is why he took her away.

We have one more room besides this one, but we have to cross an open passage to get to it. This is a nuisance during the rains, when sometimes we have to use an umbrella to go from our bedroom to our sitting room. We run across the passage under the umbrella, holding each other close. Now he was taking Sudha through our passage. I heard him shut the door and draw the big metal bolt from inside.

I was left alone with Daddy, who was sleeping with his mouth dropped open. He looked an old, old man. The clock ticked, loud as a hammer. I tried not to think of Rajee and Sudha in our bedroom, just as I always tried not to think of them in her house on Tuesday and Thursday afternoons (the days her husband goes to visit his factory at Saharanpur). Sometimes it is not good to think too much. Why dwell on things that can't be helped? Or on those that are over and done with? That is why I also don't look back on the past very much. There was a time when I didn't know Rajee but Sudha did. Of course she often spoke to me about him—I was her best friend— but I didn't meet him till I had to start taking letters between them. That was the time her family was arranging her marriage, and she and Rajee were planning to elope together. Well, it all turned out differently, so what is the use of thinking back now to what was then?

Daddy woke up. He looked around the room and asked where the other two were. I said Sudha had gone home and Rajee was sleeping in the bedroom because he was very tired after last night.

Daddy groaned at the mention of last night. He said, "Do you know what it could mean? Seven years rigorous imprisonment."

"No, no, Daddy," I said. I wasn't a bit frightened; I didn't believe it for a moment.

"You may look in the penal code. Cheating and impersonation, Section four twenty."

"It was all a mistake, Daddy. While you were sleeping, he explained everything to me."

I didn't want to hear anything more, and there was only one way I knew to keep him quiet. Although I couldn't find anything except one rather soft banana, he was glad to have even that. I watched him peeling it and chewing slowly, mulling it around in his mouth to make the most of every bite. Whenever I watch him eat nowadays, I feel he is not going to live much longer. I feel the same when I see him looking at the leaves moving on a tree. He enjoys these things like a person for whom they are not going to be there much longer.

He said, "How will you stay alone for seven years?"

I said, "No, Daddy."

I was saying no, it wouldn't happen, Rajee wouldn't be away for seven years, and also I was saying no, Daddy, I won't be alone, you won't die.

But he went on. "Yes, alone. You will be alone. I won't be here."

He turned away his face from me. I strained my ears toward the bedroom. But of course it was too far away, with the passage in between, to hear anything.

Daddy said, "These government regulations are very unfair. If there is a widow, the pension is paid to her, but otherwise it stops. Often I think if I had saved, but how was it possible? With high rent and college fees and other expenses?"

Daddy used to spend a lot of money on me. He sent me to the best school and college, where girls from much richer families went. He also tried to buy me the same sort of clothes that those girls had, so that I should not feel inferior to them.

I said, "I'm all right. I have my job."

"Your job!"

Daddy has always hated it that I work as cashier in a shop. Of course, from his point of view, and after all that expense and education, it isn't very much, but it is enough for Rajee and me to live on.

"They wanted a graduate. I couldn't have got it if I weren't a graduate." I said this to make him feel better and show him his efforts had not been wasted. "And sometimes there are some quite difficult calculations, so it's good I did all that maths at college."

"For this?" Daddy said, making the grubbing movement of counting coins with which he always refers to my job.

"Never mind," I said. "It doesn't matter."

Whenever we speak about this subject, we end up in the same way. Daddy used to have very high hopes for me. There were only the two of us, because my mother had died when I was born and Daddy didn't care for the rest of the family and had broken off relations with them. He cared only for me. He was proud because I did well at school and always stood first in arithmetic and English composition. At that time he used to read a lot. It's funny: nowadays he doesn't read at all; you would think in his retirement he would be reading all the time, but he doesn't—not even the newspaper. But at that time he was particularly fond of reading H. G. Wells and Bernard Shaw, and was keen for me to become like the women in their books. He said there was no need for me to get married; he said why should I be like the common run of girls. No, I must be free and independent and the equal of men in everything. He wanted me to smoke cigarettes, and even began to smoke himself so as to encourage me. (I didn't like the taste, so we both stopped.)

Now he said, "If he has to go, it would be better to give up this place and stay somewhere as paying guest."

"He doesn't have to go!"

"Or perhaps you can stay with a friend. What about her? What is her name?"

"Sudha? You want me to go and stay with her?"

I laughed and laughed; only at some point I stopped. I don't know if he noticed the difference. He may not have, because I was sitting on the floor with my knees drawn up and my face buried in them. All he would be able to see was my shoulders shaking, and that could be laughing *or* crying.

But I think he wasn't taking much notice of me. I think he was more interested in his own thoughts. He has a lot of thoughts always; I can tell because I can see him sunk into them and mumbling to himself and sometimes mumbling out loud. Perhaps that's the reason he doesn't read anymore. I looked at him; he was shaking his head and smiling to himself. Well, at least he was thinking something pleasant that made him happy.

And I could think only of Sudha and Rajee in there in our bed-room! You would have said—anyone would have said—that I had the right to go and bang on the door and shout, "What are you doing! Come out of there!" I should have done it.

Daddy said, "The time I liked best was the exams. I watched you go in with the others and I knew you would do better than any of them. I was sure of it."

He chuckled to himself in the triumphant way he used to when the results came out and I had done well. He had always accompanied me right up to the door of the examination hall, and as I went in he shouted after me, "Remember! First Class first!" flexing the muscles of his arm as if to give me strength. It used to be rather embarrassing—everyone stared—and I hurried in, pretending not to be the person addressed. But I was glad to see him when I came out again and he was standing there waiting, always with some special thing he knew I liked, such as a bag of chili chips.

He had stopped chuckling. Now his face was sad. He turned up his hand and held it out empty. "In the end, what is there?" he said. "Nothing. Ashes."

Well, I couldn't sit there listening to such depressing talk! I jumped up. I went straight through the passage, and now I did bang on the door. The bolt was drawn back and Rajee opened the door. He said, "One minute. She is going now."

I said, "I told Daddy she has gone home."

Rajee understood the problem at once. We have only one entrance door, and to get to that Sudha would have to pass through the sitting room and walk past Daddy. He would be surprised to see her back again.

Rajee told me to wait till he called. He went into the sitting room. I heard him talk to Daddy in a loud, cheerful voice. I went into the bedroom. Sudha was buttoning up her blouse. She didn't take much notice of me but only glanced at me over her shoulder and went on straightening her sari and fixing her hair. She did not look happy or satisfied; on the contrary, her eyes and cheeks were swollen with tears, and I think she was still crying, without making any sound.

At last Rajee called. Sudha and I walked through the passage and into the sitting room. I made her walk on the far side of Daddy, along the wall, and Rajee had also got between us and Daddy to shield us from view. He was stirring something in a cup. "Just wait till you taste this, Daddy," he was saying. "It is called Rajee's Special. Once tasted, never forgotten." Daddy's attention was all on this cup, and he had even stretched out his hands for it. Sudha walked along the wall with her sari pulled over her head, not looking right or left. I think she was still crying. I took her as far as the stairs and I said, "Be careful," because there was no light on the stairs. She managed to grope her way down, though I didn't wait to see. I was in a hurry to get back into the room.

I said, "Daddy had better go home now, before it gets too late." "How can he go?" Rajee said. "He is not well; he must stay here with us."

Suddenly I became terribly angry with Rajee. Perhaps I had been angry all the time—only now it came out. I began to shout at him. I shouted about the disgrace of getting arrested, but it wasn't only that; in fact, that was the least of it. Once I get angry, I find it very difficult to stop. New thoughts keep coming up, making me more angry, and I feel shaken through and through. I said many things I didn't mean.

Daddy joined in from time to time, saying what a disgrace it was to the family. The worse things I said the better pleased he was. When I showed signs of running down, he encouraged me to start up again. He listened attentively with his head to one side, so as not to miss anything, and whenever he thought I had scored a good point he thrust his forefinger up into the air and shouted, "Right! Correct!" He had become quite bright and perky again.

But Rajee sat there hunched together and with his head bowed, letting me say whatever I wanted, even when I called him a cheat and a liar and a thief. He sat there quiet and looking guilty. Then I wished that he would speak and rouse himself and perhaps get angry in return. I stopped every time I had said something very bad, so that he might defend himself. But it was always Daddy who spoke. "Right," he said. "Correct," till at last I cried, "Oh, please be quiet, Daddy!"

"No," Rajee said. "He is right. I deserve everything you say, all the names you are calling me, for having worried you so much."

"Worried me about what?"

Rajee looked up in surprise. He made a vague gesture, as if too ashamed to mention what had happened.

"About what?"

Rajee lowered his eyes again.

"Oh, you think that's all," I said. "That you have been in jail. You think that's the worst thing you have done. Ha."

He looked quite blank. The idiot! Did he think that was nothing—to have been in our bedroom alone with Sudha? Was it so small a thing? Then I longed to do more than only shout at him. I longed really to strike and beat him. If only Daddy would go away!

Daddy said, "I'm very tired. I will stay here tonight."

"Yes, yes, quite right." Rajee jumped up. He got sheets and pillows and made up Daddy's bed on the sofa. Afterward he turned down the sheet like a professional nurse and helped Daddy undress and arranged him comfortably. He spent rather a long time on all this, and appeared quite engrossed in it. I realized he was putting off being alone with me.

But I could wait. Soon Daddy would be asleep and then we would be alone. He would not be able to get away from me. I crossed the passage into our bedroom. I looked around carefully. It was as usual. There seemed to be no trace of Sudha left. It is strange: she has a very strong smell—partly because she is heavy and perspires heavily and partly because of the strong perfumes she wears—but though I sniffed and sniffed the air, I found that nothing of her remained.

I stepped up close to the mirror to look at myself. I often do it—not so much because I'm interested in myself but because of a desire to check up on how I look to Rajee. I haven't changed much from the time he first knew me. I think small, skinny girls like me don't change as fast as big ones like Sudha. If it weren't for my long hair, I still could be taken either for a boy or a girl. When I was a child, people had difficulty in telling which I was because Daddy always had my hair cut short. He had a theory that it was a woman's long hair that was to blame for her lack of freedom. But later, when I grew bigger, I envied the other girls their thick, long hair, in which they wore ornaments and flowers, and I would no longer allow mine to be cut. It never grew very thick, though. Sometimes I try to wear a flower, but my hair is too thin to hold it and the flower droops and looks odd, so that sooner or later I snatch it out and throw it away.

Rajee called to ask if I wanted tea. I called back no. I realized he only wanted to put off the moment for us to be alone together. I felt angry and grim. But when he did come I stopped feeling like that. He stood in the door, trying to scan my face to see my mood. He tried to smile at me. He looked terribly tired, with rings under his eyes.

"Lie down," I said. "Go to sleep now." My voice shook, I had such deep feeling for him at that moment.

He was very much relieved that I had stopped being angry. He flung himself on the bed like a person truly exhausted. I squatted on the bed beside him and rubbed my fingers to and fro in his soft hair. He had his eyes shut and looked at peace.

After a time, I whispered, "Was it very bad?"

Without opening his eyes, he answered, "Only at first. Don't stop. I like it." I went on rubbing my fingers in his hair. "At first of course it was a shock, though everyone was quite polite. They allowed me to take a taxi, and two policemen accompanied me."

"They didn't—?" I asked. I had been thinking about this all the time, and it made me shudder more than anything. So often in the streets I had seen people led away to jail, and their wrists were handcuffed and they were fastened to a policeman with a long chain.

"Oh no," he said. He knew what I meant at once. "They could see they were dealing with a gentleman. The policemen were very respectful to me, and they accepted cigarettes from me and smoked them in the taxi, though they were on duty. And when we got there everyone was quite nice. They were quite apologetic that this had to be done." He opened his eyes and said, "I wish you hadn't taken the money from Sudha."

"Then from where?" I cried.

"Yes, I know. But I wish—"

"Should I have left you there?"

"No no, of course not." He spoke quickly, as if afraid that I would get angry again. And to prevent this from happening he pulled me down beside him and pressed me close and held me.

He seemed eager to tell me about the jail. He always likes to tell me everything, and I sit up for him at night and try to keep awake, however late he comes, because I know he is coming home with a lot to tell. Every day something exciting happens to him, and he loves to repeat it to me in every detail. Well, it seemed that even in jail he had had a good time, and it wasn't at all like what I had thought.

"You see," he explained, "before trial we are kept quite separate and we are allowed all sorts of facilities. It's really more like a hotel. Of course, there are guards, but they don't bother you at all. On the contrary, if they see you are a better-class person they like to help you. I met some very interesting people there—really some quite topnotch people; you'd be surprised."

I *was* surprised. I had no idea it could be like that. But that is one of the wonderful things about Rajee—wherever he goes, whatever he does, something good and exciting happens to him.

"As a matter of fact," he said, "I made a very good contact. Something interesting could come of it. Wait, I'll tell you."

I knew he wanted his cigarettes—he always likes to smoke when he has something nice to tell—so I got out of bed and brought them for him. He lit up, and we lay again side by side on the bed.

"There was this person in the patent-medicine line, who had been in for several days. It took time to arrange for his bail, because it was for a very big amount. There is a big case against him. Everyone—all the guards and everyone—was very respectful to him, and he was good to them too. He knew how to handle them. His food and other things came from outside, and he also had cases of beer and always saw to it that the guards had their share. Naturally, they did everything they could to oblige him. And they were very careful with me too, because they could see he had taken a great liking to me."

That was nothing new. Wherever he goes, people take a great liking to Rajee and do all sorts of things for him and want to keep him in their company.

"He insisted I should eat with him, though as a matter of fact I wasn't very hungry, I was still rather upset. But the food was so delicious—such wonderful kebabs, I wish you could have tasted them. And plenty of beer with it, and plenty of good company, because there were some other people too, all in for various things but all of them better-class. We were quite a select group. Afterward we had a game of cards, that was good fun. Why are you laughing?"

It was all so different from what I had thought! I was laughing at myself, for my fears and terrible visions. I asked, "Did you win anything?"

"No, as a matter of fact I lost, but as I didn't have the money to pay they said it didn't matter, I could pay some other time."

"How much?" I asked, suddenly suspicious.

"Oh, not very much."

But he seemed anxious to change the subject, which confirmed my suspicions. My mood was no longer so good now. I began to brood. Here I had been, and Daddy and Sudha, and there he had been all the time quite enjoying himself and even losing money at cards.

I said, "If it was so nice, perhaps I should have left you there."

He gave me a reproachful look and was silent for a while. But then he said, "I wish it had been possible to get the money from someone else."

"Why?" I said, and then I felt worse. "Why?" I repeated. "She is such a wonderful friend to you. So wonderful," I cried, "that you bring her here and lock yourself into our bedroom with her to do God knows what!"

He turned to me and comforted me. He explained everything. I began to see that he had had no alternative—that he *had* to bring her in here because of the way she felt and because of the money she had given. He didn't say so outright, but I realized it was partly my fault also, for taking the money from her.

I felt much better. He went on talking about Sudha, and I liked it, the way he spoke about her. He said, "She is not a generous person; that is why it is not good to take from her. At heart, she grudges giving—it eats her up."

"She was always like that," I said, giving him a swift sideways look. But he agreed with me; he nodded. I saw that his feelings for her had completely changed.

"Every little bit she gives," he said, "she wants four times as much in return."

"It's her nature."

I remembered what she had said about his taking money from her purse. I felt indignant. To shame him like that, before her servant! Obviously, he would never have taken the money if he had not been in great need. She should have been glad to help him out. I never hide my money from him now. I used to sometimes—I used to put away absolutely necessary amounts, like for the rent—but he always seemed to find out my hiding places, so I don't do it anymore. Now if we run short I borrow it from the cash register in the shop; no one ever notices, and I always put it back when I get my salary. Only once I couldn't put it back—there were some unexpected expenses—but they never found out, so it's all right.

"What's that?" he said. We were both silent, listening. He said, "I think Daddy is calling."

"I don't hear anything."

Rajee wanted to go and see, but I assured him it was all right. Daddy might have called out in his sleep—he often did that. I asked Rajee to tell me more about his adventures last night, so he settled back and lit another cigarette.

"You know, this person I was telling you about—in the patent-medicine line? He wants me to contact him as soon as he comes out. He says he will put some good things in my way. He was very keen to meet me again and wanted to have my telephone number . . . You know, it is very difficult without a telephone; it is the biggest handicap in my career. It is not even necessary to have an office, but a telephone—you can't do big business without one. Do you know that some of the most important deals are concluded over the telephone only? I could tell you some wonderful stories."

"I know," I said. He had already told me some wonderful stories on this subject, and I knew how much he longed for and needed a telephone, but where could I get it from?

"Never mind," he said. He didn't want me to feel bad. "When we move into a better place, we shall install all these things. Telephone, refrigerator—I think he *is* calling."

Rajee went to see. I also got off the bed and looked under it for my slippers. As I did so, I remembered a terrible dream I used to have as a child. I used to dream Daddy was dead. Then I screamed and screamed, and when I woke up Daddy was holding me and I had my arms around his neck. Afterward I was always afraid to go on sleeping by myself and got into his bed. But I would never tell him my dream. I was frightened to speak it out.

When I came into the sitting room, I found Daddy sitting up on the sofa, and Rajee was holding him up under the arms—sort of propping him up. It was that time of the night when everything looks dim and depressing. We have only one light bulb, and it looked very feeble and even ghostly and did not shed much light. Dawn wasn't far off—it was no longer quite night and it was not yet day—and the light coming in through the window was rather dreary. Perhaps it was because of this that Daddy's face looked so strange; he lay limp and lolling in Rajee's arms.

And he was very cross. He said he had been shouting for hours and no one came. In the end, he had had to get up himself and get his pills and the water to swallow them with. If it hadn't been for that—if he hadn't somehow got the strength together—then who knew what state we might have found him in later when we woke up from our deep sleep? Rajee kept apologizing, trying to soothe him, but that only seemed to make him more cross. He went on and on.

"Yes," he said, "and if something happens to me now, then what about her?" He pointed at me in an accusing way.

"Nothing will happen, Daddy," Rajee said, soothing him. "You are all right."

Daddy snorted with contempt. "Feel this," he said, guiding Rajee's hand to his heart.

"You are all right," Rajee repeated.

Daddy made another contemptuous sound and pushed Rajee's hand away. "You would have made a fine doctor. And who is going to look after her when you go? What will she do all alone for seven years?"

"He is *not going*, Daddy," I said, spacing my words very distinctly. I didn't like it, that he should still be thinking about that.

"Not going where?" Rajee asked.

That made Daddy so angry that he became quite energetic. He stopped lolling in Rajee's arms and began to abuse him, calling him the same sort of names I had called him earlier. And Rajee listened to him as he had listened to me, respectfully, with his head lowered.

I tried to bear it quietly for a while but couldn't. Then I interrupted Daddy. I said, "It is not like that at all."

"No?" he said. "To go to jail is not like that? Perhaps it's a nice thing. Perhaps we should say, 'Well done, Son. Bravo.' "

"He wasn't in jail," I said. "It was more like a hotel. And he met some very fine people there. You don't understand anything about these things, Daddy, so it's better not to talk."

Daddy was quiet. I didn't look at him, I was too annoyed with him. He had no right to meddle in things he didn't know about; he was old now, and should just eat and sleep.

"Lie down," I told him. "Go to sleep."

"All right," Daddy said in a meek voice.

But in fact he couldn't lie down, because Rajee had dropped off to sleep on the sofa. He was sitting up, but his head had dropped to his chest and his eyes were shut. Naturally, after two sleepless nights, I couldn't disturb him, so I told Daddy he had better go and sleep in our bedroom. Daddy said all right again, in the same meek voice. He carried his pillow under his arm and went away.

I lifted Rajee's legs onto the sofa and arranged his head. He didn't wake up. I looked at him sleeping. I thought that even if he had to go away for a while he would be coming back to me. And even if it were for a longer time there are always remissions for good conduct and other concessions, and meanwhile visits are allowed and I could take him things and also receive letters from him. So even if it is for longer, I shall wait and not do anything to myself. I would never do anything to myself now, never. I wouldn't think of it.

I did try it once. I got the idea from two people. One of them was Rajee. It was the time when Sudha's marriage was being arranged, and he came daily to our house and cried and said he could not bear it and would kill himself. I think he felt better with being able to talk to me, but after I told him my feelings for him he didn't come so often anymore, and after a time he stopped coming altogether. Then I began to remember all he had said about what was the use of living. It so happened that just at this time there was a girl in the neighborhood who committed suicide—not for love but because of cruel treatment from her in-laws. She did it in the usual way, by pouring kerosene over her clothes and setting herself on fire. It is a crude method and perhaps not suitable for a college girl like me, but it was the only way I could think of and also the easiest and cheapest, so I decided on it.

Only that day, when everything was ready, Daddy came home early and found me. Although he never wanted me to get married, he saw then that there was no other way and he sent for Rajee. When Daddy saw that Rajee was reluctant to get married to me, he did a strange thing—the sort of thing he has never, never in his whole life done to anyone. He got down on the floor and touched Rajee's feet and begged him to marry me. Rajee, who is always very respectful to elders, was shocked, and he bent down to raise him and cried, "Daddy, what are you doing!" As soon as I heard him say Daddy, I knew it would be all right. I mean, he wouldn't call him Daddy, would he, unless he was going to be his son-in-law?

IN THE MOUNTAINS

When one lives alone for most of the time and meets almost nobody, then care for one's outward appearance tends to drop away. That was what happened to Pritam. As the years went by and she continued living by herself, her appearance became rougher and shabbier, and though she was still in her thirties, she completely forgot to care for herself or think about herself as a physical person.

Her mother was just the opposite. She was plump and pampered, loved pastries and silk saris, and always smelled of lavender. Pritam smelled of—what was it? Her mother, enfolded in Pritam's embrace after a separation of many months, found herself sniffing in an attempt to identify the odor emanating from her. Perhaps it was from Pritam's clothes, which she probably did not change as frequently as was desirable. Tears came to the mother's eyes. They were partly for what her daughter had become and partly for the happiness of being with her again.

Pritam thumped her on the back. Her mother always cried at their meetings and at their partings. Pritam usually could not help being touched by these tears, even though she was aware of the mixed causes that evoked them. Now, to hide her own feelings, she became gruffer and more manly, and even gave the old lady a push toward a chair. "Go on, sit down," she said. "I suppose you are dying for your cup of tea." She had it all ready, and the mother took it gratefully, for she loved and needed tea, and the journey up from the plains had greatly tired her.

But she could not drink with enjoyment. Pritam's tea was always too strong for her—a black country brew such as peasants drink, and the milk was also that of peasants, too newly rich and warm

235

from the buffalo. And they were in this rough and barely furnished room in the rough stone house perched on the mountainside. And there was Pritam herself. The mother had to concentrate all her energies on struggling against more tears.

"I suppose you don't like the tea," Pritam said challengingly. She watched severely while the mother proved herself by drinking it up to the last drop, and Pritam refilled the cup. She asked, "How is everybody? Same as usual? Eating, making money?"

"No, no," said the mother, not so much denying the fact that this was what the family was doing as protesting against Pritam's saying so.

"Aren't they going up to Simla this year?"

"On Thursday," the mother said, and shifted uncomfortably.

"And stopping here?"

"Yes. For lunch."

The mother kept her eyes lowered. She said nothing more, though there was more to say. It would have to wait till a better hour. Let Pritam first get over the prospect of entertaining members of her family for a few hours on Thursday. It was nothing new or unexpected, for some of them stopped by every year on their way farther up the mountains. However much they may have desired to do so, they couldn't just drive past; it wouldn't be decent. But the prospect of meeting held no pleasure for anyone. Quite often there was a quarrel, and then Pritam cursed them as they drove away, and they sighed at the necessity of keeping up family relationships, instead of having their lunch comfortably in the hotel a few miles farther on.

Pritam said, "I suppose you will be going with them," and went on at once, "Naturally, why should you stay? What is there for you here?"

"I want to stay."

"No, you love to be in Simla. It's so nice and jolly, and meeting everyone walking on the Mall, and tea in Davico's. Nothing like that here. You even hate my tea."

"I want to stay with you."

"But I don't want you!" Pritam was laughing, not angry. "You will be in my way, and then how will I carry on all my big love affairs?"

"What, what?"

Pritam clapped her hands in delight. "Oh no. I'm telling you nothing, because then you will want to stay and you will scare everyone away." She gave her mother a sly look and added, "You will scare poor Doctor Sahib away."

"Oh, Doctor Sahib," said the old lady, relieved to find it had all been a joke. But she continued with disapproval, "Does he still come here?"

"Well, what do you think?" Pritam stopped laughing now and became offended. "If he doesn't come, then who will come? Except some goats and monkeys, perhaps. I know he is not good enough for you. You don't like him to come here. You would prefer me to know only goats and monkeys. And the family, of course."

"When did I say I don't like him?" the mother said.

"People don't have to say. And other people are quite capable of feeling without anyone saying. Here." Pritam snatched up her mother's cup and filled it, with rather a vengeful air, for the third time.

Actually, it wasn't true that the mother disliked Doctor Sahib. He came to visit the next morning, and as soon as she saw him she had her usual sentiment about him—not dislike but disapproval. He certainly did not look like a person fit to be on terms of social intercourse with any member of her family. He was a tiny man, shabby and even dirty. He wore a kind of suit, but it was in a terrible condition and so were his shoes. One eye of his spectacles, for some reason, was blacked out with a piece of cardboard.

"Ah!" he exclaimed when he saw her. "Mother has come!" And he was so genuinely happy that her disapproval could not stand up to him—at least, not entirely.

"Mother brings us tidings and good cheer from the great world outside," Doctor Sahib went on. "What are we but two mountain hermits? Or I could even say two mountain bears."

He sat at a respectful distance away from the mother, who was ensconced in a basket chair. She had come to sit in the garden. There was a magnificent view from here of the plains below and the mountains above; however, she had not come out to enjoy the scenery but to get the benefit of the morning sun. Although it was the height of summer, she always felt freezing cold inside the house, which seemed like a stone tomb.

"Has Madam told you about our winter?" Doctor Sahib said. "Oh, what these two bears have gone through! Ask her."

"His roof fell in," Pritam said.

"One night I was sleeping in my bed. Suddenly—what shall I tell you—crash, bang! Boom and bang! To me it seemed that all the mountains were falling and, let alone the mountains, heaven itself was coming down into my poor house. I said, 'Doctor Sahib, your hour has come.' "

"I told him, I told him all summer, 'The first snowfall and your roof will fall in.' And when it happened all he could do was stand there and wring his hands. What an idiot!"

"If it hadn't been for Madam, God knows what would have become of me. But she took me in and all winter she allowed me to have my corner by her own fireside."

The mother looked at them with startled eyes.

"Oh yes, all winter," Pritam said, mocking her. "And all alone, just the two of us. Why did you have to tell her?" she reproached Doctor Sahib. "Now she is shocked. Just look at her face. She is thinking we are two guilty lovers."

The mother flushed, and so did Doctor Sahib. An expression of bashfulness came into his face, mixed with regret, with melancholy. He was silent for some time, his head lowered. Then he said to the mother, "Look, can you see it?" He pointed at his house, which nestled farther down the mountainside, some way below Pritam's. It was a tiny house, not much more than a hut. "All hale and hearty again. Madam had the roof fixed, and now I am snug and safe once more in my own little kingdom."

Pritam said, "One day the whole place is going to come down, not just the roof, and then what will you do?"

He spread his arms in acceptance and resignation. He had no choice as to place of residence. His family had brought him here and installed him in the house; they gave him a tiny allowance but only on condition that he wouldn't return to Delhi. As was evident from his fluent English, Doctor Sahib was an educated man, though it was not quite clear whether he really had qualified as a doctor. If he had, he may have done something disreputable and been struck off the register. Some such air hung about him. He was a great embarrassment to his family. Unable to make a living, he had gone around crounging from family friends, and at one point had sat on the pavement in New Delhi's most fashionable shopping district and attempted to sell cigarettes and matches.

Later, when he had gone, Pritam said, "Don't you think I've got a dashing lover?"

"I know it's not true," the mother said, defending herself. "But other people, what will they think—alone with him in the house all winter? You know how people are."

"What people?"

It was true. There weren't any. To the mother, this was a cause for regret. She looked at the mountains stretching away into the distance—a scene of desolation. But Pritam's eyes were half shut with satisfaction as she gazed across the empty spaces and saw birds cleaving through the mist, afloat in the pure mountain sky.

"I was waiting for you all winter," the mother said. "I had your room ready, and every day we went in there to dust and change the flowers." She broke out, "Why didn't you come? Why stay in this place when you can be at home and lead a proper life like everybody else?"

Pritam laughed. "Oh but I'm not like everybody else! That's the last thing!"

The mother was silent. She could not deny that Pritam was different. When she was a girl, they had worried about her and yet they had also been proud of her. She had been a big, handsome girl with independent views. People admired her and thought it a fine thing that a girl could be so emancipated in India and lead a free life, just as in other places.

Now the mother decided to break the news. She said, "He is coming with them on Thursday."

"Who is coming with them?"

"Sarla's husband." She did not look at Pritam after saying this. After a moment's silence Pritam cried, "So let him come! They can all come—everyone welcome. My goodness, what's so special about him that you should make such a face? What's so special about any of them? They may come, they may eat, they may go away again, and good-bye. Why should I care for anyone? I don't care. And also you! You also may go—right now, this minute, if you like—and I will stand here and wave to you and laugh!"

In an attempt to stop her, the mother asked, "What will you cook for them on Thursday?"

That did bring her up short. For a moment she gazed at her mother wildly, as if she were mad herself or thought her mother mad. Then she said, "My God, do you ever think of anything except food?"

"I eat too much," the old lady gladly admitted. "Dr. Puri says I must reduce."

Pritam didn't sleep well that night. She felt hot, and tossed about heavily, and finally got up and turned on the light and wandered around the house in her nightclothes. Then she unlatched the door and let herself out. The night air was crisp, and it refreshed her at once. She loved being out in all this immense silence. Moonlight lay on top of the mountains, so that even those that were green looked as if they were covered in snow.

There was only one light—a very human little speck, in all that darkness. It came from Doctor Sahib's house, some way below hers. She wondered if he had fallen asleep with the light on. It happened sometimes that he dozed off where he was sitting and when he woke up again it was morning. But other times he really did stay awake all night, too excited by his reading and thinking to be able to sleep. Pritam decided to go down and investigate. The path was very steep, but she picked her way down, as sure and steady as a mountain goat. She peered in at his window. He was awake, sitting at his table with his head supported on his hand, and reading by the light of a kerosene lamp. His house had once had electricity, but after the disaster last winter it could not be got to work again. Pritam was quite glad about that, for the wiring had always been uncertain, and he had been in constant danger of being electrocuted.

She rapped on the glass to rouse him, then went around to let herself in by the door. At the sound of her knock, he had jumped to his feet; he was startled, and no less so when he discovered who his visitor was. He stared at her through his one glass lens, and his lower lip trembled in agitation.

She was irritated. "If you're so frightened, why don't you lock your door? You should lock it. Any kind of person can come in and do anything he wants." It struck her how much like a murder victim he looked. He was so small and weak—one blow on the head would do it. Some morning she would come down and find him lying huddled on the floor.

But there he was, alive, and, now that he had got over the shock, laughing and flustered and happy to see her. He fussed around and invited her to sit on his only chair, dusting the seat with his hand and drawing it out for her in so courtly a manner that she became instinctively graceful as she settled herself on it and pulled her nightdress over her knees.

"Look at me, in my nightie," she said, laughing. "I suppose you're shocked. If Mother knew. If she could see me! But of course she is fast asleep and snoring in her bed. Why are you awake? Reading one of your stupid books—what stuff you cram into your head day and night. Anyone would go crazy."

240

Doctor Sahib was very fond of reading. He read mostly historical romances and was influenced and even inspired by them. He believed very strongly in past births, and these books helped him to learn about the historical eras through which he might have passed.

"A fascinating story," he said. "There is a married lady—a queen, as a matter of fact—who falls hopelessly in love with a monk."

"Goodness! Hopelessly?"

"You see, these monks—naturally—they were under a vow of chastity and that means—well—you know . . ."

"Of course I know."

"So there was great anguish on both sides. Because he also felt burning love for the lady and endured horrible penances in order to subdue himself. Would you like me to read to you? There are some sublime passages.

"What is the use? These are not things to read in books but to experience in life. Have you ever been hopelessly in love?"

He turned away his face, so that now only his cardboard lens was looking at her. However, it seemed not blank but full of expression.

She said, "There are people in the world whose feelings are much stronger than other people's. Of course they must suffer. If you are not satisfied only with eating and drinking but want something else . . . You should see my family. They care for nothing—only physical things, only enjoyment."

"Mine exactly the same."

"There is one cousin, Sarla—I have nothing against her, she is not a bad person. But I tell you it would be just as well to be born an animal. Perhaps I shouldn't talk like this, but it's true."

"It is true. And in previous births these people really were animals."

"Do you think so?"

"Or some very low form of human being. But the queens and the really great people, they become—well, they become like you. Please don't laugh! I have told you before what you were in your last birth."

She went on laughing. "You've told me so many things," she said.

"All true. Because you have passed through many incarnations. And in each one you were a very outstanding personality, a highly developed soul, but each time you also had a difficult life, marked by sorrow and suffering."

Pritam had stopped laughing. She gazed sadly at the blank wall over his head.

"It is the fate of all highly developed souls," he said. "It is the price to be paid."

"I know." She fetched a sigh from her innermost being.

"I think a lot about this problem. Just tonight, before you came, I sat here reading my book. I'm not ashamed to admit that tears came streaming from my eyes, so that I couldn't go on reading, on account of not being able to see the print. Then I looked up and I asked, 'Oh, Lord, why must these good and noble souls endure such torment, while others, less good and noble, can enjoy themselves freely?'"

"Yes, why?" Pritam asked.

"I shall tell you. I shall explain." He was excited, inspired now. He looked at her fully, and even his cardboard lens seemed radiant. "Now, as I was reading about this monk—a saint, by the way—and how he struggled and battled against nature, then I could not but think of my own self. Yes, I too, though not a saint, struggle and battle here alone in my small hut. I cry out in anguish, and the suffering endured is terrible but also—oh, Madam—glorious! A privilege."

Pritam looked at a crack that ran right across the wall and seemed to be splitting it apart. One more heavy snowfall, she thought, and the whole hut would come down. Meanwhile he sat here and talked nonsense and she listened to him. She got up abruptly.

He cried, "I have talked too much! You are bored!"

"Look at the time," she said. The window was milk-white with dawn. She turned down the kerosene lamp and opened the door. Trees and mountains were floating in a pale mist, attempting to surface like swimmers through water. "Oh my God," she said, "it's time to get up. And I'm going to have such a day today, with all of them coming."

"They are coming today?"

"Yes, and you needn't bother to visit. They are not your type at all. Not one bit."

He laughed. "All right."

"Not mine, either," she said, beginning the upward climb back to her house.

*   *   *

Pritam loved to cook and was very good at it. Her kitchen was a primitive little outbuilding in which she bustled about. Her hair fell into her face and stuck to her forehead; several times she tried to push it back with her elbow but only succeeded in leaving a black soot mark. When her mother pointed this out to her, she laughed and smeared at it and made it worse.

Her good humor carried her successfully over the arrival of the relatives. They came in three carloads, and suddenly the house was full of fashionably dressed people with loud voices. Pritam came dashing out of the kitchen just as she was and embraced everyone indiscriminately, including Sarla and her husband, Bobby. In the bustle of arrival and the excitement of many people, the meeting went off easily. The mother was relieved. Pritam and Bobby hadn't met for eight years—in fact, not since Bobby had been married to Sarla.

Soon Pritam was serving a vast, superbly cooked meal. She went around piling their plates, urging them to take, take more, glad at seeing them enjoy her food. She still hadn't changed her clothes, and the smear of soot was still on her face. The mother—whose main fear had been that Pritam would be surly and difficult—was not relieved but upset by Pritam's good mood. She thought to herself, why should she be like that with them—what have they ever done for her that she should show them such affection and be like a servant to them? She even looked like their servant. The old lady's temper mounted, and when she saw Pritam piling rice onto Bobby's plate—when she saw her serving *him* like a servant, and the way he turned around to compliment her about the food, making Pritam proud and shy and pleased—then the mother could not bear any more. She went into the bedroom and lay down on the bed. She felt ill; her blood pressure had risen and all her pulses throbbed. She shut her eyes and tried to shut out the merry, sociable sounds coming from the next room.

After a while Pritam came in and said, "Why aren't you eating?"

The old lady didn't answer.

"What's the matter?"

"Go. Go away. Go to your guests."

"Oh my God, she is sulking!" Pritam said, and laughed out loud—not to annoy her mother but to rally her, the way she would a child. But the mother continued to lie there with her eyes shut

Pritam said, "Should I get you some food?"

"I don't want it," the mother said. But suddenly she opened her eyes and sat up. She said, "You should give food to him. He also should be invited. Or perhaps you think he is not good enough for ʲour guests?"

"Who?"

"Who. You know very well. You should know. You were with him the whole night."

Pritam gave a quick glance over her shoulder at the open door, then advanced toward her mother. "So you have been spying on me," she said. The mother shrank back. "You pretended to be asleep, and all the time you were spying on me."

"Not like that, Daughter—"

"And now you are having filthy thoughts about me."

"Not like that!"

"Yes, like that!"

Both were shouting. The conversation in the next room had died down. The mother whispered, "Shut the door," and Pritam did so.

Then the mother said in a gentle, loving voice, "I'm glad he is here with you. He is a good friend to you." She looked into Pritam's face, but it did not lighten, and she went on, "That is why I said he should be invited. When other friends come, we should not neglect our old friends who have stood by us in our hour of need."

Pritam snorted scornfully.

"And he would have enjoyed the food so much," the mother said. "I think he doesn't often eat well."

Pritam laughed. "You should see what he eats!" she said. "But he is lucky to get even that. At least his family send him money now. Before he came here, do you want to hear what he did? He has told me himself. He used to go to the kitchens of the restaurants and beg for food. And they gave him scraps and he ate them—he has told me himself. He ate leftover scraps from other people's plates like a sweeper or a dog. And you want such a person to be my friend."

She turned away from her mother's startled, suffering face. She ran out of the room and out through the next room, past all the guests. She climbed up a path that ran from the back of her house to a little cleared plateau. She lay down in the grass, which was alive with insects; she was level with the tops of trees and with the birds that pecked and called from inside them. She often came here. She looked down at the view but didn't see it, it was so familiar to her. The only unusual sight was the three cars parked outside her house.

A chauffeur was wiping a windshield. Then someone came out of the house and, reaching inside a car door, emerged with a bottle. It was Bobby.

Pritam watched him, and when he was about to go back into the house, she aimed a pebble that fell at his feet. He looked up. He smiled. "Hi, there!' he called.

She beckoned him to climb up to her. He hesitated for a moment, looking at the bottle and toward the house, but then gave the toss of his head that she knew well, and began to pick his way along the path. She put her hand over her mouth to cover a laugh as she watched him crawl up toward her on all fours. When finally he arrived, he was out of breath and disheveled, and there was a little blood on his hand where he had grazed it. He flung himself on the grass beside her and gave a great "Whoof!" of relief.

She hadn't seen him for eight years, and her whole life had changed in the meantime, but it didn't seem to her that he had changed all that much. Perhaps he was a little heavier, but it suited him, made him look more manly than ever. He was lying face down on the grass, and she watched his shoulder blades twitch inside his finely striped shirt as he breathed in exhaustion.

"You are in very poor condition," she said.

"Isn't it terrible?"

"Don't you play tennis anymore?"

"Mostly golf now."

He sat up and put the bottle to his mouth and tilted back his head. She watched his throat moving as the liquid glided down. He finished with a sound of satisfaction and passed the bottle to her, and without wiping it she put her lips where his had been and drank. The whisky leaped up in her like fire. They had often sat like this together, passing a bottle of Scotch between them.

He seemed to be perfectly content to be there with her. He sat with his knees drawn up and let his eyes linger appreciatively over the view. It was the way she had often seen him look at attractive girls. "Nice," he said, as he had said on those occasions. She laughed, and then she too looked and tried to imagine how he was seeing it.

"A nice place," he said. "I like it. I wish I could live here."

"You!" She laughed again.

He made a serious face. "I love peace and solitude. You don't know me. I've changed a lot." He turned right around toward her, still very solemn, and for the first time she felt him gazing full into

245

her face. She put up her hand and said quickly, "I've been cooking all day."

He looked away, as if wanting to spare her, and this delicacy hurt her more than anything. She said heavily, "I've changed."

"Oh no!" he said in haste. "You are just the same. As soon as I saw you, I thought: Look at Priti, she is just the same." And again he turned toward her to allow her to see his eyes, stretching them wide open for her benefit. It was a habit of his she knew well; he would always challenge the person to whom he was lying to read anything but complete honesty in his eyes.

She said, "You had better go. Everyone will wonder where you are."

"Let them." And when she shook her head, he said, in his wheedling voice, "Let me stay with you. It has been such a long time. Shall I tell you something? I was so excited yesterday thinking: Tomorrow I shall see her again. I couldn't sleep all night. No, really—it's true."

Of course she knew it wasn't. He slept like a bear; nothing could disturb that. The thought amused her, and her mouth corners twitched. Encouraged, he moved in closer. "I think about you very often," he said. "I remember so many things—you have no idea. All the discussions we had about our terrible social system. It was great."

Once they had had a very fine talk about free love. They had gone to a place they knew about, by a lake. At first they were quite frivolous, sitting on a ledge overlooking the lake, but as they got deeper into their conversation about free love (they both, it turned out, believed in it) they became more and more serious and, after that, very quiet, until in the end they had nothing more to say. Then they only sat there, and though it was very still and the water had nothing but tiny ripples on it, like wrinkles in silk, they felt as if they were in a storm. But of course it was their hearts beating and their blood rushing. It was the most marvelous experience they had ever had in their whole lives. After that, they often returned there or went to other similar places that they found, and as soon as they were alone together that same storm broke out.

Now Bobby heaved a sigh. To make himself feel better, he took another drink from his bottle and then passed it to her. "It's funny," he said. "I have this fantastic social life. I meet such a lot of people, but there isn't one person I can talk with the way I talk with you. I mean, about serious subjects."

"And with Sarla?"

"Sarla is all right, but she isn't really interested in serious subjects. I don't think she ever thinks about them. But I do."

To prove it, he again assumed a very solemn expression and turned his face toward her, so that she could study it. How little he had changed!

"Give me another drink," she said, needing it.

He passed her the bottle. "People think I'm an extrovert type, and of course I do have to lead a very extrovert sort of life," he said. "And there is the business too—ever since Daddy had his stroke, I have to spend a lot of time in the office. But very often, you know what I like to do? Just lie on my bed and listen to nice tunes on my cassette. And then I have a lot of thoughts."

"What about?"

"Oh, all sorts of things. You would be surprised."

She was filled with sensations she had thought she would never have again. No doubt they were partly due to the whisky; she hadn't drunk in a long time. She thought he must be feeling the way she did; in the past they had always felt the same. She put out her hand to touch him—first his cheek, which was rough and manly, and then his neck, which was soft and smooth. He had been talking, but when she touched him he fell silent. She left her hand lying on his neck, loving to touch it. He remained silent, and there was something strange. For a moment, she didn't remove her hand—she was embarrassed to do so—and when at last she did, she noticed that he looked at it. She looked at it too. The skin was rough and not too clean, and neither were her nails, and one of them was broken. She hid her hands behind her back.

Now he was talking again, and talking quite fast. "Honestly, Priti, I think you're really lucky to be living here," he said. "No one to bother you, no worries, and all this fantastic scenery." He turned his head again to admire it and made his eyes sparkle with appreciation. He also took a deep breath.

"And such marvelous air," he said. "No wonder you keep fit and healthy. Who lives there?" He pointed at Doctor Sahib's house below.

Pritam answered eagerly. "Oh, I'm very lucky—he is such an interesting personality. If only you could meet him."

"What a pity," Bobby said politely. Down below, there was a lot of activity around the three cars. Things were being rolled up and stowed away in preparation for departure.

"Yes, you don't meet such people every day. He is a doctor, not only of medicine but all sorts of other things too. He does a lot of research and thinking, and that is why he lives up here. Because it is so quiet."

Now people could be seen coming out of Pritam's house. They turned this way and that, looking up and calling Pritam's name.

"They are looking for you," Bobby said. He replaced the cap of his whisky bottle and got up and waited for her to get up too. But she took her time.

"You see, for serious thinking you have to have absolute peace and quiet," she said. "I mean, if you are a real thinker, a sort of philosopher type."

She got up. She stood and looked down at the people searching and calling for her. "Whenever I wake up at night, I can see his light on. He is always with some book, studying, studying."

"Fantastic," Bobby said, though his attention was distracted by the people below.

"He knows all about past lives. He can tell you exactly what you were in all your previous births."

"Really?" Bobby said, turning toward her again.

"He has told me all about my incarnations."

"Really? Would he know about me too?"

"Perhaps. If you were an interesting personality. Yes all right, coming!" she called down at last.

She began the steep climb down, but it was so easy for her that she could look back at him over her shoulder and continue talking. "He is only interested in studying highly developed souls, so unless you were someone really quite special in a previous birth he wouldn't be able to tell you anything."

"What were you?" Bobby said. He had begun to follow her. Although the conversation was interesting to him, he could not concentrate on it, because he had to keep looking down at the path and place his feet with caution.

"I don't think I can tell you," she said, walking on ahead. "It is something you are supposed to know only in your innermost self."

"What?" he said, but just then he slipped, and it was all he could do to save himself from falling.

"In your innermost self!" she repeated in a louder voice, though without looking back. Nimbly, she ran down the remainder of the path and was soon among the people who had been calling her.

*　　*　　*

They were relieved to see her. It seemed the old lady was being very troublesome. She refused to have her bag packed, refused to get into the car and be driven up to Simla. She said she wanted to stay with Pritam.

"So let her," Pritam said.

Her relatives exchanged exasperated glances. Some of the ladies were so tired of the whole thing that they had given up and sat on the steps of the veranda, fanning themselves. Others, more patient, explained to Pritam that it was all very well for her to say let her stay, but how was she going to look after her? The old lady needed so many things—a masseuse in the morning, a cup of Horlicks at eleven and another at three, and one never knew when the doctor would have to be called for her blood pressure. None of these facilities was available in Pritam's house, and they knew exactly what would happen—after a day, or at the most two, Pritam would send them an SOS, and they would have to come back all the way from Simla to fetch her away.

Pritam went into the bedroom, shutting the door behind her. The mother was lying on her bed, with her face to the wall. She didn't move or turn around or give any sign of life until Pritam said, "It's me." Then her mother said, "I'm not going with them."

Pritam said, "You will have to have a cold bath every day, because I'm not going to keep lighting the boiler for you. Do you know who has to chop the wood? Me, Pritam."

"I don't need hot water. If you don't need it, I don't."

"And there is no Horlicks."

"Tcha!" said her mother. She was still lying on the bed, though she had turned around now and was facing Pritam. She did not look very well. Her face seemed puffed and flushed.

"And your blood pressure?" Pritam asked.

"It is quite all right."

"Yes, and what if it isn't? There is no Dr. Puri here, or anyone like that."

The mother shut her eyes, as if it were a great effort. After a time, she found the strength to say, "There is a doctor."

"God help us!" Pritam said, and laughed out loud.

"He *is* a doctor." The mother compressed her little mouth stubbornly over her dentures. Pritam did not contradict her, though she was still laughing to herself. They were silent together but not in disagreement. Pritam opened the door to leave.

"Did you keep any food for him?" the mother said.

"There is enough to last him a week."

She went out and told the others that her mother was staying. She wouldn't listen to any arguments, and after a while they gave up. All they wanted was to get away as quickly as possible. They piled into their cars and waved at her from the windows. She waved back. When she was out of sight, they sank back against the car upholstery with sighs of relief. They felt it had gone off quite well this time. At least there had been no quarrel. They discussed her for a while and felt that she was improving; perhaps she was quietening down with middle age.

Pritam waited for the cars to reach the bend below and then— quite without malice but with excellent aim—she threw three stones. Each one squarely hit the roof of a different car as they passed, one after the other. She could hear the sound faintly from up here. She thought how amazed they would be inside their cars, wondering what had hit them, and how they would crane out of the windows but not be able to see anything. They would decide that it was just some stones crumbling off the hillside—perhaps the beginning of a landslide; you never could tell in the mountains.

She picked up another stone and flung it all the way down at Doctor Sahib's corrugated tin roof. It landed with a terrific clatter, and he came running out. He looked straight up to where she was standing, and his one lens glittered at her in the sun.

She put her hands to her mouth and called, "Food!" He gave a sign of joyful assent and straightaway, as nimble as herself, began the familiar climb up.

HOW I BECAME
A HOLY MOTHER

On my twenty-third birthday when I was fed up with London and all the rest of it—boyfriends, marriages (two), jobs (modeling), best friends that are suddenly your best enemies—I had this letter from my girlfriend Sophie who was finding peace in an ashram in South India:

> . . . oh Katie you wouldn't know me I'm such a changed person. I get up at 5—a.m.!!! I am an absolute vegetarian let alone no meat no eggs either and am making fabulous progress with my meditation. I have a special mantra of my own that Swamiji gave me at a special ceremony and I say it over and over in my mind. The sky here is blue all day long and I sit by the sea and watch the waves and have good thoughts . . .

But by the time I got there Sophie had left—under a cloud, it seemed, though when I asked what she had done, they wouldn't tell me but only pursed their lips and looked sorrowful. I didn't stay long in that place. I didn't like the bitchy atmosphere, and that Swamiji was a big fraud, anyone could see that. I couldn't understand how a girl as sharp as Sophie had ever let herself be fooled by such a type. But I suppose if you want to be fooled you are. I found that out in some of the other ashrams I went to. There were some quite intelligent people in all of them but the way they just shut their eyes to certain things, it was incredible. It is not my role in life to criticize others so I kept quiet and went on to the next place. I went to quite a few of them. These ashrams are a cheap way to live in India and there is always company and it isn't bad for a few days provided you don't get involved in their power politics. I was amazed to come across quite a few people I had known over the years and would never have expected to meet here. It is a shock when you see someone you had last met on the beach at St. Tropez now all dressed up in a saffron robe and meditating in some very dusty ashram in Madhya Pradesh. But really I could see their point because they were all as tired as I was of everything we had been doing and this certainly was different.

I enjoyed myself going from one ashram to the other and traveling all over India. Trains and buses are very crowded—I went third class, I had to be careful with my savings—but Indians can tell when you want to be left alone. They are very sensitive that way. I looked out of the window and thought my thoughts. After a time I became quite calm and rested. I hadn't brought too much stuff with me, but bit by bit I discarded most of that too till I had only a few things left that I could easily carry myself. I didn't even mind when my watch was pinched off me one night in a railway restroom (so-called). I felt myself to be a changed person. Once, at the beginning of my travels, there was a man sitting next to me on a bus who said he was an astrologer. He was a very sensitive and philosophical person—and I must say I was impressed by how many such one meets in India, quite ordinary people traveling third class. After we had been talking for a time and he had told me the future of India for the next forty years, suddenly out of the blue he said to me "Madam, you have a very sad soul." It was true. I thought about it for days afterward and cried a bit to myself. I did feel sad inside myself and heavy like with a stone. But as time went on and I kept going around India—the sky always blue like Sophie had said, and lots of rivers and fields as well as desert—just quietly traveling and looking, I stopped feeling like that. Now I was as a matter of fact quite light inside as if that stone had gone.

Then I stopped traveling and stayed in this one place instead. I liked it better than any of the other ashrams for several reasons. One of them was that the scenery was very picturesque. This cannot be said of all ashrams as many of them seem to be in sort of dust bowls, or in the dirtier parts of very dirty holy cities or even cities that aren't holy at all but just dirty. But this ashram was built on the slope of a mountain, and behind it there were all the other mountains stretching right up to the snow-capped peaks of the Himalayas; and on the other side it ran down to the river, which I will not say can have been very clean (with all those pilgrims dipping in it) but certainly looked clean from up above and not only clean but as clear and green as the sky was clear and blue. Also along the bank of the river there were many little pink temples with pink cones and they certainly made a pretty scene. Inside the ashram also the atmosphere was good, which again cannot be said of all of them, far from it. But the reason the atmosphere was good here was because of the head of this ashram who was called Master. They are always called something like that—if not Swamiji then Maharaj-ji or Babaji or Maharishiji or Guruji; but this one was just called plain Master, in English.

He was full of pep and go. Early in the morning he would say "Well what shall we do today!" and then plan some treat like all of us going for a swim in the river with a picnic lunch to follow. He didn't want anyone to have a dull moment or to fall into a depression, which I suppose many there were apt to do, left to their own devices. In some ways he reminded me of those big business types that sometimes (in other days!) took me out to dinner. They too had that kind of superhuman energy and seemed to be stronger than other people. I forgot to say that Master was a big burly man, and as he didn't wear all that many clothes—usually only a loincloth—you could see just how big and burly he was. His head was large too and it was completely shaven so that it looked even larger. He wasn't ugly, not at all. Or perhaps if he was one forgot about it very soon because of all that dynamism.

As I said, the ashram was built on the slope of a mountain. I don't think it was planned at all but had just grown: there was one little room next to the other and the Meditation Hall and the dining hall and Master's quarters—whatever was needed was added and it all ran higgledy-piggledy down the mountain. I had one of the little rooms to myself and made myself very snug in there. The only furniture provided by the ashram was one string bed, but I bought a handloom rug from the Lepers Rehabilitation Center and I also put up some pictures, like a Tibetan Mandala, which was very colorful. Everyone liked my room and wanted to come and spend time there, but I was a bit cagey about that as I needed my privacy. I always had lots to do, like writing letters or washing my hair and I was also learning to play the flute. So I was quite happy and independent and didn't really need company though there was plenty of it, if and when needed.

There were Master's Indian disciples who were all learning to be swamis. They wanted to renounce the world and had shaved their heads and wore an orange sort of toga thing. When they were ready, Master was going to make them into full swamis. Most of these junior swamis were very young—just boys, some of them—but even those that weren't all that young were certainly so at heart. Sometimes they reminded me of a lot of school kids, they were so full of tricks and fun. But I think basically they were very serious—they couldn't not be, considering how they were renouncing and were supposed to be studying all sorts of very difficult things. The one I liked the best was called Vishwa. I liked him not only because he was the best looking, which he undoubtedly was, but I felt he had a lot going for him. Others said so too—in fact, they all said that Vishwa was the most advanced and was next in line for full initiation. I always let him come and talk to me in my room whenever he wanted to, and we had some interesting conversations.

Then there were Master's foreign disciples. They weren't so different from the other Europeans and Americans I had met in other ashrams except that the atmosphere here was so much better and that made them better too. They didn't have to fight with each other over Master's favors—I'm afraid that was very much the scene in some of the other ashrams, which were like harems, the way they were all vying for the favor of their guru. But Master never encouraged that sort of relationship, and although of course many of them did have very strong attachments to him, he managed to keep them all healthy. And that's really saying something because, like in all the other ashrams, many of them were not healthy people; through no fault of their own quite often, they had just had a bad time and were trying to get over it.

Once Master said to me "What about you, Katie?" This was when I was alone with him in his room. He had called me in for some dictation—we were all given little jobs to do for him from time to time, to keep us busy and happy I suppose. Just let me say a few words about his room and get it over with. It was *awful*. It had linoleum on the floor of the nastiest pattern, and green strip lighting, and the walls were painted green too and had been decorated with calendars and pictures of what were supposed to be gods and saints but might as well have been Bombay film stars, they were so fat and gaudy. Master and all the junior swamis were terribly proud of this room. Whenever he acquired anything new—like some plastic flowers in a hideous vase—he would call everyone to admire and was so pleased and complacent that really it was not possible to say anything except "Yes very nice."

When he said "What about you, Katie?" I knew at once what he meant. That was another thing about him—he would suddenly come out with something as if there had already been a long talk between you on this subject. So when he asked me that, it was like the end of a conversation, and all I had to do was think for a moment and then I said "I'm okay." Because that was what he had asked: was I okay? Did I want anything, any help or anything? And I didn't. I really was okay now. I hadn't always been but I got so traveling around on my own and then being in this nice place here with him.

This was before the Countess came. Once she was there, everything was rather different. For weeks before her arrival people started talking about her: she was an important figure there, and no wonder since she was very rich and did a lot for the ashram and for Master when he went abroad on his lecture tours. I wondered what she was like. When I asked Vishwa about her, he said "She is a great spiritual lady."

We were both sitting outside my room. There was a little open space around which several other rooms were grouped. One of these—the biggest, at the corner—was being got ready for the Countess. It was the one that was always kept for her. People were vigorously sweeping in there and scrubbing the floor with soap and water.

"She is rich and from a very aristocratic family," Vishwa said, "but when she met Master she was ready to give up everything." He pointed to the room that was being scrubbed: "This is where she stays. And see—not even a bed—she sleeps on the floor like a holy person. Oh, Katie, when someone like me gives up the world, what is there? It is not such a great thing. But when *she* does it—" His face glowed. He had very bright eyes and a lovely complexion. He always looked very pure, owing no doubt to the very pure life he led.

Of course I got more and more curious about her, but when she came I was disappointed. I had expected her to be very special, but the only special thing about her was that I should meet her *here*. Otherwise she was a type I had often come across at posh parties and in the salons where I used to model. And the way she walked toward me and said "Welcome!"—she might as well have been walking across a carpet in a salon. She had a full-blown, middle-aged figure (she must have been in her fifties) but very thin legs on which she took long strides with her toes turned out. She gave me a deep searching look—and that too I was used to from someone like her because very worldly people always do that: to find out who you are and how usable. But in her case now I suppose it was to search down into my soul and see what that was like.

I don't know what her conclusion was, but I must have passed because she was always kind to me and even asked for my company quite often. Perhaps this was partly because we lived across from each other and she suffered from insomnia and needed someone to talk to at night. I'm a sound sleeper myself and wasn't always very keen when she came to wake me. But she would nag me till I got up. "Come on, Katie, be a sport," she would say. She used many English expressions like that: she spoke English very fluently though with a funny accent. I heard her speak to the French and Italian and German people in the ashram very fluently in their languages too. I don't know what nationality she herself was—a sort of mixture I think—but of course people like her have been everywhere, not to mention their assorted governesses when young.

She always made me come into her room. She said mine was too *luxurious*, she didn't feel right in it as she had given up all that. Hers certainly wasn't luxurious. Like Vishwa had said, there wasn't a stick of furniture in it and she slept on the floor on a mat. As the electricity supply in the ashram was very fitful, we usually sat by candlelight. It was queer sitting like that with her on the floor with a stub of candle between us. I didn't have to do much talking as she did it all. She used her arms a lot, in sweeping gestures, and I can still see them weaving around there by candlelight as if she was doing a dance with them; and her eyes, which were big and baby-blue, were stretched wide open in wonder at everything she was telling me. Her life was like a fairy tale, she said. She gave me all the details though I can't recall them as I kept dropping off to sleep (naturally at two in the morning). From time to time she'd stop and say sharply "Are you asleep, Katie," and then she would poke me till I said no I wasn't. She told me how she first met Master at a lecture he had come to give in Paris. At the end of the lecture she went up to him—she said she had to elbow her way through a crowd of women all trying to get near him—and simply bowed down at his feet. No words spoken. There had been no need. It had been predestined.

She was also very fond of Vishwa. It seemed all three of them—i.e. her, Master, and Vishwa—had been closely related to each other in several previous incarnations. I think they had been either her sons or her husbands or fathers, I can't remember which exactly but it was very close so it was no wonder she felt about them the way she did. She had big plans for Vishwa. He was to go abroad and be a spiritual leader. She and Master often talked about it, and it was fascinating listening to them, but there was one thing I couldn't understand and that was why did it have to be Vishwa and not Master who was to be a spiritual leader in the West? I'd have thought Master himself had terrific qualifications for it.

Once I asked them. We were sitting in Master's room and the two of them were talking about Vishwa's future. When I asked "What about Master?" she gave a dramatic laugh and pointed at him like she was accusing him: "Ask him! Why don't you ask him!"

He gave a guilty smile and shifted around a bit on his throne. I say throne—it really was that: he received everyone in this room so a sort of dais had been fixed up at one end and a deer skin spread on it for him to sit on; loving disciples had painted an arched back to the dais and decorated it with stars and symbols stuck on in silver paper (hideous!).

When she saw him smile like that, she really got exasperated. "If you knew, Katie," she said, "how I have argued with him, how I have fought, how I have begged and pleaded on my *knees*. But he is as stubborn as—as—"

"A mule," he kindly helped her out.

"Forgive me," she said (because you can't call your guru names, that just isn't done!); though next moment she had worked herself up again: "Do you know," she asked me, "how many people were waiting for him at the airport last time he went to New York? Do you know how many came to his lectures? That they had to be turned away from the *door* till we took a bigger hall! And not to speak of those who came to enroll for the special three-week Meditation-via-Contemplation course."

"She is right," he said. "They are very kind to me."

"Kind! They want him—need him—are crazy with love and devotion—"

"It's all true," he said. "But the trouble is, you see, I'm a very, very lazy person." And as he said this, he gave a big yawn and stretched himself to prove how lazy he was: but he didn't look it—on the contrary, when he stretched like that, pushing out his big chest, he looked like he was humming with energy.

That evening he asked me to go for a stroll with him. We walked by the river, which was very busy with people dipping in it for religious reasons. The temples were also busy—whenever we passed one, they seemed to be bursting in there with hymns, and cymbals, and little bells.

Master said: "It is true that everyone is very kind to me in the West. Oh they make a big fuss when I come. They have even made a song for me—it goes—wait, let me see—"

He stopped still and several people took the opportunity to come up to ask for his blessing. There were many other holy men walking about but somehow Master stood out. Some of the holy men also came up to be blessed by him.

"Yes, it goes: *'He's here! Our Master-ji is here! Jai jai Master! Jai jai He!'* They stand waiting for me at the airport, and when I come out of the customs they burst into song. They carry big banners and also have drums and flutes. What a noise they make! Some of them begin to dance there and then on the spot, they are so happy. And everyone stares and looks at me, all the respectable people at the airport, and they wonder 'Now who is this ruffian?' "

He had to stop again because a shopkeeper came running out of his stall to crouch at Master's feet. He was the grocer—everyone knew he used false weights—as well as the local moneylender and the biggest rogue in town, but when Master blessed him I could see tears come in his eyes, he felt so good.

"A car has been bought for my use," Master said when we walked on again. "Also a lease has been taken on a beautiful residence in New Hampshire. Now they wish to buy an airplane to enable me to fly from coast to coast." He sighed. "She is right to be angry with me. But what am I to do? I stand in the middle of Times Square or Piccadilly, London, and I look up and there are all the beautiful beautiful buildings stretching so high up into heaven: yes I look at them but it is not them I see at all, Katie! Not them at all!"

He looked up and I with him, and I understood that what he saw in Times Square and Piccadilly was what we saw now—all those mountains growing higher and higher above the river, and some of them so high that you couldn't make out whether it was them, with snow on top, or the sky with clouds in it.

Before the Countess's arrival, everything had been very easygoing. We usually did our meditation, but if we happened to miss out, it never mattered too much. Also there was a lot of sitting around gossiping or trips to the bazaar for eats. But the Countess put us on a stricter regime. Now we all had a timetable to follow, and there were gongs and bells going off all day to remind us. This started at 5 A.M. when it was meditation time, followed by purificatory bathing time, and study time, and discussion time, and hymn time, and so on till lights-out time. Throughout the day disciples could be seen making their way up or down the mountainside as they passed from one group activity to the other. If there was any delay in the schedule, the Countess got impatient and clapped her hands and chivied people along. The way she herself clambered up and down the mountain was just simply amazing for someone her age. Sometimes she went right to the top of the ashram where there was a pink plaster pillar inscribed with Golden Rules for Golden Living (a sort of Indian Ten Commandments): from here she could look all around, survey her domain as it were. When she wanted to summon everyone, she climbed up there with a pair of cymbals and how she beat them together! Boom! Bang! She must have had military blood in her veins, probably German.

She had drawn up a very strict timetable for Vishwa to cover every aspect of his education. He had to learn all sorts of things; not only English and a bit of French and German, but also how to use a knife and fork and even how to address people by their proper titles in case ambassadors and big church people and such were drawn into the movement as was fully expected. Because I'd been a model, I was put in charge of his deportment. I was supposed to teach him how to walk and sit nicely. He had to come to my room for lessons in the afternoons, and it was quite fun though I really didn't know what to teach him. As far as I was concerned, he was more graceful than anyone I'd ever seen. I loved the way he sat on the floor with his legs tucked under him; he could sit like that without moving for hours and hours. Or he might lie full length on the floor with his head supported on one hand and his ascetic's robe falling in folds around him so that he looked like a piece of sculpture you might see in a museum. I forgot to say that the Countess had decided he wasn't to shave his hair anymore like the other junior swamis but was to grow it and have long curls. It wasn't long yet but it was certainly curly and framed his face very prettily.

After the first few days we gave up having lessons and just talked and spent our time together. He sat on the rug and I on the bed. He old me the story of his life and I told him mine. But his was much petter tnan mine. His father had been the station master at some very small junction, and the family lived in a little railway house

near enough the tracks to run and put the signals up or down as required. Vishwa had plenty of brothers and sisters to play with, and
friends at the little school he went to at the other end of town; but
quite often he felt like not being with anyone. He would set off to
school with his copies and pencils like everyone else, but halfway he
would change his mind and take another turning that led out of
town into some open fields. Here he would lie down under a tree and
look at patches of sky through the leaves of the tree, and the leaves
moving ever so gently if there was a breeze or some birds shook their
wings in there. He would stay all day and in the evening go home
and not tell anyone. His mother was a religious person who regularly visited the temple and sometimes he went with her but he
never felt anything special. Then Master came to town and gave a
lecture in a tent that was put up for him on the parade ground.
Vishwa went with his mother to hear him, again not expecting anything special, but the moment he saw Master something very pecu-
liar happened: he couldn't quite describe it, but he said it was like
when there is a wedding on a dark night and the fireworks start and
there are those that shoot up into the sky and then burst into a huge
white fountain of light scattering sparks all over so that you are
blinded and dazzled with it. It was like that, Vishwa said. Then he
just went away with Master. His family were sad at first to lose him,
but they were proud too like all families are when one of them re-
nounces the world to become a holy man.

Those were good afternoons we had, and we usually took the
precaution of locking the door so no one could interrupt us. If we
heard the Countess coming—one good thing about her, you could
always *hear* her a mile off, she never moved an inch without shouting
instructions to someone—the moment we heard her we'd jump up
and unlock the door and fling it wide open: so when she looked in,
she could see us having our lesson—Vishwa walking up and down
with a book on his head, or sitting like on a dais to give a lecture and
me showing him what to do with his hands.

When I told him the story of *my* life, we both cried. Especially
when I told him about my first marriage when I was only sixteen
and Danny just twenty. He was a bass player in a group and he was
really good and would have got somewhere if he hadn't freaked out.
It was terrible seeing him do that, and the way he treated me after
those first six months we had together, which were out of this world.
I never had anything like that with anyone ever again, though I got

260

involved with many people afterward. Everything just got worse and worse till I reached an all-time low with my second marriage, which was to a company director (so-called, though don't ask me what sort of company) and a very smooth operator indeed besides being a sadist. Vishwa couldn't stand it when I came to that part of my story. He begged me not to go on, he put his hands over his ears. We weren't in my room that time but on top of the ashram by the Pillar of the Golden Rules. The view from here was fantastic, and it was so high up that you felt you might as well be in heaven, especially at this hour of the evening when the sky was turning all sorts of colors though mostly gold from the sun setting in it. Everything I was telling Vishwa seemed very far away. I can't say it was as if it had never happened, but it seemed like it had happened in someone else's life. There were tears on Vishwa's lashes, and I couldn't help myself, I had to kiss them away. After which we kissed properly. His mouth was as soft as a flower and his breath as sweet; of course he had never tasted meat nor eaten anything except the purest food such as a lamb might eat.

The door of my room was not the only one that was locked during those hot afternoons. Quite a few of the foreign disciples locked theirs for purposes I never cared to inquire into. At first I used to pretend to myself they were sleeping, and afterward I didn't care what they were doing. I mean, even if they weren't sleeping, I felt there was something just as good and innocent about what they actually *were* doing. And after a while—when we had told each other the story of our respective lives and had run out of conversation—Vishwa and I began to do it too. This was about the time when preparations were going on for his final Renunciation and Initiation ceremony. It's considered the most important day in the life of a junior swami, when he ceases to be junior and becomes a senior or proper swami. It's a very solemn ceremony. A funeral pyre is lit and his junior robe and his caste thread are burned on it. All this is symbolic—it means he's dead to the world but resurrected to the spiritual life. In Vishwa's case, his resurrection was a bit different from the usual. He wasn't fitted out in the standard senior swami outfit—which is a piece of orange cloth and a begging bowl—but instead the Countess dressed him up in the clothes he was to wear in the West. She had herself designed a white silk robe for him, together with accessories like beads, sandals, the deer skin he was to sit on, and an embroidered shawl.

Getting all this ready meant many trips to the bazaar, and often she made Vishwa and me go with her. She swept through the bazaar the same way she did through the ashram, and the shopkeepers leaned eagerly out of their stalls to offer their salaams, which she returned or not as they happened to be standing in her books. She was pretty strict with all of them—but most of all with the tailor whose job it was to stitch Vishwa's new silk robes. We spent hours in his little shop while Vishwa had to stand there and be fitted. The tailor crouched at his feet, stitching and restitching the hem to the Countess's instructions. She and I would stand back and look at Vishwa with our heads to one side while the tailor waited anxiously for her verdict. Ten to one she would say "No! Again!"

But once she said not to the tailor but to me: "Vishwa stands very well now. He has a good pose."

"Not bad," I said, continuing to look critically at Vishwa and in such a way that he had a job not to laugh.

What she said next however killed all desire for laughter: "I think we could end the deportment lessons now," and then she shouted at the tailor: "What is this! What are you doing! What sort of monkey work do you call that!"

I managed to persuade her that I hadn't finished with Vishwa yet and there were still a few tricks of the trade I had to teach him. But I knew it was a short reprieve and that soon our lessons would have to end. Also plans were now afoot for Vishwa's departure. He was to go with the Countess when she returned to Europe in a few weeks' time; and she was already very busy corresponding with her contacts in various places, and all sorts of lectures and meetings were being arranged. But that wasn't the only thing worrying me: what was even worse was the change I felt taking place in Vishwa himself, especially after his Renunciation and Initiation ceremony. I think he was getting quite impressed with himself. The Countess made a point of treating him as if he were a guru already, and she bowed to him the same way she did to Master. And of course whatever she did everyone else followed suit, specially the foreign disciples. I might just say that they're always keen on things like that—I mean, bowing down and touching feet—I don't know what kick they get out of it but they do, the Countess along with the rest. Most of them do it very clumsily—not like Indians who are *born* to it—so sometimes you feel like laughing when you look at them. But they're always very solemn about it and afterward, when they stumble up again, there's a sort of holy glow on their faces. Vishwa looked down at them with a benign expression and he also got into the habit of blessing them the way Master did.

Now I stayed alone in the afternoons, feeling very miserable, specially when I thought of what was going on in some of the other rooms and how happy people were in there. After a few days of this I couldn't stand being on my own and started wandering around looking for company. But the only person up and doing at that time of day was the Countess, who I didn't particularly want to be with. So I went and sat in Master's room, where the door was always open in case any of us needed him any time. Like everybody else, he was often asleep that time of afternoon but it didn't matter. Just being in his presence was good. I sat on one of the green plastic benches that were ranged round his room and looked at him sleeping, which he did sitting upright on his throne. Quite suddenly he would open his eyes and look straight at me and say "Ah, Katie" as if he'd known all along that I was sitting there.

One day there was an awful commotion outside. Master woke up as the Countess came in with two foreign disciples, a boy and a girl, who stood hanging their heads while she told us what she had caught them doing. They were two very young disciples; I think the boy didn't even have to shave yet. One couldn't imagine them doing anything really evil, and Master didn't seem to think so. He just told them to go away and have their afternoon rest. But because the Countess was very upset he tried to comfort her, which he did by telling about his early life in the world when he was a married man. It had been an arranged marriage of course, and his wife had been very young, just out of school. Being married for them had been like a game, specially the cooking and housekeeping part, which she had enjoyed very much. Every Sunday she had dressed up in a spangled sari and high-heeled shoes and he had escorted her on the bus to the cinema where they stood in a queue for the one-rupee seats. He had loved her more than he had ever loved anyone or anything in all his life and had not thought it possible to love so much. But it only lasted two years, at the end of which time she died of a miscarriage. He left his home then and wandered about for many years, doing all sorts of different jobs. He worked as a motor mechanic, and a salesman for medical supplies, and had even been in films for a while on the distribution side. But not finding rest anywhere, he finally decided to give up the world. He explained to us that it had been the only logical thing to do. Having learned during his two years of marriage how happy it was possible for a human being to be, he was never again satisfied to settle for anything less; but also seeing how it couldn't last on a worldly plane, he had decided to look for it elsewhere and help other people to do so with him.

I liked what he said, but I don't think the Countess took much of it in. She was more in her own thoughts. She was silent and gloomy, which was *very* unusual for her. When she woke me that night for her midnight confessions, she seemed quite a different person: and now she didn't talk about her fairy-tale life or her wonderful plans for the future but on the contrary about all the terrible things she had suffered in the past. She went right back to the time she was in her teens and had eloped with and married an old man, a friend of her father's, and from there on it was all just one long terrible story of bad marriages and unhappy love affairs and other sufferings that I wished I didn't have to listen to. But I couldn't leave her in the state she was in. She was crying and sobbing and lying face down on the ground. It was eerie in that bare cell of hers with the one piece of candle flickering in the wind, which was very strong, and the rain beating down like fists on the tin roof.

The monsoon had started, and when you looked up now, there weren't any mountains left, only clouds hanging down very heavily; and when you looked down, the river was also heavy and full. Every day there were stories of pilgrims drowning in it, and one night it washed over one bank and swept away a little colony of huts that the lepers had built for themselves. Now they no longer sat sunning themselves on the bridge but were carted away to the infectious-diseases hospital. The rains came gushing down the mountain right into the ashram so that we were all wading ankle-deep in mud and water. Many rooms were flooded and their occupants had to move into other people's rooms, resulting in personality clashes. Everyone bore grudges and took sides so that it became rather like the other ashrams I had visited and not liked.

The person who changed the most was the Countess. Although she was still dashing up and down the mountain, it was no longer to get the place in running order. Now she tucked up her skirts to wade from room to room to peer through chinks and see what people were up to. She didn't trust anyone but appointed herself as a one-man spying organization. She even suspected Master and me! At least me—she asked me what I went to his room for in the afternoon and sniffed at my reply in a way I didn't care for. After that one awful outburst she had, she didn't call me at night anymore but she was certainly after me during the day.

She guarded Vishwa like a dragon. She wouldn't even let me pass his room, and if she saw me going anywhere in that direction, she'd come running to tell me to take the other way around. I wasn't invited anymore to accompany them to the bazaar but only she and Vishwa set off, with her holding a big black umbrella over them both. If they happened to pass me on the way, she would tilt the umbrella so he wouldn't be able to see me. Not that this was necessary as he never seemed to see me anyway. His eyes were always lowered and the expression on his face very serious. He had stopped joking around with the junior swamis, which I suppose was only fitting now he was a senior swami as well as about to become a spiritual leader. The Countess had fixed up a throne for him at the end of Master's room so he wouldn't have to sit on the floor and the benches along with the rest of us. When we all got together in there, Master would be at one end on his throne and Vishwa at the other on his. At Master's end there was always lots going on—everyone laughing and Master making jokes and having his fun—but Vishwa just sat very straight in the lotus pose and never looked at anyone or spoke, and only when the Countess pushed people to go and touch his feet, he'd raise a hand to bless them.

With the rains came flies and mosquitoes, and people began to fall sick with all sorts of mysterious fevers. The Countess—who was terrified of germs and had had herself pumped full of every kind of injection before coming to India—was now in a great hurry to be off with Vishwa. But before they could leave, he too came down with one of those fevers. She took him at once into her own room and kept him isolated in there with everything shut tight. She wouldn't let any of us near him. But I peeped in through the chinks, not caring whether she saw me or not. I even pleaded with her to let me come in, and once she let me but only to look at him from the door while she stood guard by his pillow. His eyes were shut and he was breathing heavily and moaning in an awful way. The Countess said I could go now, but instead I rushed up to Vishwa's bed. She tried to get between us but I pushed her out of the way and got down by the bed and held him where he lay moaning with his eyes shut. The Countess shrieked and pulled at me to get me away. I was shrieking too. We must have sounded and looked like a couple of madwomen. Vishwa opened his eyes and when he saw me there and moreover found that he was in my arms, *he* began to shriek too, as if he was frightened of me and that perhaps I was the very person he was having those terrible fever dreams about that made him groan.

It may have been this accidental shock treatment but that night Vishwa's fever came down and he began to get better. Master announced that there was going to be a Yagna or prayer-meet to give thanks for Vishwa's recovery. It was to be a really big show. Hordes of helpers came up from the town, all eager to take part in this event so as to benefit from the spiritual virtue it was expected to generate. The Meditation Hall was repainted salmon pink and the huge holy *OM* sign at one end of it was lit up all around with colored bulbs that flashed on and off. Everyone worked with a will, and apparently good was already beginning to be generated because the rains stopped, the mud lanes in the ashram dried up, and the river flowed back into its banks. The disciples stopped quarreling, which may have been partly due to the fact that everyone could move back into their own rooms.

The Countess and Vishwa kept going down into the town to finish off with the tailors and embroiderers. They also went to the printer who was making large posters to be sent abroad to advertise Vishwa's arrival. The Countess often asked me to go with them: she was really a good-natured person and did not want me to feel left out. Especially now that she was sure there wasn't a dangerous situation working up between me and Vishwa. There she was right. I wasn't in the least interested in him and felt that the less I saw of him the better. I couldn't forget the way he had shrieked that night in the Countess's room as if I was something impure and dreadful. But on the contrary to me it seemed that it had been *he* who was impure and dreadful with his fever dreams. I didn't even like to think what went on in them.

The Great Yagna began and it really was great. The Meditation Hall was packed and was terribly hot not only with all the people there but also because of the sacrificial flames that sizzled as more and more clarified butter was poured on them amid incantations. Everyone was smiling and singing and sweating. Master was terrific—he was right by the fire stark naked except for the tiniest bit of loincloth. His chest glistened with oil and seemed to reflect the flames leaping about. Sometimes he jumped up on his throne and waved his arms to make everyone join in louder; and when they did, he got so happy he did a little jig standing up there. Vishwa was on the other side of the hall also on a throne. He was half reclining in his spotless white robe; he did not seem to feel the heat at all but lay there as if made out of cool marble. He reminded me of the god Shiva resting on top of his snowy mountain. The Countess sat near him, and I saw how she tried to talk to him once or twice but he took no notice of her. After a while she got up and went out, which was not surprising for it really was not her scene, all that noise and singing and the neon lights and decorations.

It went on all night. No one seemed to get tired—they just got more and more worked up and the singing got louder and the fire hotter. Other people too began to do little jigs like Master's. I left the hall and walked around by myself. It was a fantastic night, the sky sprinkled all over with stars and a moon like a melon. When I passed the Countess's door, she called me in. She was lying on her mat on the floor and said she had a migraine. No wonder, with all that noise. I liked it myself but I knew that, though she was very much attracted to Eastern religions, her taste in music was more for the Western classical type (she loved string quartets and had had a long *affaire* with a cellist). She confessed to me that she was very anxious to leave now and get Vishwa started on his career. I think she would have liked to confess more things, but I had to get on. I made my way uphill past all the different buildings till I had reached the top of the ashram and the Pillar of the Golden Rules. Here I stood and looked down.

I saw the doors of the Meditation Hall open and Master and Vishwa come out. They were lit up by the lights from the hall. Master was big and black and naked except for his triangle of orange cloth, and Vishwa was shining in white. I saw Master raise his arm and point it up, up to the top of the ashram. The two of them reminded me of a painting I've seen of I think it was an angel pointing out a path to a pilgrim. And like a pilgrim Vishwa began to climb up the path that Master had shown him. I stood by the Pillar of the Golden Rules and waited for him. When he got to me, we didn't have to speak one word. He was like a charged dynamo; I'd never known him like that. It was more like it might have been with Master instead of Vishwa. The drums and hymns down in the Meditation Hall also reached their crescendo just then. Of course Vishwa was too taken up with what he was doing to notice anything going on around him, so it was only me that saw the Countess come uphill. She was walking quite slowly and I suppose I could have warned

Vishwa in time but it seemed a pity to interrupt him, so I just let her come on up and find us.

Master finally settled everything to everyone's satisfaction. He said Vishwa and I were to be a couple, and whereas Vishwa was to be the Guru, I was to embody the Mother principle (which is also very important). Once she caught on to the idea, the Countess rather liked it. She designed an outfit for me too—a sort of flowing white silk robe, really quite becoming. You might have seen posters of Vishwa and me together, both of us in these white robes, his hair black and curly, mine blond and straight. I suppose we do make a good couple—anyway, people seem to like us and to get something out of us. We do our best. It's not very hard; mostly we just have to sit there and radiate. The results are quite satisfactory—I mean the effect we seem to have on people who need it. The person who really has to work hard is the Countess because she has to look after all the business and organizational end. We have a strenuous tour program. Sometimes it's like being on a one-night stand and doing your turn and then packing up in a hurry to get to the next one. Some of the places we stay in aren't too good—motels where you have to pay in advance in case you flit—and when she is very tired, the Countess wrings her hands and says "My God, what am I doing here?" It must be strange for her who's been used to all the grand hotels everywhere, but of course really she likes it. It's her life's fulfillment. But for Vishwa and me it's just a job we do, and all the time we want to be somewhere else and are thinking of that other place. I often remember what Master told me, what happened to him when he looked up in Times Square and Piccadilly, and it's beginning to happen to me too. I seem to *see* those mountains and the river and temples; and then I long to be there.

DESECRATION

It is more than ten years since Sofia committed suicide in the hotel room in Mohabbatpur. At the time, it was a great local scandal, but now almost no one remembers the incident or the people involved in it. The Raja Sahib died shortly afterward—people said it was of grief and bitterness—and Bakhtawar Singh was transferred to another district. The present Superintendent of Police is a mild-mannered man who likes to spend his evenings at home playing card games with his teenage daughters.

The hotel in Mohabbatpur no longer exists. It was sold a few months after Sofia was found there, changed hands several times, and was recently pulled down to make room for a new cinema. This will back on to the old cinema, which is still there, still playing ancient Bombay talkies. The Raja Sahib's house also no longer exists. It was demolished because the land on which it stood has become very valuable, and has been declared an industrial area. Many factories and workshops have come up in recent years.

When the Raja Sahib had first gone to live there with Sofia, there had been nothing except his own house, with a view over the ruined fort and the barren plain beyond it. In the distance there was a little patch of villagers' fields and, huddled out of sight, the village itself. Inside their big house, the Raja Sahib and Sofia had led very isolated lives. This was by choice—his choice. It was as if he had carried her away to this spot with the express purpose of having her to himself, of feasting on his possession of her.

Although she was much younger than he was—more than thirty years younger—she seemed perfectly happy to live there alone with him. But in any case she was the sort of person who exudes happi-

269

ness. No one knew where the Raja Sahib had met and married her. No one really knew anything about her, except that she was a Muslim (he, of course, was a Hindu) and that she had had a good convent education in Calcutta—or was it Delhi? She seemed to have no one in the world except the Raja Sahib. It was generally thought that she was partly Afghan, perhaps even with a dash of Russian. She certainly did not look entirely Indian; she had light eyes and broad cheekbones and a broad brow. She was graceful and strong, and at times she laughed a great deal, as if wanting to show off her youth and high spirits, not to mention her magnificent teeth.

Even then, however, during their good years, she suffered from nervous prostrations. At such times the Raja Sahib sat by her bedside in a darkened room. If necessary, he stayed awake all night and held her hand (she clutched his). Sometimes this went on for two or three weeks at a time, but his patience was inexhaustible. It often got very hot in the room; the house stood unprotected on that barren plain, and there was not enough electricity for air-conditioning—hardly even enough for the fan that sluggishly churned the hot air. Her attacks always seemed to occur during the very hot months, especially during the dust storms, when the landscape all around was blotted out by a pall of desert dust and the sky hung down low and yellow.

But when the air cleared, so did her spirits. The heat continued, but she kept all the shutters closed, and sprinkled water and rose essence on the marble floors and on the scented grass mats hung around the verandas. When night fell, the house was opened to allow the cooler air to enter. She and the Raja Sahib would go up on the roof. They lit candles in colored glass chimneys and read out the Raja Sahib's verse dramas. Around midnight the servants would bring up their dinner, which consisted of many elaborate dishes, and sometimes they would also have a bottle of French wine from the Raja Sahib's cellar. The dark earth below and the sky above were both silver from the reflection of the moon and the incredible numbers of stars shining up there. It was so silent that the two of them might as well have been alone in the world—which of course was just what the Raja Sahib wanted.

Sitting on the roof of his house, he was certainly monarch of all he surveyed, such as it was. His family had taken possession of this land during a time of great civil strife some hundred and fifty years before. It was only a few barren acres with some impoverished vil-

lages thrown in, but the family members had built themselves a little fort and had even assumed a royal title, though they weren't
much more than glorified landowners. They lived like all the other
landowners, draining what taxes they could out of their tenant villagers. They always needed money for their own living, which became very sophisticated, especially when they began to spend more
and more time in the big cities like Bombay, Calcutta, or even London. At the beginning of the century, when the fort became too
rough and dilapidated to live in, the house was built. It was in a
mixture of Mogul and Gothic styles, with many galleries and high
rooms closed in by arched verandas. It had been built at great cost,
but until the Raja Sahib moved in with Sofia it had usually remained empty except for the ancestral servants.

On those summer nights on the roof, it was always she who read
out the Raja Sahib's plays. He sat and listened and watched her.
She wore colored silks and the family jewelry as an appropriate cos-
tume in which to declaim his blank verse (all his plays were in
English blank verse). Sometimes she couldn't understand what she
was declaiming, and sometimes it was so high-flown that she burst
out laughing. He smiled with her and said, "Go on, go on." He sat
cross-legged smoking his hookah, like any peasant; his clothes were
those of a peasant too. Anyone coming up and seeing him would not
have thought he was the owner of this house, the husband of
Sofia—or indeed the author of all that romantic blank verse. But he
was not what he looked or pretended to be. He was a man of considerable education, who had lived for years abroad, had loved the
opera and theater, and had had many cultivated friends. Later—
whether through general disgust or a particular disappointment, no
one knew—he had turned his back on it all. Now he liked to think of
himself as just an ordinary peasant landlord.

The third character in this story, Bakhtawar Singh, really did
come from a peasant background. He was an entirely self-made
man. Thanks to his efficiency and valor, he had risen rapidly in the
service and was now the district Superintendent of Police (known as
the S.P.). He had been responsible for the capture of some notorious
dacoits. One of these—the uncrowned king of the countryside for almost twenty years—he had himself trapped in a ravine and shot in
the head with his revolver, and he had taken the body in his jeep to
be displayed outside police headquarters. This deed and others like
it had made his name a terror among dacoits and other proscribed

criminals. His own men feared him no less, for he was known as a ruthless disciplinarian. But he had a softer side to him. He was terribly fond of women and, wherever he was posted, would find himself a mistress very quickly—usually more than one. He had a wife and family, but they did not play much of a role in his life. All his interests lay elsewhere. His one other interest besides women was Indian classical music, for which he had a very subtle ear.

Once a year the Raja Sahib gave a dinner party for the local gentry. These were officials from the town—the District Magistrate, the Superintendent of Police, the Medical Officer, and the rest—for whom it was the greatest event of the social calendar. The Raja Sahib himself would have gladly dispensed with the occasion, but it was the only company Sofia ever had, apart from himself. For weeks beforehand, she got the servants ready—cajoling rather than commanding them, for she spoke sweetly to everyone always—and had all the china and silver taken out. When the great night came, she sparkled with excitement. The guests were provincial, dreary, unrefined people, but she seemed not to notice that. She made them feel that their presence was a tremendous honor for her. She ran around to serve them and rallied her servants to carry in a succession of dishes and wines. Inspired by her example, the Raja Sahib also rose to the occasion. He was an excellent raconteur and entertained his guests with witty anecdotes and Urdu couplets, and sometimes even with quotations from the English poets. They applauded him not because they always understood what he was saying but because he was the Raja Sahib. They were delighted with the entertainment, and with themselves for having risen high enough in the world to be invited. There were not many women present, for most of the wives were too uneducated to be brought out into society. Those that came sat very still in their best georgette saris and cast furtive glances at their husbands.

After Bakhtawar Singh was posted to the district as the new S.P., he was invited to the Raja Sahib's dinner. He came alone, his wife being unfit for society, and as soon as he entered the house it was obvious that he was a man of superior personality. He had a fine figure, intelligent eyes, and a bristling moustache. He moved with pride, even with some pomp—certainly a man who knew his own value. He was not put out in the least by the grand surroundings but enjoyed everything as if he were entirely accustomed to such entertainment. He also appeared to understand and enjoy his host's anecdotes and poetry. When the Raja Sahib threw in a bit of Shakespeare, he confessed frankly that he could not follow it, but wnen his host translated and explained, he applauded that too, in real appreciation.

After dinner, there was musical entertainment. The male guests adjourned to the main drawing room, which was an immensely tall room extending the entire height of the house with a glass rotunda. Here they reclined on Bokhara rugs and leaned against silk bolsters. The ladies had been sent home in motorcars. It would not have been fitting for them to be present, because the musicians were not from a respectable class. Only Sofia was emancipated enough to overlook this restriction. At the first party that Bakhtawar Singh attended, the principal singer was a well-known prostitute from Mohabbatpur. She had a strong, well-trained voice, as well as a handsome presence. Bakhtawar Singh did not take his eyes off her. He sat and swayed his head and exclaimed in rapture at her particularly fine modulations. For his sake, she displayed the most delicate subtleties of her art, laying them out like bait to see if he would respond to them, and he cried out as if in passion or pain. Then she smiled. Sofia was also greatly moved. At one point, she turned to Bakhtawar Singh and said, "How good she is." He turned his face to her and nodded, unable to speak for emotion. She was amazed to see tears in his eyes.

Next day she was still thinking about those tears. She told her husband about it, and he said, "Yes, he liked the music, but he liked the singer too."

"What do you mean?" Sofia asked. When the Raja Sahib laughed, she cried, "Tell me!" and pummeled his chest with her fists.

"I mean," he said, catching her hands and holding them tight, "that they will become friends."

"She will be his mistress?" Sofia asked, opening her eyes wide.

The Raja Sahib laughed with delight. "Where did you learn such a word? In the convent?"

"How do you know?" she pursued. "No, you must tell me! Is he that type of man?"

"What type?" he said, teasing her.

The subject intrigued her, and she continued to think about it to herself. As always when she brooded about anything, she became silent and withdrawn and sat for hours on the veranda, staring out over the dusty plain. "Sofia, Sofia, what are you thinking?" the Raja Sahib asked her. She smiled and shook her head. He looked into her strange, light eyes. There was something mysterious about them. Even when she was at her most playful and affectionate, her eyes seemed always to be looking elsewhere, into some different and distant landscape. It was impossible to tell what she was thinking. Perhaps she was not thinking about anything at all, but the distant gaze gave her the appearance of keeping part of herself hidden. This drove the Raja Sahib crazy with love. He wanted to pursue her into the innermost recesses of her nature, and yet at the same time he respected that privacy of hers and left her to herself when she wanted. This happened often; she would sit and brood and also roam around the house and the land in a strange, restless way. In the end, though, she would always come back to him and nestle against his thin, gray-matted chest and seem to be happy there.

For several days after the party, Sofia was in one of these moods. She wandered around the garden, though it was very hot outside. There was practically no shade, because nothing could be made to grow, for lack of water. She idly kicked at pieces of stone, some of which were broken garden statuary. When it got too hot, she did not return to the house but took shelter in the little ruined fort. It was very dark inside there, with narrow underground passages and winding steep stairs, some of which were broken. Sometimes a bat would flit out from some crevice. Sofia was not afraid; the place was familiar to her. But one day, as she sat in one of the narrow stone passages, she heard voices from the roof. She raised her head and listened. Something terrible seemed to be going on up there. Sofia climbed the stairs, steadying herself against the dank wall. Her heart was beating as loudly as those sounds from above. When she got to the top of the stairs and emerged on to the roof, she saw two men. One of them was Bakhtawar Singh. He was beating the other man, who was also a policeman, around the neck and head with his fists. When the man fell, he kicked him and then hauled him up and beat him more. Sofia gave a cry. Bakhtawar Singh turned his head and saw her. His eyes looked into hers for a moment, and how different they were from that other time when they had been full of tears!

"Get out!" he told the policeman. The man's sobs continued to be heard as he made his way down the stairs. Sofia did not know what to do. Although she wanted to flee, she stood and stared at

Bakhtawar Singh. He was quite calm. He put on his khaki bush jacket, careful to adjust the collar and sleeves so as to look smart. He explained that the man had been derelict in his duties and, to escape discipline, had run away and hidden here in the fort. But Bakhtawar Singh had tracked him down. He apologized for trespassing on the Raja Sahib's property and also—here he became courtly and inclined his body toward Sofia—if he had in any way upset and disturbed her. It was not a scene he would have wished a lady to witness.

"There is blood on your hand," she said.

He looked at it. He made a wry face and then wiped it off. (Was it his own or the other man's?) Again he adjusted his jacket, and he smoothed his hair. "Do you often come here?" he asked, indicating the stairs and then politely standing aside to let her go first. She started down, and looked back to see if he was following.

"I come every day," she said.

It was easy for her to go down the dark stairs, which were familiar to her. But he had to grope his way down very carefully, afraid of stumbling. She jumped down the last two steps and waited for him in the open sunlight.

"You come here all alone?" he asked. "Aren't you afraid?"

"Of what?"

He didn't answer but walked around the back of the fort. Here his horse stood waiting for him, grazing among nettles. He jumped on its back and lightly flicked its flanks, and it cantered off as if joyful to be bearing him.

That night Sofia was very restless, and in the morning her face had the clouded, suffering look that presaged one of her attacks. But when the Raja Sahib wanted to darken the room and make her lie down, she insisted that she was well. She got up, she bathed, she dressed. He was surprised—usually she succumbed very quickly to the first signs of an attack—but now she even said that she wanted to go out. He was very pleased with her and kissed her, as if to reward her for her pluck. But later that day, when she came in again, she did have an attack, and he had to sit by her side and hold her hand and chafe her temples. She wept at his goodness. She kissed the hand that was holding hers. He looked into her strange eyes and said, "Sofia, Sofia, what are you thinking?" But she quickly covered her eyes, so that he could not look into them. Then he had to soothe her all over again.

Whenever he had tried to make her see a doctor, she had resisted him. She said all she needed was him sitting by her and she would get well by herself, and it did happen that way. But now she told him that she had heard of a very good doctor in Mohabbatpur, who specialized in nervous diseases. The drive was long and wearying, and she insisted that there was no need for the Raja Sahib to go there with her; she could go by herself, with the car and chauffeur. They had a loving quarrel about it, and it was only when she said very well, in that case she would not go at all, would not take medical treatment, that he gave way. So now once a week she was driven to Mohabbatpur by herself.

The Raja Sahib awaited her homecoming impatiently, and the evenings of those days were like celebrations. They sat on the roof, with candles and wine, and she told him about her drive to Mohabbatpur and what the doctor had said. The Raja Sahib usually had a new passage from his latest blank-verse drama for her to read. She would start off well enough, but soon she would be overcome by laughter and have to hide her face behind the pages of his manuscript. And he would smile with her and say, "Yes, I know, it's all a lot of nonsense."

"No, no!" she cried. Even though she couldn't understand a good deal of what she was reading, she knew that it expressed his romantic nature and his love for her, which were both as deep as a well. She said, "It is only I who am stupid and read so badly." She pulled herself together and went on reading, till made helpless with laughter again.

There was something strange about her laughter. It came bubbling out, as always, as if from an overflow of high spirits, but now her spirits seemed almost too high, almost hysterical. Her husband listened to these new notes and was puzzled by them. He could not make up his mind whether the treatment was doing her good or not.

The Raja Sahib was very kind to his servants, but if any of them did anything to offend him, he was quick to dismiss him. One of his bearers, a man who had been in his employ for twenty years, got drunk one night. This was by no means an unusual occurrence among the servants; the house was in a lonely spot, with no amusements, but there was plenty of cheap liquor available from the village. Usually the servants slept off the effects in their quarters, but this bearer came staggering up on the roof to serve the Raja Sahib and Sofia. There was a scene. He fell and was dragged away by the other servants, but he resisted violently, shouting frightful obscenities, so that Sofia had to put her hands over her ears. The Raja Sahib's face was contorted with fury. The man was dismissed instantly, and when he came back the next day, wretchedly sober, begging pardon and pleading for reinstatement, the Raja Sahib would not hear him. Everyone felt sorry for the man, who had a large family and was, except for these occasional outbreaks, a sober, hardworking person. Sofia felt sorry for him too. He threw himself at her feet, and so did his wife and many children. They all sobbed, and Sofia sobbed with them. She promised to try and prevail upon the Raja Sahib.

She said everything she could—in a rushed, breathless voice, fearing he would not let her finish—and she did not take her eyes off her husband's face as she spoke. She was horrified by what she saw there. The Raja Sahib had very thin lips, and when he was angry he bit them in so tightly that they quite disappeared. He did it now, and he looked so stern and unforgiving that she felt she was not talking to her husband at all but to a gaunt and bitter old man who cared nothing for her. Suddenly she gave a cry, and just as the servant had thrown himself at her feet, so she now prostrated herself at the Raja Sahib's. "Forgive!" she cried. "Forgive!" It was as if she were begging forgiveness for everyone who was weak and had sinned. The Raja Sahib tried to make her rise, but she lay flat on the ground, trying over and over again to bring out the word "Forgive" and not succeeding because of her sobs. At last he managed to help her up; he led her to the bed and waited there till she was calm again. But he was so enraged by the cause of this attack that the servant and his family had to leave immediately.

She always dismissed the car and chauffeur near the doctor's clinic. She gave the chauffeur quite a lot of money—for his food, she said—and told him to meet her in the same place in the evening. She explained that she had to spend the day under observation at the clinic. After the first few times, no explanation was necessary. The chauffeur held out his hand for the money and disappeared until the appointed time. Sofia drew up her sari to veil her face and got into a cycle rickshaw. The place Bakhtawar Singh had chosen for them was a rickety two-story hotel, with an eating shop downstairs. It was in a very poor, outlying, forgotten part of town, where there was no danger of ever meeting an acquaintance. At first Sofia had been shy about entering the hotel, but as time went on she became bolder. No one ever looked at her or spoke to her. If she was the first to arrive, the key was silently handed to her. She felt secure that the hotel people knew nothing about her, and certainly had never seen her face, which she kept veiled till she was upstairs and the door closed behind her.

In the beginning, he sometimes arrived before her. Then he lay down on the bed, which was the only piece of furniture besides a bucket and a water jug, and was at once asleep. He always slept on his stomach, with one cheek pressed into the pillow. She would come in and stand and look at his dark, muscular, naked back. It had a scar on it, from a knife wound. She lightly ran her finger along this scar, and if that did not wake him, she unwound his loosely tied dhoti, which was all he was wearing. That awakened him immediately.

He was strange to her. That scar on his back was not the only one; there were others on his chest and an ugly long one on his left thigh, sustained during a prison riot. She wanted to know all about his violent encounters, and about his boyhood, his upward struggle, even his low origins. She often asked him about the woman singer at the dinner party. Was it true what the Raja Sahib had said—that he had liked her? Had he sought her out afterward? He did not deny it, but laughed as at a pleasant memory. Sofia wanted to know more and more. What was it like to be with a woman like that? Had there been others? How many, and what was it like with all of them? He was amused by her curiosity and did not mind satisfying it, often with demonstrations.

Although he had had many women, they had mostly been prostitutes and singers. Sometimes he had had affairs with the wives of other police officers, but these too had been rather coarse, uneducated women. Sofia was his first girl of good family. Her refinement intrigued him. He loved watching her dress, brush her hair, treat her skin with lotions. He liked to watch her eat. But sometimes it seemed as if he deliberately wanted to violate her delicacy. For instance, he knew that she hated the coarse, hot lentils that he loved from his boyhood. He would order great quantities, with coarse bread, and cram the food into his mouth and then into hers, though it burned her palate. As their intimacy progressed, he also made her perform acts that he had learned from prostitutes. It seemed that he could not reach far enough into her, physically and in every other way. Like the Raja Sahib, he was intrigued by the look in her foreign eyes, but he wanted to seek out that mystery and expose it, as all the rest of her was exposed to him.

The fact that she was a Muslim had a strange fascination for him. Here too he differed from the Raja Sahib who, as an educated nobleman, had transcended barriers of caste and community. But for Bakhtawar Singh these were still strong. All sorts of dark superstitions remained embedded in his mind. He questioned her about things he had heard whispered in the narrow Hindu alleys he came from—the rites of circumcision, the eating of unclean flesh, what Muslims did with virgin girls. She laughed, never having heard of such things. But when she assured him that they could not be true, he nodded as if he knew better. He pointed to one of his scars, sustained during a Hindu-Muslim riot that he had suppressed. He had witnessed several such riots and knew the sort of atrocities committed in them. He told her what he had seen Muslim men do to Hindu women. Again she would not believe him. But she begged him not to go on; she put her hands over her ears, pleading with him. But he forced her hands down again and went on telling her, and laughed at her reaction. "That's what they did," he assured her. "*Your* brothers. It's all true." And then he struck her, playfully but quite hard, with the flat of his hand.

All week, every week, she waited for her day in Mohabbatpur to come around. She was restless and she began to make trips into the nearby town. It was the usual type of district town, with two cinemas, a jail, a church, temples and mosques, and a Civil Lines, where the government officers lived. Sofia now began to come here to visit the officers' wives whom she had been content to see just once a year at her dinner party. Now she sought them out frequently. She played with their children and designed flower patterns for them to embroider. All the time her thoughts were elsewhere; she was waiting for it to be time to leave. Then, with hurried farewells, promises to come again soon, she climbed into her car and sat back. She told the chauffeur—the same man who took her to Mohabbatpur every week—to drive her through the Police Lines. First there were the policemen's barracks—a row of hutments, where men in vests and shorts could be seen oiling their beards and winding their turbans; they looked up in astonishment from these tasks as her saloon car drove past. She leaned back so as not to be seen, but when they had driven beyond the barracks and had reached the Police Headquarters, she looked eagerly out of the window again. Every time she hoped to get a glimpse of him, but it never happened; the car drove through and she did not dare to have it slow down. But there was one further treat in store, for beyond the offices were the residential houses of the police officers—the Assistant Deputy S.P., the Deputy S.P., the S.P.

One day, she leaned forward and said to the chauffeur, "Turn in."

"In here?"

"Yes, yes!" she cried, mad with excitement.

It had been a sudden impulse—she had intended simply to drive past his house, as usual—but now she could not turn back, she had to see. She got out. It was an old house, built in the times of the British for their own S.P., and now evidently inhabited by people who did not know how to look after such a place. A cow was tethered to a tree on what had once been a front lawn; the veranda was unswept and empty except for some broken crates. The house too was practically unfurnished. Sofia wandered through the derelict rooms, and it was only when she had penetrated to the inner courtyard that the life of the house began. Here there were children and noise and cooking smells. A woman came out of the kitchen and stared at her. She had a small child riding on her hip; she was perspiring, perhaps from the cooking fire, and a few strands of hair stuck to her forehead. She wore a plain and rather dirty cotton sari. She might have been his servant rather than his wife. She looked older than he did, tired and worn out. When Sofia asked whether this was the house of the Deputy S.P., she shook her head wearily, without a smile. She told one of her children to point out the right house, and turned back into her kitchen with no further curiosity. A child began to cry.

At their next meeting, Sofia told Bakhtawar Singh what she had done. He was surprised and not angry, as she had feared, but amused. He could not understand her motives, but he did not puzzle himself about them. He was feeling terribly sleepy; he said he had been up all night (he didn't say why). It was stifling in the hotel room, and perspiration ran down his naked chest and back. It was also very noisy, for the room faced onto an inner yard, which was bounded on its opposite side by a cinema. From noon onward the entire courtyard boomed with the ancient sound track—it was a very poor cinema and could afford to play only very old films—filling their room with Bombay dialogue and music. Bakhtawar Singh seemed not to care about the heat or the noise. He slept through both. He always slept when he was tired; nothing could disturb him. It astonished Sofia, and so did his imperviousness to their surroundings—the horribly shabby room and smell of cheap oil frying from the eating shop downstairs. But now, after seeing his home, Sofia understood that he was used to comfortless surroundings; and she felt so sorry for him that she began to kiss him tenderly while he slept, as if wishing to make up to him for all his deprivations. He woke up and looked at her in surprise as she cried out, "Oh, my poor darling!"

"Why?" he asked, not feeling poor at all.

She began for the first time to question him about his marriage. But he shrugged, bored by the subject. It was a marriage like every other, arranged by their two families when he and his wife were very young. It was all right; they had children—sons as well as daughters. His wife had plenty to do, he presumed she was content—and why shouldn't she be? She had a good house to live in, sufficient money for her household expenses, and respect as the wife of the S.P. He laughed briefly. Yes, indeed, if she had anything to complain of he would like to know what it was. Sofia agreed with him. She even became indignant, thinking of his wife who had all these benefits and did not even care to keep a nice home for him. And not just his home—what about his wife herself? When she thought of that bedraggled figure, more a servant than a wife, Sofia's indignation rose—and with it her tender pity for him, so that again she embraced him and even spilled a few hot tears, which fell on to his naked chest and made him laugh with surprise.

A year passed, and it was again time for the Raja Sahib's annual party. As always, Sofia was terribly excited and began her preparations weeks beforehand. Only this time her excitement reached such a pitch that the Raja Sahib was worried. He tried to joke her out of it; he asked her whom was she expecting, what terribly important guest. Had she invited the President of India, or perhaps the King of Afghanistan? "Yes, yes, the King of Afghanistan!" she cried, laughing but with that note of hysteria he always found so disturbing. Also she lost her temper for the first time with a servant; it was for nothing, for some trifle, and afterward she was so contrite that she could not do enough to make it up to the man.

The party was, as usual, a great success. The Raja Sahib made everyone laugh with his anecdotes, and Bakhtawar Singh also told some stories, which everyone liked. The same singer from Mohabbatpur had been called, and she entertained with the same skill. And again—Sofia watched him—Bakhtawar Singh wept with emotion. She was deeply touched; he was manly to the point of violence (after all, he *was* a policeman), and yet what softness and delicacy there was in him. She reveled in the richness of his nature. The Raja Sahib must have been watching him too, because later, after the party, he told Sofia, "Our friend enjoyed the musical entertainment again this year."

"Of course," Sofia said gravely. "She is a very fine singer."

The Raja Sahib said nothing, but there was something in his silence that told her he was having his own thoughts.

"If not," she said, as if he had contradicted her, "then why did you call for her again this year?"

"But of course," he said. "She is very fine." And he chuckled to himself.

Then Sofia lost her temper with him—suddenly, violently, just as she had with the servant. The Raja Sahib was struck dumb with amazement, but the next moment he began to blame himself. He felt he had offended her with his insinuation, and he kissed her hands to beg her forgiveness. Her convent-bred delicacy amused him, but he adored it too.

She felt she could not wait for her day in Mohabbatpur to come around. The next morning, she called the chauffeur and gave him a note to deliver to the S.P. in his office. She had a special expressionless way of giving orders to the chauffeur, and he a special expressionless way of receiving them. She waited in the fort for Bakhtawar Singh to appear in answer to her summons, but the only person who came was the chauffeur, with her note back again. He explained that he had been unable to find the S.P., who had not been in his office. Sofia felt a terrible rage rising inside her, and she had to struggle with herself not to vent it on the chauffeur. When the man had gone, she sank down against the stone wall and hid her face in her hands. She did not know what was happening to her. It was not only that her whole life had changed; she herself had changed and had become a different person, with emotions that were completely unfamiliar to her.

Unfortunately, when their day in Mohabbatpur at last came around, Bakhtawar Singh was late (this happened frequently now).

She had to wait for him in the hot little room. The cinema show had started, and the usual dialogue and songs came from the defective sound track, echoing through courtyard and hotel. Tormented by this noise, by the heat, and by her own thoughts, Sofia was now sure that he was with the singer. Probably he was enjoying himself so much that he had forgotten all about her and would not come.

But he did come, though two hours late. He was astonished by the way she clung to him, crying and laughing and trembling all over. He liked it, and kissed her in return. Just then the sound track burst into song. It was an old favorite—a song that had been on the lips of millions; everyone knew it and adored it. Bakhtawar Singh recognized it immediately and began to sing, *"O my heart, all he has left you is a splinter of himself to make you bleed!"* She drew away from him and saw him smiling with pleasure under his moustache as he sang. She cried out, "Oh, you pig!"

It was like a blow in the face. He stopped singing immediately. The song continued on the sound track. They looked at each other. She put her hand to her mouth with fear—fear of the depths within her from which that word had arisen (never, never in her life had she uttered or thought such abuse), and fear of the consequences.

But after that moment's stunned silence all he did was laugh. He took off his bush jacket and threw himself on the bed. "What is the matter with you?" he asked. "What happened?"

"Oh I don't know. I think it must be the heat." She paused. "And waiting for you," she added, but in a voice so low she was not sure he had heard.

She lay down next to him. He said nothing more. The incident and her word of abuse seemed wiped out of his mind completely. She was so grateful for this that she too said nothing, asked no questions. She was content to forget her suspicions—or at least to keep them to herself and bear with them as best she could.

That night she had a dream. She dreamed everything was as it had been in the first years of her marriage, and she and the Raja Sahib as happy as they had been then. But then one night—they were together on the roof, by candle- and moonlight—he was stung by some insect that came flying out of the food they were eating. At first they took no notice, but the swelling got worse and worse, and by morning he was tossing in agony. His entire body was discolored; he had become almost unrecognizable. There were several people around his bed, and one of them took Sofia aside and told her that the Raja Sahib would be dead within an hour. Sofia screamed out loud, but the next moment she woke up, for the Raja Sahib had turned on the light and was holding her in his arms. Yes, that very same Raja Sahib about whom she had just been dreaming, only he was not discolored, not dying, but as he was always—her own husband, with gray-stubbled cheeks and sunken lips. She looked into his face for a moment and, fully awake now, she said, "It's all right. I had a nightmare." She tried to laugh it off. When he wanted to comfort her, she said again, "It's all right," with the same laugh and trying to keep the irritation out of her voice. "Go to sleep," she told him, and pretending to do so herself, she turned on her side away from him.

She continued to be haunted by the thought of the singer. Then she thought, if with one, why not with many? She herself saw him for only those few hours a week. She did not know how he spent the rest of his time, but she was sure he did not spend much of it in his own home. It had had the look of a place whose master was mostly absent. And how could it be otherwise? Sofia thought of his wife—her neglected appearance, her air of utter weariness. Bakhtawar Singh could not be expected to waste himself there. But where did he go? In between their weekly meetings there was much time for him to go to many places, and much time for her to brood.

She got into the habit of summoning the chauffeur more frequently to take her into town. The ladies in the Civil Lines were always pleased to see her, and now she found more to talk about with them, for she had begun to take an interest in local gossip. They were experts on this, and were eager to tell her that the Doctor beat his wife, the Magistrate took bribes, and the Deputy S.P. had venereal disease. And the S.P.? Sofia asked, busy threading an embroidery needle. Here they clapped their hands over their mouths and rolled their eyes around, as if at something too terrible, too scandalous to tell. Was he, Sofia asked—dropping the needle, so that she had to bend down to pick it up again—was he known to be an ... adventurous person? "Oh! Oh! Oh!" they cried, and then they laughed because where to start, where to stop, telling of *his* adventures?

Sofia decided that it was her fault. It was his wife's fault first, of course, but now it was hers too. She had to arrange to be with him more often. Her first step was to tell the Raja Sahib that the doctor said she would have to attend the clinic several times a week. The

Raja Sahib agreed at once. She felt so grateful that she was ready to give him more details, but he cut her short. He said that of course they must follow the doctor's advice, whatever it was. But the way he spoke—in a flat, resigned voice—disturbed her, so that she looked at him more attentively than she had for some time past. It struck her that he did not look well. Was he ill? Or was it only old age? He did look old, and emaciated too, she noticed, with his skinny, wrinkled neck. She felt very sorry for him and put out her hand to touch his cheek. She was amazed by his response. He seemed to tremble at her touch, and the expression on his face was transformed. She took him in her arms. He *was* trembling. "Are you well?" she whispered to him anxiously.

"Oh yes!" he said in a joyful voice. "Very, very well."

She continued to hold him. She said, "Why aren't you writing any dramas for me these days?"

"I will write," he said. "As many as you like." And then he clung to her, as if afraid to be let go from her embrace.

But when she told Bakhtawar Singh that they could now meet more frequently, he said it would be difficult for him. Of course he wanted to, he said—and how much! Here he turned to her and with sparkling eyes quoted a line of verse that said that if all the drops of water in the sea were hours of the day that he could spend with her, still they would not be sufficient for him. "But . . ." he added regretfully.

"Yes?" she asked, in a voice she tried to keep calm.

"Sh-h-h—Listen," he said, and put his hand over her mouth.

There was an old man saying the Muhammedan prayers in the next room. The hotel had only two rooms, one facing the courtyard and the other the street. This latter was usually empty during the day—though not at night—but today there was someone in it. The wall was very thin, and they could clearly hear the murmur of his prayers and even the sound of his forehead striking the ground.

"What is he saying?" Bakhtawar Singh whispered.

"I don't know," she said. "The usual—*la illaha il lallah* . . . I don't know."

"You don't know your own prayers?" Bakhtawar Singh said, truly shocked.

She said, "I could come every Monday, Wednesday, and Friday." She tried to make her voice tempting, but instead it came out shy.

"You do it," he said suddenly.

"Do what?"

"Like he's doing," he said, jerking his head toward the other room, where the old man was. "Why not?" he urged her. He seemed to want it terribly.

She laughed nervously. "You need a prayer carpet. And you must cover your head." (They were both stark naked.)

"Do it like that. Go on," he wheedled. "Do it."

She laughed again, pretending it was a joke. She knelt naked on the floor and began to pray the way the old man was praying in the next room, knocking her forehead on the ground. Bakhtawar Singh urged her on, watching her with tremendous pleasure from the bed. Somehow the words came back to her and she said them in chorus with the old man next door. After a while, Bakhtawar Singh got off the bed and joined her on the floor and mounted her from behind. He wouldn't let her stop praying, though. "Go on," he said, and how he laughed as she went on. Never had he had such enjoyment out of her as on that day.

But he still wouldn't agree to meet her more than once a week. Later, when she tried ever so gently to insist, he became playful and said didn't she know that he was a very busy policeman. Busy with what, she asked, also trying to be playful. He laughed enormously at that and was very loving, as if to repay her for her good joke. But then after a while he grew more serious and said, "Listen—it's better not to drive so often through Police Lines."

"Why not?" Driving past his office after her visits to the ladies in the Civil Lines was still the highlight of her expeditions into town.

He shrugged. "They are beginning to talk."

"Who?"

"Everyone." He shrugged again. It was only her he was warning. People talked enough about him anyway; let them have one more thing. What did he care?

"Oh nonsense," she said. But she could not help recollecting that the last few times all the policemen outside their hutments seemed to have been waiting for her car. They had cheered her as she drove past. She had wondered at the time what it meant but had soon put it out of her mind. She did that now too; she couldn't waste her few hours with Bakhtawar Singh thinking about trivial matters.

But she remembered his warning the next time she went to visit the ladies in the Civil Lines. She wasn't sure then whether it was her imagination or whether there really was something different in the way they were with her. Sometimes she thought she saw them turn aside, as if to suppress a smile, or exchange looks with each other that she was not supposed to see. And when the gossip turned to the S.P., they made very straight faces, like people who know more than they are prepared to show. Sofia decided that it was her imagination; even if it wasn't, she could not worry about it. Later, when she drove through the Police Lines, her car was cheered again by the men in underwear lounging outside their quarters, but she didn't trouble herself much about that either. There were so many other things on her mind. That day she instructed the chauffeur to take her to the S.P.'s residence again, but at the last moment—he had already turned into the gate and now had to reverse—she changed her mind. She did not want to see his wife again; it was almost as if she were afraid. Besides, there was no need for it. The moment she saw the house, she realized that she had never ceased to think of that sad, bedraggled woman inside. Indeed, as time passed the vision had not dimmed but had become clearer. She found also that her feelings toward this unknown woman had changed completely, so that, far from thinking about her with scorn, she now had such pity for her that her heart ached as sharply as if it were for herself.

Sofia had not known that one's heart could literally, physically ache. But now that it had begun it never stopped; it was something she was learning to live with, the way a patient learns to live with his disease. And moreover, like the patient, she was aware that this was only the beginning and that her disease would get worse and pass through many stages before it was finished with her. From week to week she lived only for her day in Mohabbatpur, as if that were the only time when she could get some temporary relief from pain. She did not notice that, on the contrary, it was on that day that her condition worsened and passed into a more acute stage, especially when he came late, or was absentminded, or—and this was beginning to happen too—failed to turn up altogether. Then, when she was driven back home, the pain in her heart was so great that she had to hold her hand there. It seemed to her that if only there were someone, one other living soul, she could tell about it, she might get some relief. Gazing at the chauffeur's stolid, impassive back, she realized that he was now the person who was closest to her. It was as if she had confided in him, without words. She only told him where she wanted to go, and he went there. He told her when he needed money, and she gave it to him. She had also arranged for several increments in his salary.

The Raja Sahib had written a new drama for her. Poor Raja Sahib! He was always there, and she was always with him, but she never thought about him. If her eyes fell on him, either she did not see or, if she did, she postponed consideration of it until some other time. She was aware that there was something wrong with him, but he did not speak of it, and she was grateful to him for not obtruding his own troubles. But when he told her about the new drama he wanted her to read aloud, she was glad to oblige him. She ordered a marvelous meal for that night and had a bottle of wine put on ice. She dressed herself in one of his grandmother's saris, of a gold so heavy that it was difficult to carry. The candles in blue glass chimneys were lit on the roof. She read out his drama with all the expression she had been taught at her convent to put into poetry readings. As usual she didn't understand a good deal of what she was reading, but she did notice that there was something different about his verses. There was one line that read "Oh, if thou didst but know what it is like to live in hell the way I do!" It struck her so much that she had to stop reading. She looked across at the Raja Sahib; his face was rather ghostly in the blue candlelight.

"Go on," he said, giving her that gentle, self-deprecating smile he always had for her when she was reading his dramas.

But she could not go on. She thought, what does he know about that, about living in hell? But as she went on looking at him and he went on smiling at her, she longed to tell him what it *was* like.

"What is it, Sofia? What are you thinking?"

There had never been anyone in the world who looked into her eyes the way he did, with such love but at the same time with a tender respect that would not reach farther into her than was permissible between two human beings. And it was because she was afraid of changing that look that she did not speak. What if he should turn aside from her, the way he had when she had asked forgiveness for the drunken servant?

"Sofia, Sofia, what are you thinking?"

She smiled and shook her head and with an effort went on reading. She saw that she could not tell him but would have to go on bearing it by herself for as long as possible, though she was not sure how much longer that could be.

FOR THE BEST IN PAPERBACKS, LOOK FOR THE 🐧

In every corner of the world, on every subject under the sun, Penguin represents quality and variety – the very best in publishing today.

For complete information about books available from Penguin – including Pelicans, Puffins, Peregrines and Penguin Classics – and how to order them, write to us at the appropriate address below. Please note that for copyright reasons the selection of books varies from country to country.

In the United Kingdom: Please write to *Dept E.P., Penguin Books Ltd, Harmondsworth, Middlesex, UB7 0DA*

In the United States: Please write to *Dept BA, Penguin, 299 Murray Hill Parkway, East Rutherford, New Jersey 07073*

In Canada: Please write to *Penguin Books Canada Ltd, 2801 John Street, Markham, Ontario L3R 1B4*

In Australia: Please write to the *Marketing Department, Penguin Books Australia Ltd, P.O. Box 257, Ringwood, Victoria 3134*

In New Zealand: Please write to the *Marketing Department, Penguin Books (NZ) Ltd, Private Bag, Takapuna, Auckland 9*

In India: Please write to *Penguin Overseas Ltd, 706 Eros Apartments, 56 Nehru Place, New Delhi, 110019*

In Holland: Please write to *Penguin Books Nederland B.V., Postbus 195, NL-1380AD Weesp, Netherlands*

In Germany: Please write to *Penguin Books Ltd, Friedrichstrasse 10-12, D-6000 Frankfurt Main 1, Federal Republic of Germany*

In Spain: Please write to *Longman Penguin España, Calle San Nicolas 15, E-28013 Madrid, Spain*

In France: Please write to *Penguin Books Ltd, 39 Rue de Montmorency, F-75003, Paris, France*

In Japan: Please write to *Longman Penguin Japan Co Ltd, Yamaguchi Building, 2-12-9 Kanda Jimbocho, Chiyoda-Ku, Tokyo 101, Japan*

RUTH PRAWER JHABVALA

Three Continents

'A writer of genius . . . a writer of world class . . . a master story-teller' –
Sunday Times

Last-of-line scions of a prominent American family, Harriet and her twin
brother, Michael, have so far resisted the whirligig of adulteries and
diplomatic cocktail parties that seem to be their sole inheritance. Spoilt,
blindly idealistic and extremely rich, they seem set to prove perfect fodder
for the charismatic Rawul and his sinister Fourth World Movement . . .

'The clash of cultures has always been a central theme in Ruth Prawer
Jhabvala's fiction. In her new novel the clash is pleasingly puzzling: the
easternised West meeting the westernised East . . . marvellously acute' –
Observer

'She excels in describing the confrontation between the old world and the
new . . . she has done it before, but never so well. *Three Continents* is
stunningly good . . . rich and constantly enthralling' – *London Evening
Standard*

Also published

A Backward Place
Esmond in India
Get Ready for Battle
The Householder
How I Become a Holy Mother and other stories
In Search of Love and Beauty
The Nature of Passion
To Whom She Will